"Can you get up?"

Will shook his head. "Get out of here, Chance, before you get yourself killed. You can't help me. I'm dying."

"Save the heroics," Chance told him. "Come on."

"Go on, Chance. Get out of here while you can."

Chance ignored him. He half hauled, half pushed Will to his horse. He started to lift him into the saddle, then he stopped and let him back down.

"It's too late to get out," he said.

Will looked. The Indians had gotten around them. They were forming a wide circle.

Will and Chance were surrounded.

TEXAS KINGDOMS

Robert W. Broomall

FAWCETT GOLD MEDAL • NEW YORK

A Fawcett Gold Medal Book
Published by Ballantine Books
Copyright © 1989 by Robert W. Broomall

Library of Congress Catalog Card Number: 89-91231

ISBN 0-449-13395-8

Manufactured in the United States of America

First Edition: October 1989

Part I

1

1851

On an April morning in 1851, two young men rode along the Clear Fork of the Brazos River, in Texas.

The young men led packhorses. Like thousands that year, they were bound for California. They maintained a steady pace, but they were alert. This was Indian country.

Chance Evans was in the lead. Chance was twenty, compactly built, with a solid chin and dark hair cut very short for travel. His eyes were close set and hooded. He wore weatherbeaten buckskins and a faded slouch hat. A Sharps carbine lay across the pommel of his big Texas saddle. At his waist were two Walker Colt revolvers in embossed Mexican holsters.

Will Cooper, riding behind, was a year younger. He was tall and rangy, coltish yet, unlike Chance, whose fluid movements were those of a grown man. Honey-blond hair poked from beneath Will's stiff, wide-brimmed hat. He wore a sturdy red flannel shirt, wool pants, and high boots. A flintlock rifle was strung across his back, and he carried a brand-new Colt's Dragoon .44 in his belt.

Will and Chance had met at Fort Worth. Each had gone there hoping to join one of the companies forming for California, only to find that they had missed the season's last group by five days. That was not too much time to make up, and Chance had invited Will to join him in riding after the company. Though Chance talked a lot, all that Will had really learned about him was that he'd been born in Louisiana and that he'd served with the Texas Rangers in the war with Mexico. Chance seemed genial by nature, but Will had looked into those hooded eyes, and he had decided that this was not a man to have angry at you.

3

The two men crossed the river at a shallow ford, following the rutted wagon tracks of what was called the California Road. To the sides of the trail, where it hadn't been grazed off by the many animals that had passed before them, the grass grew high as a horse's belly. It rippled playfully in the breeze.

Ahead of the riders was a flat, mesquite-covered hill, the highest elevation in these parts. Chance turned to Will. "Let's go up there. I want to look around."

They left the trail and worked their way up the hill. Chance's shaggy pony moved lightly among the sharp rocks and prickly pear cactus. Will's heavier, grain-fed horse lumbered behind. A pick, shovel, and miner's outsized pan were tied on Will's pack. The pick handle banged against the pan. Will's tin mess utensils rattled.

Chance stopped and waited for Will to catch up. "You and that noisy outfit. Don't see why you need it."

Will replied in his Kentucky drawl, "I need it to pan gold, of course."

"Sounds like hard work," Chance said. "Too hard for me."

Will was surprised. "Ain't that why you're going to California? To mine gold and make your fortune?"

Chance grinned his big, easy grin. He tapped a pocket of his buckskin shirt. He kept a deck of cards in there, and he practiced with them every night. "I got my fortune right here, brother. Ace through deuce, four suits to the deck. You mine the gold, and I'll relieve you of it."

"Not me, you won't. I don't gamble. Money's too scarce where I come from. I mean to hang on to mine."

Chance laughed. "Famous last words." He turned his horse and moved on.

They halted below the hill's flat summit. There they dismounted, stretching their cramped legs and backs, staking their animals to a clump of stunted mesquite. Will's stomach was sore where the Colt's hammer had been pressing into it. He had wanted to put the weapon in his saddlebags, but the saddlebags were full, and there was no place on the old army saddle to tie it. Not for the first time, he wished he'd had the sense to use his last few dollars and buy some kind of holster. He envied Chance's fancy Mexican ones.

Will followed Chance to a rocky outcrop. Chance's moccasined feet moved silently on the grass and rocks. His eyes never stopped moving, studying the ground before them, looking around.

Will caught his breath at the sweeping vista that was opening before them. There was the river, its twisting course marked by a narrow belt of trees and undergrowth. Undulating green hills stretched to the horizon, splotched yellow, white, and red with fields of wildflowers. Will smelled the fresh grass and the flowers. He even caught the musky scent of a distant buffalo herd that drifted northwest under a cloud of dust. Above him, white clouds fluffed high. A hawk wheeled lazily. Insects whirred in the brush. Birds chirped.

Chance had no time for the view. He studied the hillside below them, then he quartered the horizon, looking for signs of trouble. Now he concentrated his gaze to the southwest, in the direction of the river. He looked that way a long time, and his expression was sour. "I thought we'd see the dust of that company from here. I wanted to catch them today. I don't want to spend another night in Comanche country by ourselves." He rubbed his unshaven chin. "What's wrong with that wagon boss, anyway? This isn't the Overland Trail. They're not in a race against winter. The way he's driving them, those animals will be worn out before they reach El Paso. They'll never make it across the Great Desert."

Chance realized that Will was barely listening to him. "What's got you so interested?"

Will waved a hand at the vast landscape. "This. This country. It's so big, so empty. So free. I reckon a man could be anything he wants in country like this."

"I reckon," Chance said. "Come on, we got ground to cover."

They mounted their horses and started down the hill's far side. The pitch was steep. The horses picked their way, slipping at times. Will was not an expert rider. He concentrated on his animal and on the ground before them. He was so intent that he almost ran into Chance, who was halted with a warning hand up.

"Stop!" Chance hissed.

Will reined in. He followed his companion's gaze. Then his stomach went cold.

Ahead of them was a smaller hill, with a scattering of trees at its base. Emerging from behind the trees was a file of mounted Indians.

Will had never seen wild Indians before. There must have been two dozen of them, squat men on small horses, about three-quarters of a mile off. From this distance, he couldn't tell much about them, except that they were nearly naked and they carried lances and bows.

"Comanches?" Will whispered.

Chance nodded.

He leaned down and pinched his horse's nostrils, to keep him quiet. Will did the same. They had to take their chances with the packhorses.

The Indians had not seen the two white men. They were following the buffalo herd to the north. Will and Chance were downwind, so the Indians wouldn't be able to smell them. Chance looked around. He and Will were in an open space, with no cover for a hundred yards in any direction. It would be impossible to move without attracting the attention of the keen-eyed hunters.

"Keep still," Chance said. "Maybe they won't see us."

Will held his breath. The sun was suddenly very hot. His mouth was dry and tasted of salt. He smelled horse sweat and leather and the steaming wool of his shirt.

The Comanches rode on. Will had started to think they might get out of this, when his packhorse snuffled. It had smelled the Indian horses and was nervous. Will tugged the lead line, trying to draw the beast closer, but the horse balked. It pawed the ground, tossing its head. It started to kick, and the rattling and banging of Will's gear sounded unnaturally loud in the spring air.

"Keep that animal still," Chance said savagely.

But it was too late. The Indians had heard. One or two looked in the white men's direction, then the whole file stopped. Some of them motioned toward the hill.

Chance swore. Will's heart was pounding. Now Chance's packhorse was kicking and neighing, as well, but neither man tried to stop them.

"Stay where you are," Chance said. "It's not a war party.

Maybe they'll let us be. Maybe they need those buffalo bad, or maybe it's not worth the effort of picking a war chief.''

The two sides stared at one another. Will saw the Indians gesturing. Some appeared to be laughing. Then they began drifting apart, spreading toward Will and Chance in a lazy semicircle.

"It's not our day," Chance said.

Will had never been so scared in his life. His teeth chattered as he spoke. "Do we go back up the hill? Make a stand?"

"Last thing we want is to get ourselves surrounded, especially up there, where there's not likely to be water. We'll have to try and outrun them.''

Chance looked at Will's horse with quick pity, then he slung the Sharps carbine across his back. He pulled down his hat and jammed his pistols deep in their holsters. "Let go that packhorse," he told Will. He had already dropped the reins of his own.

Will said, "But everything I own is on—"

"It won't do you any good if you're missing your scalp. Let it go.''

Will unwrapped the line from his hand. Before he could drop it, the frightened horse pulled away and ran down the hill, followed by Chance's packhorse. The metallic banging of Will's pack faded.

The Indians were coming on. They rode casually, as if disinterested.

Chance took a deep breath. "You ready?"

Will thought his heart would explode through his chest. "I guess," he said.

"See you back at Fort Worth."

Chance dug in his heels, and his little pony bounded away. Will kicked his own horse and followed. Across the valley, the Indians sent up a whoop and started in pursuit.

The two white men galloped down the hill and around its base, heading back the way they had come. They kept to the side of the trail, avoiding the dangerous ruts that could break a horse's leg or trip it and send a rider sprawling. They lashed the animals with their reins, pointing them for the ford in the river. Will had all he could do to stay in the saddle. Ahead of him, Chance rode easily, low on his horse's neck. The pony's hoofs sent clods of earth flying past Will. The sound of the Indians' horses was a heavy drumming in Will's head.

The riders plowed through a field of red-and-brown gaillardias, scattering flowers in their path. Despite its nondescript appearance, Chance's pony had a deal of speed. Chance was drawing steadily away from Will. Will saw Chance glance quickly over his shoulder, and he ventured his own look.

Two of the Indians were well in front of the others. They had more than halved the initial distance between themselves and the white men. One carried a bow, the other a lance, and they were quirting their ponies furiously. Will turned back, lashing his horse with every ounce of his strength. "Go! Go!" he yelled.

On they raced, toward an ancient pin oak, spreading its wide branches like a mute sentinel. The two closest Indians were yelling now, savage, blood-chilling cries. They sensed the kill. The first notched an arrow to his bow. He carried spare arrows in his mouth. His long hair streamed behind him.

Will passed the pin oak. Chance was getting farther away. Will heard the Indian horses closing on him.

Something punched Will between the shoulder blades, knocking him onto his horse's neck. The reins slipped in his hands, and as he fumbled to get them back, he realized that he'd been shot with an arrow.

Without warning, the world spun. Will bounced hard, and the brass trigger guard of the slung flintlock dug into his kidney, making him cry out.

He was on the ground, lying in tall saw grass, and for a second he wondered why. Then the Indian who had shot him galloped past, carried by the momentum of his horse. The Indian reined in. The animal pawed the air as it wheeled around.

Will struggled to clear his head. He sat up, and a shaft of pain almost made him pass out. Clumsily he pulled the revolver from his belt. As he did, the second Indian drew up his horse. The Indian threw himself from the horse's back and ran forward, lance raised. He was laughing, because he was going to count first coup, not the bowman. There was a jagged scar on his stomach, with a design tattooed around it in black.

Will lifted the heavy pistol, cocking it. He'd fired the pistol only once, and it felt unfamiliar in his hand. He pointed it at the Indian and fired almost point blank.

He missed.

The Indian laughed again. Feverishly Will tried to recock the weapon. The Indian's lance started its downward stroke.

A rifle banged. A hole spouted in the Indian's chest, and he was knocked onto his back, twitching.

Will turned, stunned. He saw Chance sitting his horse nearby. Smoke drifted from the barrel of Chance's carbine. He must have turned back as soon as Will was hit. Now he kicked in his heels and charged forward.

The Indian with the bow had wheeled again, to face Chance. Before the Indian could loose an arrow, Chance was on him, with his big revolver drawn. He shot the Indian in the face. The Indian screamed and dropped the bow. Then he slid from his wicker saddle into the long grass.

Chance hung his rifle from his pommel and galloped over to Will. With two of their number down, the rest of the Indians had grown wary of their prey. They veered well off to the sides.

Chance jumped from the saddle beside Will, holstering the revolver as he did. He bent to look at Will's wound. "Where the hell did you learn how to shoot?" Chance said.

Will started to reply, but Chance cut him off. "Tell me about it later." The arrow shaft had been splintered in Will's fall. Chance snapped it off clean. "Can you get up?"

Will shook his head. "Get out of here, before you get yourself killed. You can't help me. I'm dying."

"Save the heroics," Chance told him. "Come on." He gripped Will under the arms and heaved him to his feet. Will bit back a cry of pain. There seemed to be no strength in his legs.

"Go on, Chance. Get out of here while you can."

Chance ignored him. He half hauled, half pushed Will to his horse. He started to lift him into the saddle, then he stopped and let him back down.

"It's too late to get out," he said.

Will looked. The Indians had gotten around them. They were forming a wide circle.

Will and Chance were surrounded.

2

The Indians sat their horses out of rifle shot, waiting.

Will was steadier on his legs now. His flannel shirt was wet and sticky with blood. His back felt numb and strangely heavy from the arrow buried in it. He gripped Chance's saddle horn for support.

"We're in for it," Chance said.

Will turned. "Why did you come back, Chance? You must have known this would happen. You could have saved yourself. You barely know me."

Chance ignored the question. He was studying the flat terrain, looking for a place to make a fight. The Indians had them cut off from the riverbank. "It's not likely we'll get much better acquainted either," he concluded. He drew Will's arm over his shoulder. "Come on."

Chance hurried Will forward, tugging the horse's reins with his free hand. "Make for that buffalo wallow. It's the closest thing to cover we'll find." He led them toward a shallow, grassless depression in the plain, about a hundred yards off, formed by buffalo rolling and scratching themselves.

Each step was agony for Will, whose lip bled where he was biting it. They waited for the Comanches to swoop down on them, but the Indians remained motionless. "Why are they holding off?" Will asked.

Chance strained under Will's weight. Will was taller than Chance, and that made him awkward to carry, as well. "Time isn't right to attack," Chance said. "The chief must still be making his medicine."

They reached the wallow, and Chance lay Will down. In great pain, Will unslung the flintlock from his back. Chance brought his nervous horse to the edge of the wallow. He yanked his saddlebags free and tossed them in the depression. Then he pulled one of his big revolvers, cocked it, and put a bullet in the horse's brain.

The shot made Will jump with surprise. The horse's legs dropped from under him. He fell first to his knees, then onto his side, as Chance helped pull him down. He quivered once, violently, then he was dead.

Will was shaken. "Why'd you do that?" he asked. "If we get out of this, we're going to need a horse."

Chance laid his rifle barrel across the dead horse's neck. From the saddlebags, he took two spare revolver cylinders, along with boxes of cartridges and percussion caps, and he lined them up, using the animal's body as a breastwork. "We'd never get out with the horse. First thing the Comanches would do is run him off or kill him. I don't want to see a good horse like this in their hands, and if he's going to die, he might as well die where he can do us some good."

The Comanche circle had begun to move, slowly. Chance never paused. He took his canteen from the saddle and handed it to Will, who drank gratefully. "Easy," Chance said. "That water might have to last us awhile."

Chance examined the arrow in Will's back. He tugged the broken shaft, testing it. Will gasped. His fingers stiffened. "It's in too deep," Chance said. "There's no time to get it out."

Chance took a plug of tobacco from his saddlebags. He bit off a big piece and began chewing it vigorously. The Indians were circling faster now. They waved bows and lances at the white men, yelling insults.

"They're working themselves up to fight," Chance explained.

Chance extricated the wad of half-chewed tobacco from his mouth. He packed the tobacco around the arrow in Will's back, working the juice into the wound. "Best I can do right now," he said. Unsheathing his bowie knife, he dropped to his knees in the wallow's shallow bottom, and he began chopping the hard earth, breaking it up. He looked at Will. "You're not hurt so bad you can't help. Build a parapet."

Will took his knife and hacked dirt from the wallow's side and bottom, using his good left shoulder. Waves of pain washed over him. The dirt was hard and dry at first, but it became moist as they dug more of it away. Chance packed the uncovered earth in an emptied saddlebag. When the bag was full, he piled the earth in a mound on the lip of the wallow. Then he went back for more.

Both men were soon breathing heavily. Sweat rolled down their faces in the hot morning sun. Chance took off his buckskin shirt and wiped his forehead. As he did, one of the Indians broke the circle.

The Indian trotted toward the wallow. He was leading a big horse with an army saddle. Well inside rifle range, to show his boldness, he stopped. He shook his long lance and hurled insults at the white men, gesturing at the horse.

Chance kept digging. "They got your horse," he said.

"I see."

"They'll get our packs, too, if they haven't already." Chance couldn't resist a grin. "There goes that fancy prospector's outfit of yours."

Will was undaunted. "I'll get another outfit in California."

Chance plopped a saddlebagful of earth on the parapet. There was now a circle of mounds around the wallow. Chance began adding a second layer, packing the moist earth. "Dead set on California, aren't you?"

"Sure I am. California's the land of opportunity. Ain't that why everybody goes there?"

Chance said, "I'm going 'cause of some trouble I had in Nacogdoches. Something to do with another fellow's wife. Her relatives were making things unhealthy for me back there."

Will stopped working. "Ain't you kind of young to be fooling with other people's wives?"

Chance grinned again, wider. "Women are a weakness of mine."

Around them, the Indian circle began picking up speed.

Chance's grin faded. "They'll be coming now. Look to your weapons."

Chance wiped his muddy hands on his pants. He took his place behind the dead horse. Will covered the other side. He crouched in the shallow depression, propping the flintlock's barrel on the earthen parapet. He felt weak, alternately hot and cold.

The Comanches came out of the sun. A line of five charged from the moving circle. Chance pushed back the brim of his hat.

The line of his jaw was set. The Indians' wild yells raised goose bumps on Will's arms and neck.

"Make sure they're in range before you fire," Chance said. "They want us to waste ammunition."

The five Indians rode at the wallow, weaving their horses so that the white men couldn't get a good shot. Then, abruptly, while still at long range, they veered off. They returned to the circle, still yelling, while another group broke forward.

Will stared down the barrel of the old flintlock. Sweat dripped from his eyebrows and he blinked it away. These Indians came closer than the first group, then they, too, veered off.

Will wiped his dry mouth. He tried to ignore the growing pain in his back. Now two groups of Indians came at them. The first group weaved their horses and turned as before, but the second group came in closer, racing past the wallow at about a hundred yards. One by one, they loosed arrows, arcing their bows high and ducking behind their horses' necks after they fired. Behind Will, Chance fired the Sharps. Will hugged the parapet, eyes clenched, muscles taut, as the arrows thumped around him. Please, God, he did not want to be hit again. He did not want to die. Then he steadied himself. The alternative to death was capture, and he knew what that meant. If he had to die, it was better to die fighting.

Chance had missed his shot. An Indian was sitting his horse out front, laughing at him. Chance ignored the taunts. He opened the breech of the Sharps and calmly pushed in another paper cartridge, as the Indian rode away.

"Why are they doing this?" Will asked. "Why don't they just rush us?"

"Comanches don't fight that way. They could lose a lot of men in a rush. That circle of theirs is supposed to represent a grinding wheel, and that's just what they'll do to us. Grind us down. This could go on all day."

"We got any chance of getting out?"

"One. If we hold them off long enough, they might get tired of the game and leave us alone. Indians do that sometimes."

As Chance spoke, the Comanches came again. Two groups from opposite sides. One file rode right at Will. Will adjusted his grip on the flintlock, aiming at the first Indian in the line. At fifty yards, the Indians swerved gracefully and galloped past the wallow, firing arrows. Will followed the move. He drew breath, making himself ignore the falling arrows. He squeezed the trigger.

The rifle's recoil almost tore his wounded shoulder apart, and he jumped with the pain. He smelled the acrid powder smoke. When he looked, the lead Indian was riding back to the circle with his fellows, but he was bent double.

"That gave 'em something to think about," Chance said. "Maybe you can shoot after all."

Will handed his rifle and powder to Chance. "You'll have to use this. One more time, and my arm will fall off."

The Indian circle stopped. The Comanches sat in little groups on the plain, occasionally communicating with hand gestures.

Chance resumed work on the parapet, digging earth and piling it in ever higher layers. Will tried to help, but he no longer had the strength. He felt flushed. He was drenched with sweat. Chance dropped his bowie knife as the next attack started.

The rumble of the Comanche horses filled Will's ears. It grew louder as the Indians approached. Will hefted the Dragoon Colt in his left hand, cocking it, trying to feel comfortable with it. Revolving pistols had started selling well only in the last year or so, mainly to the thousands of young men caught up in the California gold madness. Will had felt foolish carrying one himself. He'd never dreamed he would need it. He'd never pictured his trip west ending this way—murdered by Indians three days out of Fort Worth. This was the kind of thing that happened in stories. It was the kind of thing that happened to other people, not to him.

Arrows whooshed. Chance's rifle banged. The Indians charged past. Will aimed his revolver and fired, cursing at the same moment, because his target was out of range. It had been a wasted shot.

The battle continued this way for an hour, then another, until Will and Chance lost all sense of time. The Comanches attacked in small groups, one after another, so that there was barely time to reload. After a spate of attacks, there would be a lull. Then the Indians would move in again, gingerly, testing whether the white men still had fight in them. They played with Will and Chance, like a cat playing with a wounded snake—striking, jumping back, waiting to strike again. They were patient and respectful of the white men's superior weapons, but with each series of attacks, they came a bit closer. Each volley of arrows struck with greater accuracy. The parapet and the dead horse were peppered with feathered shafts. Arrows stuck at all angles in the wallow's deepening bottom. Will and Chance were both bleeding from minor wounds.

The Indians themselves were almost impossible to hit. They weaved their horses; they crisscrossed them. They made dust clouds and charged out of the dust. Sometimes they hung beneath their horses' necks as they shot their bows or rifles. Chance shot the horse from under one. The animal rolled head over heels, but its rider bounced to his feet, apparently unhurt. While Will and Chance blazed away, two more Indians galloped down on their companion at full speed. With the precision of circus riders, they lifted him from the ground and carried him to safety.

It was midafternoon. The sun burned down on Will and Chance, punishing them. The dead horse began to smell. The blood had been drained from its carcass by arrows, and flies swarmed over the blood and the horse. Already ants streamed in and out of the horse's wounds, in and out of its eyes and mouth. The ants and flies were so bad that Chance had to shift to another part of the wallow. Both men's faces were streaked with powder and dirt and sweat. Their lips swelled and cracked. Will grew weaker and weaker, and the burden of the battle fell on Chance. Chance used up the rifle bullets, first for the Sharps, then the flintlock, until all that was left to the men were the shorter-ranged pistols.

During one attack, an Indian broke loose from the outer circle and rode in with his lance, hoping to catch the white men looking the other way. At the last moment, Chance heard him. He turned and drilled the Indian through the chest. The .44 slug knocked the Indian from his saddle, but the rawhide thong that bound his wrist to his horse's neck did not break, and the horse ran away, dragging the Indian along the ground until other tribesmen caught up with it.

The Indian's death brought another lull in the attacks. Hurrying, keeping an eye on the Indians, Chance broke the cylinders from his cannonlike Walker Colts. He fixed an oily patch to a rammer, and he ran it down first the cylinders, then the barrels, which had become fouled from so much firing. Chance wrenched spent percussion caps from the cylinder nipples, and he stuck a pin through each nipple's flash hole, to clear it. He stuffed one of the new paper cartridges into each cylinder and rammed it home. He seated new caps on the nipples, then snapped the cylinders back into the weapons. Chance took another look at the Indians, then he said to Will, "Give me your six-shooter. I'll reload for you."

Will was light-headed, more tired than he could have believed possible. He wanted to lie down and sleep. Chance loaded Will's pistol and handed it back. "That's five rounds left for you. Eight for me."

"How many Indians have we gotten so far?" Will said.

"Three dead that I know of. A couple more wounded, and a bunch of horses hurt. Not much to show for all the bullets we used."

Chance took his canteen and swished it, listening to the hollow sounds inside. "It's a toss-up which'll do for us first, the Indians or thirst. I'll tell you, it's times like this that make a man get religion."

He gave the canteen to Will, who drank sparingly. The water did little for his thirst. It was like sprinkling raindrops on a forest fire. He was short of breath. The earth seemed to be spinning. So did the sky. He tried to concentrate. "You fought Indians a lot?"

Chance took the canteen and drank. "Not really. I never fight anybody unless I have to."

Everything seemed confused to Will. "But you were in the Rangers, in the war . . ."

"I joined the Rangers for the card games. Those boys always had one going. There wasn't much money involved, but it was a good place to practice my trade."

"You didn't see action?"

Chance's eyes narrowed as he remembered. "I didn't say that. I saw action, all right, a lot more than I cared to."

There was a shot, and a bullet kicked up dirt from the parapet near Chance's head. He ducked instinctively. Then he peered over the parapet's rim. "Sniper," he said. "They got somebody in close. I saw his powder smoke, but I can't make him out in that tall grass."

Chance began digging again, adding another layer to the

earthen parapet. Will didn't know how he still had the energy. "Why don't you just give up?" Will asked. "It won't change the end."

"Don't believe in giving up," Chance said.

All day a line of gray clouds had been building to the northwest, until they stretched across the horizon in a gloomy mass. Now the first wisps of cloud reached across the sun. Within minutes, the flaming orb was lost to sight.

Sheltered from the sun, the men in the wallow breathed with relief. The breeze picked up. It began to gust. The temperature dropped, chilling their sweaty bodies. A drop of cold rain splashed on Chance's hand. Another drop struck the brim of Will's hat. More rain fell, spattering around them at first, then beating with rhythm, until suddenly it was raining very hard.

The rain was welcome after the blistering heat. It washed away dirt and blood. It cleansed the foul-smelling powder smoke from the air. Will and Chance were soaked. They sucked rainwater from their grimy shirts to slake their thirsts.

The rain continued to fall. By now Will and Chance were chilled through and through, shivering and longing for the sun's return. But the sun did not return. Visibility dropped; the far reaches of the valley were lost to sight. The rain battered away the top of the parapet even as Chance added to it. The sides of the wallow turned to mud. They ran with rivulets of brown water. The wallow was filling up.

Chance watched the Indians, who were huddled in groups on the rainswept plain. Chance had placed his pistols under his buckskin shirt, to keep them as dry as possible. His moccasined feet were freezing in the water. Hunger gnawed at him. There was a bit of jerked beef in his saddlebags, but he might need that later, so he bit off another hunk of the rank-tasting tobacco and chewed it glumly.

"There's one consolation," he said. "It's raining as hard on them as it is on us."

Will made no answer. His legs were drawn up in the water. His arms were wrapped around himself. He was shaking. Chance felt Will's forehead. It was burning up. He would be no more help in this fight.

Chance gave Will the remaining water in the canteen. He

scooped muddy rainwater from the wallow for himself. He thought how easily he could have escaped this fate, and he wondered, why *had* he come back?

He didn't know. It hadn't been an act of honor, because he didn't believe in honor. It hadn't been loyalty to a friend, because he didn't know Will enough for him to be a friend. It had been instinct, something he'd done without thinking. He couldn't abandon Will to the Comanches.

With a yell, a group of Comanches broke from the circle. Chance spit out the tobacco.

The Indians splashed toward the wallow. Their naked chests and legs glistened in the rain. Their yells sounded less enthusiastic than before. They didn't like this weather. They weren't going to let this go on much longer.

The Indians rode by the wallow. Arrows plopped into the mud beside Chance, but he held his fire. The Indians would note that lack of return fire. They would know that the whites were low on ammunition. Soon they would come for the kill.

The hidden sniper fired again. The ball tore a gash in Chance's upper arm. He swore and gritted his teeth against the pain. He crouched low behind the parapet, and his chin touched water. The level in the wallow had risen precipitously. Even when he straightened, it was halfway up his chest. The brown water was tinged red with blood.

Chance took off his hat and began bailing, throwing the water over the top of the parapet. His muscles screamed with agony. The gash in his arm was streaming blood. He stopped to gulp some of the filthy water, then he continued bailing. The sniper fired again, but he took no notice.

Across from him, Will lapsed into semiconsciousness. He slumped and began to slide under the water.

Chance floundered across the wallow. As Will's nose disappeared into the muddy water, Chance grabbed him beneath the arms. He lifted Will's head from the water. He held Will awkwardly and slapped his face. "Wake up! Wake up! Christ, you're the only person I know that could drown in a buffalo wallow."

Will mumbled. He was pale and hollow-cheeked. Sodden blond hair was plastered across his forehead.

Hoofbeats thudded in the mud. The Indians were attacking again. Chance got one arm around Will's chest, straining to keep his companion from sliding back under water. With the other hand, he pulled a Colt from beneath his buckskin shirt and cocked it.

The Indians came within twenty-five yards before releasing their arrows. Chance fired back, a bad shot because he was dragged off balance by Will's dead weight. He couldn't hold Will much longer. His tired muscles were strained to their limit.

With difficulty, Chance heaved Will over to the lip of the parapet. If the sniper got him there, it couldn't be helped. He took his hat and started bailing again. He was glassy-eyed, drawing on unknown reserves of strength. Despite his exertions, he was freezing in the chest-deep water. His blood slowed, paralyzed by the cold.

The Indians' circle was moving closer. Now they were just a short dash from the wallow. They were bunched up, ready to end it.

Chance stood, defiant at the end. He took his fully loaded pistol and Will's Dragoon Colt. To Will he said, ''Looks like this is where we say *adios, amigo*. I won't let them take you alive.''

Will's eyelids fluttered. Chance doubted that he'd heard.

Chance turned this way and that, waiting for the Indians' final attack. His defiance began to crumble. He licked his cracked lips. The Indians would be on them quickly when they came. Maybe he should shoot Will and himself right now. He might not have time otherwise.

The wind shifted. It whipped the rain into Chance's eyes. He turned his head, blinking against the needlelike drops. When he looked again, the Indians were riding away, disappearing into the storm.

3

Chance stood still. His right hand was shaking, but he did not try to stop it. His stomach felt hollow.

Was it possible? Had the Comanches given up the fight just when they were on the point of winning?

It must be a trick. Any minute, they'd come charging back.

But the minutes passed, and the valley remained empty and silent, save for the steady hiss of the rain.

"They *are* gone," Chance said at last. "Damn them, they are."

He sagged against the parapet, overcome by exhaustion and emotional release. He stared blankly at the mud. He was freezing in the rising water of the buffalo wallow, but he did not care. He began laughing.

Then Chance remembered Will, lying on the parapet next to him, and his laughter evaporated. He fought down weariness. He fought down the urge to let his mind go mercifully blank. "All right. Let's have a look at you."

He hauled himself from the flooded buffalo wallow, wincing with pain from his wounded arm. His sleeve was dark with blood. He knelt beside Will, who was shivering, looking at Chance with fever-bright eyes.

"What happened?" Will asked weakly.

Chance looked at Will's pale, sunken cheeks. He forced himself to grin for Will's sake. "This rain saved us. The Indians got tired of it. They said the hell with it and went somewhere to get dry. Indians do that kind of thing, I told you."

"Will they be back?"

"Not that bunch. They probably figure we're bad medicine. 'Cause of us, they lost at least three men, they lost the buffalo herd, and now they're getting soaked. All they've got to show for it is a couple horses and what's in our packs. They'll want to leave us be.''

Chance fingered the broken arrow in Will's back. "How are you holding up?"

"All right. Is there water?"

Chance swirled mud and blood from the water in the wallow, and he dipped in his canteen. The river water would be nearly as muddy in a storm like this, and he dared not wander that far from Will, in case he was wrong and the Comanches did return.

He held the canteen to Will's lips. Will drank, making a face at the taste. "What now?" he asked.

"Now we get this arrow out of your back." Chance hoped he sounded more confident than he felt.

Chance wrapped his bandanna around the bullet wound in his arm. Luckily the slug had only gouged the skin. He turned Will over gently and straddled his back. "Get ready. This is going to hurt."

Will went taut. Chance scraped mud from the arrow shaft. He wiped his hands dry on his undershirt. He set himself, bracing his knee in Will's back. Chance gripped the slippery arrow, testing his hands in various positions until he was satisfied. He rocked the arrow back and forth, trying to loosen it, feeling Will squirm beneath him. "It's in there good," he said. "Those Comanche bows are strong as hell."

Chance pulled on the arrow. He pulled harder. He felt something give, deep in Will's back. Will's fists clenched and unclenched in the mud. He was holding his breath.

Chance strained. Inside Will's body, the arrow suddenly ripped free, and Will gasped with pain. Slowly Chance pulled out the blood-smeared shaft, careful not to jolt Will more than necessary. Then he gave a last tug, and the shaft was out.

Will exhaled his breath with a rush. He rested his head in the mud, panting. "All done? That wasn't . . . that wasn't so bad."

Chance looked at the broken arrow shaft for a second, then he threw it away. "The head didn't come out," he said. "It broke off inside you. I'll have to cut it out."

Will didn't say anything.

"Sorry," Chance told him. "But I've got to do it right here. Right now. If I don't, you'll die."

Chance looked around. They couldn't have picked a worse

spot. There was no shelter. It was cold and wet. He wished they hadn't lost their packs, with the tents and supplies. Most of all, he'd have liked a fire. There were plenty of trees by the river-bank, but the wood would be too wet to burn. His tinder was soaked through, anyway.

Chance splashed into the wallow. He picked his bowie knife from the litter of arrows and weapons and empty cartridge boxes that stood above the rising water. Then he saw Will's smaller knife, and he picked that up. He tested the point and blade. They were sharp. He decided to use that one.

Will watched him, trying to be brave. "Tell me you've done this before."

"I'd be lying if I did," Chance told him.

From the saddle of his dead horse, Chance took his rope of braided Mexican leather, his reata. He wandered afield until he found a good-sized stick, probably blown from the old pin oak. He came back, and he rinsed his hands and the knife in the muddy water of the hollow. He dried them on his sodden un-dershirt. His hands were white and wrinkled from the rain. His feet felt shriveled. Everything smelled wet, and his teeth were chattering with cold.

"Let's get on with it," he said.

He settled himself beside Will in the mud. With the knife, he slit Will's shirt and undershirt, and he tore them away from Will's upper back.

"I don't know if I'm going to like this," Will joked ner-vously.

"You won't," Chance assured him. He wished that Will would pass out from fever. He was having a hell of a time for an alert period. Chance handed Will the stick. "Bite on this."

Will put the wet stick in his mouth, sliding it around until he got a good grip on it with his teeth. The gritty bark flaked off in his mouth, but it was a strong stick.

"For your hands," Chance said, giving Will the reata.

Will took two turns of the reata around each hand, with a short length in between.

Chance's mouth was dry. He wished he'd thought to drink before he started, but now that he'd come this far he wanted to keep going. He bent over the angry, puckered arrow wound.

The rain was helping to wash away the blood. That was one good thing, anyway.

"Here we go."

He felt Will's body tense. He inserted the knife point into the wound, probing for the arrowhead. Deeper and deeper he inched, cutting through muscle. Blood bubbled out.

He heard Will's boots digging the mud. He heard Will's labored breathing. The length of reata was stretched tight. Will's knuckles were white.

Then the knife point struck an object—the arrow head. It was stuck behind the shoulder bone. Will squealed through the stick in his mouth. He arched his back, straining.

Chance licked his lips and took a firmer grip on the knife. He began to cut around the arrowhead, trying to pry it out.

In Will's mouth, the stick snapped.

4

Will smelled woodsmoke. It tickled his nostrils.

He opened his eyes. The rain had stopped. The sun was out, but he was shielded from it. He was in a shelter, a framework of saplings with some kind of hide stretched overhead. A rolled-up blanket was his pillow. Outside the shelter, he saw another frame of saplings, with long strips of meat drying on it.

Will sat up, and he moaned sharply, because his back hurt, and he remembered that there had been an arrow in it. His shirt was gone, and he felt a bandage, so the arrow must be out. He had been there awhile. The ground beneath him was firm, even after the rain, and he could see where the shelter poles had been moved inward as the drying hide had shrunk.

He was burning with thirst. His tongue felt swollen and fuzzy. He looked around the shelter for some water. He saw his Dragoon Colt revolver. He saw the small fire, buried in a pit for further shelter. There was piled brush nearby. He saw Chance's saddle and their two rifles.

Chance. Where was Chance? He had no idea.

Chance's wooden canteen leaned against his saddle blanket. Slowly, because of his back, Will reached for the canteen. It was full. Will remembered the muddy taste of the water in the buffalo wallow, but any taste would be fine now. Just so it was wet. He unscrewed the top and took a sip. To his surprise, the water was cool and fresh.

He drank again, a long gulp this time, then another. He could have emptied the canteen, but he rested, because that little bit of activity had started him breathing faster. He felt weak and limp, as if every ounce of strength had been drained from him.

He heard footsteps. He dropped the canteen and picked up his revolver.

Someone laughed, and he looked. It was Chance.

Chance was coming from the river. He carried a pole over one shoulder, from which dangled two fat bass. His undershirt was covered with dirt and old blood. One sleeve was missing, where it had been cut away to expose his gunshot wound to the air. He looked different, and Will realized it was because his dark beard had grown.

"Well, well, look who's awake," Chance said. He flashed his big grin. "How do you feel?"

Will put down the pistol and straightened the canteen. "Awful. How long was I out?"

Chance slung the fish to the ground. "Four days. Tell you the truth, I didn't think you were going to make it. Your head was hot enough to fry eggs. You're tough, though, I'll give you that."

Chance dug in his pants pocket. "Here, I saved this for you."

He handed Will a flint arrowhead.

"This the one that got me?" asked Will.

Chance nodded. Will turned the triangular arrowhead over curiously. He ran a finger along the sharp, chiseled blade. He started to toss the arrowhead away, then he changed his mind.

"Thanks," he said. "I'll keep it."

He put the arrowhead in his own pocket. His movement was too sudden, and he winced. "My back sure hurts," he said.

"That'll be the stitches pulling," Chance told him. "I sewed you with thread from my carryall. I rinsed your undershirt in the river and made bandages from it.'' He grinned again. "A real professional job, if I do say. Maybe I should hang out my shingle.''

Will drank from the canteen again. He indicated the hide stretched overhead. "What'd you do, shoot a buffalo?''

"Wild cow,'' Chance said. "The woods hereabouts are full of 'em. I stumbled on a bunch by accident. This old girl must have thought I was after her calf, because she came at me like a bat out of hell. Took me three slugs to bring her down.''

Chance grew serious. He changed the subject. "Can you stand?''

"I—I think so,'' Will said.

The two men crawled from beneath the hide shelter. Will blinked in the bright sunlight. Chance gave him a hand up. Will staggered, bracing himself. Looking around, he saw the buffalo wallow, where they had made the fight against the Comanches, about seventy-five yards away, toward the river. There was no sign of Chance's dead horse, and Will was guessing where some of that meat had come from, when the world began to spin. The blood rushed from his head. His legs wobbled and he sat, heavily. He was sweating, breathing hard.

Chance gave Will some more water. After a minute he helped Will up again, but Will didn't do much better. Chance caught him before he fell and sat him down.

"I was afraid of this,'' Chance said. He squatted beside Will. "I won't lie to you, Will. We're in a tight spot here. Besides the three cartridges it took to bring down that cow, I used another one starting this fire. That leaves me eight. That isn't much for hunting, and if serious trouble comes along, it's even worse. I suppose we could make bows and arrows if we had time to season the wood and shape arrowheads, but they wouldn't be any help if the Comanches come back. We'd be dead men. We've got to get you well and get out of here, quick.''

"I'll be all right,'' Will promised. "We got some moving to do if we're to catch that train for California.''

"You're not catching any train. Not this year.''

"What do you . . . ?''

"It'll be a long time before you're strong enough to travel to

California. Right now you just better pray you can make it back to Fort Worth."

Chance let the truth of this sink in, then he lightened. "First off, we better get you something to eat. I hope you like fish."

5

The next few days were spent trying to get Will in shape to march back to Fort Worth. By late the first afternoon, Will was able to walk to the river, where Chance cut a hickory branch and fashioned him a fishing pole. Fish was their main meal, because Chance wanted to stretch the beef and horsemeat as far as they could, and he did not want to use more cartridges hunting fresh meat.

Gradually they went farther afield. Chance was always pushing, urging Will to do better. Chance was worried, nervous, constantly on guard. He was afraid the Indians would come back.

Will, on the other hand, was unusually content. He loved exploring the land. He reveled in the ever-changing vistas, in the play of light and shadow over the rugged hills. This was a hunter's paradise. There were herds of buffalo and antelope. There were quail and prairie chickens and jackrabbits. In the woods were deer and wild turkeys, and cattle, too, though these were heard more often than seen. Wild horses, or mustangs, could sometimes be seen running free in the distance.

The days were warm and the nights cool. Chance did most of the work around camp, while Will lay under the shelter. Will still couldn't walk more than a half mile without resting. He wondered if his strength would ever return.

In the evenings, the two men would sit by the fire and enjoy the quiet beauty of the scene. "Days like this, I wish I hadn't lost my pack," Chance said on one such occasion. "There was some whiskey in there, and a drink would go down nice about now.''

Will said, "I don't see how folks can drink whiskey, especially in hot weather like this. I like a nice cool glass of beer, myself.''

Chance gave him a sidelong look. "I bet you don't drink too many beers, neither. You've got that sober look about you.''

"Never had time for drinking," Will said, "nor the money to do it with. With eleven brothers and sisters, I was too busy trying to stay alive.''

"Eleven?'' Chance laughed. "No wonder you wanted to leave home.''

"With me being next youngest, there wasn't nothing to inherit—even if Pa had anything worth inheriting, which he don't. Land was all taken up in them parts. The only work was in the lumber mill over to Booneville. I worked there just long enough to buy my outfit, then I lit out.''

The sun was setting in an orange ball, casting long shadows across the valley. Caught in its glow, chirring insects rose in luminescent clouds from the grass. The two men could smell the river. Chance said, "Was it hard leaving your family?''

"It was real hard. I didn't always get along with them, but they was my family. We went through a lot together. I don't expect I'll ever see none of them again.'' Will paused. "What about you? You leave anybody behind?''

Chance shook his head. "I didn't have brothers or sisters. My parents are dead. I was born in New Orleans. That's where I lived, mostly, when I was a boy. My dad was a gambler, my mom had been an actress before they got married. Mom died of yellow jack when I was fourteen. After that, me and Dad moved around a lot.''

"What happened to your dad?''

Chance's mouth became a grim line. "He got killed in a card game, in Austin. Just before the war with Mexico.''

Will tried to imagine a life such as Chance must have lived, but he could not. He had never known anything but the farm.

Chance built up the fire. He had cut some strips of the dried horsemeat, and they stuck them on sharp sticks and roasted them. Will didn't mind the sweetish taste of the meat. He could remember times at home when horsemeat would have been a delicacy.

As Chance chewed his meat, he seemed to be debating something in his mind. Finally he said, "Will, I can't wait for you any longer. I'm going back to Fort Worth. I'll get ammunition and horses, and I'll come back for you."

They looked at each other, and Chance went on. "There's no choice. It's too dangerous to stay here. It's a good five days' walk to Fort Worth, and it'll be weeks before you could make it. After I get the horses, we'll go back and winter in Dallas. You can get a job there while you get well and wait for the spring trains to California."

An idea that had been floating around the back of Will's mind for the last few days suddenly came to the forefront. On the spot, he made his own decision. "I ain't going to California," he said.

Chance looked surprised. "What?"

"I'm staying here."

Chance stared.

"Why go all the way to California, when everything I want is right here? Land's dear in California, they say. I only meant to mine enough gold to buy me some. This land here is free, as much as a man can take."

Chance ran his tongue around the inside of his jaw. He looked at a loss for words. At last he said, "Why? I'm no farmer, but I'd be willing to bet this country doesn't get enough regular rain for crops."

"I wasn't thinking about farming," Will said. "I was thinking about ranching. There's all these cattle around, and they don't belong to nobody."

"You know anything about raising cattle?" Chance said.

"I can learn."

"What are you going to do with them?"

"Sell 'em for beef, I guess."

"To who?"

"All right, then, I'll sell 'em for the hides and tallow. There's a market in New Orleans."

"How're you going to get them there?"

"I'll find a way. I'm staying, Chance, and that's that."

"What about the Indians? They're bound to come back eventually."

"My grandpa fought Indians. I reckon I can, too. Indians ain't usually a problem for more'n a couple years after whites move in. I figure I got that much luck left in me."

"You'll never last out here by yourself," Chance said.

Somehow Chance's opposition only made Will more stubborn. "I'll take that chance."

"At least tell me you've got sense enough to go back to Dallas for the winter."

"I don't like Dallas. I don't like any town much. This land is mine, and I'm staying here." Then Will had another idea. "Why don't you stay, too, Chance? God knows, there's enough land. It's an opportunity to get in at the start of something big."

Chance rose and took a turn around the twilit camp. Then he stopped. "This is without a doubt the stupidest idea I ever heard in my life. But I'll tell you what. If you want, when I come back, I'll bring provisions to see you through the winter and get you started next year."

"But you won't stay?"

Chance smiled ruefully. "Wilderness living isn't really my style. I like a place where there's women and card games. Music."

Will nodded. "Sure." Then he faltered. "Chance, I . . . I never got to thank you. For what you done for me. I—I don't know how to put it in words good, but I wouldn't be alive if it wasn't for you. I don't know how I'll ever—"

"Forget it," Chance said.

It was an awkward moment. Then Will said, "When will you leave?"

"First light tomorrow. No sense putting it off. These provisions of yours are going to cost a lot of money, by the way. Better give me everything you have."

Will hesitated. "I ain't got all that much."

"How much?"

"Eleven dollars and forty-seven cents, if I ain't lost none since last I counted."

Chance looked at him. Then he put back his head and laughed. "You were going to California on eleven dollars and forty-seven cents?"

Will shrugged.

"And now you expect to start a ranch with that? You've got some hide, my friend."

Will squirmed. "Actually, I was hoping I could borrow the money from you."

Chance laughed louder. "That's rich. I was hoping to borrow from *you*. I've got less than ten dollars. I had to leave Nacogdoches in a hurry."

Chance stooped under the shelter. From his buckskin shirt, he brought out his deck of cards. He flipped the dog-eared edges, listening to them rustle. "It's time to trust to the gods of the green felt, William. What we have won't give me much of a stake, but it'll get me in a game for one hand, at least."

"What if you lose?" Will said.

"I won't."

Chance set out the next morning after breakfast. Sunlight was just pushing through the scattered clouds. Both men were chilled and stiff from sleep. The long grass was wet with dew.

Chance carried a pistol loaded with four rounds. His saddlebags were stuffed with dried meat, and he slung them over his shoulder. "I'll be back in two weeks, at the latest," he told Will. "Keep your eyes open. Don't use your powder unless you have to, and make sure that fire doesn't go out."

Will nodded. His stomach was tight. He wished Chance wasn't going, but he knew it had to be done.

Chance held out his hand. Will took it. With his free hand, Chance gripped Will's shoulder. "Good luck, Will."

"You, too."

Chance turned and started off, striding purposefully toward the river crossing. He looked back once and waved.

Will waved, too. He watched Chance as long as his friend was in view, and he kept watching long after Chance had crested the hill on the stream's far side. He wondered if Chance would make it. Chance faced danger from Indians, from the elements, from the outlaws who infested a virtually lawless state like Texas.

Then Will stiffened. He suddenly wondered if Chance intended to come back, at all. Had this just been a painless way of abandoning him? No. Chance wouldn't do that, would he?

Will turned and walked back to the hide shelter.

6

Will was scared. With Chance gone, this empty land seemed bigger, more threatening. Maybe Chance would get back before the two weeks were up, Will thought hopefully.

If Chance came back at all.

Will kept close to camp that first day. He caught a large bass, roasted it on the embers of the fire, and ate it. As the sun started dropping in the west, he grew nervous. He dreaded the coming of night. He dreaded the darkness and what it might bring.

The sun set. Gray dusk deepened over the valley. The last crimson flush faded from the western sky, and it was night.

Will let the fire burn low. What if Comanches were around? What if they saw the flames?

Then he remembered what Chance had said—"Don't let the fire go out." He took dried brush from the pile and fed the fire stick by stick, until it was again burning brightly. The still air was filled with the crackle of flames, the pop and hiss of cinders.

As the darkness deepened, the night came alive with sounds—small scurryings, the flappings of wings, a faraway howl. The yell of a panther. There were other noises, too, indefinable ones. Some of them were close.

Will put his heavy revolver in his lap. He was too scared to sleep. He resolved to stay awake all night. He edged just outside the fire's glow, occasionally adding a small branch or some twigs to keep it going. At last, exhaustion and pain overcame him. His head nodded. He curled onto one side, the pistol still in his hand.

He woke with a start. The sun was up. He sat up and looked around, the pistol poised for use. At first he was mad at himself for falling asleep, then he realized it was all right. He was still alive. There had been no danger, after all.

He looked at the fire. It was out. Frantically he poked through the pit, hoping to find some embers to blow back to life. But the ashes were cold. He cursed. One of the few things Chance had told him to do, and he'd bungled it right away. Chance had been right—he'd never make it out here.

Then he composed himself. He had sworn not to leave this land. If that was the case, he was going to be alone here for a long time, so he'd better get used to it. He couldn't just cower by the fire. He had to make do.

The first thing was to start a new fire. Will cleaned out the pit, then he put in a fresh layer of twigs and small branches. He tore a strip from what was left of his flannel shirt, crumpled it, and built the twigs around it. He broke the cylinder from his revolver. With much effort, he pried the bullet from one of the chambers, and he poured the chamber's powder onto the flannel. He took the flint from his rifle, put it on the powder, and struck it with his knife blade. A spark leaped out, igniting the powder. He fed twigs onto the burning powder until he had a good fire going. Then he cut some beef strips and cooked them. He was tired of fish.

He had three cartridges left.

Next Will began thinking about a more permanent shelter. The easiest thing would be to build a dugout, he decided, probably in the side of that flat-topped hill. He would be more protected there, from the elements and from the Indians, if they came.

He found a spot at the base of the hill, partly screened by scrub oak, with good drainage and a view of the river. He began work, hacking away with his knife. He worked slowly, carving out a few inches at a time, stopping to rest, then going on. The work took a lot out of him, but he enjoyed it. It gave him something to do, something to take his mind off the loneliness. He sweated at it, and he grew stronger.

He planned the dugout to be seven feet high, with four feet above ground and the rest below. When he had excavated a fair-sized dwelling, he moved the fire and his gear up from the river. He set up the hide and poles as an entranceway. He fashioned some snares and trapped a jackrabbit. He even managed to kill a few squirrels by chucking rocks at them—he was glad to see he hadn't lost his boyhood skill. He got used to being alone, and he grew more confident in himself. He felt like Adam in the Garden of Eden.

He used his fishing pole for a calendar. There were twelve notches carved on it now. It was nearly May. The weather had turned hot. It had rained only once since Chance had left, and the prairie had a parched, brown look. Will went down to the river, to collect some of the big pieces of driftwood that he used to keep the fire going while he was out exploring or hunting.

His path took him through a field of yellow-and-white daisies, holding bravely forth against the heat. Then something caught his eye.

It was a large set of deer antlers, or rather two sets, locked together and yellowing. Will examined them. They were heavy and splintered, and though he could move them a bit, he could not pry them apart. He would have to break them to do that. He tried to picture what had happened. Two great bucks, each master of his own domain, had battled for supremacy here beside the river. They had clashed with such violence that their antlers had become entangled. Unable to free themselves, they had died together, mortal enemies joined forever. Will wondered if it had been a lingering death or a quick one. Quick, probably. These hills were filled with predators.

He decided to keep the antlers. He would put them over the entrance to the ranch house that he would someday build, and he would call his ranch the Double Horn.

He started back to camp with his prize. He saw the dugout ahead. A trio of lean, gray shapes were tearing at his rabbits, snapping down his remaining cache of dried beef and horsemeat. Coyotes.

Will dropped the antlers and drew his revolver, running forward. "Hey! Get out of there!" He fired the revolver once, twice. The coyotes dropped their tails and scampered off, carrying the meat with them.

Will cleaned up the camp. The meat could be replaced. The bad part was that he was now down to one shot. Again he'd acted stupidly. There had been no need to fire those shots. He had wasted them.

Chance was supposed to be back no later than the day after tomorrow. Would he come? Will had been worried to start with, and his unease was growing.

Chance was not there when Will carved the two-week notch on the fishing pole. He was not there when Will carved the three-week notch, either. Will's worry deepened into resignation. In his heart, he had known this would happen. Chance was not coming back. He was dead, or he had lost their money, or he'd simply chosen not to brave the return journey.

Will couldn't stay here now. With one pistol shot and a dull knife, he was in poor condition to tame the wilderness. He'd have to swallow his big talk and go back to Fort Worth, then Dallas. He'd get a job in Dallas, load up on supplies, and return next spring.

Just making it to Fort Worth was going to take some doing, though. He had gotten stronger, but he wasn't sure he was up to a five-day hike. For certain he was in no shape to take on Indians or outlaws, should he encounter them. No matter, he had to go, and the sooner the better. He just hoped he didn't find Chance living it up when he got there.

First he needed food. There wasn't enough meat on rabbits and squirrels to pack, and he wouldn't be able to hunt on the way. He took his revolver and went upriver, to a spot where he'd seen fresh deer tracks yesterday. One of the few supplies Chance had carried in his saddlebags was a quantity of salt. Will put the salt in one of his socks, and he hung the sock from a tree branch. With his canteen, he ran water through the sock, until there was a salty pool on the ground below. As the water dried, Will settled in the nearby undergrowth to wait. Insects buzzed around him, biting his face and arms. The revolver was cocked. He'd hunted deer before, but always with a rifle. He hadn't shown much skill with the Dragoon Colt so far. He'd hoped to save this last bullet for himself in case he was captured by Indians, but there was no chance of that now.

He was half asleep when he heard a rustle in the bushes. Very slowly he looked up. Not twenty yards away, a fine doe was licking the salt from the ground. Her nose and ears twitched alert for danger.

Will raised the pistol, holding it with both hands to steady it. The doe looked up for a second, as if something were not right but she couldn't decide what. She began licking the salt again. Will aimed at a spot just behind the left shoulder. He fired.

The doe leaped and fell on her side. Will rushed forward with his knife to end her struggles.

Will skinned the deer and cut up the meat. He cooked some of it and dried the rest. He made a sack from the skin of the deer's haunch, and when the venison was dried, he filled the sack and closed it with a rawhide thong.

Before leaving, he laced the double-horned antler to the poles that formed the dugout's entranceway. He took a last look. The dugout had already begun to feel like home. He'd be back, though. He swore it.

He swung the sack over his shoulder and started away, walking down the gentle slope to the river. Suddenly he stopped.

In the distance, a wagon was approaching. The wagon had a white canvas top. It was drawn by four horses, and it looked heavily loaded. A big yellow dog trotted alongside. The wagon was headed for the river crossing, and when its driver saw Will, he stood in the box, took off his hat, and waved.

It was Chance.

7

Chance started the wagon across the ford. Will sat on a hummock of earth to wait for him.

Chance wore new clothes—a dark-red shirt with a shield in front, dark-blue trousers, and expensive boots. Will's clothes were now little more than rags. Chance was clean shaven, in comparison to Will's scraggly, month-old beard. Chance braked the wagon in front of Will. He rested his arms on his knees, and he grinned. "Where were you going?"

"To Fort Worth," Will said, "where do you think? I couldn't stay here no more. Where have you been all this time? Did it take you this long to win the money?"

Chance looked down guiltily. "Actually, I won the money right away. The truth is, I was kind of . . . delayed."

"Delayed? Delayed how?" Then Will understood. "You mean a woman?"

Chance's look said everything.

"Not somebody's wife again?"

"No. No, she was a whore, but she was pretty, and it sure was hard to tear myself away."

Will pushed his hat back. He kicked the wagon wheel, fuming. "Why, you son of a . . . You spent all this time with a whore? I almost died out here!"

Chance grinned again and made a dismissive gesture with his hand. "I knew you'd be all right. And you are all right, aren't you? Stop turning red in the face and climb on up here."

Chance moved over in the wagon box, while Will joined him. Will was trying to stay mad, trying to resist his friend's infectious good humor. Will had not smelled horses in a while, and at first their odor seemed unusually strong. He glanced behind him under the canvas. The wagon bed was filled to the top, but he couldn't make out what any of the items were.

The big yellow dog ambled alongside. He was about nine months old, all floppy legs and eagerness. He heard something in the high grass and ran off to investigate.

"What's the dog for?" Will asked.

"To warn us in case our red brothers decide to pay us a visit. I bought him off a fellow in Fort Worth. I call him Jaundice, because of his yellow color."

Chance looked ahead. "You move the camp?"

Will said, "Yeah. Keep driving. I'll show you where."

He directed Chance to the base of the hill and the half-completed dugout.

"You've been busy," Chance said as they drove up.

"I had enough time," Will said sarcastically.

Chance ignored the barb. "How are you feeling, by the way? You look better than I expected. Isolation must agree with you."

Will snorted in reply. Then he said, "How 'bout you? You have any trouble getting to Fort Worth?"

"Almost got bit by a rattler, but that was about it."

Chance stopped the wagon in front of the dugout. He climbed down, stretching, while the big yellow dog sniffed the dugout's entrance and urinated on it. Chance examined the locked deer antlers mounted on the poles. Then he looked in the dugout. "This'll do," he said. "This'll do fine."

He took a buckskin jacket from the wagon box and tossed it in the dugout. He turned to Will. "Help me with this wagon."

Chance had packed more into the small wagon than Will thought possible. There were cords of rope. There were kegs of nails and tools of all description. There were casks of gunpowder and salt and sugar, along with a pig of lead. There were fifty-pound sacks of corn. There was even a cast-iron stove, with a tin chimney in sections.

For Will, there was a big Texas-style saddle. "I see you still have my saddle," Chance said.

"I been using it for a pillow," Will told him.

Chance dragged a bulging carpetbag to the edge of the wagon bed. He pulled out a wool coat, hickory shirt, and pair of stout Kentucky jeans, and he handed them to Will. "I had to guess your size." He tossed Will a boxed shaving kit and grinned. "Get rid of that beard, too. It looks like hell."

Will went over the material from the wagon. "We didn't have a stove this good back in Kentucky," he said, running his fingers over the stove's ornate grill. He put down the clothes and picked up an ax, testing the weight and balance, giving it a few half swings. "These tools, too. We never had nothing like this. Your luck must have been awful good in that card game."

"I was brought up to make my own luck," Chance said.

"You've still got things in the wagon. What are they for?"

Chance's dark eyes glittered with mischievous humor. "Come on." He motioned Will back onto the wagon. They drove back toward the river, to a broad, level spot just off the deep ruts of the California Road. He stopped the wagon and scrambled from the box. Will followed.

"What is this?" Will asked.

"You'll see. Give me a hand."

Will helped Chance unload a large tent from the wagon. They set up the tent poles. They guyed and pegged the new white canvas. Next they lifted a fifty-gallon barrel of whiskey from the wagon. Chance rolled the barrel into the tent, and he placed it with the tap facing the tent's front flap. He put a tin cup atop the barrel, and from the wagon he got a sign that he'd had specially painted.

Chance hammered the sign into the ground in front of the tent. It said SALOON.

"I'm staying," he announced.

Will laughed out loud with pleasure, and he pumped Chance's hand. "What made you change your mind?"

"I got to thinking about what you said. About this being country where a man could do anything he wants. I got to thinking maybe you were right. So I thought I'd give it a try. I always wanted my own saloon."

"That's great," Will said. "I'll run the ranch, and you run the saloon. We'll split the profits fifty-fifty."

"Sounds fair to me," Chance said.

The two men shook hands firmly, sealing the bargain.

Chance picked up the tin cup. "Let's drink on it. Look in the wagon. There's one more thing for you."

Will stuck his head under the canvas and saw two wooden crates tucked in the back corner. He pulled one of the crates closer. They were full of dark bottles, packed in wood shavings so they wouldn't break. He took one out. They were beer bottles.

"Your private stock," Chance told him. "It's brewed by some Germans in Fredericksburg, so it should be good."

Chance poured himself a large cup from the barrel whiskey, while Will unwired the beer bottle's cork. They raised a toast.

"Here's to you, partner," said Chance.

"You, too—partner," Will said.

Chance downed his whiskey with practiced ease, and he poured himself another cup. He leaned against the barrel, settling in for a long day.

Will finished the beer slowly. He savored its robust taste. "That's good," he said. He set the empty bottle back in the case. "We better get to work. There's a lot to do."

Chance looked pained.

8

First they cut poles from mesquite, and they built a corral for the horses. Next they went hunting out past Buzzard Peak, as Will had named the flat-topped hill, and they shot a buffalo. They set some of the buffalo meat to dry, and they built a smoke-house to preserve the tongue and other choice cuts. They dug a well and deepened the dugout. The dugout's entrance of poles and cowhide was replaced by walls of picket logs. The roof was earthed over and covered with thatch. A stable was thrown together, along with sheds for tools and firewood. When the jerked buffalo meat was ready, Will and Chance packed it, along with cornmeal, salt, coffee, and a can to make the coffee in. They took the yellow dog Jaundice and they set off to catch cattle.

They rode southeast, turning up a pleasant, well-wooded creek that fed into the Clear Fork. Chance told Will what he knew about ranching, remembered from observations in Mexico and south Texas during the war. "Have you thought about what brand to put on the cattle?" he asked.

"No, I ain't," Will said. Even back in Kentucky, the first thing they did with a cow was brand it. "Been too busy, I guess." He pondered a moment. "Double Horn Ranch. Double Horn. Double H. That's it—a double H—two H's joined together. That's our brand. And this creek will be Double Horn Creek."

"You sure like to name things, don't you?" Chance said. "I'd better give out a few myself, or you'll have this state all named up."

In a grassy area near the creek, they built a pen for the cattle they would catch. Unfortunately, the cattle didn't want to be caught. They were smart and quick and ornery, and their long horns could get a man or horse in an instant. They stayed in the thickets and woods, and Will, Chance, and the dog had to go in and chase them out. The men dodged trees while trying to throw their reatas over the cattle's plunging, twisting horns. When that proved fruitless, the two men tried waiting by the creek and jumping the cattle at night, when the animals were heavy from drinking. That worked no better. In the dark, their horses stepped in holes and threw them. Unseen branches knocked them out of their saddles.

They moved up the creek, hoping to change their luck. Near the creek's head, they came upon a salt spring. Will remembered the deer he'd shot. "Cattle love salt. We'll build a pen around this spring and trap all the cattle that come here."

So they took their axes, and they laboriously constructed another pen of poles and brush. When it was done, they hid in the nearby undergrowth and waited. Jaundice slept in the shade beside them. Many cattle came close to the pen that first day, longing for salt, but all refused to go through the gate. More cattle were heard that night, lots of them, and Will and Chance shut the gate, certain that they had caught a big bunch. Yet when dawn came, the pen was empty.

"Why won't they go inside?" Chance said.

"Don't know," Will said. "Too much man smell, maybe."

The next day was the same. Many cattle came near, but none would enter the pen. Finally one old black bull, after a good hour of sniffing the fence poles and whirling around, looking for enemies, decided to take the chance. He trotted through the gate toward the salt spring, still looking around suspiciously. He reached the spring and, after sniffing around some more, began to lick contentedly.

Will rose from hiding and started for the pen's gate. His movement caused Jaundice to wake up and start barking. The bull heard the dog and turned. He saw Will. Will ran for the gate. The bull charged. Will reached the gate and fumbled with the rawhide latch. The dog kept barking. The bull thundered close. Will finished with the gate and stepped away, just as the bull slammed into it. The mesquite posts shook dust from the tremendous impact, but they held.

Chance came running out to join Will. The black bull stood off from the gate, snorting and pawing his hoofs and glaring at the two men with red eyes. The bull weighed only about eight hundred pounds, but he packed enough meanness for twice that weight.

"We got one!" Will exulted.

Chance was more realistic. "Now that we've got him, what do we do with him?"

They gave the bull some time to get used to his new surroundings, then they entered the pen on their horses. After playing out their reatas, they twirled the loops experimentally.

"You ever done this before?" Will said.

"Nope," said Chance.

They approached the bull from two sides, intending to catch him from the front and back. The bull didn't give them time. He leaped forward and charged at Will. Will's horse reared, terrified. If the bull got them down, he would gore them to death. Desperate, Chance cast his loop. As the bull lowered his head, the loop settled over his horns. More from instinct than anything else, Chance took a couple turns with the rope around his saddle horn, and he turned his horse away.

There was a collision. Will's horse squealed as the bull's horns sliced open its stomach. Will and the horse went crashing down. At the same moment, the bull was drawn up short by Chance's rope and flipped on his back. Chance's horse was not prepared for the drag on the other end of the rope. It was pulled off its feet. Chance jumped clear of the falling horse. He scrambled to his feet, drawing one of his six-shooters, hoping to kill the bull before it killed him. But Will had managed to get to his feet, with the rope still in his hands. While the bull still lay on the ground, struggling against the weight of Chance's horse, Will flipped his loop around the bull's rear legs. He quickly tied the rope's end around a branch of an elm tree that peeked over the wall of the pen. Just as the bull righted himself, his rear legs went from under him, and he banged onto his chin. He lay there, snorting and squirming and trying to kick free with his front legs.

Will's horse was thrashing in a puddle of its own blood and intestines. Will drew his revolver and shot the animal. Chance limped over. He had lost his hat, and his face was streaming sweat. Will bent over with his hands on his knees, red faced, trying to catch his breath.

Chance put a hand on Will's shoulder for support. He looked at the enraged bull. "He's steaming, isn't he? Now what?"

"Leave him," Will rasped. "Let him think things over."

When Will and Chance came back the next day, the black bull was as full of fight as before, so they left him another day. When they came back again, he wasn't much better. Will didn't want him hurt, so he threw a line around the bull's horns and fixed it to the stout tree branch. By a process of shortening this line and lengthening the line around the bull's feet, they dragged the beast head first to the tree. Will cut the leg rope, then jumped away from the inevitable kick. The bull staggered to his feet, shaking and pawing and bellowing, slobber dripping from his mouth.

Will and Chance left him like that for three days. When they came back the next time, the black bull was gaunt, on his knees, his tongue hanging out. The ground around him could not have been more dug up if an infantry platoon had been set loose upon it.

"That took the starch out of him," Will said.

Will made a little fire of dried cow chips. He and Chance threw the bull. While Chance held the bull down, Will branded him with a hot cinch ring held between bent green sticks. Then he tied a bell around the bull's neck. He shook free the line from the bull's horns, and both men scrambled over the fence. Will opened the pen's gate, and he got out of the way.

The bull rose slowly. He shook himself. Then he bellowed loudly and lit out of the open gate for all he was worth.

Will and Chance got their horses. They followed the bull at a distance. They had no trouble hearing the bell. After a long drink at the creek, the bull disappeared into a dense thicket of chaparral. "That's where his cows will be," Will said.

They heard the bell, but they could not see the bull. Will looked down at the yellow dog eagerly. "Jaundice. Go on and . . ."

The dog seemed to understand without being told. He went tearing into the thicket, barking madly. The bell tinkled again, then the thicket erupted with cattle—cows, calves, and yearlings. Will and Chance charged down on them, ropes flying. Chance caught a big heifer by one horn. He took a couple turns around a tree trunk, and the heifer was securely tied. After a good chase, Will missed his throw at a slab-sided yearling, and his quarry turned sharply and vanished back into the chaparral.

Will rode over to Chance, coiling his leather reata. Both men were torn and bleeding from their dash through the thorny chaparral. Sweat only made the cuts feel worse. Their horses were cut up, too, especially around the knees. Chance looked beat, but Will was full of enthusiasm. "This is good. Even if we only catch one cow a day, we'll have a nice herd before long."

In the thicket, they heard the bell tinkling again. Will said, "We'll bring this heifer later. Let's go catch some more. Come on, Jaundice." He rode off with the dog. Chance followed reluctantly.

Through the summer and early fall the two men worked. That first day had been lucky. Often as not they came up empty-handed, and another one of their horses had to be killed, after he broke a leg. Gradually, however, they built up a herd. The black bull led them to a good many cattle, and after that, Jaundice learned how to find them. Jaundice became an expert at turning the running animals toward the pursuing riders. He loved his work. Will and Chance became proficient at roping and branding. They learned how to tail a herd breaker. This happened when there was not room or time to throw a rope. The rider came alongside the bolter and grabbed its tail. He held the tail under his right leg and turned his horse sharply left, depositing the cow on its head and, with luck, making it think twice before running again.

As new cattle were caught, they were added to the herd. Will and Chance day herded the cattle along Double Horn Creek and penned them at night, with fires around the pen to keep the animals from stampeding and breaking down the poles. They castrated the calves and yearlings to prepare their first crop of steers. Long before fall came, the clothes of both men had been ripped to shreds. Their bodies were a mass of cuts and bruises, and they'd both been near-killed a dozen times. They made new shirts and leggings from buckskin and new trousers from the canvas wagon cover. Their two remaining horses were half dead, so they had to catch some of the mustangs that roamed the country. They walked the wild horses down, working in relays, never giving the mustangs time to rest or graze or drink, eventually driving them into yet another pen. They kept the herd's stallion along with the best mares and colts. The rest they set loose. During all these months, they returned to the dugout infrequently. Most nights they slept under the stars, and they lived on fried cornbread, strong coffee, and whatever game they could hunt.

"I hate ranching," Chance announced one evening, after the mustangs had been penned. "I hate cows. I used to like horses, but I'm starting to hate them, too." The nights were growing crisp, and Chance wrapped his blanket around himself as he sipped coffee.

"Come on," Will replied, "this is the opportunity of a lifetime. Look how big a herd we got already. Think how many we'll catch next year."

Chance looked up. "Next year? You don't expect me to do this again, do you?"

"If you want a ranch, you got to build a herd."

"What I want to know is, when do we do the saloon keeping? We've been killing ourselves for months, and what do we have to show for it? Sixty-two cattle, worth exactly nothing. Hell, mining gold would have been easier than this. And we still have to break those horses."

Will was in good spirits. "Hard work is good for you," he said.

"Good for you, maybe. Not for me."

Will laughed, as if he didn't believe Chance meant it.

9

Winter. A howling norther beat against the dugout.

Inside, Will and Chance kept close to the iron stove, with Jaundice at their feet. Sleet rattled against the rawhide window. The wind shrieked through chinks in the wall.

Will and Chance wore their buffalo coats, unbuttoned. Their razors had been used up, and their beards were long and matted. A tallow candle burned on the table between them. It was a sturdy table. Will had made it from oak.

The rest of the dugout was in shadow. It reeked of smoke and stale sweat and moldy earth. From time to time, loose dirt dribbled from the roof. In one corner, a small mesquite tree was propped. The tree was decorated with cutout paper stars and half-moons. Atop the stove, a Dutch oven steamed seductively.

Will and Chance sat on chairs made from rawhide and cattle horns they had found. Chance was in his drawers. The seat of his canvas trousers had worn through, and he was patching them with a square of the ubiquitous rawhide. He drank whiskey from a tin cup. The bottle was on the table. A pannikin of molten lead hung over the fire. From time to time, Will tipped some of the lead into the bullet mold for his flintlock rifle, which he held with large tongs. When the lead was set, he cooled it in a rawhide bucket of water, then he set the new bullet alongside the others on the table before him.

Will picked his beer bottle from the floor. He took a drink of the beer, then held the bottle to the weak light. It was three-quarters empty.

As if on signal, Jaundice rose. He shook himself vigorously, his long ears flapping. He sat at Will's side, looking up with big brown eyes. Will made him wait a second, then he tilted the bottled and let the dog lap up the last drops.

Chance grinned. "You're feeling no pain, are you?"

Will reached for another beer bottle and unwired the cork. "I didn't say I *never* drink. If you can't get drunk today, when can you do it?"

Chance finished with his trousers. He put them on, satisfied. He shivered and peeked through a crack in the window. It was midafternoon, and what little light there had been was rapidly diminishing.

Chance shook his head. "Been blowing like this for a day and a half now, as far as I can make out. Doesn't look like it'll ever stop."

Will said, "I wonder how the horses are doing. I wish we'd built the stable stronger."

"I wonder where the cattle are," Chance said. "We haven't

seen most of them since we turned them loose for the winter. By the time this weather stops, they'll have drifted halfway to Mexico.''

Will was confident. "We'll find them in the spring. You'll see.''

Chance shook his head. He turned toward the cast-iron stove. "My nose tells me this is done.''

He wrapped a hand with the skirt of his buffalo robe coat, and he lifted the lid of the Dutch oven. Steam flooded out. Inside the oven was a turkey that Chance had shot yesterday, just before the storm struck. The bird was stuffed with cornbread, wild onions, and pecans, and Chance had seasoned the basting juices with whiskey. He tested the turkey with a fork. "It's done, all right.''

Will held a wooden plate next to the Dutch oven. Chance gripped the turkey with his fork and bowie knife, and he lifted it onto the plate. Will carried the plate to the table. Prompted half by the season and half by the unaccustomed glow of alcohol, he began to sing: "God rest you merry gentlemen, Let nothing you dismay . . .''

Will sang out. Singing had always been part of his life. Many times the family sing had been the only entertainment they'd had. Chance grinned at him self-consciously. He hesitated, then he joined in: "Oh, tidings of comfort and joy, Comfort and joy . . .''

Will grinned at him. Chance grinned back.

They went through another verse of the song together, putting their arms around each other, waving their free hands in time to the music, finishing with a flourish: "Oo-o-h, ti-idings of co-omfort and joy.''

There was silence for a moment, then Will said, "Sure hope you cook better than you sing.''

Chance laughed and punched his friend's arm.

Jaundice stood with his forepaws on the table, sniffing the turkey, but Will pushed him down. "Don't worry, Jaundice, you'll get some. We should have named this dog Bottomless Pit.''

Chance honed his bowie knife on a whetstone. "Christmas dinner, who would have thought it? I was supposed to be in San Francisco by now, or one of the big gold camps, living off the fat of the land.''

He braced the turkey with the fork and began slicing the breast.

He balanced the long slice of meat on his knife point, then flipped it to the expectant dog, who caught it in midair and snapped it down. Chance kept carving. "This is the longest I've stayed in one place since Mom died," he said. "I'm used to being around a lot of people. It's funny, but being alone out here hasn't bothered me like I thought it would. I figured we'd be at each other's throats by now."

"True," said Will, "we haven't had many problems among ourselves." He grinned. "Outside of the fact that you don't like to work."

Chance ignored him. He put a heap of turkey on Will's plate. "That enough?"

"Yeah," said Will, who was busy scooping out stuffing for himself.

Chance said, "I don't know why I like you so much. You don't even play poker."

"If I did, I sure wouldn't play it with you."

"A wise decision," Chance said.

When their plates were filled, they dragged their chairs close to the table. Chance poured himself more whiskey. He lifted his tin cup. "Well, partner. Merry Christmas."

Will touched his beer bottle to the cup. "Merry Christmas." He drank, then he raised his bottle again. "May the new year be better."

Chance scratched at a sudden flea bite on his bearded cheek. He looked around at the smelly dugout. He listened to the wind shrieking outside. "It couldn't get much worse," he said.

10

Spring came early on the Clear Fork. The days were warm. The grass was up. The mesquites were green with new leaves. The prickly pear cactus had sprouted waxy blossoms.

Will and Chance had rounded up most of last year's cattle herd. There had been a fine crop of calves as a bonus. Soon they would go out to catch more cattle, but right now they were in the corral, trying to break a red roan stallion they had caught. The stallion threw first Will, then Chance, then Will again.

"Your turn," Will told Chance.

Chance looked less than enthusiastic. Will wobbled on his feet. Blood trickled out his nose from the pounding the roan had given him. "We're wearing him down," he said confidently.

"Sure we are," said Chance. "My knee feels like it's broken from the first time he threw me." He sighed and took a deep breath. "Come on. Let's catch him."

Something had captured Will's attention. He was gazing to the northeast. "What's that?" he said, and he pointed to a long plume of dust.

Chance saw the dust, and he grinned as if he'd just been reprieved from a hanging. "It's an emigrant train," he said. "Customers for the saloon." He slapped Will's arm. "Come on."

The two men left the roan to his own devices, saddled and all. They hurried from the corral to the dugout. Inside, Chance got out his carpetbag. He pulled out a folded suit of black broadcloth. He shook the suit out and began putting it on.

He saw Will staring, and he said, "You don't think I dress like Daniel Boone all the time, do you? If you're going to take people's money, you've got to show them some style. Besides, this is a special day. These are our first paying customers."

He buttoned the new white shirt. "This didn't fit so tight when I bought it."

"You've added muscle," Will told him. "That happens when you work."

Chance took out a dark-red silk cravat. "Get the shears, will you?"

Will got the shears from the shed. When he came back, Chance had tied the cravat and put on a brocaded vest. He sat on one of the cattlehorn chairs. "Cut my beard for me."

Will sliced through Chance's beard, working slowly because the hair was stiff with dirt and knotted. He squared off Chance's long hair in back. When he was done, Chance brushed hair from his suit, and he felt his shortened beard, seemingly satisfied. He took a shiny plug hat from the carpetbag, and he grinned. "All right, my friend, now I'll show you my line of work."

They walked down to the tent. Chance had been working on his saloon. He'd fashioned a rough bar from the trunk of a post oak, and he'd set the whiskey barrel on it. There were a crude table and chairs in the back, where the two men sat while they waited for the wagons. Will rubbed his bloodshot eyes. He hadn't slept well the last few nights. It was full moon, and he and Chance were alternating periods on guard, watching for Comanches.

Slowly, the ox-drawn wagons crossed the river and started up the bank. There were twenty wagons in all, with about five men to each, walking alongside or riding horseback. There were three families with the column, and they had been given the lead position, to avoid the dust. A herd of oxen and some spare horses brought up the rear. Three or four dogs were with the company, and they ran around barking.

The emigrant men were young, eighteen to twenty-five, from all walks of life. They carried rifles and revolvers, and they were dressed as Will had once been, in flannel shirts, high boots, and flowing bandannas. It shocked Will to realize how much he'd changed, with his beard and buckskins.

The emigrant company was not road broken yet. The men were footsore and saddlesore, and they let out a whoop when they saw the SALOON sign. "Let's stop a while, Cap'n," they yelled.

Chance stood and walked toward the wagons. "Morning, gents."

The captain, whose name was Richmond, was a practical man. He knew he couldn't prevent the men from staying. "This looks like a good place to water out the stock," he said. "It's early yet, but we'll noon here." The three married couples were unhappy about the delay, but there was nothing they could do.

Some of the men hurriedly tended the wagons and stock, while the rest rushed toward the tent with their mess cups. Chance moved behind the bar. He drew one of his big six-guns and laid it on the bar beside him, so that everyone would know he wasn't fooling. "All right, boys, belly up. Two bits a shot. Have your money ready when you get to the front."

Chance poured the drinks. Will took the money. Will was unused to handling money, and he had a hard time making the right change at first. The emigrants had monstrous thirsts, and it was awhile before the crush at the bar diminished. The men sat in the grass around the saloon, drinking and laughing. Some distance off, the three families had made camp, along with Captain Richmond and the guide. Under the eyes of their wives, the married men despondently watched the bachelors having fun, pretending to be outraged at the single men's behavior and secretly wishing they could join in. The children ran screaming around the wagons. In the background, range cows were bawling, set off no doubt by the smell of the oxen.

Chance finished pouring drinks and wiped his hands on a towel. He pulled a new deck of cards from his frock coat, and he raised his voice. "Anybody for a friendly game?"

Some of the better-heeled emigrants were eager to play, and Chance showed them to the table and chairs inside the tent. "You handle the booze," he told Will. "Make sure all of 'em pay." He looked around the milling crowd. "It's a pity you don't deal faro bank. Course if you did, you'd feel sorry for the customers and let them win, and we'd lose our shirts."

Chance set his plug hat at a rakish angle, and he went to join the card players. It was a good-natured game. Chance was careful not to take too much from anyone. Several men left the game for drinks, and others joined in. A big group of men watched, guzzling whiskey, smoking pipes and cigars, sweating as they filled the back of the small tent.

Once Captain Richmond looked in on the game. "Say, you men. Don't go losing all your money now. We've got a long way to go."

"Don't worry, Captain," Chance said, waving a cigar that someone had given him. "We're playing for small stakes. This is nothing to what it'll be like when they go up against those gold camp card sharps."

He turned to the players and shuffled the cards. "Mind what I tell you, gents. Those Californios will beat you out of every ounce of dust you mine, if you let them. Always make sure you're in a game that's not rigged." Smiling, he propped the cigar in his mouth and tossed some coins to the center of the table. "Ante up."

After two hours, the married couples persuaded the captain and guide to get the company moving again. Animals were rounded up. Wagons were hitched. The emigrants fell—literally, in a few cases—into line. They started southwest, following the river.

Will and Chance watched the company plod away. Some of the men were singing "Oh, Susanna." Snatches of the song drifted back.

"Got the itch to be with them?" Will asked his friend.

Chance hadn't realized that it showed. "A little, I guess. But I won't have it long if these emigrants keep coming."

Chance counted their profits. "Including everything, it comes to four hundred and forty-two dollars and fifty cents. We made more off whiskey and cards in two hours than we have off cows in ten months."

"The cows'll pay," Will said defensively.

Chance wasn't listening. "I wish we had a whore. Then we could really rake it in. I tell you, Will, if the California trade stays strong, a man could do right well here."

The wagon train faded into the distance. On an impulse, Chance got his paint bucket. Under the fancily scrolled word SALOON on the tent's sign, he painted in smaller letters: AND WHOREHOUSE.

Toward day's end, more dust was sighted in the east, but this time it belonged to a lone wagon, not a train. A man and woman walked alongside the wagon, with their two girls. A milk cow was tethered to the rear, and there was a terrier bitch who promptly ran off with Jaundice.

The man and woman wore homespun. Their equipment was not the best. The man was wiry and active, with an intelligent face. The woman was rather plain, with stringy brown hair, but she looked prettier because of the good humor that lit her face.

The family's name was Clayton. They were from Tennessee. Nothing seemed to faze them. They could laugh about anything. The girls, Melody and June, were ten and eight. For Will and Chance's benefit, they struck poses like those they imagined young ladies to use, but they kept breaking down in giggles.

"We're members of Captain Horace Richmond's company," Mr. Clayton said. "We had wagon trouble, and we stayed at that new army post downriver—Fort Belknap—to get it fixed. How long since the main body passed this way?"

"Not more than six hours," Will told him.

Mr. and Mrs. Clayton exchanged looks of relief. "Good," said the woman, "I didn't want to go much farther by ourselves."

"We slowed 'em up for you," Chance added. "You're bound to catch them tomorrow." Chance knew the woman and girls had seen the word "whorehouse" on his sign, and he was hugely embarrassed.

Will said, "We was in the same situation as you all last year, but we got sidetracked and stayed here."

"We can't do that," Mrs. Clayton said. "My sister and her husband live in California. They've optioned a piece of land for us, but if we're not there by November, we'll lose it."

Chance said, "Why don't you camp here tonight? Grazing's good, and we'd enjoy the conversation."

Mr. Clayton looked at the westering sun, and he shook his head. "Thank you, boys, but I believe we'll keep moving. There's a good two hours of daylight left, and now that we're this close, I don't want to lose any time on them. Makes it all the earlier we'll catch them tomorrow."

Mrs. Clayton reached into the wagon and pulled out an enormous tin. She opened it. It was full of cookies. "I made these to help pacify the children on the journey. You boys take some. You must work hard, running your . . . establishment."

She flicked her eyes toward the sign and grinned. Will laughed, and Chance went red in the face. They reached for the cookies.

"Lemon drop, my favorite," Chance said. "Thank you, ma'am."

"Yes, ma'am, thank you," said Will, taking a few more.

"Please, don't call me 'ma'am.' You make me feel a hundred. I ain't but a few years older than you, after all."

The Claytons said good-bye. Melody and June whistled up the terrier. Mr. Clayton popped his long bullwhip, and the wagon groaned forward. Mr. and Mrs. Clayton were still joking about their ages. The girls looked back and waved shyly.

"Nice folks," Will said.

"Not exactly good for business, though," Chance observed. He sighed. "I had a good time today. I wonder how long we'll have to wait before we get more customers?"

His question was answered the next afternoon, when five riders approached the saloon. The riders did not come from the east. They came from upriver, out of the southwest.

"Who would be coming from that direction?" Will said, watching them. "Soldiers?"

Chance observed the riders' loose formation. "No, they're not soldiers. You best look to your six-gun, Will. I don't know who they are, but I think there's going to be trouble."

11

Chance drew one of his pistols. He levered the hammer up and down with his thumb, loosening the mechanism, checking the percussion caps. "Follow my lead," he said. "Act like nothing's the matter."

Will made sure his revolver was in good working order. He'd been wearing the big Colt at his waist for so long that he hardly noticed it, but now it felt unnaturally heavy on his hip. His muscles were tight, and he loosened them as best he could.

The five riders drew close. They were young and bearded and tough looking. Their buckskins had seen hard travel. They were armed with rifles, shotguns, pistols, and knives, and they looked like they knew how to use them. Their horses were gaunt and predatory, like the men themselves. They led two pack mules and a string of spare horses.

Will and Chance exchanged glances. Will realized how alone they were. There was no law out here, no restraint of civilization. What happened here in the next few minutes would go unnoticed by the outside world.

The riders halted a short distance from the tent. Their leader had a gotch eye. One lid opened only halfway, giving him an oddly sleepy appearance. He was a big man, with long, dirty-blond hair and beard. He wore no hat, only a Mexican headband of red silk. To his right was a strange-looking young man, with hair so pale that it was almost white.

The riders dismounted. Despite his size, the leader moved well. He flipped his reins to a young man in a blue coat and flat cap. As he did, Chance caught Will's eye. Chance motioned toward the pale-haired man.

Will looked. Decorating the pale-haired man's bridle were hanks of what looked like dried hair. Will's stomach turned as he realized they were human scalps. But that was not the worst. The scalp that dangled from the horse's bit ring was fresh. The brown hair was long and stringy, like a woman's.

Will's gorge rose. In a loud whisper he said, "That's Mrs. Clayton's . . ."

He stopped. Chance seemed to have changed. He looked cold and calculating in a way that Will had never seen him. Chance nodded once. He knew whose scalp it was.

The newcomers' leader started toward the tent. His men staked out their horses and the string of spares, and they followed. The pale-haired man and another, with a pinched, ratlike face, carried shotguns. Just then, Jaundice appeared. The dog's ears and tail went down. A menacing growl rose in his throat.

"Shut up!" yelled the rat-faced man. The pale-haired man picked up a rock and hit the dog with it, making him yelp. His friends laughed.

Will's anger surged. Jaundice stood his ground. He showed his teeth. The pale-haired man now swung his shotgun toward the dog. Will ran out of the tent and yelled, "Jaundice, stop! Stop. It's all right, boy."

The dog hesitated. "Lay down," Will told him. Jaundice obeyed, but he continued to watch the newcomers suspiciously.

"Good dog," mocked a skinny man in a coonskin cap and red pants.

"Lucky dog," muttered the pale-haired man. He kept the shotgun pointed at Jaundice.

"Leave the dog alone, Whitey," said the gang's sleepy-eyed leader.

"Sure, Squirrel Eye," said Whitey.

The five men swaggered into the tent, looking around as if they'd already taken over the place. Whitey's gaze fell on Will. Whitey's eyes were as pale as his hair. There was a coldness in those eyes that Will had only seen once in his life, and that was a few minutes before, with Chance.

All traces of Chance's earlier look had vanished, however. He greeted the newcomers with a greenhorn's grin. "Afternoon, gents. Light your hosses and set a spell, as they say in this part of the world. What'll it be? Hope it's whiskey, 'cause that's all we got." He smacked the barrel and laughed, the very model of the genial tapster. Will did not see how he kept so cool. Will was scared, and he knew that it showed. He could feel sweat running down his neck and the palms of his hands.

Squirrel Eye leaned against the bar. He wore a necklace of wolf's claws. His silk headband was crusted with dried sweat. "Whiskey's all right with us."

"Got your own cups?" Chance asked.

"We'll use yours."

"Sure," Chance said. He dug out some tin cups and filled them, passing one to each man. "That'll be two bits," he said.

"We'll run a tab," Squirrel Eye said. Some of his men looked at each other and snickered. They had decided that Chance and Will were no danger, and they would take their time before killing them. It occurred to Will that this was how Chance wanted them to feel. Chance wanted to fill them with whiskey before the trouble started. Whiskey slowed the reflexes.

The men drank deeply, used to raw liquor. Buck, the one in the coonskin cap, spit out his whiskey. "This stuff tastes like pig shit."

"How do you know?" said Whitey. "You ever eat pig shit?"

The others laughed. The rat-faced fellow, whose name was Danny, looked at Chance threateningly. "You sure this is whiskey, mister? You sure it ain't grain alcohol with a plug of tobacco in it for flavor?"

Chance spoke evenly, as if taking no offense. "Whiskey's what it says on the barrel, friend. I don't make the stuff. I just buy it."

Buck said, "You shouldn't be charging no two bits for this puke. Should he, Squirrel Eye?"

Squirrel Eye looked amused, in his sleepy fashion. His voice was low, but there was no mistaking the challenge. "Sign outside says this is a whorehouse. Where's the whore?"

Chance pushed back his hat and scratched his head, grinning ruefully. "We're still working on that part, I admit."

"I don't know if I like that," Squirrel Eye said. "I could use a whore."

Danny rapped his shotgun on the bar. "I think we got us some liars here, Squirrel Eye."

"Let's have some more drinks," said the youth in the flat cap, as if trying to restore good spirits. He looked like a decent boy who had fallen in with bad companions.

While Chance refilled the cups, Squirrel Eye turned his gaze on Will, who tried to appear unworried. "You want a drink?" Squirrel Eye said.

"No, thanks," Will replied. "I don't like—"

"Have one anyway," Squirrel Eye ordered. He turned to Chance. "You, too."

Chance passed Will a tin cup full of whiskey. Will held it to his lips and pretended to drink. Squirrel Eye walked around the tent, restless. "Surprised to find anybody this far into Indian country. You boys been here long?"

"A year this month," Chance told him.

"You lasted longer than I would have expected," Squirrel Eye said. He stepped to the front of the tent and looked out. "You done right much work here. Building corrals, rounding up stock. What do you figure it's worth?"

Chance shook his head, as if he had no idea. So did Will.

Squirrel Eye said, "Is that so? Well, the cows are worth a dollar or maybe two a hide, that's if you can get 'em somewhere to sell the hides. The horses, you'd get about ten bucks each for them, twenty—maybe even fifty for that red roan. That's a couple hundred worth of stock, plus tools and weapons and cash— and however much of the whiskey we don't drink."

Squirrel Eye's men laughed as their leader brazenly figured the potential value of their plunder.

Chance seemed unaware of what was happening. "You gents horse traders?"

"You could say that," Squirrel Eye told him. "You could say we just come up from Mexico."

Actually, Squirrel Eye and his gang had followed a party of surveyors from Austin, and had killed and robbed them down on the Concho. Now the gang was making a swing along the frontier, snapping up an isolated farm or ranch on the way. Such crimes were relatively risk-free, and if you cut up the bodies enough, it was almost always blamed on Comanches. The five men had come across the Clayton wagon last night. They had taken it more for the woman and two girls than for anything of value the family might possess.

Chance refilled the gang's cups. "Drink up. It's a long ride to the next saloon."

Danny and the flat-capped boy were laughing and joking. Buck was carving his initials into the bar with a bowie knife. Will saw a smile pass between Squirrel Eye and Whitey. They were ready to make their move. Squirrel Eye was the leader, but Whitey was the triggerman. Unobtrusively, Will backed a few steps down the bar, to a spot where he had the outlaws better covered.

Squirrel Eye downed his third cup of whiskey. In his quiet voice he said, "Where do you boys keep the cash hid? You need a safe spot in country like this."

"Oh, we got one," Chance said. He smiled self-consciously, like a man embarrassed by his own riches.

"You think we could borrow some?" Squirrel Eye said. Will heard Buck snicker. "Not much, just a little, to get us on our feet. You see, we didn't have such good luck in Mexico, and we're kind of short just now."

Will knew that if the gang couldn't locate the cash this way, they were prepared to use other methods. Whitey had loosened the shotgun in his arms. His thumb was on the hammers.

Chance looked at Squirrel Eye reluctantly. Squirrel Eye affected an injured tone. "Come on, what's that look for? It's only a loan. We'll pay you back, I swear it. You'd think we was robbers or something."

Squirrel Eye's men laughed out loud at that. Their leader turned to acknowledge his joke.

"That's exactly what I think you are," Chance said quietly.

"What?"

The outlaws stopped laughing. They looked, and Chance was holding his cannonlike Walker Colts on them. Chance was smiling. He fired, hitting Whitey in the chest, knocking him onto his back.

"Now, Will!"

There was no time for Will to think. Fear took over. Dropping his cup of whiskey, he pulled his revolver and cocked it. As he did, the inside of the tent dissolved in motion. Closest to Will, Danny turned with his shotgun, cocking the hammers, fumbling because of the whiskey he had consumed. Will pointed the pistol and fired, hitting Danny in the neck. Blood spurted. The shotgun boomed into the tent roof, and Danny fell, banging into the boy Pete, who was drawing his own pistol. Will snapped a shot at Pete but missed.

While this was happening, Chance stepped to his right and put a slug into Squirrel Eye's shoulder. Squirrel Eye was blasting away with his own pistol by then, and Chance fired his second round while diving for the packed earth floor behind the bar. He thought he'd hit Squirrel Eye, but he wasn't sure where.

Chance came up on one knee. He didn't see Squirrel Eye. The outlaw leader must be down. Buck fired a pistol at him. The bullet zipped by his cheek. Chance turned and fired back, but a bullet from Will's gun hit Buck first, jolting the coonskin cap over his eyes, even as Chance's bullet spun him around and sent him crashing into the side of the tent.

Only the boy Pete was left. He dropped to his knees, throwing away his pistol and raising his hands over his head. "Don't shoot," he cried. "Please. Don't shoot."

The only sounds were Pete's frightened sobbing and someone moaning in pain. Jaundice was barking madly at the front of the tent. The breeze cleared the powder smoke from the tent, along with the smell of spilled whiskey. Part of the tent's canvas roof had been shredded by Danny's shotgun blast.

Chance rose to his feet, pistols cocked and ready. He looked around. Whitey and Buck were dead, so was Danny. Squirrel Eye was still alive. He was the one moaning, holding a thigh that had been shattered by the heavy slug from Chance's .44. There were blotches of blood from the wounds in his shoulder and leg.

Chance stepped over Whitey's body, holstering one of his pistols. He stood over Squirrel Eye. He aimed his other pistol between the outlaw's eyes. He saw fear in Squirrel Eye's sleepy face. He started to squeeze the trigger, then Will grabbed his arm away. "Stop, Chance! You can't shoot a wounded man."

"The hell I can't," Chance said. He jerked his arm free and pointed the pistol back in Squirrel Eye's face.

Will grabbed his arm again, hard. "I mean it, Chance. It's wrong, and I won't let you do it."

Chance turned on Will, and his hooded eyes blazed with anger. Their intensity was frightening. He hurled his words. "What do you think he was going to do to us? Or have you forgotten what they did to Mrs. Clayton? What do you think happened to Mr. Clayton? What do you think happened to their girls?"

Will met Chance stare for stare, surprising himself. "I'm forgetting nothing. But we ain't no judge and jury. We sure ain't no executioners. That's what makes us different from men like Squirrel Eye." He let that sink in, then he added, "Squirrel Eye'll lose that leg, if he don't die from it first. He's no more threat to us. Seems that's punishment enough."

Chance's chest rose and fell. He glared at Will. His jaw was clenched. His gun wrist was tight as steel where Will was holding it. At last he let out his breath. "All right. All right. Have it your way, this time. But don't ever cross me like that again."

Chance continued to look at Will for a second, then he turned to the boy. "You. Get him on a horse"—he indicated Squirrel Eye—"and both of you get out of here."

Pete scrambled gratefully to his feet. His cheeks were wet. "Yes," he said. "Thank you." He hurried from the tent.

Will said, "What about their other horses and packs?"

"Keep 'em," Chance said.

"But they ain't ours."

"We've as much call on 'em as anybody. People they belonged to are all dead now."

Pete readied two horses. Will helped him load Squirrel Eye onto one. Chance kicked Squirrel Eye in the rear as he mounted, making him cry out. The outlaw leader was pouring sweat, groaning with pain. He clung to the horse's mane. Pete took Squirrel Eye's reins, and the two men rode away, heading northeast along the river.

Chance went back into the tent. Will followed reluctantly. He looked at the scene inside. The three bodies lay sprawled in the twisted attitudes of violence. There was blood and spilled whiskey everywhere.

"What you did with Whitey," Will told Chance, "shooting him in cold blood. I couldn't have done that. I mean, you didn't hesitate."

"Don't believe in hesitating," Chance said. "My dad hesitated once. That's what got him killed." He looked at Will. "I ought to know. I was there."

Chance poured a cup of whiskey and downed a good slug of it. He collected the dead men's weapons. He went through their pockets, taking money and anything of value. From a fringed pouch at Danny's side, he pulled something else. It was one of Mrs. Clayton's lemon drop cookies.

Chance stared at the cookie for a long minute. Then he stood. He drank more whiskey, and he said, "Let's get these three buried, before they start to smell."

Part II

12

1856

The outlines of the three graves were long gone on a gray, chilly morning in November, as Will and Chance led their saddled horses from the corral. Both men had waist-length beards. They wore buffalo robe coats, buckskins, and stiff rawhide hats. Will still had his Colt Dragoon revolver, but Chance now carried a pair of .36 Navy Colts.

Two of their hands, the Mexican Fulgencio and sixteen-year-old Rusty Harding, waited outside the corral with their own mounts. Their other hand, Fulgencio's younger brother Rodolfo, stood in front of the picket cabin that had replaced the dugout. The locked pair of deer antlers were over the cabin's rawhide door. The cabin's sides were adorned with assorted cattle skulls that the men had found.

Outside the cabin, the big yellow dog Jaundice ran back and forth excitedly. From down by the river came the lowing of a trail herd of seventy-three steers that had been rounded up and brought there the day before. A bull bellowed in the distant thickets.

The four men swung into their saddles, shivering against the wind's bite. Rodolfo, who was taller than his older brother, raised a hand in farewell. "Good luck, *mi amigos*."

"Thanks," Will said. "We should be back in three days."

Chance shook his head. "I still think that's a long time for a twenty-mile trip. Hell, I can walk it faster than that."

Will said, "The government's paying us two dollars and fifty cents the hundredweight for these steers. I don't intend to work a single ounce off of 'em if I can help it. Nice and slow, that's the way."

Rodolfo knelt and held Jaundice, to prevent him from following, as the four men turned their horses and rode toward the herd. They trotted past the huge pin oak, whose last faded orange leaves clung stubbornly to its branches, as if in a vain attempt to ward off the oncoming winter. They passed the saloon, which had been rebuilt as a picket house with a canvas roof. Over the entrance, Chance had placed a sign that said CHANCE'S KINGDOM. On the side of the roof facing east, where travelers would come, was a large sign that said FIRST CHANCE. On the far side of the roof, where travelers would depart, was a sign that said LAST CHANCE. They passed the spot where the buffalo wallow had been, but the shaggy beasts no longer came here. This land had been taken over by cattle, and by men.

They took positions around the herd. Fulgencio was on the point. Beneath his heavy beard, Fulgencio had a flat, pockmarked face. He and his brother had been raised on a hacienda near Matamoros. Their father had been killed in the Mexican war, and their family had been displaced. The brothers had taken to odd jobs, eventually following the U.S. Army north from the border as cooks and teamsters. Chance had found them at Fort Worth on one of his yearly trips there.

Will and Chance took the herd's flanks. Young Rusty brought up the rear. "All right," Will called. "Move 'em out."

Fulgencio waved his reata. With whoops and cries, the men got the herd under way. The beasts strung out and started slowly down river. They were headed for the new army post called Camp Cooper. Will had contracted to sell the steers to the government there, for distribution to the Penateka Comanche reservation that had been established along the Clear Fork two years back. The previous beef contractor had defaulted, and Will and Chance had gotten the job through the efforts of some friends among the fort's officers.

They were soon within the reservation boundaries. They passed scattered groups of tipis and the fields where Indian agents attempted to teach the reluctant Comanches how to grow corn. They were followed by an ever-growing procession of Indians—men, women, and children. Some were afoot, some on horseback.

Chance eased his red roan across the herd's path to Will. He and Will had flipped a coin to see who would get the roan.

Chance had named it Chinaco. Chance drew up alongside Will and indicated the Indians. "They look hungry enough."

"They probably are," Will said. "Lieutenant Hood says that when the ration herd didn't come through last winter, the Indians had to eat their dogs and horses to keep from starving." He watched the Indians trailing them, begging silently, like dogs. "You know, it's sad to see people like this—proud people, hunters—reduced to a starving rabble living on handouts."

"I'd reduce 'em to more than that, if it was up to me."

"You don't object to taking money for feeding them, though."

Chance shrugged. "Money's money. If we didn't sell the government these cows, somebody else would."

Will swung around in the saddle. He looked to the rear of the herd, where Rusty rode, kerchief pulled around his freckled face to keep out the dust. Rusty glanced at the Indians apprehensively. He touched one of the old Walker Colts that Chance had given him, as if for reassurance.

"Rusty's scared," Will said.

Chance's voice was harsh. "Do you blame him? There's a good chance some of these Indians you're feeling so sorry for are the same ones that murdered his family."

Both men remembered the day, nearly three years ago, when Chance had brought the shy, devastated orphan boy to the Double Horn Ranch. Chance had found the boy at Fort Belknap, the only survivor of an Indian raid, and he'd offered to take him in. It had taken Rusty a long time to come out of his shell. The sight of these Indians brought back memories of his family and their awful deaths.

The herd reached Camp Cooper before noon the next day. The post was a collection of tents and log cabins, placed with geometrical precision around a square parade ground. It was garrisoned by the newly created Second Cavalry. These men were Secretary of War Jefferson Davis's pets. They wore black hats with one brim turned up and ostrich feathers in the bands.

The steers were weighed out and paid for. Then they were set loose on the plain outside the fort, where waiting Indians chased them on horseback, shooting them with arrows as if in memory of bygone buffalo hunts. The squaws and children followed behind, butchering the dead animals on the spot, stuffing the hot livers in their mouths, squeezing the intestines between their teeth, singing songs of thanksgiving. They cut up the meat and carried it off, wrapped in the bloody hides, while the whites, especially the new post commander, an aristocratic Virginia colonel named Lee, looked on in disbelief.

The four men started home the next morning. The ranch's take had been over fifteen hundred dollars. The men had bathed, shaved, bought new clothes, and gotten drunk, even Rusty. For Will, it had been his first hot bath since leaving Kentucky and his first shave in years, and when he'd looked at himself in a mirror, he could hardly believe it. He'd forgotten what he looked like. He felt on top of the world in his new checked flannel shirt and corduroys, and the soft felt hat was a great improvement over the rawhide one he'd worn so long. Fulgencio and Rusty nursed headaches. Even the weak autumn sunlight seemed to hurt their eyes. Chance looked preoccupied. He was chewing on his lip.

"Our first sale," Will said, as if he still couldn't believe it. "After all these years, things are starting to break our way."

"*Sí,*" said Fulgencio, grinning through the pain in his head. "And we have the contract for next year, too."

"And the year after that, if we uphold our end of it. We're on our way, men."

Only Fulgencio seemed to share a degree of Will's enthusiasm. Rusty said nothing. The swaying motion of the boy's horse was having an adverse effect on his stomach. He looked green around the edges.

Will smiled at the sight and turned to his partner. "What's the matter with you, Chance? You're supposed to be happy. This is *money* we're talking about. Say, you didn't get skinned playing cards with them soldiers, did you?"

"That'll be the day," Chance said. He'd spent the better part of yesterday afternoon and evening playing poker in the sutler's store. "No, I beat them down for about fifty dollars, probably all the loose change there was at that fly-bitten place." He hesitated. "Look, I—I've got something to tell you, Will."

Chance was serious, but Will found it impossible to be anything but light-hearted just now. "What is it?"

"I'm leaving."

Will reined in. "What do you mean? Leaving what? The ranch, the saloon?"

" 'I'm leaving Texas. I've been thinking about it awhile. I made up my mind last night.''

"But why? Especially now, just when we—"

"Because there's no future for me here, Will. For you and your cows, maybe, but not me. I was wrong about this country, about what it could become. I've given it five years, and it's no more civilized now than it was when we came here. Not only that, but the California trade's dying out. We haven't had a big emigrant train all this year, and only one last year. All we get is small parties of freighters or soldiers, and the money they have to spend isn't worth talking about. I could stay here till the end of time and never get rich. Even if I did get rich, there's no place to spend it. I'm tired of living like a hermit. I want bright lights. I want people around me. I want women.''

Will didn't know what to say. He looked at Fulgencio and Rusty, and they were just as stunned. "We can't change your mind?''

Chance shook his head.

"But . . . how are we going to get along without you?''

"Hell, you'll do fine. You've got these two and Rodolfo to help you. You don't need me.''

Fulgencio said, "Where will you go, *Señor* Chance?''

"San Francisco, I guess, like I planned from the start.''

"When?'' said Will.

"Next spring. Too late in the year now. I'll hook on with the first freight train heading west.''

"I'll miss you,'' Will said.

"I'll miss you, too. But it's something that's got to be.''

Will's lips formed a thin line. His high spirits had vanished. The little party rode on in silence.

The day after they returned to the ranch, Will and Chance loaded a kettle onto their wagon. They took axes for cutting firewood, and they started up Double Horn Creek to the salt spring, to lay in a winter's supply of salt.

It was another chill, overcast day. As they neared the spring, they saw smoke. Chance halted the wagon, and they proceeded on foot. Gray tendrils curled above the nearly leafless trees ahead.

"Indians?'' Will said.

"Could be,'' said Chance.

They moved slowly, rifles ready. They rounded a bend, and the spring became visible through a gap in the trees.

Will and Chance looked at each other.

Beside the spring was now a cabin. Smoke rose from its stone chimney. In a cleared space in front of the cabin were two large copper vats, with fires underneath and salt water bubbling within, reducing. Scrawny pigs rooted among the fallen leaves. There was a stable with a milk cow and oxen inside. There was a chicken coop, built above the ground to avoid rattlesnakes. The horse corral was empty.

"Settlers," said Will. "Well, I'll be."

Chance wrinkled his brow. "We should have figured somebody would show up here eventually. Hell, we should have sent Rodolfo or somebody to file a claim on this spring."

They walked forward, still carrying their rifles. "Hello!" they called. "Hello, the cabin!"

There was no answer. The pigs and squawking chickens scattered before them.

Will said, "I wonder where everybody—"

There was a rifle shot, and Will's hat went flying.

From the trees, a woman's voice called, "Drop those rifles and get your hands up!"

13

Will and Chance looked at each other. There was no telling how many people might be out there with weapons trained on them. They laid their rifles on the ground, and they raised their hands.

"Your pistols, too," called the woman's voice. The voice sounded young but unafraid.

Chance started to protest. "Hey, now, wait a—"

There was another shot, and a bullet kicked up dirt at Chance's feet.

"All right, all right," Chance yelled. Slowly the two men lifted the revolvers from their holsters and put them down.

"Now step away," ordered the voice.

Will and Chance obeyed, hands once again raised.

Branches parted, and a tall girl emerged from the trees, squinting down the barrel of a Sharps rifle. She was about seventeen, slender but sturdy looking, with a longish face and reddish blond hair. She wore a hat of braided wheat straw and a homespun dress. Her shoes looked homemade, too.

Chance was nervous. "Put that thing down before it goes off, will you? We're not Indians."

The girl kept the rifle aimed. "You might be renegades, pretending to be Indians. It's been known to happen."

"We just come for some salt," Will said. "We own a ranch down on the river."

The girl looked from one to the other. "You the fellas with the H's on the cows?"

"That's right," Will said.

The girl lowered her rifle a bit. "Well, I guess you can put your hands down."

Will and Chance did. "All right if we get our guns?" Chance asked.

"Not yet."

Chance looked amused. He spread his hands in a pacific gesture. "You got the artillery, lady."

Will picked up his hat. He looked at the bullet hole in the crown. "This was a new hat," he said ruefully.

The girl turned her green eyes full on him, and he got a prickly feeling at the base of his neck. "I'm sorry about that," she said. "I hadn't really meant to come so close."

Will put the hat back on. He felt himself blushing, the way he always did when he was around girls. "It wasn't even broke in yet."

"It is now," Chance said, laughing. He grinned at the girl with self-assurance. "You're a spunky little vixen, aren't you? What's your name?"

"It's Hope, Hope Sommerville, and I'll thank you to keep a civil tongue in your head."

Chance spread his hands again. "Whatever you say, Hope. I'm Chance Evans, and this is my partner, Will Cooper."

Will nodded shyly.

There was noise from the trees, and four men rode into the clearing, an older man and three younger ones. Like the girl, they wore homespun. Like the girl, as well, they carried rifles.

"What's the shooting about, Hope?" said the eldest one. He was about forty, though he looked fifty. He had a good-humored face, but there was a determined set to his jaw. Sparse gray whiskers stuck like pieces of straw from his cheeks.

"These fellas say they're our neighbors from down the river," Hope replied. "The ranchers."

The man studied Will and Chance for a moment. "Like as not they are," he said. "We seen that Double H brand on their horses down the path a piece. Go ahead, boys, pick up your guns. That was good work, Hope. You can't be too careful."

Hope lowered her rifle, but not all the way. She was still taking no chances. Will and Chance retrieved their weapons.

The older man dismounted and held out his hand. "I'm Jack Sommerville. These are my boys—Curt, Sammy, and Todd. You done met Hope."

Will and Chance introduced themselves, and they shook hands all around. Curt was about twenty-one. Sam was fifteen or sixteen, and Todd a few years younger. Curt and Sam were dark like their father. Todd had his sister's reddish hair and fair complexion.

Jack said, "You boys come inside a spell, get out of the chill. Curt, you bring their wagon along and take care of the horses. Todd, you go back and bring in that buck we killed. Sammy will fix up your salt. You'll stay to supper, of course."

"Thanks," Will said. "We didn't bring no money with us for the salt. We didn't know that—"

"Oh, hell, that's all right. Pay me any time. Ain't like none of us is going nowhere."

Jack led the way across the clearing to the cabin. Hope looked at Will and Chance without expression. Up close, Will saw that she had a clear, milky complexion. Her green eyes were framed by long lashes. Her reddish hair was brushed to a sheen, and her apron was freshly starched. Will touched his chin, self-conscious about his new growth of whiskers.

"We knew there was white folks around," Jack was saying. "We could see the salt had been worked, and there's these branded cows everywhere." He shook his grizzled head. "At first we thought about settling down by the river, too. Then we found this spring. The Sommerville Salt Works, I call it. Should give us a nice source of income."

The cabin was a plain affair of green wood, two rooms separated by a covered dog walk. Inside, the chinked walls kept out little of the November wind, and everyone huddled near the stone fireplace. The cabin was neat and clean. The furniture consisted of a crude table and some chairs, along with an old, much-used hand loom and spinning wheel. The other room would be the kitchen.

Will said, "How long you been here, Mr. Sommerville?"

"Jack, son, call me Jack. We ain't been here but a month or so. We come up from Burke's Prairie in Bastrop County. Left right after the harvest. Traveled by way of Pecan Bayou and the old fort at Phantom Hill."

Hope had come quietly in, and Will sneaked a glance at her. Her big green eyes looked back at him, and he quickly dropped his gaze. She made him feel funny inside. It was a tingly feeling, something he'd never experienced before.

Jack produced an earthenware jug and handed it to Chance. Chance pulled out the stopper and drank. His eyes opened wide and he gave his head a half twist.

"Gets your attention, don't it?" Jack said. "I make it myself."

Chance gave the jug to Will. Will didn't want it, but he felt it would be impolite to refuse. He tilted the heavy jug and drank. It was like swallowing a hot branding iron. The breath was scalded out of him. He bent over and coughed, and his eyes watered. Chance, Jack, and his sons laughed.

As Will handed the jug to Jack, Chance said, "Late in the year to be moving."

The elder Sommerville drank. He wiped the back of his mouth with his hand. His geniality seemed somewhat forced. "Bastrop County's getting too filled up. It was time to be heading west again." He laughed. "I been traveling west all my life, since I was a boy in Georgia. Don't want to look back when I die, neither. No, sir, bury me standing up, with my face to the setting sun. That's what I say.''

Hope said, ''You know that wasn't the only reason, Pa.''

Jack looked at her.

''Go on. Tell them.''

Jack rubbed his whiskery chin. Then he said, ''Too many of the 'better sort' of folks was moving to Bastrop. They was bringing slaves with them. Why, they run old Doc Burke right out of his own town. Doc was a veteran of the Revolution, just like me. He come to that spot when there wasn't nothing there but Comanches and rattlers. It was men like him made it safe for the others to follow. But he made the mistake of marrying hisself a black woman, and, boy, them high-and-mighty types couldn't abide that. So they run him out. I refuse to be around folks like that.'' He hesitated. ''You boys don't own no slaves, do you?''

Will and Chance laughed. ''Not likely,'' Chance said.

Jack passed the jug again. ''Did you say you fought in the Revolution?'' Will asked.

''Yes, sir,'' Jack said proudly. ''I was dispatch rider from Sam Houston to the Alamo. I reckon I was the last Texian to see them boys alive.'' He shook his head and had another drink. ''Ol' Sam, he didn't want them to stay there, you know. Ordered them to leave. But Buck Travis wouldn't hear it. Wanted to be a hero. I always thought he got them boys killed for nothing.''

''You at San Jacinto?'' Chance asked.

''Nope, missed her by half an hour. My company had been on detached duty. We caught up with the main bunch just as the fighting ended. I was pretty worked up about it at the time, but it don't seem to matter much anymore.''

Supper was fried venison and gravy, corn fritters and molasses, followed by pecan pie. ''That sure was tasty, Miss Hope,'' said Chance, pushing himself back from the table. ''I haven't eaten that good in years.''

''Me, neither,'' Will said.

Hope smiled, lowering her eyes.

Jack said, ''Hope's something, ain't she? She's got fire in her. Takes after her ma, you know.'' He grew misty-eyed. ''Last baby Ma had died and took Ma with it. We surely miss her.''

He put his arm around his daughter. ''Here's Hope now. All of seventeen, and she ain't married yet.''

Hope had heard this before. "Pa . . ."

"Well, it ain't right. Girl your age should be married. Your ma was, and she had a baby to boot." Jack looked at Will and Chance, and he winked. "Maybe one of you boys'll oblige her. You're a likely-looking pair."

"Pa!" Hope said again, and this time she blushed.

Jack and his boys laughed. Hope rose and began clearing the table. "I'm going to do the dishes."

Later, Jack, Chance, and the oldest boy, Curt, got out the jug again. The younger boys went to sleep, while everyone else clustered around the fire. Jack and Curt had both served with the Texas Rangers, and they swapped tall tales with Chance for what seemed like hours. Will sat withdrawn, wishing he could think of something to say to Hope, wishing she would speak to him. All too soon, she excused herself from the conversation and left. Presumably she slept in the kitchen. The talk went on till the jug had been well dented and everyone was heavy-eyed. Then Jack and Curt unrolled cow hides from the corner. "You two can have these beds," Jack told his guests. "Me and Curt'll sleep on the floor."

After breakfast next morning, Will and Chance lashed their cask of fresh salt onto the wagon. They hitched their team and prepared to leave. Chance removed his hat to Hope and smiled broadly. "Well, good-bye, Miss Hope. It's been a real pleasure meeting you. You certainly have an interesting way of introducing yourself."

Hope laughed. "Good-bye, Chance. Good-bye, Will."

"Bye," Will said, nodding and taking off his own hat awkwardly. He wished he could be glib like Chance. He wished he didn't feel so tongue-tied and stupid around women.

Will and Chance climbed onto the wagon and drove off, waving to their new neighbors.

As they made their way home, Chance said, "That Hope's some looker, isn't she?"

"I . . . I guess," Will said.

Chance laughed. "What do you mean, you *guess*? You didn't take your eyes off her all night." He grew reflective for a moment, then he said, "Yes, sir, she's a fine looker, with spirit to match. I'm looking forward to seeing a lot more of Miss Hope Sommerville.''

Will was surprised. "I thought you was leaving Texas."

Chance looked at Will, and he grinned. "A fellow can change his mind, can't he?''

14

1858

A low growl rose from Jaundice's throat. Then another, a note higher.

Will rolled from his blankets in the darkness, rubbing sleep from his eyes.

"What is it?'' he heard Rusty mumble.

"There's something out there,'' Will said.

Around him, the others were waking, rising from their cowhide beds and shivering in the night chill. They reached for their rifles.

Jaundice's growling grew louder. He crouched by the door, nose to the crack. He scratched the dirt floor in agitation.

The four men spoke in whispers. "Is it a lion?'' asked Rodolfo.

"I don't think so,'' Will said.

Rusty's voice trembled. "Oh, Jesus, not . . .''

He left the word unsaid, but everyone knew what he meant.

Rodolfo said, "They would not come so early. It is only March.''

His older brother, Fulgencio, said, "They could have traveled by creeks and valleys where there is grass all year.''

"Full moon tonight,'' Will added. "Be up soon, too. This is when they like to do it.''

Outside, the silence had grown unnaturally intense. All the

men could hear were Jaundice's growls and scratching. Quickly they dressed themselves, pulling on boots, buckling their six-shooters. Will loaded his double-barreled shotgun and stuffed extra shells in his pockets. He looked out the front window of the picket house. He could see nothing, just the vague outline of the trees by Double Horn Creek and the darker mass of the hills beyond. They had moved the ranch headquarters last year, to get away from the growing settlement around Chance's saloon. With the establishment of Camp Cooper and the placing of the Penateka Comanches on a reservation, more and more settlers had been moving into the Clear Fork valley. At first all had been peaceful, then last summer most of the Second Cavalry had been ordered to Utah. With the country unprotected, the Indian raids had started again. Horses were stolen, men and women murdered, children kidnapped. The Double H had its horses taken, but the ranch had been spared an all-out attack, and Will now wished they'd built the house more securely.

"See anything at the back?" Will whispered.

"No," said Fulgencio, peering out the small rear window.

Jaundice grew more agitated. His growls started low in his throat, then rose, threatening to explode out of him. He was standing now, pawing the door, trying to open it and get out. From the corrals, the men heard nickering and stamping, as the horses picked up the foreign scent.

"What are we going to do?" Rusty said. There was terror in his voice. He was trembling. It was all happening again for him, the nightmare of his family's massacre relived.

Rodolfo said, "Maybe they only take the horses, like last time."

"They'll take that Kentucky stud for sure," said Fulgencio. "He cost you five hundred dollars, *Señor* Will."

Will thought about taking his rifle to the corrals and waiting in ambush, trying to pick them off. Then he remembered last year's raid. That night the horses had been galloping into the darkness before anybody knew what was happening. That night the horses and dog had given no warning. Tonight the Indians must be coming from downwind. That meant they had the house surrounded, which meant there were a lot of them. This was a war party.

Will's stomach tied itself in a hard knot. He felt very cold.

"I wish *Señor* Chance was here," Fulgencio murmured.

"So do I," Will said. His eyes strained into the darkness, but still he saw nothing. He wondered if anybody else's place would be hit tonight. He wondered about the Sommervilles upstream. He wondered about Hope, and his fingers brushed his clean-shaven face, as they frequently did when he thought about her.

"The house will be hard to defend against many," Fulgencio went on.

Will hesitated. He hated to give up what he'd built here without a fight.

Just then Jaundice got the door opened enough to wedge himself through. He burst outside, erupting in a cross between a bark and a high-pitched yowl. The horses were very agitated now, banging against the corral poles.

Will heard the dog's furious barking race past the corrals. Then, abruptly, it stopped.

The white men looked at one another.

In the southeast, the moon rose. The ranch and surrounding land were bathed in a mosaic of silver glow and black shadow. Will saw a form flit across the open ground by the corral. Then another. He saw another by the hayrick.

"Out the back window," he said, pushing his friends. He counted on most of the Indians congregating toward the front of the house. "Make for the creek bottom, and hide in the trees. Hurry!"

Rodolfo went first, then Fulgencio. They seemed to be taking forever. Will's heart was pounding. His palms were sweating. Sweat rolled down his back in the cold night.

It was Rusty's turn next. He climbed into the window. Half-way through, he froze. He was shaking with fear.

There were noises outside the front door.

Desperate, Will shoved Rusty the rest of the way through the window. He heard him hit the ground, and he started through himself. There was a whoop and yells, and the door crashed open behind him. Half in the window, half out, Will turned and fired both barrels of the shotgun into the house. The powder flash momentarily blinded him. He heard screams.

Then he was on the ground and running. He drew his pistol. Rusty was running beside him. There were yells behind them. Will didn't know where the others had gone. To his right, he saw vague shapes in the moonlight. He circled around the cattle pen, heading for the creek. Somewhere to his left a pistol went off. There was more gunfire, yells. Rusty was gone, Will didn't know where. Shadowy forms appeared ahead of him. One was carrying a bow. Will turned away, firing his pistol at them.

He kept running, stumbling over unseen rocks and folds in the ground, lungs burning for breath. The blessed darkness of the trees was just ahead. He wondered why the Indians weren't chasing him. Then, behind him, he heard someone screaming. It sounded like a white man.

A squat figure rose before him. It was too late to get out of the way. The two men collided and fell to the ground. The Indian stank. Will thrashed frantically, grappling with the Indian. He heard himself crying. His hands slipped on the Indian's greasy buckskin shirt. The Indian got Will on his back. He squeezed Will's throat so hard that Will saw stars. Will jammed his thumb in the Indian's eye, and he dug as hard as he could. Something popped loose, and there was an agonized cry. The grip on Will's throat released. Will threw the screaming Indian off, then he was on his feet and running again. He had lost his pistol and shotgun. Footsteps pounded behind him now. There were tears in his eyes. Animal noises welled in his throat.

He tripped and went sprawling into a brush-strewn gully, hitting his shoulder hard. He burrowed facedown in the icy mud of the gully's bottom, praying that the shadows would hide him. Above him were scattered shots and yells. Moccasined feet leaped the gully and ran on, one pair then another, searching for him. He heard guttural expletives. He scarcely dared to breathe, willing himself to become one with the earth.

Beneath him, the ground rumbled as the horses were driven from the corrals. Through the icy mud that clogged his nostrils, he smelled smoke. The smell grew stronger. He heard the crackle of flames. The sound seemed to come from all around. He pushed his face deeper into the mud as a store of cartridges inside the burning ranch house exploded. The Indians must have missed the ammunition when they ransacked the house.

The night was split by a burst of savage cries. Then the cries, like the hoofbeats of the stolen horses, receded into the distance.

The Indians were gone. Will waited, giving them plenty of time to get away. He realized how cold he was. The gully's mud was frozen from recent snow. He lay shivering in the shadows, while above him the flames soared high in the moonlit sky. He smelled burning wood, burning leather and hay.

Finally he raised his head and peered from the gully. Everything was burning—the house, the stable, the sheds, the hayrick. Everything was lost.

He stood. His joints were cramped and aching from cold and wet and fear. One hand was badly scraped, and his shoulder hurt where he had fallen. His shirt was torn and he was caked with mud. He climbed stiffly from the gully, shielding his eyes from the glare of the flames. The heat was comfortably warm at first, but it became suffocating as he got closer to the burning house.

There was no sign of his companions. He looked for his pistol and shotgun, but he couldn't find them. There was a dark object on the ground before him. It was the body of a man, stretched out. It was young Rodolfo. Rodolfo's throat was slit, and he'd been scalped and carved by Comanche knives. One of his arms was hacked off.

There was a roar as the ranch house collapsed in a shower of sparks and cinders. Will flinched. He saw two men coming from the creek, heads bent against the glare of the fire. One was supporting the other.

"Fulgencio! Rusty!" Will called.

He met them, and the three men clasped each other's shoulders gratefully. Rusty's legs were shaking, and Fulgencio held him up. "*Señor* Will," said Fulgencio, "thank God you are alive. Have you seen my brother?"

With his head, Will motioned toward the burning ruins. "He's over there," he said quietly.

For a moment Fulgencio's face brightened, then he understood. With a little cry, he moved forward.

"No!" Will said, holding him back.

Fulgencio struggled to pull away. "I must!"

"No, Fulgencio. It won't do any good. You don't want to see."

The pockmarked Mexican turned. His dark eyes were wild.

"As a friend," Will said, "I ask you not to go."

Fulgencio sank down, crying. *"Mi madre,"* he moaned. "He will never see our homeland again."

Will put his hand on Fulgencio's shoulder, feeling useless. "Stay with him," he told Rusty.

Will went back and covered Rodolfo's face with his own torn shirt. Then he completed his search of the ranch. He found dark splotches of blood on the ground, but no bodies. Comanches carried off their dead, so there was no way of knowing if any of the Indians had been killed. By what remained of the corral, he stopped. Jaundice was there. The big yellow dog was lying on his side, with a lance embedded in his chest.

"Oh, no," Will said.

He knelt and hung his head. He remembered Jaundice as an eager pup, as a valued companion on cow hunts. If it hadn't been for Jaundice raising the alarm, they might have been butchered in their beds tonight . . .

Hoofbeats sounded in the darkness. A rider was approaching from the direction of the settlement.

"Will!" It was Chance's voice. "Will! Fulgencio!"

"Over here," Will said wearily, rising.

Chance galloped up. He was riding the red roan Chinaco. He reined in, looking around. Chinaco was nervous because of the flames, and Chance had a hard time holding him. Chance wore his ranging outfit—buckskin jacket, wine-colored shirt, dark pants and hat, with hand-tooled and painted Mexican *botas* to protect his lower legs.

"I saw the flames," he said. "I came as fast as I could. The others are on their way."

"Rodolfo's dead," Will told him. "So's Jaundice. They got all the horses."

"Damn," Chance said. He shook his head, tightlipped. "We'll get after 'em as soon as it's light enough to pick up a trail. We'll get you a horse from the stage remounts."

Fulgencio and Rusty came up. "I am going, also," said Fulgencio.

"Sure you're up to it?" Will asked him.

"I am sure," Fulgencio said grimly.

Will turned to the boy. "You be all right here by yourself, Rusty?"

"I—I reckon so," Rusty said. He was shaking with cold and fright.

"You'll be fine," Chance told him. "The Indians won't come

back here. No reason for 'em to. This is probably the safest place in Texas right now.''

More hoofbeats sounded from the settlement. Chance swung from his saddle. ''Let's clean up here and get ready to move out.''

15

They buried Rodolfo as dawn streaked the eastern sky. They had dug the grave by torchlight. Smells of charred and smoldering wood from the burned ranch filled the air. Stray wisps of smoke made the men's eyes water.

Will had managed to retrieve only two items from the house— the locked deer antlers, which were smoke-blackened but still intact, and the flint arrowhead that Chance had pulled from his back years ago. The arrowhead had been on the fireplace's stone mantel, and it was still there after the house collapsed.

Rodolfo's body had been wrapped in a blanket. Will helped lower it into the earth. Will's mud-caked clothes were not yet dry. He had borrowed a shirt from Chance. He shivered with cold. He could not wait for the sun to rise.

Fulgencio prayed briefly over the grave in Spanish. Chance stood outside the little group of mourners, impatient to be off. Chance didn't hold much with prayer.

Fulgencio ended his prayer. As the men began shoveling earth into the grave, Chance put on his hat. ''Todd and Rusty can finish that,'' he said, and he started for the horses. ''Let's go.''

Eight men started in pursuit of the Comanches, with two packhorses. Besides Will, Chance, and Fulgencio, there was Curt Sommerville, whose youngest brother Todd had come to the ranch to stay with Rusty. There was Colonel George Vestry, the lawyer-merchant from Austin. There were the farmers Amos

Blaine and big Tom Nye, and a little Frenchman named Jules Villette, who had just moved into the community.

Aside from Chance's red roan Chinaco and Colonel Vestry's white Arabian, the men's horses were not the best. All of the settlement's good horses had been stolen by Indians. Most of the men rode Spanish ponies that had been used as farm hacks. Will and Fulgencio had big stagecoach remounts. The horses belonged to Chance, who had obtained one of Butterfield's Overland Mail contracts when that service had been inaugurated last year. The stagecoaches ran from St. Louis to San Francisco, twice a week in each direction. Chance supplied the coaches with fresh horses and grain and the passengers with food, drink, and a quick card game. It was more work than one man could handle, and Sam Sommerville helped Chance run the business now.

The men rode along, muffled in long coats against the biting March wind. Will and Fulgencio had lost their coats in the fire. They wore Saltillo blankets with holes cut in the center, which they had borrowed from some of the other settlers. In the growing light, they followed the broad trail left by the raiders and the stolen horses. The tracks led northeast, roughly paralleling the Clear Fork.

In the last year, Will and Chance had been called out on these pursuits time and again, as war parties cut a bloody swathe across the Texas frontier. Sometimes Will and Chance had been called Rangers, sometimes militia, sometimes minute men, but it was all the same. Both men had developed reputations, but Chance was the one to whom the others instinctively looked for leadership. He'd spent half the last year in the saddle.

"I make it thirty or so braves," Chance said, looking at the tracks. "A big party."

George Vestry said, "It's those reservation Indians, you mark my words." Vestry spoke in clipped, precise tones, with a slight flourish to his *r*'s.

Will said, "What are you talking about, Vestry? Reservation Indians didn't hit my ranch."

"Of course they did," Vestry said. Vestry was tall and dark, with arched eyebrows and high cheekbones. He had slicked-back hair, with a thin mustache and goatee, and he affected the dress and manners of the planter aristocracy. "These tracks lead to the reservation, don't they? The tracks always lead here, and there's nothing we can do about it, because the Indians are protected by the government. I say the devil with the government. I say kill the first Indians we come to. They're all in it together. We've got to show them that when they attack white men, there's going to be retribution.''

There was a chorus of support from Amos Blaine and Tom Nye. The Frenchman Villette looked unsure.

"Vestry, you're crazy," Will said.

Vestry sneered down his long, aquiline nose. "Of course. I see. It's in your interest to protect these government pets, isn't it? You've got that fat contract to feed them. It's all money to you. Maybe you can overlook their depredations, but it's our families who are in danger, and we're not going to permit—"

"You idiot," Will said. "It was my ranch that got burned. It was my friend they scalped and cut up. I want revenge, but I want to get the ones who did it, not the first peaceful village we come to. I ain't big on killing people just for the sake of doing it."

Vestry turned. "Where do you stand on this, Evans?"

Chance gave Vestry an ironic smile. Chance didn't like George Vestry. Vestry had been involved in Austin politics, and talk had it that he'd left the capital after shooting an opponent in the back. No charges had been filed against him, but Vestry had evidently decided that a change of scenery was in order.

Chance remembered the day that Vestry had arrived in town, late last spring. Chance had been standing in front of his saloon. Vestry had been riding that big white Arabian, with his high-born wife at his side. Vestry had stopped in front of the saloon. He'd signaled his Negro teamster to halt the wagon with his belongings and small children. Vestry had cast an arrogant eye around the tiny settlement. He'd looked at the saloon's sign, then he'd looked down at Chance, much as a great nobleman might regard a wayside peasant. He'd said, "Kingdom, eh? Is that the name of the town or the saloon?"

Chance had regarded him with a level gaze. "Never much thought about it. Both, I guess."

Vestry had built his general store and law office across from the saloon. It was the largest structure in the community, and

Vestry seemed to assume that he was now the settlement's leader, as if by divine right.

Now Chance said, "Well, I don't know if I consider Indians people, but Will's right. Reservation Indians didn't burn his ranch. That bunch led the tracks here deliberately. They're angry at the Penatekas for making peace. They want them blamed for what's going on. They want to provoke us into just the kind of dumb act you're talking about."

Vestry bristled. He looked around. Blaine and Nye were willing to follow him, but nobody else was, and that made him all the madder. "Very well," he said. "There will be time enough to take care of these reservation savages. And I'll do it, too. Believe me. I'll have this reservation closed, if it's the last thing I ever do."

The little column strung out. Chance and Will were in the lead. Fulgencio followed, sombrero pulled down, looking grim. Beside him rode Curt Sommerville. At a distance came George Vestry, with Blaine and Nye just behind him in a little group. The Frenchman brought up the rear, riding by himself.

Chance eased Chinaco closer to Will. Will spoke first. "Think we'll catch them?"

"We never have before," Chance said. "Their horses are too good, and they have too many of them. No reason to think this time will be any different."

"It will be if I have anything to say about it," Will said. He had chased Comanches before, but he had never wanted to catch them as much as he wanted to catch this bunch. Rodolfo had been killed, so had Jaundice. His ranch had been burned and his horses stolen, including his prize Kentucky stud. He felt violated, shamed, and enraged at the same time. He could begin to understand men who lived only to kill Indians. No. No, he couldn't. He couldn't imagine what he'd be feeling now if that were his wife and children dead back there. That might have plunged him into the kind of black abyss from which there was no emergence.

"I ain't letting them get away with this," he told Chance.

"That's been said before. The Comanches have to be stopped, all right, but this isn't the way to do it."

"What do you mean?"

"These reactionary pursuits are no threat to the Comanches.

The government's policy of passive resistance is useless. We have a governor now who knows that. Will, Texas is going on the offensive. I just found out yesterday, I would have been over today to tell you. Governor Runnels is raising a force of Rangers. We're going to cross the Red River and hit the Indians up in the Territories, where they live. We're going to destroy their villages and kill their horses. We're going to keep the survivors so busy running, they won't have time to think about raiding in Texas.''

Chance looked at Will, and there was a cold light in his eyes. ''My old *compadre* Rip Ford is on the Brazos right now. He's to be in command. I'm joining him as soon as we've finished this little business. I'm going to be one of his officers.''

''I'm going, too,'' Will said immediately.

Chance shook his head. ''We can't both go. Somebody's got to watch things here. Fulgencio's got problems right now, and there's nobody but you that can handle Vestry. I don't trust that snake as far as I can throw him.''

Will felt hurt at being left out. ''How long you going to be gone?''

''Long as it takes. If I had my way, we'd stay all winter and exterminate the bastards.'' He saw Will's look, and his eyebrows rose. ''You don't agree?''

''About extermination? I don't know. Part of me says yes, but another part . . . Believe it or not, I feel sorry for the Indians sometimes.''

Chance gave him a look. ''Oh, I believe it, all right. It sounds just like you. They burn your ranch, and you're sorry for them.''

''We're at war with them, Chance, and it's a war we started. Let's face it, we're taking their land. They're fighting back the only way they know how. Their way of life is disappearing, and they're desperate to stop it. White people are no saints when it comes to making war, you know. My great-grandpa was in the war against England and I heard stories about some of the things they done to the Tories and their families. It wasn't pretty.''

''Oh, come on, Will. They didn't steal Tory children. They didn't rape Tory women to death and burn the men alive.''

''I ain't saying I'm on the Indians' side. I wouldn't be here if I was. I'm just saying you got to look at it like they do. What would we do if we was in their places?''

Chance looked exasperated. "Since we're not likely to be in their place, that's not my concern," he said. He eased his horse away, content to ride on in silence.

The day had dawned sunny, but it gradually turned cloudy and cold, with a wind that chilled the bones. They were on the Penateka reservation now. The tracks of the fleeing Indians were easy to read. About nine miles from the ranch, the little party came across a bunch of Double H longhorns stuck in a bog. The animals were soaked with blood. The Comanches had herded them into the bog, then cut slices of meat from their living bodies. The poor beasts were lowing, quivering with pain and fright. The Indians had left the bloody meat slices beside the bog, uneaten, to show their contempt for these animals.

The whites took their six-shooters and put the cattle out of their agony. "Still feeling sorry for the Indians?" Chance asked Will.

On the far side of the reservation, the Comanches' trail turned west, toward the Double Mountain Fork of the Brazos. The little party of white men followed it the rest of that day. They camped that night along a shallow creek. The next morning broke with thick gray mist. The white men watered their horses, gave them some grain, and rode on.

Chance had gone ahead. Will dropped down the line, beside Jules Villette. The Frenchman had dark features and thick, expressive eyebrows. He wore a caped tweed coat and a hat with the kind of elaborately curled wide brim that Will had thought existed only in the minds of magazine illustrators.

"How you bearing up?" Will said.

"Bien," the Frenchman said brightly. He tried to show the ebullience for which his country was famous, but he had seen Rodolfo's body, and he could not help being scared.

"It's good of you to ride with us."

"Ah, that is no mention. I am an American now. It is my duty as a citizen, *n'est-ce pas*?"

Jules had lived in Texas for several years. Before coming to Kingdom, as the settlement was being called, he had been part of an experimental community of his countrymen near Dallas, called La Réunion. La Réunion had been founded to demonstrate in a practical way the virtues of socialism, but it had broken up in arguments over who was to do the work. Jules had planted vineyards on the southeast slope of a hill outside Kingdom.

"How's the grapes coming?" Will asked. "Going to have a big crop this year?"

"Mais oui," said Jules. "And then I bottle my first wines. This country has excellent possibilities, I believe. The climate is mindful of the Côtes du Rhone, except that it is, perhaps, *un petit chaud* in the summer."

Will had never tasted wine, though he had heard of it. Until he had met Jules, he had no idea that it came from grapes. "Who's going to drink this wine?"

"Ah. As to that, I think we shall have to educate your American tastes."

Will grinned. "Well, maybe you'll be some competition for Chance and that hair tonic he calls whiskey."

The Frenchman was about to say something, when Chance whistled from up ahead. As the men rode up, his ghostly figure materialized out of the fog. Near him was the remains of a campfire.

"This is where they camped last night," Chance said. "Looks like they scattered from here."

It was true. The Indians had roasted one of Will's colts here. Colt was one of their favorite dishes. From this point, the tracks of the Indians and of the stolen horses took off in every direction, save the one from which they had come.

"Well, that does it," said Colonel Vestry, not without some relief. "We'll never catch them now. There's no telling which way their village is."

Amos Blaine said, "Hell, I wouldn't be a bit surprised if they ain't all doubled back to that reservation." Blaine was an angular, balding farmer from Alabama. He'd always been ambitious and a bit tight-fisted, and since his wife and young son had died from fever last fall, he'd become bitter, as well.

"Well said," Vestry told him. "I still maintain we've more chance of finding Will's animals there than anywhere else. I think we should go back and search for them."

Chance had dismounted. He was sifting the remains of the fire. Then he stopped. Buried among the ashes was a twig, set upright in the ground, with its lone branch pointing toward the northwest.

"They haven't gone to the reservation," he said. "This is a sign for stragglers, or for friends from another war party. It means they're to join up later, in that direction." He pointed in the direction of the tiny branch. "This bunch must be Quohadas. Their camps are supposed to be somewhere on the Staked Plains, but white men have never found them."

The little party crowded around Chance. After some initial skepticism, even Vestry was convinced that the sign was genuine. They picked up a set of Indian tracks—two braves and six horses—running in the general direction that the branch had indicated, and they followed them. Will recognized the tracks of his Kentucky Thoroughbred among them, and that made him all the more determined to catch up. He'd bought the Thoroughbred to mate to his Spanish mares. The horse would make an excellent foundation on which to rebuild the ranch, and he wanted it back.

The fog gradually lifted, revealing a bleak, rolling prairie. The trees thinned out, then disappeared. Water grew scarcer; the creeks became trickles. It was as if they were on an ocean, dotted with sage and buffalo grass. A cold wind sprang up, blowing down from Canada with nothing to break its force. The men huddled in their saddles, freezing and dispirited.

They crossed the Double Mountain Fork of the Brazos. They camped that night along the Salt Fork. They sat shivering around the fire.

At last, George Vestry broke the silence. "See here, Cooper, we've come too far. Few white men have ever seen this country before. It's Comanche country. I think we should turn back, before we're all killed."

He looked around the little group for support. "I'm with you," said Amos Blaine.

Tom Nye said, "Me, too." Nye was a big, bearded fellow with patched clothing. He'd come to Texas after losing his Georgia farm in the panic of 1857. In his slow voice, he added, "We want to help you, Will, but it ain't no sense getting ourselves scalped while we're about it."

Blaine said, "Best say good-bye to that stud horse, Will. Start over. It's all you can do. It ain't like the rest of us ain't had to do the same this last year."

Will stared at the fire, watching it flicker, feeling its thin warmth on his face while the freezing wind blew against his back. "You're all for turning back?"

"That's right," Vestry said.

Blaine and Nye grunted. Will looked at Jules Villette. The Frenchman hesitated, then said in a small voice, "*Oui.*" He added, "I am sorry, Will."

"That's all right," Will told him.

"What are you going to do, Will?" asked Nye.

Will looked determined. "I'm going on."

Fulgencio said, "I go with you. I want a scalp, for Rodolfo."

Curt Sommerville said, "I guess I'll go, too."

Vestry said, "What about you, Evans?"

Chance had been playing with his bowie knife. He ran his thumb along the blade. "If Will goes, I go."

The next morning, Vestry and his three men took one of the packhorses and turned back for Kingdom. Will, Chance, and the two others pushed on, following the Indians' tracks northwest.

16

The four men entered a country of gyp water, where there was any water at all. It was a country of rugged arroyos, of rocks and sand, of flat-topped buttes rising in the distance, like giant watchtowers guarding some devil's realm.

At noon Chance looked at the tracks. "We're catching up to those two. They think they're safe, and they're taking it easy."

Then, crossing a steep gully, Fulgencio's horse misstepped, fell, and cracked a foreleg. Fulgencio raged in Spanish, hurling his sombrero to the ground, but it did no good. The horse had to be put down. Fulgencio cut the animal's throat with his knife. They did not want to risk the sound of a gunshot. Afterward, Fulgencio started back to Kingdom with Curt Sommerville. They took turns riding the slower packhorse. Will and Chance went on, after the two Comanches.

It was cold, but the sun was bright. Chance took off his coat. Will removed the Saltillo blanket from his shoulders. "We're getting close," Chance said, watching the tracks.

In midafternoon, the Comanche trail crossed a dry streambed and turned down a narrow canyon. At a bend, the canyon opened. There, before Will and Chance, were not only the six horses they'd been trailing, but Will's entire herd, plus the spare Comanche war horses, grazing peacefully on what little forage they could find.

Will and Chance reined in. They looked around. Chance's breath was coming in short bursts. Will felt the hair on the back of his neck rising. His stomach had felt bad, and he was feverish from drinking gyp water, but that was forgotten now.

"What do you think?" Will said.

"Does the word 'trap' mean anything to you?" Chance said. " 'Cause I think we just walked into one."

Even as he spoke, there was movement ahead of them and to their right. Mounted Indians appeared along the rocky canyon rim. There were about two dozen of them. The squat coppery figures carried lances and bows that stood in stark outline against the cloudless blue sky. Even at this distance, the two white men could see that the Indians were painted for war. Their horses' tails were tied up.

Chance let out a deep breath. "They knew we were following them. They slowed up just to draw us on." He pulled his hat down, and he drew his Sharps carbine from its pommel scabbard. "You know what to do." He wheeled his red roan and dug in his spurs. "Come on!"

Will followed him. The two men galloped around the bend of the canyon. There was a cry, and the Indians came charging along the rim after them.

Will and Chance left the canyon and crossed the streambed, onto open ground. The red roan Chinaco quickly drew ahead of Will's heavy stagecoach remount. Chinaco could outrun most things on four legs, but Chance knew there was no way that Will would be able to outpace the swift Indian ponies. There was no cover ahead, no place to take refuge, and even if there was, they could not count on a rainstorm to save them this time.

Chance slowed his horse. He turned and dropped back alongside Will. He could buy them some time, if nothing else.

"What are you doing?" Will cried.

Chance waved him on. "Keep riding!"

Chance drew in Chinaco and steadied the animal. The Indians were coming straight at him, yelling now. Chance's heart was thumping wildly, yet he felt a queer elation. He realized that he was enjoying himself. He raised the long-ranging Sharps. Chance reckoned the range at just over half a mile. He aimed the rifle at the charging mass of Indians. He drew his breath and squeezed the trigger.

There was a bang. One of the lead Indians reeled crazily on his horse's back, slewing the animal sideways and nearly bowling over several of his fellows. The other Indians swerved out of his way.

Chance jammed another paper-wrapped cartridge into the carbine's breech. Across from him, the Indians stopped. Some milled around their wounded tribesman, who slumped on his pony's neck, then slowly slid to the ground. Chance raised the carbine, as if to shoot again. The remaining Indians backed their horses off. They did not wish to court death from the white man's fire stick.

Chance kept the Indians at bay, while behind him Will lathered the barrel-chested stagecoach horse for all it was worth. Chance was sweating heavily. It was hard to believe he'd been cold just a little while before. When Will had put some distance between them, Chance turned Chinaco and galloped after. Almost immediately he heard the yipping cries again as the Comanches started in pursuit.

Chance put his head down. He gained rapidly on Will. He came up beside Will, stayed with him for a furlong, then turned his horse again, raising his Sharps at the onrushing Indians.

The Indians halted in a cloud of dust. As the dust blew away, Chance saw the Indians drifting out of what they hoped was the range of his carbine. Chance thought about firing, but if he missed, it would only give the Indians the confidence to come ahead, so he held off. Let them think he was a dead-eye shot.

Once again Will got a substantial lead, while Chance stood off the Comanches. When Will was about a half mile off, Chance turned and galloped away again. Again the Comanches pursued.

Chance followed Will down a long rocky slope. He felt bad because they were almost certainly leading the Comanches onto Fulgencio and Curt, but there was nothing else to be done.

Chance drew even with Will. Will's big bay clumped along gamely, but its pace was slowing. Its neck and shoulders were lathered with sweat. Its tongue was hanging out. It had been three days since the animal had had a full ration of grain. Will looked over at him. Chance shouted, "Keep riding, Will! Don't stop!"

Once more Chance slowed and turned to face their pursuers. Once more the Indians stopped. The Indians were losing their patience, though. They now sent flank riders far to both sides, out of range of Chance's rifle, to cut the white men off. The rest spread out and started forward, challenging Chance to repeat his marksmanship. They wished to end this game before night fell.

Ahead, Will steered his faltering bay toward a conical, boulder-strewn hill. The horse was about done, and the hill was the best spot for a stand. Suddenly puffs of smoke issued from the rocks. Rifle and pistol shots cracked. Will ducked, but the rapid burst of firing was aimed over his head, at the Indians.

Will glanced over his shoulder. Chance was riding hard toward him. Behind Chance, as the gunfire from the hill continued, the Indians halted. With upraised lance, their chief signaled the flank riders, and they halted, too. Abruptly, the whole group of Indians turned their horses and jogged away. They had taken a scalp. They had a fine herd of stolen horses. It had been a successful raid. There was no point in fighting an unknown number of white men to get more.

Will slowed his exhausted mount. He could hardly believe what had happened. Then from behind the boulders stepped Fulgencio and Curt Sommerville, grinning and waving their rifles.

Will dismounted, laughing from sheer relief. "I was wondering where you two had got to. You made enough noise for an army."

"That was the idea," Curt said. "We wanted them to think there was more of us than there was."

"I only wish we could have hit some of the devils," said Fulgencio, whose clothes were covered with dried blood from his horse.

Chance came trotting up. He was grinning at their narrow escape.

"Good shooting," Will said.

"Good luck, you mean," Chance told him. "Hell, I couldn't make that shot again in a hundred . . ."

Chance's red roan looked down. There was the ear-splitting hiss of a rattle. Chinaco leaped sideways, all four legs leaving the ground at once. Chance was caught off guard. He flew from the saddle. He hit the ground, and his left leg bent beneath him at an unnatural angle. There was a loud snap. "Ow!" Chance yelled.

Will and Curt ran over to Chance. He lay on the ground gripping his leg. He was biting his lips and cursing. Fulgencio shot the rattlesnake with his pistol.

"Oh, Christ," Chance said. "Oh, God damn." His normally tan face had turned pale, and his features were screwed up with pain. Sweat dripped from his temples. As the others gathered around him, he tried to laugh. "That horse always was a hammerhead."

With his knife, Will cut away Chance's hand-tooled *bota* and the top of his boot. He heard Chance gasp with pain, and he tried not to pay attention. The others held Chance down. The leg of Chance's dark corduroy pants was wet with blood. Will cut that away, too, to see the jagged white tip of the tibia sticking through the skin.

Will let out his breath. He pushed up his hat. The leg was broken about a third of the way between the knee and the ankle. "It's a clean break, anyway. It's got to be set. There ain't nothing for splints, though."

Fulgencio said, "There is mesquite not far from here."

"How's Chance going to travel?" Curt said. "He'll never be able to sit a horse."

Will said, "If we get wood, we'll make a stretcher, tie it between the horses."

Chance shook his head. "Make a travois," he rasped. "Like the Indians. Less chance of me getting kicked or thrown out."

Will nodded. He looked for Fulgencio and Curt. "Ever set a break like this?"

Fulgencio said, "Like this one? No." Curt shook his head.

"Guess that means I have to do it. Roll your coats up tight

and tie them. We'll use them for splints till we get wood. Give me your belts. Chance, you ain't got no whiskey, do you?"

"For me or for you?" Chance joked.

"You need it more than me, I'm afraid," Will said.

"Well, I'm fresh out for once."

"For once I wish you wasn't. Fulgencio, hold his thigh. Right there, that's good. Curt, grab his shoulders."

Will took off his belt. He looked his friend in the eye. He said, "I guess the tables are turned this time."

"I guess they are," Chance said.

"I ain't got a stick for you to bite. You'll have to use this." Will doubled the belt and gave it to Chance.

Chance bit into the sweat-stiffened leather as Will knelt. Gently Will took hold of the broken leg. Chance stiffened under his touch. Chance's breathing was harsh and rapid, like a frightened rabbit's. Will said, "All right, partner. Count to three. When you hit three, I'll do it."

Chance nodded. His face was wet and drawn. He looked at the sky, and he began counting, mumbling through the belt in his mouth, "One, two . . ."

At that moment, Will forced the broken bone back under the skin. He pulled the fractured leg together. Chance screamed in agony. He tried to rise, and it was all that Fulgencio and Curt could do to hold him down. Then he passed out.

Will looked at Fulgencio and Curt. "Never could count good," he explained.

Fingers slippery with blood, Will adjusted the bones until they felt in place. A bad set would leave his friend a cripple. When he was satisfied, he placed the rolled-up coats as temporary splints, then he bound the leg tightly with Fulgencio's and Curt's belts.

Will sat back, flushed. The wind felt cold on his sweaty body. "All right, Fulgencio, go for the wood. Curt, find some chips for a fire. It'll be dark soon. I'll wait here with Chance."

"What about the Indians?" Curt said.

"What about them? We got to hope they're gone. There's nothing we can do if they ain't. Curt, your place is nearest to here. We'll take Chance there."

Curt nodded. He and Fulgencio set off. Will wiped his bloody hands on his pants, then he covered Chance with a couple of blankets. He unsaddled Chance's red roan and propped Chance's head on the saddle. The horses needed to be watered and fed, but that could wait. Will was exhausted. He thought about tomorrow, and about the long trip back to the Sommervilles'.

At the end of that trip, he would see Hope. That thought made Will excited and nervous at the same time. Chance would see Hope, too, and that thought made Will worried.

17

The trip back was long, hard, and cold. Chance's broken leg was splinted with mesquite. The men fashioned a rude travois from cottonwood saplings that they found on the first day.

Late that day, Chance came to. He was semidelirious with fever and in great pain, both from the leg itself and from the constant jolting of the journey. He bore it well, though, joking about his condition, and his leg stayed miraculously free from infection.

They took it as easy on Chance as they could. There were frequent stops, to lift the rear of the travois as they crossed ravines or exceptionally broken ground, or when they forded streams. On the second day, they shot a buffalo, which provided them with meat and with nourishing broth for Chance. There was no sign of the Comanches, but the men stayed vigilant.

The pace was slow, sometimes agonizingly so; but as every mile brought them closer to the Sommervilles', Will found himself thinking more and more about Hope. He had thought about Hope a lot in the last year and a half, more than he'd admit to anyone but himself. Dreams of Hope filled his mind, and he wondered if it was because she was the only girl he'd seen in seven years, or because he was in love with her. The worst part was that he didn't know how to—or was afraid to—express these thoughts to her. She made him tongue-tied. She made him feel foolish.

He knew that Chance thought about her, too. There had been few excuses for either of them to see her, though. Work at the ranch and the saloon, plus this business of chasing Indians, had kept them far busier than either of them, especially Chance, had anticipated.

Will still felt embarrassed when he remembered Chance's trip to Dallas last year, to purchase whiskey and other supplies. Chance had stopped by the ranch to get Will's order. Will gave him the usual list—ammunition, flour, horseshoes—and Chance said, "Anything else?"

Will had hemmed and hawed, pulling his beard. Then he'd said, "Bring me a razor, will you? And maybe a small mirror?"

Chance had stared at him a second, then he had thrown back his head and started laughing. "Ha, ha, ha. Something tells me you and me are going to be buying a lot of salt this year, aren't we, partner?"

Chance had been right. Both men had stored enough salt at their places to last them the next five winters, though Will's had been destroyed in the Indian raid. Old Jack Sommerville smiled whenever they showed up. He knew why they were there. Will shaved every day—as did Chance—when he wasn't out after Indians, on the off chance of an encounter with Hope.

Those encounters were all too rare. There were few social functions that they could attend to meet her. The lack of a church had a lot to do with that. Will remembered the settlement's big Fourth of July celebration last year. He and Chance had preened themselves, which for Will had meant washing his everyday clothes and having Fulgencio cut his hair with the horse shears. When the music had started, Will and Chance had faced off like a couple of banty roosters, prepared to cut in on each other at every opportunity, only to watch Hope monopolized by a group of bachelor officers from Camp Cooper, in glittering dress uniforms. Will and Chance had been astonished at first, then angry, then they had ended up laughing at themselves.

This rivalry between Will and Chance was not entirely friendly, at least on Will's part. Will knew about Chance and women. He liked Chance better than any friend he'd ever had, but he prayed that Hope would refuse him, even if she chose someone other than Will. He didn't want to see Hope used and discarded. Love should mean more than that. He hoped she would not let herself be taken advantage of. He liked to think she wasn't that kind of girl. He liked to think she was something special.

There had been just one time when Will had been alone with Hope. He could recall it as if it had just happened. He doubted that he would ever forget. It had been last August. The heat had been intense; the land had seemed to shrivel under its withering assault. Will had taken Jaundice up along the upper reaches of Double Horn Creek, looking for unbranded cattle. It had been a fruitless search, and in midafternoon they had entered the belt of trees bordering the creek, to rest.

It was like entering another world. Oaks, elms, and cottonwoods engulfed the creek in cool green shade. Water gurgled soothingly in the rocks. Blue jays called from the branches. The air was fragrant with leafy growth.

Will cupped the cold water with his hands and drank. The horse and dog drank alongside him. The filtered light made the creek look green, too; though here and there it foamed white where the current swirled it around outcrops of rock.

There was a crackle of undergrowth. Jaundice barked. Will scrambled to his feet, drawing his revolver. Nearby, a shaft of sunlight slanted through the trees. Motes of dust floated in its diffused rays. Out of this light stepped Hope Sommerville.

She was wearing her homemade hat and carrying a wicker basket. "Hello, Will," she said, smiling. "I didn't mean to startle you."

Hastily Will holstered the revolver. "Oh, hello, Miss Hope."

"Don't be so formal," she admonished, knitting her brows in mock anger. "It's not like we don't know each other."

"No, ma'am, no," Will said. "Thanks." He could not take his eyes from the set of her oval face, the lines of her graceful neck, the thick reddish hair that fell about her shoulders. He had never seen a woman so beautiful.

Hope petted Jaundice, who had raised his paws against her legs for attention. "What are you doing here?" she asked Will.

"Come to get out of the heat, mostly," he said. "What about you? This is a fair walk from your place."

"I come here a lot. There's a grove of wild plums back there.

They're just ripening now; I came to pick some." She held out the wicker basket to show him. "Try one."

Will picked a plum and bit into it. "Good," he said.

"I'm going to bake them in a pie. Plum pie is Pa's and Curt's favorite. Why don't you come to the house and have some?"

"Thanks," Will said, and his heart soared. "I'd like that."

They started back for the Sommerville place. Will walked beside Hope, leading his horse. Jaundice trotted alongside them happily.

"How's the ranch?" Hope said.

"Fine, I reckon."

"Pa says you'll be an important person one day."

Will looked away. "Oh, I doubt that." Chance would be the important person, if anyone was, but Will didn't tell her that. He didn't want to give Chance any advantage.

"You work hard," she said. "We never see you."

"Can't afford not to work hard. You all work just as hard, I reckon."

As they walked, she drew him out, and he found himself talking far more than he was used to, about his life in Kentucky, about his family and how he missed them, about his dreams for the ranch and the future he hoped to build here.

She listened raptly, and at one point she said, "You know, you're very nice. I always thought you were standoffish, but you're really just shy, aren't you?"

"I don't know," Will said. "I reckon I never had much to say. I never thought you'd be interested in anything I had to say."

She gave him that mock pout again. "Do I seem that horrible?"

"Oh, no," he said hurriedly. "No, you ain't horrible. I didn't mean for you to think that."

She smiled. It was the prettiest smile, captivating, for him alone. Will allowed himself to hope—to think—that she liked him. Maybe she even thought about him the way he thought about her. His feet no longer felt the ground. He wished that this walk to her house would never end.

But it had ended, and when they got back, Chance was there—come for some more salt. Chance had taken over the conversation, the way he always did. Will had gradually been left out, and at last he had drifted away, leaving the two of them alone, talking and laughing. He hadn't stayed for the pie.

After five days, the little party reached the head of Double Horn Creek. Jack Sommerville and Hope came out to welcome them in, along with George Vestry and Amos Blaine, whose saddled horses were tied in front of the Sommerville house.

They rode in slowly. Chance lay on the travois with a blanket over him. He was making an effort not to show his pain. The horses were gaunt and hungry. They had barely enough strength to make the last steps. The men were dirty and disheveled, and they suffered rheumatic pains from days of bad water. They were in low spirits because their pursuit of the Comanches had failed. They smelled the salt in the bubbling kettles by the spring. They heard the pigs rooting, the chickens squawking. They were vaguely aware of green buds on the trees around the Sommerville place.

Old Jack Sommerville ran to his son. "Curt. Thank God you're alive, boy. We been praying for you every day."

Curt dismounted. He embraced his father and sister. Will had eyes only for Hope. She gave him a quick smile, warm and dazzling, a smile that made the whole expedition worthwhile. Then she turned with a worried look to Chance.

"How is he?" she asked Will.

"His leg's broke. His horse throwed him after a brush with the Comanches."

Jack bent down. He lifted the blanket and looked at Chance's leg. "You won't be going nowheres for a while," he said. He rose again. "Reckon you'll have to stay here till that leg mends. There's nowhere else you can go, not by yourself. Hope here can look after you."

Chance looked up at Will, and he smiled smugly.

"You can have the kitchen," Jack told Chance. "Hope, you move in the front room with us. We'll rig a blanket to give you some privacy."

Blaine and Curt unhitched the travois and carried it onto the gallery. Will and Fulgencio climbed off their horses, while Jack took their reins. "I'll get you boys something to eat," Hope said, and she went inside.

Vestry slapped Will's shoulder. The comradely gesture

seemed out of place for him. "Glad you're back, Cooper. No hard feelings about before, eh? By all that's holy, we'd given you men up for dead. Blaine and I came here to comfort the family and help them . . . well, plan for the future."

As Vestry strode inside, he heard someone snort. He turned. It was Jack Sommerville, who led the horses close to Will. In a low voice he said, "What he really wanted was for me and my boys to join him in a raid on the Penateka reservation."

Will shut his eyes. "What did you tell him?"

Jack snorted again. "What do you think? That sort of thing ain't my style, 'specially for a skunk like Vestry. He's got designs on that reservation land, you know. Wouldn't be surprised if he wasn't eyeing your place and the saloon, too."

Will nodded wearily, then he changed the subject. "How's Rusty making out?"

"He was a little shook up at first, but he seems fine now. Him and Todd was up here yesterday. Them two has hit it off just like brothers. You go inside now, get some vittles. I'll follow directly."

Inside the house, Curt, Fulgencio, and Will seated themselves at the trestle table. Chance was off to one side, with his injured leg propped on a chair. The fire felt good after the chill wind. Hope brought out the food. There was side pork and a cold haunch of venison. There was cornbread with butter. There was hot coffee and plenty of it. Jack and Blaine came in from tending the horses. Cups and utensils clattered. The house buzzed with conversation, as Chance and Curt answered questions about the arduous pursuit and the fight with the Comanches.

Will kept out of the talk. He watched the play of Hope's long fingers as she worked. He watched the movements of her strong, slender body. She seemed so competent, so in control of things. There was nothing she couldn't do, he decided. She could probably build a house or repair a wagon as easily as she sewed a new dress or served coffee. She always kept something in reserve, too. She had dignity. She was a real lady. Once she caught him staring at her, and he looked away, self-conscious, as he always was around her. Then he laughed at himself. His heart hadn't been beating this fast when the Comanches were chasing him.

Even before they were done eating, Jack pulled out the jug of corn liquor. Pretty soon he, Fulgencio, and Curt were laughing, along with Vestry and Blaine. Chance had eaten little. His face was thin, and his dark eyes looked even more deep-set than usual. He was flushed with fever. He sipped from a wooden cup full of the whiskey, and he motioned to Will. "Help me outside, will you? I'm burning up in here."

Fulgencio rose to help, too, but Chance waved him off. "That's all right. Will can do it. Finish your meal."

Will helped Chance from the chair. Chance put an arm around Will's neck, and he hopped outside on his good leg. He sat in a crude chair on the gallery, out of breath and sweating. He let the chill breeze blow over him. "That's better," he said. "Thought I was going to pass out in there."

"You going to be all right?" Will asked.

"Sure. It only hurts when I breathe." Chance sipped more whiskey, glancing around. "So this is home for a while, eh?" He looked up at Will with mock innocence, "You look mad, partner."

"I am mad. You probably broke that leg on purpose, just so's you could be alone here with Hope."

Chance laughed. He shifted the leg, giving an exaggerated gesture from the pain. "Yes, I'd say it's going to be a long convalescence. Very long. I'm going to require lots of close, personal attention. The feminine touch."

"You son of a . . ." Will poined a finger in his friend's face. "I won't let you get away with this. I'm going to visit you every day."

"You can't," Chance told him.

"Why not?"

"Because you have to take my place with Rip Ford's Rangers."

Will stared at him.

"Rip's expecting somebody from Kingdom," Chance said. "He's expecting our best man. That's you now."

There was a silence, then Will said, "I know I told you I wanted to go, but that was when you were going, too. By myself, well . . ." Will wanted to say that he lacked confidence, but he was ashamed to.

Chance struggled up in the chair. His feverish eyes burned. "Look, Will, this is important. Believe me, I'd go if I could.

Hell, it's killing me to miss it. If we can lick the Indians on their own ground, we can make this country safe for a long time. Think of your neighbors. Think of Hope. Rip needs every good man he can get, if he's going to be successful. You're the only one around here with the Ranger stamp. You've got to go.''

Will gave in. He let out his breath slowly. "When do I leave?''

"Soon as you can. Rip's at the Brazos Reserve. You know where that is, about twelve miles below Belknap, on the river. He'll march as soon as the grass is up. You'll need a first-class horse. Take Chinaco. Take my rifle, too, if you want.''

Will pushed back his hat, and he scratched his dirty hair. "Out of the frying pan . . .'' he said. "Guess I'll go back and see the ranch, or what's left of it, then leave from there. I better go soon if I want to get there before dark.'' He shook his head. "I was looking forward to a few days sleep, too.''

"That's all right, I'll do the sleeping for both of us. If Hope lets me, of course.''

Will gave his friend a dirty look, but Chance just smiled. "You can't hit a wounded man. You said so yourself.''

The men had eaten. The horses were fed and rested. Vestry and Blaine mounted. They would ride partway back with Will and Fulgencio. Fulgencio shook Chance's hand. "I would like to keep this stagecoach horse awhile, *Señor* Chance, if it is all right with you. Until Rusty and I can catch some of the *mesteños* and break them.''

"Keep him as long as you like," Chance said. "If Mr. Butterfield doesn't like it, that's his problem.''

"Get Todd to help you at the ranch,'' Jack added. "There's no rush for him to come back here.''

It was Will's turn to say his farewells. By now everyone knew he was riding with the Rangers. He shook hands with Jack and Curt, then he took off his hat and turned to Hope, who was standing beside Chance. "Good-bye, Hope.''

"Good-bye, Will.'' She touched his hand. "Be careful.''

The spot where she touched him seemed to glow. He felt himself blush. "I will,'' he mumbled, putting his hat back on.

Chance reached up his hand, and Will took it. *"Vaya con Dios, compadre,"* Chance said. "Don't forget to duck.''

Jack Sommerville said, "Give them red devils hell, Will.''

"Good luck,'' Curt added.

Will walked to Chance's red roan and mounted. The tired horse pitched a bit under the new rider, then he was all right. Will waved, then he joined the others and rode off.

On the gallery, the Sommervilles and Chance watched Will's party until they were out of sight behind the trees.

Hope shivered. She turned and felt Chance's forehead. It was red hot. She took the cup of whiskey from him, and she looked at her father and brother. "We'd better get him to bed. Carry him inside for me, will you, please?"

18

Hope's bed was the best in the house. It was made of rails run between four posts, with a cowhide stretched in between. On top was a mattress stuffed with straw. Jack and Curt lay Chance on the bed, then withdrew. Hope had already removed her things from the room, which, because of the kitchen stove, was warmer than the room on the other side of the dog run.

Hope placed a blanket over Chance. His face was wet and flushed. He looked as if he were asleep. She stood straight, hands on hips. She spoke to herself. "So, Chance Evans, you're to be my patient. Well, what shall we do first?"

His feverish eyes opened. "How about this?" he said. With a surprisingly quick motion for one in his condition, he grabbed her and pulled her down on top of him, kissing her.

She responded, involuntarily at first, then with eagerness. Then she remembered herself, and with an effort, she broke his grasp and pushed herself away from him.

"You . . . you . . ." She raised a hand to slap him, then stopped. "I can't. Not when you're sick."

Chance grinned. "Come on, there was no harm. Admit it, you liked it."

"I'll admit no such thing, and I'll thank you to keep your hands off me in the future. As a matter of fact, it was vile."

Chance was still grinning as Hope smoothed the front of her dress. Her brows were knit. Her usually pale cheeks were red. "I suppose you've kissed a lot of girls," she said tartly.

"A few."

"More than a few, I'll bet."

"What about you?" Chance said.

Hope lowered her gaze. "That was . . . it was the first time."

Chance's eyes opened wide. "A girl as pretty as you, and it's the first time you been kissed? What's wrong with the boys around here?"

"There aren't any boys, save for you and Will Cooper."

Chance laughed. "Well, you'll grow old waiting for Will to kiss you." He reached for her again. "Let's get you some more experience."

She stepped back, out of his grasp. "Are you going to be like this the whole time you're here? Because if you are, you can get well on your own."

Chance lay back on the mattress. That little bit of effort had taken a lot out of him. He felt very tired, and cold. "All right. All right. You can't blame a fellow for trying. I've been wanting to do that since the first time I saw you."

"For real?" she said. She'd long been wondering what it would be like to be kissed by Chance, but she'd never let him know it.

"For real," he said. He closed his eyes, and he mumbled, "You don't have any of your pa's whiskey around, I suppose?"

"No more whiskey for you, Mr. Evans. You're a sick man. Now, you go to sleep, and I'll be in to see you later."

But Chance was already asleep. Hope stood for a minute, studying his tousled dark hair and full, sensual lips, watching the rise and fall of his thick chest. She could still taste his kiss. Then she went out, shutting the door softly behind her.

19

When Chance awoke, Hope was sitting in the chair beside the bed, looking at him. It was near noon, as close as he could judge from the light in the room. The smell of broth came from the stove.

"Hello," Hope said brightly. "How do you feel today?"

Chance struggled up, hindered by the splinted leg. "I've felt worse. Felt better, too."

"How's the leg?"

"It hurts. Course with Will setting it, I'm lucky it's not pointed backward."

"Will did a good job. As far as I can see, you've got a good chance of walking normally again."

Chance indicated a pitcher and cup on the bedstand. "Is that water? I've a fair thirst."

She poured him some water, and as he reached for it, he realized something. "Hey, my clothes are gone!"

Hope was amused. "I washed them. You do know what it is to have clean clothes, don't you?"

Chance looked down at himself. "This isn't my undershirt, either."

"It's one of Curt's. A little small on you, but it'll do."

Chance was aghast. "You mean I been undressed . . . ?"

Hope's amusement grew. "Yes, and if you look, you'll see you've been bathed and shaved, too."

"Bathed? By . . . by you?"

"Chance Evans, I've got three brothers. Don't you think they were ever sick? Do you think a man is something I've never seen before?"

Blushing in spite of himself, Chance took the cup of water

and drank it. She poured him some more and he drank that, too, for the thirst burned in him.

Hope felt his forehead, his cheek, his hand. "The fever's down. Feel like eating?"

Refreshed by the water, Chance showed his old spirit. "I could eat. Especially if you did the cooking."

Hope took a bowl and scooped some of the thick broth into it. "Smells like beef," Chance said.

"It is. Will told us to take one of his steers. You don't see wild cattle on this range anymore."

Chance laughed. "Will and his cows. He'd own every cow in Texas, if he had his way."

Hope resumed her seat. She spooned some broth from the bowl. "Do you think you can keep your hands off me this time?"

"It won't be easy," Chance said.

"Then maybe I should get my brother to do this."

Chance sighed. "You win. I'll be good. It still won't be easy, though."

Chance was in bed for ten days. It was Hope's bed, and that made him think about her even more than he did normally. He looked forward to Hope's visits, and so did she. She spent as much time in the kitchen as she could, to be near him. She was infatuated with Chance's charm, with his humor, with his knowledge of life and the world, a world she could only dream about. She quizzed him about the places he'd been, the things he'd seen. He taught her to play cards, using pebbles for chips, and she laughed excitedly when she won, which was often, though she suspected that Chance somehow manipulated the cards. She could read and write well, despite being largely self-taught, and sometimes she read to him from the Bible, which was the only book in the house. Chance's interest in Scripture was negligible, but he listened to her clear, firm voice as raptly as another man might listen to great music.

One rainy afternoon Chance was by himself, playing solitaire, when there was a scraping of feet on the gallery and a knock at the door. "Come in," he said.

The door opened, and out of the storm stepped Jules Villette and Sam Sommerville.

"Sammy! Jules!" Chance cried. He gathered the cards and

set them aside "Come in! It's good to see you." He reached up and clasped their hands. Sam grinned. Jules took off his preposterously curled hat. They shook the water from their coats. "How's the saloon, Sam?"

The dark-haired boy dropped his grin. "It was all I could do to leave Kingdom, Chance. That's why I ain't been to see you before. I got as much work as I can handle when them stages come in. I been able to take care of the animals, and Jules here, he helps with the passengers' food when he can, but the booze and card games I've pretty much abandoned till you get back."

He hesitated. "Tell the truth, I hated to leave this long."

"Afraid Indians'll steal the horses?" Chance said.

"It ain't so much the Indians I worry about as some of the whites. I know there's men helping themselves to free whiskey right now. And I knew better than to leave any money around. I brung the cash box with me."

"Who do you think would steal it?"

"There's a couple I don't trust, but that fellow Blaine, Colonel Vestry's friend, is the one I'd reckon most likely."

"Well, like your pa says, that's what happens when 'the better sort' of people move in. Reckon we'll have to get us a safe. There been any word of Will?"

"I heard the Rangers left their camp on the Brazos. I don't know no more than that."

Chance fell silent, looking at his splinted leg ruefully.

"When are you coming back, Chance?"

"When I can, Sam." Chance felt guilty about leaving the boy with all that work, but at the same time he was in no hurry to leave Hope. He didn't want to get well too quickly, or even to seem much improved, in case she started paying him less attention.

Jules Villette might have sensed this, for his eyes twinkled as he said, "You are not lonely here, *non*?"

Chance dodged the question. "Not at all. There's always somebody around. Jack and Curt, of course; and Fulgencio, Todd, and Rusty have ridden up a couple of times. Then there's these settlers that come for salt. By God, old Jack does a land-office business here. It's like having a gold mine. I've seen folks come from sixty miles and more."

"I have brought you a book," Jules said.

From a deep pocket inside his wet tweed coat, he produced a leather-bound volume. Chance took it. *"Ivanhoe,"* he said.

"I used it to help me practice the English."

"Well, it's got to beat the hell out of what I've been reading," Chance said.

"There is something else," Jules said. He reached in his coat again and held out a bottle.

"Brandy." Chance grinned. "Now we're getting somewhere. Thanks, Jules."

"It is nothing. I feel the guilt, you know . . . for having left you out there . . ."

Chance waved him off. "Hell, you did the smart thing. If we'd had any brains, we'd have turned back with you. It's only a miracle we didn't lose our scalps."

He uncorked the brandy. "Let's have a snort. You boys staying for supper?"

"Yeah," Sammy said. "We're heading back in the morning."

They were passing the bottle around when the door opened, and Hope came in.

"Hi, Sis," said Sammy, with the bottle frozen to his lips.

Jules rose and bowed elaborately. "Mademoiselle Hope."

She nodded to them. "Sammy, what's Pa going to say?"

"Oh, Hope. I'm seventeen now. I can have a drink."

Hope raised one eyebrow doubtfully. Then she went to work in the kitchen, mixing dough for biscuits. Sam was ready for a long set-to with the brandy, but Jules motioned toward the door. "Let us go visit your father and brother."

"But . . ."

With his eyes, Jules indicated Chance and Hope. At last Sam got the hint, and the two of them departed.

After they left, there was an awkward silence. Hope kneaded the biscuit dough, conscious of Chance watching her. The rain rattled on the roof and walls of the cabin. In places it leaked onto the earthen floor.

"Rotten weather," Chance said at last.

"We can sure use it, though," Hope said.

Finished with the dough, she wiped her hands on her apron and crossed the room. "Do you need anything?" There were dark circles under her eyes. Her hair was out of place and matted from the rain. Her face drooped with fatigue, as it frequently did by this time of day.

"Sit down awhile," Chance said.

"I've got to—"

"Oh, go ahead."

She sat, and her shoulders slumped. She shut her eyes because it felt so good to be off her feet.

"Jules brought me a book. I was hoping you'd read it to me."

Hope turned the volume over curiously. She had never read anything but the Bible. She opened it and looked at the frontispiece. "What's that?"

"That's Ivanhoe. He's a knight." He saw that she didn't understand. "That's kind of an old-time soldier. A nobleman."

"Oh," she said. She turned to the first page, settled the book, and began to read.

Suddenly Chance reached out. "God, Hope, look at your hands."

He took one. The hand was beautifully proportioned, with long slender fingers, but the skin, which should have been smooth and white, was red and sore and cracked, and there were hard calluses on the palms and backs of the fingers. "What's this from?"

She shrugged. "Take your pick. Scrubbing, tending the stock, sewing, churning butter. It would take me too long to tell you everything I've done today. The same things I do every day."

Chance massaged the raw fingers gently. "You shouldn't have to put up with this, Hope. You were meant for better things. You know, if I could, I'd buy you gowns from Paris and jewels that would sparkle so bright, men would be afraid to look at you."

"Would you look at me?"

"I'd be the only one allowed to. I'd make it a law."

She lowered her eyes and smiled. She began reading. She let him keep holding her hand.

20

When Chance's fever was gone and the broken bone had been given time to knit, it was time to get on his feet.

Jack Sommerville made him a crutch. Jack and Curt tried to help him up, but Chance said, "I'll do it."

Using the bedpost, he pulled himself up. He tucked the crutch under his arm. It took a minute to get used to the balance, keeping the broken leg bent behind him. He hopped around the kitchen as Hope, Jack, and Curt watched.

"All right?" Hope asked.

Chance nodded.

He went into the yard, blinking in the warm spring sunshine. "Sure feels good to be outdoors again," he said. "My back hurts from being in bed so long."

Jack said, "Curt and me have to get to work. Hope, don't forget to hoe them crops. That last rain made the weeds come up something fierce."

"Yes, Pa." She turned to Chance. "You're welcome to come with me."

"I'd like that," Chance said.

He went with her first while she tended the vegetable garden behind the house. He tired quickly, though. "I better sit a spell," he said, sweating profusely.

"Use my shoulder," Hope told him. He put his arm around her, and she guided him to a bench that had been placed beneath a Spanish willow for use on hot days. She sat down with him. He kept his arm around her shoulder. His fingers played with her thick, reddish hair.

An electric thrill ran through Hope at the feel of his strong arm around her, of his fingers in her hair. Her heart was beating furiously. She wanted Chance, even though something told her that

109

she shouldn't. She had thought for some time that she would one day have to make a decision between Chance and Will Cooper. Will was solid and dependable. He was hard working. He would always be there for her, and that was a powerful attraction.

There was an element of danger about Chance, however, and that was an even more powerful attraction. Maybe Hope got that attraction to danger from her mother. Maybe it was something ingrained in the pioneer breed. Chance brought out a reckless feeling in her. It was a wild feeling, of running free before the wind. It was a feeling she found hard to control, and she was afraid that it would get the best of her. Even worse, she sometimes hoped that it would.

"Better now?" she said.

"Yeah," Chance said.

She helped him to his feet. She got her hoe, and they set off for the cornfields.

Jack and Curt were by one of the big salt kettles. They fed the fire with cords of wood. Inside were barrels of the briny water that they had trapped in seepage holes around the spring. They would boil the water until the white, bitter salt caked on top and fell to the bottom. Then they would scoop it out and dry it. Jack paused in his work to watch Hope and Chance going to the fields. Chance said something, and Hope laughed, touching his arm.

Jack said, "I wouldn't be surprised, we had us a wedding before long."

"Wouldn't be surprised, neither," Curt said, wiping sweat from his brow. "Don't know I'd be so happy, though. I'd sooner she was with Will."

Jack hadn't been expecting that. "Chance is a good boy. Sammy worships him. So does Will, for that matter."

"Chance is a gambler, Pa. You know what they're like. He ain't one of us. Not like Will is."

Jack scratched his strawlike whiskers thoughtfully. "I don't know. There's times I think Hope ain't one of us, neither."

21

The weeks became a month. It was May. The weather was warm. The leaves were thick on the trees. The meadows were splashed with wildflowers. Birds chirped merrily. Squirrels and rabbits scampered in the tall grass.

Chance was going for longer walks now. Hope went, too, when she could. She went not because she was needed anymore, but because she wanted to be with him.

One morning they wandered along Double Horn Creek. They stopped in a sheltered glade among the trees, not far from where the wild plums grew. "Watch this," Chance said. He leaned his crutch against a tree. He lowered his left leg to the ground and put his weight on it. He grimaced at first, then felt comfortable enough to limp a few steps on the injured limb. He turned back to her. "*Voilà*, as Jules would say."

He came back to her, and his tone grew somber. "I'll be able to go home soon."

Hope averted her eyes. "I know," she said quietly.

"If I'd wanted, I could have gone home already."

Hope said nothing.

"You know why I've stayed, don't you?"

Hope nodded.

Chance sighed. He turned away, and he broke a piece of dead bark from the tree. He tossed it in the creek, watching it splash in the shallow water. He turned back to Hope. "You know, I've really liked being here. You all have made me feel part of your family. I never had that kind of feeling before, even when my mom and dad were alive. I never knew what I'd been missing. The saloon and card table get pretty lonely, even with all those people around. Still, that's the life I was cut out for, I guess."

Hope smiled shyly at him. "I'm glad you've been here, too. You're the first person I've had to talk to since Ma died."

"What about your dad and brothers?"

"They wouldn't understand the things I feel. They think all I want to do is cook and clean for them. They think that's all any woman wants."

"And you don't?"

She shook her head. "I don't know what I want, exactly. Something more, that's all."

"Like what?"

"I don't know. I want to do something, to be something more than a slave, like my mother was. I love Pa and my brothers, but I don't want to marry a man like them. I want a future. I want real clothes and real shoes, not these ones Pa makes. I want a real education for my children." She turned to Chance. "Is that so wrong?"

"No," Chance said. "It's not wrong. It's not wrong at all."

He took her hand. He stroked it. Hope looked down. "I knew you'd understand. Ma might have understood, too, I think. I think she dreamed of a better life when she was young."

She walked a few steps off. She looked away from him, and her lips trembled. "It's strange. I've wanted you to get well, but at the same time I've hated seeing it happen. Because . . . because it means you'll leave."

Chance came up behind her. "And you don't want me to go?"

Her voice was barely a whisper. "No."

She turned and looked at him for a long second. Then she kissed him on the cheek. "We'd better go," she said.

She started away, and Chance smiled to himself.

He limped after her. He pulled her around, and he kissed her. She kissed him back, running her fingers through his hair. His hands moved across her back, behind her neck. Her straw hat fell off. She was carried away on a wave of passion and yearning that she had not known existed within her. Her tongue darted in and out of his mouth. She ran her hands along his muscular back and shoulders.

Then she caught her breath, and she pushed him away. "No. No, Chance, we can't . . ."

"Yes, we can," he said in a husky voice, and he drew her to him again.

She tried to fight him off, but he pressed himself upon her, awkwardly because of his splint. They stumbled, and then they were rolling in the long grass. His hands were under her dress, caressing her long legs. She wanted him so badly that it hurt. She felt like an animal, and the feeling surprised her and shamed her, but not enough to make her stop. Her dress had risen to her waist. He was fondling her breasts, kissing her neck and ears.

She made a last effort at self-control. With a little cry, she managed to shove him back again. "No. Chance. Darling."

He came forward, but she held him off. "A gentleman wouldn't do this," she said.

His dark eyes looked deep into hers. "I'm no gentleman," he said, and he lowered himself onto her.

She made a last feeble effort to stop him, then she let herself go. There was no longer a tomorrow. There was only the present.

22

Afterward, Hope was not sated. If anything, she was more aroused. She had discovered something within her whose existence she had scarcely suspected, and she was eager to explore its limits. She was in love, and love was everything she had dreamed it would be. She and Chance stole kisses and secret touches around the house and yard. They traded soulful looks. They made love every time they were alone. They made love in the sheds and in the stable. Once they even did it in the kitchen, while Jack and Curt were in the other room waiting for their supper. Their walks became passionate trysts in the glades along Double Horn Creek. She came to his bed each night, after the others were asleep, and it seemed as if she awoke in the morning impatiently yearning for the sun to go down. Curt was beginning to look at her oddly, but she did not care. Chance himself was surprised by her recklessness and the depth of her desire. He was surprised that someone with such a cool exterior could behave at times like a heedless wanton.

Three weeks passed. There was word that the Texas Rangers had fought the Comanches on the Canadian River, and that Chief Iron Shirt and many of his braves had been killed. Chance was helping out around the Sommerville house as best he could now, trying to make himself useful, but he could no longer stay without arousing suspicion. His leg was good enough for him to ride, and he had a business to look after. It was time to leave.

On Chance's last night, he and Hope lay in her sweat-stained bed. Her head rested on his chest, and she listened to the beating of his heart. They spoke in whispers, so as not to awaken the sleepers next door.

"I don't want you to leave tomorrow," Hope said. "I can't stand the thought of losing you, not even for a minute."

Chance stared at the roof. "I feel the same," he said. He hesitated then he added, "I can't live without you, Hope."

"Or me without you."

His fingers stroked her sleek back, still beaded with perspiration from their lovemaking. He broached an idea that he had been forming for some time. "Let's run away together."

She struggled up in bed beside him. "Are you serious?"

"Yes."

"Run away to where?"

"New Orleans, San Francisco—who cares? Anywhere, as long as we're together. I have money and horses in Kingdom. We'll be miles away from here before anybody knows we're gone."

She looked at him, her green eyes trying to pierce the darkness and the veil of his intentions. "Darling, I don't know what to say. I—"

"Say you'll do it," Chance told her. He smoothed back her wet hair. "I'll show you the way life was meant to be lived. I'll make you the finest lady in New Orleans. By God, you've got the beauty and style for it."

He kissed the hollow of her neck, and she sighed.

"What do you say?" he asked.

"I'll go. You know I'll go. I'd do anything for you. When do we leave?"

"Tomorrow night. After I leave here, I'll double back and wait for you—by that big post oak that was split by lightning."

"All right. I'll pack my clothes."

"Don't bother. I'll buy you new clothes. Good ones."

They kissed, and she said, "I hate to leave my family, Chance, especially without being able to say good-bye."

"Some things have to be done, Hope."

"What about Will? You two have been together so long. Can you leave without saying good-bye to him?"

Chance laughed. "Will will understand."

They kissed again, running their hands over each other's naked bodies. Chance said, "I love you, Hope."

"I love you, too," she breathed. "I'll love you forever." She lay down and drew him to her hungrily.

It was almost time to wake up when Hope stole across the dog run to the cabin's other room. She was dead tired, but she couldn't sleep. She lay on the cold cowhide, listening to the faint noises from the other side of the blanket partition and thinking about the future. This was her last night at home. This time tomorrow she would be gone, possibly never—probably never—to see her family again. Tomorrow was the start of a new life. It was so sudden. It was too sudden. She had to do it, though, even if a part of her was saying that it was foolhardy. She pushed the cautionary voice from her mind.

It was time to get up. She stood wearily, wrapping her shawl around her in the predawn chill. Her limbs seemed to lack strength and coordination. Her eyes stung from lack of sleep. She lighted the lantern, and she started from the cabin to the barn. She would milk the cow, then go back to the kitchen to start breakfast. Suddenly there was an odd feeling in the pit of her stomach, a queasy feeling. She stopped, and she threw up.

She stood straight again and kept walking. It must have been excitement about the coming night that had made her sick. Then she stopped again. A prickly feeling crept over her scalp. It spread over her entire body as she became aware of the new life that was growing within her. And even as the joy of that awareness began to manifest itself, she came crashing back to cold reality.

"Oh, God," she said.

She was going to have a baby.

Was it possible? It had only been three weeks. Her monthly time was late, but that happened frequently with her. No, she could tell. The woman in her knew. She was pregnant. The child must have been conceived that first time she and Chance were together.

She started walking again. She felt deathly ill. It was all she could do to reach the barn. With her last bit of strength, she found her milking stool and sat on it, reaching out to the barn wall for support. Her head was spinning. Her stomach heaved. The musty smells of animals and soiled straw made her gag.

She had to tell Chance. That was the first thing. And then what? Marry him?

A thrill came over her at the thought of being married to Chance. Then it died.

With a clearheadedness that she had not known in some time, she realized that Chance was not the marrying kind. He might run away with her, but he would never offer to marry her. He loved her, but not in that way. If he married her, it would be because he had to, not because he wanted to. Hope didn't want that, and she loved Chance too much to ever force him into such a situation.

Chance was like the wild mustangs. Part of his beauty was his freedom. She didn't want to tame that out of him; indeed, she doubted that he could be tamed. If she married Chance, she knew there would always be other women in his life. A marriage like that would never work. It would not be worth having. What would Chance have done if she had discovered she was pregnant after they had run away? She did not want to think.

She would have to do something before the baby started to show. Everyone would figure out who had given it to her. If Chance didn't marry her, and if he didn't run away, Pa and Curt would go after him with guns, and Hope didn't fancy anyone's odds against Chance with guns.

Everything in the barn was spinning. She had to milk the cow, she told herself. She had to get going. Pa and Curt would be up. They would want coffee and breakfast. She couldn't get off the stool, though. If she did, she would faint. She felt the blood draining from her head. She eased herself from the stool to the firmer support of the barn floor, closing her eyes and breathing heavily, with sweat running down her hot face. Oh, God, what was she going to do?

She could run away—not with Chance, but by herself. She would be penniless then, and without friends, and she would probably have to turn to whoring to support herself and the baby. Or she could get rid of the child before it was born. She heard there were doctors who did that sort of thing. But she didn't have money, and she wouldn't know how to find those doctors, though Chance probably would. But this was her *baby* she was thinking about, and she already felt fiercely protective of it. She could never let harm come to it, much less have it killed.

Should she stay here and have it, then? She pictured the shame, the humiliation she would endure from family and neighbors. With a bastard child, she would probably never marry. She would be lucky if Pa didn't kick her out of the house. Any way she cut it, her life was ruined, ended before it had fairly begun. All for a few hours of passion.

She could kill herself. That would solve a lot of problems. It would end the pain. Things might be bad now, but they were only going to get worse. Suicide was a form of quitting, however, and Hope was no quitter. One way or the other, she was going to see this through.

Hope pulled herself to her feet. She managed to get a little milk from the cow, though she didn't know how, because she couldn't see right and her fingers were fumbling, and the smell of the cow and the raw milk nauseated her. She tottered back to the house, and if it had been one step more, she wouldn't have made it.

Somehow Hope got through breakfast. She moved slowly, as in a waking nightmare, taking it a minute at a time, because she was afraid she didn't have more than a minute left in her. She was pale and trembling, and she didn't eat. It was hard to look at the food, and cooking it almost killed her. Her father and brother asked if she was sick, but Chance acted unconcerned. She knew that he attributed her state to nervousness about that night.

Chance departed after breakfast. He shook hands with Jack and Curt. "So long. Thanks for everything. I'll return this horse and saddle as soon as I can."

"No rush," Jack said. "We've enjoyed your company. You've livened the place up a bit." He grinned. "I know Hope thinks so."

Chance grinned back. He limped over to where Hope waited on the gallery. "Good-bye, Hope," he said, taking her hand. He gave the hand a slight squeeze and was surprised to get no response. "I'd never have pulled through without you."

She gave him a funny look. Sad, it seemed. "It was nothing," she murmured. "Good-bye."

"Maybe I'll see you soon," he said. His back was to Jack and Curt, and he winked at her.

"Yes, maybe."

He gave her a puzzled look, then shrugged it off. He mounted the horse from the gallery, because of his leg. He waved his hat in farewell, and he rode away.

Hope did not meet Chance that night. She lay in her bed, the bed that still smelled of him. She thought of him out beyond the trees, waiting for her and wondering why she was not there. She thought of what they had shared, of what was now lost. She started crying, and at last, exhausted, she fell asleep.

Hope awoke at her usual time. She stumbled to the barn in the last of the night's darkness. She hung the lantern on its nail. As she reached for her milking stool, someone grabbed her arm.

She stifled a scream and turned. It was Chance.

He looked angry, and he stood uneasily on his injured leg. "Where were you?" he hissed.

Before Hope could answer, he pulled her toward the door. "Come on. Let's go."

She resisted, pulling her arm away. "I'm not going."

"What do you mean, not going? Have you lost your nerve?"

Her head was whirling. Her stomach was queasy, and she thought she was going to be sick again. "I'm just not going, that's all."

He grabbed her shoulders. "I thought you loved me."

"I do. You know I do."

"Then why . . . ?"

"I can't. Don't ask any more. I just can't." Hope fought back waves of nausea. She did not want to be sick in front of Chance. She did not want him to guess her real reason. It was important to her that he not be forced into anything.

"Hope, I'm not leaving here without you."

She slipped free of him again. "Yes, you are. You're leaving now. Pa's up. If he sees you, there'll be trouble."

"Don't play games with me, Hope. What's the matter with you? When will I see you again?"

"I don't know. Please, just go."

"Maybe I won't see you at all, then," he threatened, growing angrier. "Maybe that's what you want."

"Maybe it is!" she retorted, and she was crying now.

He reached for her, "Hope, wait . . ."

But she was past him and out the barn door, hurrying back to the house. She stopped and was sick in the grass, and then she kept going, and she never looked back.

Chance did not come to the Sommerville house that day, or any day thereafter. Hope missed him terribly. She was sick nearly every morning, but by afternoons she was all right. She felt the secret life grow within her, a part of her, and she was awed by the miracle of it. Still, she had to do something. Every day that she put off a decision brought her closer to the day when the decision would no longer be hers to make. Once the baby started to show, there would be trouble. Maybe her first idea had been the best. Maybe she should run away, to Dallas, or Austin if she could get that far. Yes, that was the best way out. It was the only way. If she had to whore, so be it. Perhaps that was a fitting punishment for her sin. Pa had some money buried behind the house. She would take some to get her started. She didn't like the idea, but she felt entitled to a share. She would also take her one set of spare clothes, along with a blanket, some food, and that old horse pistol that Pa kept over the fireplace. She bided her time, waiting for an opportunity when Pa and Curt were gone from home.

Then, on a beautiful morning at the beginning of June, a buckskinned figure rode out of the sun toward the Sommerville house, with a carbine slung across the pommel of his saddle. The figure seemed even taller and more spare than Hope remembered. There was something in the way he rode, too, an authority that had not been there before.

"Will," she said, stepping off the gallery into the dust. "Will, you're all right."

As Will swung from the saddle of Chance's red roan Chinaco,

Jack and Curt came from the new harness shed they'd been building.

"Will," Curt cried, shaking his hand. "It's good to see you back."

Jack shook Will's hand, too. "We heard they was a big fight on the Canadian."

"Big enough," Will said. He looked like there was something on his mind.

"Injuns licked good?" Jack said.

"That bunch was."

Curt said, "How'd you come out of it? Don't appear like you was wounded."

Will shrugged. "They made me a lieutenant."

"Well, how about that," Jack said. The old veteran stepped back and looked at Will proudly. "Lieutenant Cooper. Lieutenant Cooper of the Texas Rangers. That's a hell of an honor, boy. This calls for a celebration. Come on in."

"I've really come to speak to Miss Hope," Will said. "In private, if it's all right."

Jack and Curt looked at each other, then at Hope, who had no idea what Will wanted. "Why, sure, Will," Jack said. "We'll talk later. Come on, Curt, let's get back to work."

As her father and brother walked away, Hope looked at Will wonderingly. His buckskins had seen hard service. He wore two pistols now. His face seemed more deep-set than before, more serious.

"Yes?" she said.

Will took off his hat, the hat through whose crown Hope had once put a bullet. He fixed her with his blue eyes. "Hope, I done a lot of thinking while I was gone. About how quick life can end. About how, if you want something, you got to go after it, because if you don't, you may not get a second chance. I'm done with daydreaming. I mean to tell you straight and get it off my chest. I love you, Hope. I always have, and I always will. Hope, I . . . I'm asking you to marry me."

Hope caught her breath. She was saved. Her heart leaped, and a thousand thoughts went whirling around her mind. She felt weak-kneed and giddy, poised on the brink of a high precipice, deciding whether to jump. Deciding whether she could afford not to jump.

Then she smiled at him. "Yes," she said.

"I don't have much to . . . what did you say?"

"I said yes."

"You mean . . . you mean, you will?"

Her smile broadened, and she nodded.

Will looked as if he couldn't believe it. "I never expected . . . I mean, Chance . . . I always thought you and him would . . ."

He shook his head, and he grinned. He stepped forward, and, in a bold move for him, he took her hand. "You've made me the happiest man in the world, Hope. I promise, I'll never give you cause to regret this."

Hope kept smiling, and a tear fell from the corner of her eye. Some might have thought it was a tear of joy.

23

Hope wanted no drawn-out, formal engagement. She wanted to have the wedding as soon as possible, which was fine with Will. The date was set for a month hence, on July 4.

Preparations began at once. The men of the neighborhood helped Will build a new house for his bride. They built the house of adobe, squat and thick like a small fort, which was what it would become if the need arose. There were two rooms with a fireproof sod roof, and windows with heavy shutters. Nearby was a picket house for Fulgencio, Rusty, and Todd, who spent most of his time at the ranch now. Chance was kept from the physical labor by his mending leg, but he supplied directions and moral support, aided by occasional drafts of whiskey. When everything was finished, Will placed the smoke-blackened pair of deer antlers over the new house's door. The only reminders of the Comanche raid were the heaps of charred wood that had been dumped by the creek and Rodolfo's headstone, on a small rise behind the house.

The women began baking well before the wedding, and on the day itself there were groaning sideboards heaped with glazed hams and fried chickens, with bowls of mustard greens and black-eyed peas, with pies and preserves of wild grape, dewberry, and plum. There were watermelons and cantaloupes, cornbread with butter, and heavy, golden pound cakes. A wagonload of corn ears was set to roasting in a shallow pit. Two steers turned on spits, along with venison and turkeys. A dance floor of split logs, or puncheons, was set up in front of the house. Chance furnished a barrel of whiskey for refreshment, and Jules Villette contributed numerous bottles of wine, the first fruits of his vineyard. Red, white, and blue bunting was hung in honor of the holiday.

The day was hot, with just enough of a breeze to make it bearable. The guests began arriving early. They came from miles around. There were old friends and more recent settlers whom Will and Hope scarcely knew. They arrived on horseback, in buckboards, and in wagons. Some set up tents, for no one would be going home until tomorrow. The weapons they had carried for their protection were left in the wagons or with their saddles. They wore their best clothes, which for most were made of homespun or buckskin. The store-bought outfits of a few, like the Vestrys, stood out. Standing out even more were the blue coats and gold braid of the officers from Camp Cooper, who were just back from Utah. Hordes of children ran screaming underfoot.

The ceremony was set for noon. Will was resplendent in new white buckskins, fringed and beaded. His hair was cut, he was freshly bathed and shaven, and he smelled of Hoyt's Cologne. Chance was his groomsman, wearing his black suit and red silk cravat. There was no regular minister in the area, so Jack Sommerville, who in addition to his other talents was a Baptist clergyman, was going to perform the service.

When the bride appeared, the crowd parted, applauding her beauty. Her dress was of white linen, her veil of lace, with a chaplet of wildflowers. She had made the garments herself. Like most frontier girls, she'd worked on her wedding wardrobe almost from the day she'd learned to sew. She did not look radiant, but rather composed and formal. Kathy Nye was her maid of honor.

Will swelled with pride when he saw her. He felt Chance stiffen at his side, and he felt sorry for his friend, because he knew that Hope meant a lot to him, too. Indeed, he was still surprised that it was he, and not Chance, who was marrying her.

The service itself was brief. The couple exchanged vows, and the beaming older man said, "I pronounce you man and wife."

Will looked at Hope. She seemed relieved to have gotten it over. Will wasn't sure what to do next.

Jack said, "Go ahead, son. Kiss the bride."

In the short time that Will and Hope had been engaged, they'd hardly ever been alone. This was the first time he'd kissed her full out, and he felt embarrassed to be doing it in front of all these people. He licked his dry lips furtively, hoping no one would notice, though many did, and some of them laughed. Hope was waiting for him, almost with trepidation. Probably the excitement of the day had overwhelmed her. Will bent and kissed her, a short kiss. He tasted her sweet lips. He smelled the rose water in which she'd bathed. The crowd erupted in a great shout.

Lifting his hands, Jack Sommerville cried above the tumult, "The hard part's over, ladies and gents. In honor of the bride and groom, we'll dispense with all the patriotic speechifying. Let's start the celebrating!"

The guests fell to the heaps of food with gusto, though Will noticed that Hope ate sparingly. The whiskey flowed. Jules's wines went untouched, however, and the little Frenchman, who wore buckskins especially made for the occasion, looked disappointed.

When everyone had stuffed themselves, the dance floor was cleared, and Jack Sommerville took up his fiddle. He was joined by Fred Thompson, one of the new people, with a clevis, a metal shackle, which he beat with its heavy pin.

Will and Hope led off the dancing, to the traditional opener, "The Old Gray Horse Came Tearing Through the Wilderness." Hope didn't know why, but she was surprised at how good a dancer her husband was. He whirled her around, clomping his boots on the wooden floor to make as much noise as possible, as was the style. The guests clapped time for them, and when the next song started, everyone joined in, stomping and spinning, whooping and shouting and singing. There were far more men than women, so the girls danced continuously, hardly getting time to catch their breaths. Because the split wood floor was full of splinters, the men who wore moccasins had to borrow boots from those who were sitting out before they could dance.

All the men wanted a dance with Hope. She was kept flying around, dodging bodies, trying to save her feet. She was not always successful, especially with big Tom Nye, who tramped her toes painfully. Hope began to feel dizzy. She was sweating. She wanted desperately to stop. She was afraid the little bit of food she'd eaten would make her sick. She had to grit her way through this, though, as if nothing were wrong and she were enjoying it. It was a relief to dance with Jules, who was a good four inches shorter than she, and who tried to lead her through something mercifully slow called a waltz.

Will stood by the drinks, beaming, watching his wife and accepting the congratulations of his friends. He drank a couple bottles of his beer. He was even emboldened to try some of Jules Villette's wine, which was bitter and made him lightheaded. Nearby, Chance swilled glass after glass of whiskey. He drank purposefully, as if trying to get drunk. Off to the side, some of the children were having a taffy pull. Others were playing games, pulling hair, fighting, and being as raucous as possible, normal for children who saw no other children, save their siblings, for months at a time.

George Vestry, whose own wife was being monopolized by the dancers, came over. Vestry held out his hand. "Will, I know we don't see eye to eye on a lot of things, but, believe me, I wish you and Hope nothing but the best. If you're half as happy as I've been with Lucinda, you'll be a lucky man."

"Thanks, George," Will said. "Have a drink."

"I believe I will." Vestry laughed. "It might be awhile before I get my wife back from these young bucks. Don't they ever get tired?"

On the dance floor, Hope's legs were shaking. She couldn't take this much longer. At last, she begged leave to get refreshment. She quaffed a life-saving cup of grape punch. She was midway through a second when a limping footstep sounded behind her.

"Hello," Chance said.

A chill went through Hope. She had known this meeting would

come, and she had not looked forward to it. Chance's dark brows were knit. He smelled of whiskey. He said, "Ordinarily I'd claim the next dance, but with this leg I seem to be at a disadvantage."

"That's all right," Hope said. She had the feeling that things were spinning again. "I don't want to dance, anyway. It's too hot in this crowd. I've got to get away. Get some shade."

She started walking toward the trees by the creek. Chance walked with her. She saw Will in conversation with Fulgencio and some other men. They were all laughing. They didn't notice her. She wanted Will to come for her, and then again she didn't. It was strange.

They entered the trees and the cool shade. Hope felt tired and unusually weak, as if something were draining the strength from her—which it was. She sat on a fallen tree trunk before she fell. Her face was pale and sweating.

Chance looked at her closely. "Are you sick? You want me to get Will?"

"No," she said. "No, don't get Will. I'll be fine. It's just that, if I don't sit down, I'm afraid I'll—" She started to say "lose the baby," and she caught herself just in time.

"You drink too much?" Chance said.

"Yes, that must be it. I had some of Jules's wine. I guess I'm not used to it."

Chance looked down at her. Her heart was fluttering. Her throat was dry. Chance came right to the point. "Well, are you happy?"

"About drinking too much?"

"You know what I mean."

She looked away.

Chance pressed on. "Why, Hope? Why did you marry Will. I thought you loved me."

"I do," she said softly.

"Then why in the name of . . . ?"

"Please, I don't want to talk about it."

"Well, I do. You get me so in love with you that I can't think about anything else, then you stand me up. Now you marry my best friend, and you won't say why. For the life of me, I can't figure out what's come over you, unless you're—"

He stopped. He looked at her. Suddenly it all fit together. The paleness, the complaints about not feeling well, the sudden change in her affections. "Hope, you're not pregnant, are you?"

She bit her lip, to keep it from trembling.

"That's it. Jesus Christ, that's it. You're pregnant. And it's mine?"

She whirled on him, crying, furious. "Of course it's yours. How can you imagine it would be anyone else's?"

Chance looked away. He rubbed his hand across his jaw, and he let out his breath slowly. He should have guessed before. He was going to be a father. He felt funny inside. He turned back to her. "Why didn't you tell me?"

"Why? Would it have made a difference? What would you have done?"

"Well . . . married you, I guess."

"You *guess*? You mean, you wouldn't have wanted to, but you'd have done it out of pity, or to keep up appearances."

"No, that's not what I mean, Hope. You know that. I love—"

"Then why didn't you ask me to marry you before? I would have. Why did you only want me to run away with you?"

"I don't know," Chance said.

"Could you offer your child a home, a future? Could you promise to stay with us?"

Chance threw up his hands. "I don't know. I never thought about it. I—"

"That's just it. You don't know. Will does know. That's why I accepted him. I had to think of my baby."

"And what if Will finds out the baby isn't his? It's not going to be nine months till the birth, you know."

She looked at him coldly. "He's not going to find out, is he? I want you to promise me that."

"You know I'd never tell him," Chance said. He hung his head, and when he looked up again he was pleading. "Look, I'll still see you, won't I? I mean, after the baby and all. Things can be like they were before. We can get off by ourselves."

"Chance, what are you saying? Don't you realize it's over?"

Chance started to lean into her, then he remembered that people could see them, and he restrained himself. His voice was intense. "Hope, you and me were meant for each other. There's no changing that. I can't give you up. I won't give you up. I'll die first.''

For a moment Hope weakened. She didn't want to give him up, either. Then she said, "There's no changing something else. I'm a married woman." She wiped the tears from her cheeks. She rose, and in a voice that was supposed to be firm but trembled noticeably, she said, "Now if you'll excuse me, I have to get back to my husband."

The music and dancing went on all afternoon. By now the more venturesome had started sampling Jules's wine. People found it of an agreeable potency and the supply was soon consumed, restoring the Frenchman's good spirits. Fortunately, Hope was considered to have done her bit and was approached for little additional dancing, except by Will. After dark, the couple was given a great sendoff, and Will carried Hope over the threshold of the house, to cheers.

The crowd gave the newlyweds time to get settled, exchanging knowing grins all the while. Then, at a signal from Chance, whose duty as groomsman this was, much as it pained him, the guests silently converged outside the windows of the house. At another signal, they began banging pans, ringing cow bells, blowing horns, setting off six-shooters, whooping and hallooing and beating the adobe walls with their fists, crying for the couple to come out and show themselves. The racket could be heard for miles, and it was a wonder that any of the children in the wagons and tents could remain asleep.

Inside the house, the fire was out, for it was a warm night. The front room was lighted by a glittering tallow candle. Long shadows flickered on the whitewashed adobe walls.

Will and Hope had been standing silently, ill at ease. The sudden, ear-shattering noise from outside gave them both a start.

"They certainly are loud," Hope said.

"Somebody's idea of a joke," Will said. He wanted to look at her, but he was scared. He could not believe that she was his wife.

"Well," she said, and her voice cracked, "it's late. If they don't knock the house down, I guess we should get ready for bed."

"I guess."

Will turned while she removed her dress. He took off his boots and his buckskin shirt. Though it was hot, his bare skin was covered with goose bumps. He felt the blood surging within him. The noise outside continued unabated, but it seemed to fade from his consciousness.

When he turned back, Hope was in her shift. She was folding her wedding dress, the one on which she'd worked so hard. She looked at it for a long second, then she laid it gently across the back of a chair, never to be worn again.

Will came up behind her. She must have felt his presence, because she turned. He stepped back.

She swallowed and seemed to force a smile. "It's all right. You're allowed to do that now, you know."

Will gazed at her, trying to lock this moment in his memory forever. He reached out tentatively and touched her long, thick hair, marveling at its silky feel. With trembling fingers, he slipped the shift from her shoulders and let it fall to the floor. She stood naked before him. In the candlelight, her pale skin gleamed, and he saw that she was trembling, too.

"Oh, God," he breathed. "God, you're beautiful."

He drew her to him, and he kissed her tenderly.

Outside, the music and dancing began again. There would be another break for food at midnight, then the revelry would continue until dawn. Everybody was happy except one man. Chance stood on the outskirts of the crowd, watching the dark house. At last he turned away, and he walked into the night, alone.

Part III

24

1861

Secession. War.

Will was driving the buckboard into Kingdom for a rally. Beside him on the seat, Hope held baby Ellen. Hope was pregnant again, due next March. Their son Tommy was skylarking in the buckboard's bed. Rusty Harding rode alongside them. Fulgencio, who had no interest in *gringo* political disputes, had stayed at the ranch. Todd Sommerville had gone into town with his family.

"How bad will it be?" Hope asked.

Will shook his head. "I don't know. I don't know why everybody thought the Yanks wouldn't fight. They seemed to think all we had to do was declare ourselves independent, and it would be over. Now they're saying one Southerner is worth ten Yanks. That's the kind of thinking that gets you in trouble."

Hope said, "I guess you won't be taking the cattle to California now?"

"Not this year. With the fighting, there won't be enough men to work a herd. Besides, California's for the Union, or so they say." He sighed and gave her an apologetic look. "This means another winter without money."

"I'm not complaining," Hope said.

"I am. You and the kids deserve more."

She gave his arm an affectionate squeeze. "Don't worry. Things will get better. At least this way, we'll have you at home instead of in California."

Through the efforts of George Vestry and others, the Penateka reservation had been closed in 1859, and the Indians removed to the Territories. Will had been left with no market for his beef, which for him and Hope had meant two years with no income, save what Chance's saloon brought in. Last year a few men from the neighboring counties had taken a herd to California to sell to the miners. Will had thought they'd never make it across the desert, but they had, with huge profits. Will had thrown together a trail herd of his own that spring, then had come the news of Fort Sumpter, and later, Manassas.

Behind them, Tommy was leaning way over the buckboard gate, watching his shadow in the dust. "Tommy, sit down," Will said sharply, "before you fall out and hurt yourself." Tommy plopped down, laughing, and Will knew it would only be minutes before he was leaning out again. Tommy had grown into a fine, healthy lad of two and a half. The winter that he'd been born had been a bad one. Grasshoppers had come that fall and eaten all the crops, and there had been unending cold and damp and snow. The privations had been hard on Hope, and the baby had come early. The baby had been surprisingly large, but there'd been no problems with his birth or his health. With his dark hair, he took after his grandfather Jack. Will sometimes resented the fact that he and Hope had started having babies so soon. They'd had so little time alone. He was happy, though. He wouldn't change a thing.

They passed the big pin oak. Its thick summer foliage rustled in the breeze. Ahead of them were the scattered houses and cultivated fields around Kingdom. As they drew closer, they saw a crowd in front of Vestry's store.

"Here's Will now," someone shouted.

Everyone was there—the Sommervilles, Jules Villette, newcomers and old-timers. Will braked the buckboard by Chance's corral. As Will saw to the horses, Chance came over. Chance was wearing his black suit, which looked somewhat the worse for wear, these days. His leg had healed well, and he walked without a limp.

"Morning, partner," Chance said. "Rusty. Morning, Hope."

"Hello, Chance," said Hope. Chance helped her from the buckboard. As his hands touched hers, their eyes met. They held the gaze for a second, then Hope looked away and stepped to the ground.

Chance went to the rear of the buckboard and lifted out his godson. "Come here, you little outlaw." Tommy squealed with delight as Chance hoisted him onto his shoulders and started for the crowd.

Will came up beside his wife. He smiled as Chance and Tommy walked off. "Chance is good with Tommy. Too bad he don't get married and have kids of his own."

Unseen by Will, Hope's lips formed a sad line. Then she said, "Who's he going to marry around here—that *woman*?"

She was referring to Chance's whore, a big healthy girl called the Kansas Cow. Nobody knew her real name. Nobody knew anything about her, except that she'd come to Texas to escape the turmoil of Bleeding Kansas. Chance had brought her from Dallas last year. She was the only whore he could find who was willing to brave the dangers of the frontier. With secession, however, the Overland Mail had stopped and the soldiers had left Camp Cooper. There was no more business for her, so she was helping out around the farms.

Will said, "Hope, you're too hard on her."

"How can you be too hard on that kind of woman? She sells herself for money."

They approached the crowd. The new flag was flying on a makeshift staff in front of Vestry's store. The Stars and Bars, they called it. It was hard to get used to. Vestry stood on the store's gallery, wearing a frock coat and looking important, holding some kind of official notice. When the Penateka reservation had closed, Vestry had somehow acquired deed to a large portion of its lands, which he had sold to new settlers, at considerable enrichment to himself. Amos Blaine, who made little pretense of farming any more, stood beside him.

The Kansas Cow came over. She had brown hair and a ruddy complexion, and she spoke with a twang. "Can I get you all something to drink? Mr. Cooper? Everything's free today."

"No, thanks," Will said.

"Mrs. Cooper? Water? Fresh buttermilk?"

Hope did not answer. She acted as if the girl weren't there. She saw the girl's face fall, and she knew that she'd hurt her. She felt badly about it, but she was sure that she was doing right. That was how you were supposed to behave with that sort of woman, wasn't it?

Was it that, she wondered, or was it jealousy? She was certain that Chance slept with this woman from time to time, and it outraged her that the body he'd shared with her would ever be shared by another, much less this whore. Still, by what right was she jealous of Chance? She was married. She still loved Chance, though, and she was careful to keep away from him, lest she give in to the emotions that raged within her.

Chance put Tommy down. Hope took the boy, and she joined the women and children. The women crowded around, admiring baby Ellen, questioning Hope about the progress of her pregnancy. Will and Chance moved to the front of the crowd, near the flagstaff.

"Is everybody here now?" Vestry asked in his clipped tones. "Good." He held the paper in the air, striking a pose like a traveling actor. "Men, I have a proclamation from Governor Lubbock. He's asking for twenty companies of infantry to be sent to Virginia. The term of enlistment is to be for the duration of the war. Apparently the Yankees want some more of what our boys gave them at Manassas."

There were cheers, and Vestry went on, "This is a glorious opportunity, men, a chance to serve our new flag. A chance to be heroes. Now, who'll be the first to sign up?"

"I will," yelled J. D. Richardson, raising his hand.

"I'm going, too," shouted Fred Thompson.

"And me," cried big Tom Nye. "Hurrah for the Confederacy!"

Rusty Harding's face was alight. He raised his hand. "I'll go. You can't keep me out of this."

Sam and Todd Sommerville had their hands raised, as well. Hope looked at her father. "Pa, are you going to let . . . ?"

"I can't stop 'em," Jack said bitterly. "They're growed men. They know how I feel about this war. It's stupid. It's suicide for the South. Sam Houston was right, we'll live to regret—"

"We all know you're a Yankee sympathizer, Sommerville," Amos Blaine sneered from the gallery. "We'll deal with you later, and all them who think like you." There were angry murmurs of approval, some from men whom Jack had counted as friends.

Will and Hope exchanged a glance. Already the war was changing things.

"All right, Amos," said Vestry. "This isn't the time for such talk. After all, Jack is giving two sons to the cause."

"That's right, Blaine," said Curt Sommerville. "And any time you want to 'deal' with my father, you better deal with me first."

Rusty turned. "What about you, Will? Chance?"

Chance and Will looked at each other. Then Chance turned to Vestry. "Are you going, George? You're the one keeps calling yourself a colonel."

Vestry cleared his throat. "No. Actually, I've been appointed to the War Production Board. I'm to do my part here, helping to keep the boys at the front supplied."

"I expected as much," Chance said. "And Amos? I suppose the Confederacy can't get along without him here, too?"

"Mr. Blaine is to be my assistant, yes. There's too much work for me to do myself." Vestry pulled the lapels of his coat, as if they needed straightening. "Well, what do you two men say? Will you do your duty and answer your country's call?"

Will calculated who would be staying behind. Besides Jack and Curt, there was Jacob Koerner, the blacksmith; Jules Villette; and Mr. Blunden, the schoolteacher. The Richardson boy, Aaron, could help out in a pinch. Not a very imposing force. He said, "Answering my country's call won't do me much good if my family gets scalped while I'm gone."

Vestry said, "The minute men will—"

"I bet you'd like to have both of us away from here, wouldn't you, George?" Chance said. "There'd be nobody to stand in your way then."

Vestry said, "If you're implying that I would put personal interests above those of my country, I—"

"Come off it, George," Will said. "We all know what a great patriot you are. You tell us every opportunity you get. Chance, let's you and me go think this over."

"Good idea," said Chance.

The two men went into Chance's saloon. Behind them, Vestry grew madder and madder. He owned the town, but people still looked to Will and Chance for leadership.

It was dim inside the saloon, with the dry, stale smell that comes from little use. The walls were untreated wood. They had become warped over the years, and sunlight glinted through the cracks between them. There was the crude bar, with the whiskey barrel. Behind the bar was a shelf, with bottles of brandy and bourbon for more discriminating customers. Above the shelf was tacked a gaudy lithograph of the battle of the Alamo. On one side of the saloon were tables for poker and faro, and in the center was a long table that had been used to feed the stagecoach passengers. All were thick with dust, as was the piano in one corner. A back door led to two shacks. In one, Chance slept. In the other, the Kansas Cow plied her trade.

Chance went behind the bar. He brought out a bottle of Will's beer. He opened the bottle and gave it to Will. Chance poured himself a cup of whiskey. He already smelled like his own best customer. He reached in his pocket and flipped a coin onto the bar. The coin hit the rough wood, spun on its edge and fell.

"There's your share of the month's profits," Chance said.

It was a quarter.

Will stared at the coin. "That's two bits more'n I have to give you," he said.

Chance sighed. He downed his drink at a gulp. "Weren't we supposed to get rich out here?"

Will laughed without mirth. " 'Supposed to' is right. A thousand head of cattle I got, and I can't raise a cent on 'em."

Chance nodded. He poured another drink. "Now, about this war."

Will said, "The way I see it, one of us has to go east and one has to stay here, to help the minute men and watch Vestry."

"That's how I see it, too. Frankly, it doesn't make a damn to me who wins the war. I don't own slaves, and I don't give a fig about states' rights, or whatever it is we're supposed to be fighting about."

Will sipped his beer thoughtfully. "I don't see much sense in it myself. Still, Vestry was right. Texas is in it, and I reckon we got to do our part."

Chance shook his head, smiling.

Will went on, "You were in the last war. What do you think will happen?"

"There'll be one more battle, two at the most," Chance said confidently. "It'll be over by Christmas, one way or the other. War has gotten too expensive for it to last any longer than that. Hell, the South is damn near bankrupt already."

Will nodded. "So how do we decide who does what?"

Chance drew a deck of cards from beneath the bar, and he slapped them on the wood. "We'll cut for it. High man stays."

"Sounds fair enough."

Chance shuffled the cards. He squared them and placed them on the bar. "You first."

Will picked about a quarter way down the deck. He turned the card over.

"Jack of hearts," Chance said. "Not bad. Not bad at all."

Will replaced the cards. Chance licked his lips. He rubbed his fingertips with his thumb, for luck. He hesitated, then he picked halfway down the deck. Slowly he turned the card over. Then he grinned.

It was the queen of diamonds.

25

Less than a week later, the new soldiers set off for the war.

In front of the ranch house, Sam and Todd Sommerville were waiting on their horses, along with Rusty. Fulgencio was with them. They would join the other volunteers in Kingdom, then ride to Fort Belknap to be mustered in. Fulgencio would bring back the horses and saddles.

Will was going in his old Ranger rank of lieutenant. It was a measure of how things had changed that there was no clamor for Chance to go, too. There was a time when people wouldn't have felt right setting out on such an undertaking without Chance, but Will was considered Chance's equal as a leader now.

Will was on the gallery with his family. He wore his buckskins. Chance was with them, looking pensive. Will took off his hat. He picked up Tommy and kissed him on top of the head. He held up baby Ellen and kissed her, too. "You kids be good for your mother and Uncle Chance."

"We will," said little Tommy, smiling manfully. The baby flapped her arms with excitement. Neither had any idea what was going on.

Will gave Ellen back to Hope. Hope's stomach was just beginning to swell with the new baby. Will put his arms around Hope, and he kissed her. It was a short kiss. Their intimate farewells had been said earlier. He went to put on his hat. Then he stopped. He stuck a finger through the bullet hole in the crown. "You put this here, remember?"

Hope's eyes brimmed with tears. "Just make sure you don't get any more," she said. "Hurry back."

"Don't worry. I'll be back long before the baby's born. Heck, I'll be back sooner than if I'd taken the cattle to California. You have a good Christmas dinner waiting for me, you hear?"

Hope nodded. She bit her lower lip.

Will put on the hat. He shook hands with Chance. "Take care of them."

"I will," Chance said. "Like they were my own."

Will mounted his horse. He looked at the group on the gallery. "Well, be seeing you."

"See you, partner," Chance said.

"Good-bye, Will," said Hope.

"Bye bye," Tommy said, waving.

Will touched his hat brim. The little troop of men turned and set off down the road.

26

Will was not back by Christmas, though, and Hope could only trust that he'd return in time for the spring cow hunt. When that didn't happen, either, she hoped to have him back by summer. Then it was going on Christmas again, and she began wondering if he'd ever come back—or if he was still alive. All the while, the names of battles sounded over the horizon, dark and ominous, like distant thunder—Gaines' Mill, Second Manassas, Sharpsburg, Fredericksburg. People cheered because most of them were Southern victories, but Hope said, "If we're doing so good, why is it still going on?"

The baby was born in March, right on time. It was a boy, and Hope named it Alex, the name she and Will had chosen before he'd left. Hope had all she could do to manage the three children. There was little time left for the ranch. Fulgencio was able to work the horses and brand the calves that roamed near the house, but the rest of the cattle were left to run wild. Chance was gone much of the time with the minute men, but he helped when he could. Hope saw the way he looked at her when he was around. His smoldering eyes pierced hers, and she was careful always to have the children or Fulgencio nearby. She did not trust herself alone with him.

With most of the men gone, the frontier was largely undefended against Indian attacks. At the urging of state officials, the citizens of Kingdom forted up. A picket stockade was erected, roughly a hundred yards square, with a blockhouse at one corner. The walls of Chance's saloon, Vestry's house, and one other house formed part of the stockade, with newly cut logs connecting them. All the settlers around Kingdom built picket cabins inside the fort, and they moved their families into them, venturing out during the day to work their fields and tend stock. Chance built Hope and the children a small house there, too, though they rarely used it.

Conscription came during the war's second year, along with martial law. George Vestry was appointed provost marshal of Kingdom County, with Amos Blaine as his assistant. This pair took Curt Sommerville, who'd become engaged to Kathy Nye, to serve in the army, along with some other men whom they didn't like. Old Jack Sommerville protested his son's loss, but his complaints fell on deaf ears. That left Jack to run the salt works and farm by himself, and Hope frequently took the children to stay with him.

They were staying with him early one morning in the spring of '63. Hope was in the kitchen, making coffee and getting breakfast together, just as she used to do. It felt comfortingly familiar, yet strange now. She smiled as she heard her father rise, stamp on his boots, and go out the door to the privy, as he'd done a thousand times before.

Then there was a ragged volley of rifle shots, a strangled cry, and a thump.

Hope ran to the kitchen door and looked out. Her father lay sprawled half off the gallery, his body oozing blood.

Hope thought it was an Indian attack. The children were scared by the shots. Tommy and Ellen ran to her, crying "Where's Grampa? I want Grampa." The baby started wailing. Hope slammed shut the kitchen door. She bolted it and the window shutter, and she armed herself with Jack's old rifle and horse pistol. She tried to hush the baby as she waited for howling savages to burst through the door. She said a quick prayer and tried not to think about their fates. The baby's cries sounded unnaturally loud in the stillness.

But no Indians appeared. At last, Hope peered through a crack in the shutter. Outside, the birds were singing once more. The animals were peaceful in the stable.

There was no one about.

Indians had not shot her father, Hope realized. It had been white men.

"Wait here," she told the children. She slipped out onto the gallery, where her father lay. She was back in a moment. Her lower lip was trembling, but she forced herself to remain steady because of the children.

"Where's Grampa?" said Tommy plaintively.

Hope knelt beside them. She wished the baby would stop screaming. "Some bad men have hurt your grandpa," she told the children.

The children looked at each other. Tommy said, "Is he dead?"

Hope nodded. There was no sugar coating it. Frontier children knew about death. They saw enough of it.

Hope made the children stay inside. When she finally got the baby quiet, she fed him and put him to sleep. Then she went outside and wrapped her father's body in a blanket. Hope would have liked to make a coffin, but with the children there was no time. She buried her father the way he had wanted. She dug a hole deep and narrow. She dragged the body to it and set it upright, facing west. She put up a rude cross for a marker, until she had time to make something more permanent.

Later that morning, there was a clatter of hoofs and a jingling of bits, and a little group of men rode up to the house. George Vestry was in the lead, wearing the gold braid of a cavalry colonel. Amos Blaine was with him, in a civilian coat; and there were three others, tough-looking men whose military accoutrements gave them to be soldiers.

The men reined in before Hope. Vestry seemed surprised to find Hope there, and he shot Blaine an angry look. Vestry's gray uniform was neat and clean in this time of privation. His high boots gleamed. Hope was conscious of her dirt-grimed face, of her sweaty homespun. She straightened a loose strand of hair. Tommy and Ellen crowded close to her. The baby was in his cradle under the big Spanish willow.

Vestry removed his plumed hat and swept it across his chest. "Good morning, Miss Hope. We've come to speak with your father."

Hope's chest rose and fell. She stared at Vestry hard. If she'd had a gun, she would have shot him. "My father's not here," she said between clenched teeth.

"Where has he gone?"

"He's dead. Shot from ambush this morning. You killed him, you and your men. This is what you wanted all along, with all your talk about him being a Yankee lover."

"Well, he was." Amos Blaine snorted. One of the tough-looking men, a drifter named Shawcross, laughed.

"Shut up, Amos," said Vestry. "This young lady has suffered a tremendous loss. I'll not have you talking against the dead."

Vestry saw the newly dug grave across the yard. He turned back to Hope, and his face showed a flash of genuine regret. Probably he had not wanted this to happen when she was around. "Miss Hope, I'm terribly sorry to hear of this. Believe me, I knew nothing of it. We will do our utmost to bring the perpetrators to justice. In the meantime, is there anything we can do . . . ?"

"You can get off my father's land," Hope told him. The children were clinging to her legs. Ellen was crying. Tommy was trying hard not to.

Vestry turned his hat in his hands. "Miss Hope, this is a bad business. Very bad. It's terrible what the war has brought people to. I had my differences with your father, but I would never have condoned his killing. You must believe that." He pursed his lips. "All this makes it doubly difficult to do what I've come here for. The country is putting forth a massive war effort, Miss Hope. We need all our resources. Salt, especially, is in short supply, and"—he hesitated—"well, by the authority vested in me as provost for Kingdom County, I'm here to confiscate your father's land."

Hope stared at him.

"I'm sorry, but it has to be done." Vestry turned to Blaine. "Gather any personal effects that Miss Hope wants removed and put them in the wagon for her. And be careful with them." To Hope, he said, "The animals, of course, are yours. My men will bring them to you later."

Blaine and his men started their horses forward.

"Don't you dare!" Hope said, blocking Blaine's way.

Blaine looked to Vestry. Vestry nodded.

Blaine's horse pushed Hope aside.

"You heard the lady," said a voice. "Stay right where you are."

Everyone turned as Chance Evans sidled around the corner of the tool shed. Chance had Vestry's men covered with his Navy Colts. He wore his buckskin jacket, red shirt, and *botas*.

"Uncle Chance!" cried the children, and they ran to him.

Chance kept his pistols trained. He said, "You kids go up to the house. Take the baby with you, and don't come out till I say so."

The children hurried off. Chance grinned at Vestry. "Well, look at you, George—a real colonel at last. Your men are all jailbirds and deserters from other units, but they're just right for your kind of work."

Vestry's look of sincerity had been replaced by one of intense dislike. He peered down his long nose. "I thought you were on a scout, Evans."

"The boys decided to break it off early and come back. Bad luck for you, wasn't it? I went to the ranch, and Fulgencio told me Hope was here. I cut your tracks on my way up. Something didn't smell right, so I circled around."

Hope cried out, "They killed Pa, Chance."

"That's a lie," snapped Vestry.

"Is it?" Chance said. "That's interesting, Vestry, because on my way here, I found four sets of tracks leaving this place. Tracks maybe six hours old. Tracks that match up real well with the horses Blaine and his friends are riding."

"I didn't come here to debate hoofprints," Vestry said. "Jack Sommerville was a Unionist, and as such his property is subject to confiscation."

"This property belongs to Jack's kids now. You can't exactly call his sons Unionists, can you? They're off dodging bullets in our so-called army, while you stay behind and try to steal their land. Maybe that's the way wars always work, but not this one. I'll make it plain, Vestry. You try to take this land, and I'll kill you."

Beneath his thin mustache, Vestry's lip curled. "And let me remind *you*, Captain Evans, that this country is under martial law, and I am its provost. I'm giving you a direct order. Stand aside in this matter. If you fail to obey, I'll have you court-martialed."

"Cut the threats, Vestry. The law out here comes from the barrel of a gun. And right now I'll wager my guns against yours."

"There's five of us. You won't win."

"Maybe not, but you won't be alive to see me go down."

Vestry shifted uneasily in the saddle. He tried a different tack. "Think of your country for once. Those boys at the front need salt. They—"

"The Yankees have closed the Mississippi, Vestry. You couldn't get that salt to the army if you tried. You're just trying to set yourself up with a steady income for when the war's over. If you're so worried about the boys at the front, why don't you confiscate some of Will's cattle and take them east? I hear the army's hungry, too."

"Maybe we'll do that," said Amos Blaine.

Chance turned, and he smiled again. "You know, Amos, you used to be a decent, hard-working fellow when you first came out here, but you've been keeping bad company. If you don't watch out, you're liable to catch lead poisoning."

Blaine acted unafraid. "I'll take my chances," he said.

Vestry said, "You can't get away with these threats, Evans."

"It's no threat, Vestry. It's a promise. And I'm a man of my word. Ask anybody. Now get out of here."

Vestry hesitated, then he waved his troop around. "Come on, men."

Hope watched them ride off, and she realized that she was shaking. Chance came to her. He put his arms around her. She buried her tearstained face in his shoulder. "Thank you," she murmured.

The feel of his body against hers once again was electric. They looked at each other. Chance moved his head close to hers.

Then Tommy and Ellen came running from the house. "Mommy, have those men gone yet? Mommy, Alex is awake."

Hope disengaged herself from Chance's embrace. She looked at him once more, then she lowered her eyes and walked to the house with the children.

27

The war dragged on. By now the early Southern victories had become an endless string of defeats, and only the most determined optimist could pretend that the Confederacy still had a chance to win.

Hope had no more trouble with Vestry. He must have decided that tangling with Chance was not worth the risk. Besides, Vestry was gone much of the time now. People said he was getting rich hauling cotton from Dallas to Matamoros, in Mexico, where it was loaded on British and French ships to be taken overseas.

In the fall of 1863, Rusty Harding was invalided home. He'd been shot through both lungs at Gettysburg and had later contracted pneumonia. He was very weak, and it was unlikely that he'd ever regain his former strength. He brought Hope a letter from Will, the first news she'd had from her husband since he'd left. Will couldn't write well, and the letter had been prepared by someone else. Will was a major now. He'd been wounded several times but was all right. Tom Nye was dead, killed in a skirmish along the Rappahannock. Fred Thompson, who'd played the clevis and pin at their wedding, was missing and believed a prisoner. Hope's brother Sam had been near death with chicken pox but was now back to duty. Young Todd was fine, and a corporal. Will wrote how he missed Hope and the children, and how he prayed for the war to end soon, though he doubted that it would.

Hope read and reread the letter, until the cheap rice paper began to crumble. Then she packed it away, with her wedding dress. Sometimes it seemed as if Will had never existed, and at other times she missed him more than she'd ever imagined she would. She had thought that Chance's presence might make up for Will's absence, but it didn't, and she was surprised by that.

Chance himself seemed to grow moodier as time passed. When he was at the ranch, Hope caught him staring at her more and more. His one joy was Tommy. He loved to take the boy fishing. They had a favorite spot on Double Horn Creek, above the cornfields, where they would while away the hours. Chance spent little time at Fort Kingdom, as it was now called. With no money in the county, there was no business for his saloon. When he was there, he mostly drank by himself and practiced cards. He'd gotten Jack Sommerville's still working again, and he kept himself supplied with corn whiskey from it.

Life at the ranch was not easy. The children got sick, as children would, and baby Alex almost died his first winter. Wolves, coyotes, and panthers preyed on the stock. The crops were alternately threatened by droughts and floods. There was literally not a dollar with which to buy provisions. Hope ground their corn by hand with a small mill. She dyed the children's homemade clothing with blackjack bark.

Hope was twenty-five, but at times she felt fifty. Her hands had grown rough and callused. Her small mirror showed lines of weariness on her face, and there were dark circles under her eyes. She hardly bothered with her hair anymore. She hadn't the time. Her youthful dreams were fading into memory. Her worst fears about life seemed to be coming true, and at times she would feel bitter. If only she hadn't gotten pregnant, she would think. If only she'd gone to New Orleans with Chance. Then she would shrug and go back to work. She had cast her lot. It was too late to change now.

The Comanches and Kiowas had been raiding since the war started, but in 1863 they seemed to realize that there were no longer soldiers or Rangers to stop them, and from then on the raids grew worse. The frontier went up in blood and flame. Whole counties were depopulated, as the shattered survivors fled to safer areas in the east. Kingdom had been left untouched save for occasional horse stealing. The inhabitants confidently attributed this to the strength of their stockade and to their vigilance. They had grown used to life in the fort. People were born and died there. There were children who could not remember any other life. Hope didn't like the fort herself. She couldn't stand the crowding, the stench, the lack of privacy. She'd grown used to the ranch, with its sweeping vistas and its sense of unlimited possibilities, and that was where she stayed.

July of 1864 was brutally hot. There had been no rain since April, and the previous year had been dry, too. The Clear Fork was a trickle, and Double Horn Creek was no more than a series of shallow pools. With the coming of the full moon, Chance came to stay at the ranch. This was the most dangerous time for Indian raids, and, despite his duties with the minute men, this was when Chance wanted to be with Hope and the children. For a week Chance, Fulgencio, and Rusty took turns at night guard, posted on the adobe house's flat roof. The hours went by with agonizing slowness. Those on guard strained their eyes into the darkness, nerves on edge. Those not on guard fared little better. They lay on their rawhide beds, tense, waiting for the war whoop, the rifle shot, the thud of the fire arrow. Saddled horses were staked in front of the house, for use in case of a pursuit.

Then the moon waned, and the inhabitants of the Double H could breathe easier, until it waxed full once more.

One day Hope sat in the front room of the house. Two-year-old Alex was asleep in the back. The afternoon heat hung like a blanket. Hope had her spare dress out. She turned it over, thinking how she could cut it down. She needed a new dress for Ellen. At four, Ellen was growing rapidly, and her dress had gotten way too short for her. Tommy was easy to clothe, because Hope could use buckskin. Ellen needed cloth, however.

Hope was determined not to have her looking like a squaw. But all of Hope's cloth had been used up, and cotton and wool were not to be had without money. She wished Will had listened when she'd said she wanted to bring some sheep here. She looked at her old dress again. The material was threadbare, but it would have to do.

She became aware of someone in the open doorway, and she turned with a start. It was Chance. He was leaning on the jamb, framed against the bright light from outside. He was watching her. She could feel the force of his eyes, and she grew uneasy.

"I thought you were cutting firewood," she said. "Is something wrong?"

"Not now."

He swung through the doorway and stood over her, looking down.

"What is it?" she said, and she put down the dress.

"This." He grasped her elbows and gently lifted her to her feet.

She stepped back. "Chance, what are you doing?"

He came after her. "You know damn well what I'm doing."

He reached for her, but she dodged aside. "Chance . . . the children."

"They've gone down the creek, playing."

He reached for her again. Again she avoided him. "Fulgencio . . ."

"Fulgencio's chasing that herd of mustangs that's been trying to run with your horses. You know that. He'll be gone at least a week."

She kept moving around the room, just out of his reach, "Rusty's here, though. He's—"

Chance smiled. "I sent Rusty into Kingdom, on business. I thought the ride would be good for him."

Hope stepped aside again and found that she had been maneuvered into a corner. Chance crowded her, smiling broadly now. "We're all alone here, except for Alex, and I don't think he'll give us any trouble." He braced his arms against the wall, blocking her escape. "I've been waiting three years to get you like this."

He leaned forward to kiss her, but she ducked under his arm. "Chance, no."

"What do you mean?" he said, coming forward again.

"We can't. *I* can't. I won't."

With a lightning-quick movement, Chance reached out and grabbed her arm.

"Chance, I'm married."

"So what?" he said, pulling her to him. "Will won't know. He's a thousand miles away."

"Yes, and I know Will is being faithful to me. How can I be any less than faithful to him? He's going through hell out there. I owe him that much."

She resisted futilely, as Chance grabbed her other arm and held her in a vicelike grip. "How about what you owe me?" he said. "You once told me you'd love me forever."

"I was a girl then, Chance. Don't hold me to a girl's promises. Anyway, there's . . . there's a part of me that will love you forever."

"Yes, and I mean to collect on that part right now."

He leaned down. He kissed her, but she turned her head, avoiding his lips. He began kissing her neck, the hollow behind her ear. She wanted to resist, but she felt herself giving in to him, inexorably. "Chance, please," she said. "Don't make this any harder on me than it already is."

"Harder on you?" he said angrily. "What about me? How do you think I feel? Six years you've been married. Six years that I've thought about nothing but you, every day. I've been going crazy, Hope. I've only stayed in Kingdom because of you. Why do you think I fixed the cards so that Will would have to go away? I did it for you . . . for us."

Hope suddenly found renewed strength. She shoved Chance back, and her voice filled with shock. "You did *what*? You mean, you're responsible for Will being out there? How could you do that, Chance? How could you betray your best friend?"

"Hell, I didn't know the war was going to last this long. I wasn't trying to get Will killed. I just wanted a chance for us to be alone, to get things like they used to be."

He leaned into her again.

"No, Chance." She was firm now, determined.

Chance pressed her against the wall. She smelled whiskey on his breath. He said, "I've waited for you, Hope, and I mean to have you."

Again she turned from his kisses. She tried to push him away, but she was helpless in his strong grasp. He grabbed her hair. He yanked her head around, and he dug his lips into hers. She squealed, hitting him with her free hand, as he forced her to the hard-packed earthen floor.

He rolled on top of her, smothering her. He was breathing heavily. The hard floor dug into her back. She felt his hands on her breasts, under her dress. She uttered little cries as she tried to get from under him, twisting her head, kicking, pulling his hair. She scratched him with what was left of her nails, but he did not notice.

He began kissing her throat. She turned her head, and she bit his ear as hard as she could, ripping it with her teeth. He roared with pain. Blood squirted. His grip on her lessened momentarily, and she sprang to her feet. She ran for the door. He was after her. She was halfway out the door when Chance caught her arm. He swung her back inside with a savage growl. He hurled her to the floor, knocking the breath out of her. Hope shook her head, dazed. When she looked again, Chance's shirt was off. Blood from his ear was all over his shoulder. Then Chance was on her, ripping her dress away, exposing her breasts. His breathing was very loud. She tried to fight, but he slapped her cheek hard. He pinned her arms with his hands. He spread her legs with his knees. He lowered himself onto her. Hope was powerless to resist him. Their eyes met, and she spit in his face.

That seemed to arouse Chance even more. His hooded eyes were on fire, and for a moment she thought he was going to kill her. His thick chest rose and fell. It glistened with sweat. His nostrils flared. His breathing filled the room.

Suddenly he let her go. He stood, and he wiped the spit from his face. He picked up his red shirt. "All right, I'll give you what you want. I'm leaving Kingdom. You won't see me again."

Chance turned and strode out the door. His boots thunked on the floor.

Hope lay there. She stared at the ceiling. She felt battered, bruised, drained of strength. Slowly her breath came back. She sat up, wrapping the rags of her dress around her. She heard Chance's horse in the yard, and she struggled unsteadily to her feet. She stumbled out the open door.

"Damn you!" she cried at the retreating figure. "Damn you, Chance!"

Then he was gone, riding away on his red roan, in the direction of town.

Hope sagged back into the house. Her knees gave way and she sank to the floor. She buried her face in her hands, and she began to cry.

28

Early the next morning, Hope went to water the corn. Rusty was back from Kingdom, and Hope left little Alex with him. Rusty couldn't handle any physical labor yet. His once-robust form was pale and wasted. He'd been shy about baby-sitting the first times he'd done it, but he'd gotten used to it. Hope thought that he secretly liked it. Fulgencio had not returned from chasing mustangs.

Hope took Tommy and Ellen with her. She carried a bucket, a hoe, and an old coffeepot that she'd rigged as a sprinkler. Will's rifle was slung across her back. She wore her old, threadbare dress. She would use the cloth from the other one—the one Chance had torn—to make that new dress for Ellen. Five-year-old Tommy brought the fishing pole that Chance had fashioned for him. Ellen was tall and blond, with long, coltish legs. She said, "Mommy, there's a hurt on your face."

Hope felt her cheek where Chance had slapped it. "Yes, I . . . I slipped yesterday and bumped against the door."

"Where's Uncle Chance?" asked Tommy.

"He had to leave, Tommy."

"Why didn't he say good-bye? He always says good-bye before he leaves."

A sudden tear sprang into Hope's eye, and she averted her head. "I don't know."

"Is he with the men again?" Ellen said, meaning the minute men.

"I . . . I guess so. He didn't say."

Ellen smiled. "I want him to come back soon. I like Uncle Chance."

"Me, too," Tommy said.

There was little likelihood of Chance's returning, Hope thought. Her fiery anger of yesterday had cooled. Now she burned with controlled rage. How could she have loved a man like Chance? And yet she had loved him, or thought she had, right up until yesterday afternoon. All she knew, in her mixed-up state of mind, was that she loved him no more. She hoped that he was really leaving Kingdom. It was better for everyone that way. She did not think she could face him again. She did not want to face him, after what he'd done to her.

Hope and the children walked along the creek to the fenced-off cornfield, which was about a mile from the house, on a level stretch of good soil. Ellen skipped along beside her mother, humming. She was barefoot. She would need shoes when the cold weather returned. The brim of Tommy's torn straw hat hung over his eyes.

Hope wanted to give her children so much. And she had nothing, nothing but love. She wondered if love was all they would ever have. If Will didn't come back . . . but that was a possibility she refused to face.

They reached the field. The corn was stunted from the drought. It was going to be another bad crop. Hope set her things down. Tommy poked his fishing pole at Ellen, and he flashed a grin. He had his father's grin, confident and contagious. "I'm going to catch lots of fish today."

"You'd better," Hope joked. "It's for our supper. If you don't catch anything, I'll have to shoot another one of your father's steers."

"Yeah," Ellen told him, "and I don't want stupid catfish, either."

"I like catfish," Tommy retorted.

"Well, I don't," Ellen said, and she stamped a foot. "I want silver perch." Tommy looked at his mother and rolled his eyes, while Ellen said, "I won't eat catfish."

"You'll eat whatever's put on your plate, young lady," Hope said, giving her a playful swat on the rear.

While Ellen and Tommy stuck out their tongues at each other, Hope told her son, "You be careful up there by yourself."

"I will, I will," Tommy said. He sounded aggrieved that his mother should remind him of such things.

Hope watched Tommy start up the creek, heading for the fishing hole that he and Chance liked so much. He was a sturdy little fellow. He twirled his pole as he walked, now pointing it like a rifle at imaginary enemies, now waving it like a sword, now using it as a spear for slaying dragons. Hope smiled. She was blessed with her children.

When Tommy was out of sight, Hope and Ellen took the bucket down to the creek. There was a bluff on this side of the creek, and they had to be careful going down. While Hope filled the bucket, Ellen chatted about her daddy and about the things the two of them had done together, though in reality she didn't remember him at all.

They carried the bucket back and filled the old coffeepot. Hope had punched holes in the pot's bottom and rigged a slide across it. By moving the slide, she could water the crops. They started down the rows. Hope broke the hard earth with the hoe, chopping the weeds, while Ellen followed, sprinkling the water. They would be at this all day, and by the end of it the corn still wouldn't have gotten sufficient water. Hope was afraid of what would happen if it didn't rain soon.

They made trip after trip to refill the bucket. Hope was hot and sweating and grimy. She straightened, easing her sore back. Ellen knelt in the corn rows, building little towers in the mud. Hope wiped her brow, leaving a film of dirt across her forehead. She would have to stay dirty, too. Water was getting too precious to use for bathing. She looked at the sun. It was almost time for the noon meal, corn dodgers and dried venison. Ellen would complain about the fare, but in the end she would eat.

Suddenly Hope stopped. She looked past the flat-topped height of Buzzard Peak, in the direction of Kingdom, where a column of gray smoke curled upward. There was a fire at the settlement.

Hope shook her head. She had always been afraid that someone would accidentally burn down the fort. Then she saw another column of smoke, some distance from the first. She heard faint pops.

Cold fear gripped her backbone. She turned. "Ellen." She jerked her daughter upright from the mud and made for the fenced edge of the field, where Will's rifle was. As she did, she heard hoofbeats. Someone was coming from the northwest, an unlikely direction. The rider hove into view on a round-bellied plow horse, and Hope recognized the ungainly form of the Kansas Cow.

The Cow saw Hope and turned the horse toward her. She rode astride like a man. Her dark hair was awry. "Indians!" she yelled. She pulled up, and Hope grabbed her reins, helping her stop the frightened animal.

"Indians, Miz Cooper." The girl gasped. Her moon face was red from the exertion of riding. Her dress was halfway up her fat legs. Her eyes were full of panic. "I come to warn you and the kids. There must be a hundred of 'em. They've killed a bunch of people, and they got the fort surrounded. I had to circle round Buzzard Peak to get away."

"Mommy," Ellen said. But Hope's thoughts were of Tommy and little Alex. She was about to tell the Cow to go upstream and get Tommy, when a party of seven or eight Indians appeared in the distance, following the Cow's trail. The Indians' bodies were painted for war. They wore a lot of feathers, and Hope thought they must be Kiowas. They caught sight of the whites and whooped with delight, kicking their ponies forward.

"Give me your gun," said the Cow. "I'll hold 'em off. You and the little girl get down to the creek and hide."

Hope said, "But you . . ."

"I'll join you when I can. Give me the gun."

Hope handed her the Sharps rifle and the kerchief full of cartridges. "Thank you," she said. "I—I'm sorry for—"

"Get out of here, will you!" The big girl was almost screaming. She checked the rifle to see that it was loaded, and she aimed it at the Indians, who were coming on fast.

Hope grabbed Ellen and started running. They didn't head for the creek, but for the house. Hope had to get to Alex. Tommy was older, he had sense enough to hide when he heard the racket. "Faster, Ellen. Run!" Behind them, the Sharps rifle banged.

There were more whoops, and another group of Indians appeared around a bend in the creek, blocking their path to the house.

"This way," Hope cried. She yanked Ellen toward the creek, running. Her lungs burned for air. She heard the Cow's rifle fire again. She heard hoofbeats and high-pitched war cries.

Ellen's coltish legs were stumbling. "Ow! Mommy!"

Hope held Ellen's wrist in an iron grip. The girl's feet barely touched the ground as Hope dragged her along. Hope didn't know where she was finding the strength. She didn't know she could run like this. She heard more shots, yelling, a confused milling of horses.

They reached the bluff. Hope didn't stop. They started down, stumbling, sliding, falling. Tearing and bruising their legs, twisting their ankles. Ellen was crying, but Hope paid no attention. They reached the bottom, out of sight to those on top. They heard yelling and screams, one more rifle shot, a different caliber this time, then whoops of triumph. Just downstream, the creek made an S curve. Filling the far bend of this curve was a large growth of reeds. The reeds were thick and green and tall as a man. Hope led Ellen across the creek, stumbling and hurting their feet on sharp rocks. They plunged into the reeds, and when they reached the middle, Hope flung her daughter to the ground and held her down.

"Mommy?" the girl whimpered, but Hope clamped a hand over her mouth.

"Don't talk," she whispered. "Don't move."

Hope's lungs pumped like a bellows. Her searing gasps for air sounded loud, and she hoped the Indians did not hear. She prayed they'd left no tracks on the creek bottom. She prayed they'd left no visible path through the reeds.

Hope and Ellen lay flat in the reeds. It was stiflingly hot. They could see no more than a foot in front of them, and the tall growth of vegetation blocked the sun. Clouds of insects swarmed around them, getting in their eyes and noses, in their hair and clothes, biting them fiercely, but they dared not move to brush them off. The razorlike stalks of the reeds had sliced their skin. A hundred cuts and scratches burned from salty sweat, but they could only grit their teeth and try to ignore the pain.

In the distance, someone was screaming. Hope realized it was the Kansas Cow. The Indians had caught her. Hope tried not to think what they were doing to her. The girl's screams rent the air, as if she were being torn apart, and Hope could feel Ellen quaking with fear. Hope felt like the lowest kind of creature for the way she'd snubbed the young whore. That girl had given her life for Hope and Ellen, and Hope had never even known her real name. If she lived through this, Hope vowed never to put on airs or look down on anyone again.

She heard horses on the bluff across the creek.

The horses came down the bluff, clattered across the creek, and clambered up the slope on the other side. The noises stopped. The riders were searching for Hope and Ellen.

Hope closed her eyes, praying. Ellen began to squirm. "Don't move, honey," Hope whispered. "Whatever you do, don't move." Her eyes met those of her daughter's, and she tried to will Ellen to immobility by the sheer force of her gaze.

She heard the horses moving slowly along the top of the slope. She heard guttural voices arguing. In the distance, the hideous screaming continued.

The horses moved back down the slope. They stopped. Hope heard the light tread of moccasins on gravel. It sounded like one man, moving around, coming closer.

Then she heard the reeds rustle.

Ellen's eyes grew large as dollars. Hope pressed her hand hard over the girl's mouth. The rustling of the reeds grew louder. The Indian was making his way into the dense vegetation. He was feeling his way, poking with something, probably his lance.

The reeds rustled louder. Louder still. Ellen's body was rigid with fear. Hope's was, too.

Louder. The Indian was very close now. Nothing could prevent them being found. Hope picked up a large rock. She gripped it with the sharp edge down, ready to strike when the Indian came in view. Please, God, she thought, let him kill me in the fight. Don't let me end up like that poor girl from Kansas. They would take Ellen prisoner. It would be a terrible life for her, but at least she would be alive, and Will might get her back one day. The screams from across the creek only made the waiting worse.

The rustle of reeds faded off to the left. For a second, Hope breathed easier. Then the noise turned again. It was coming straight for Hope and Ellen.

The stalks in front of Hope moved, sending up great clouds

of insects. Hope smelled the Indian. It was a musty smell, like an old buffalo robe. She gripped the rock harder. She tensed herself to spring.

Suddenly a loud rattle split the air.

Hope heard a guttural exclamation from just in front of her. The rustling of reeds receded rapidly as the Indian backed out of them.

Outside the thicket, there was much laughter. That surprised Hope. She had never thought of Indians as having a sense of humor. There was muffled conversation, then Hope heard the horses move back across the creek and up the bluff. They had given up the search. In the distance, the screaming had stopped.

Hope closed her eyes. She let out her breath and her body went limp. She relaxed her grip on Ellen. There was another rustling sound, as the snake that had saved them slithered indignantly away. "I never thought I'd be grateful to a rattler," Hope said.

Then reaction set in. Hope began shaking violently. Ellen started to cry, and Hope held her tightly, burying the sound of the tears in her breast, feeling the small body quiver.

The noise of the Indians' horses faded. Hope made Ellen lay there awhile longer, to be certain. At last, when nothing more could be heard, Hope said, "They're gone."

There was no time to relax. Hope still had to get to Alex. Should she leave Ellen here in the safety of the reeds? She looked at the frightened girl. No. If Ellen was older, there would be no question. But she was four. As soon as Hope left, she would probably get up and start wandering around, crying for her mother. And if the Indians heard . . .

"Come on." She took Ellen's hand. As quietly as possible, she led her to the edge of the reeds, cutting clothing and skin on the stalks and paying no attention. She looked out. The creek bed was empty. They left the reeds and moved across the stream. While Ellen waited, Hope mounted the bluff and peered cautiously over.

There was no one in sight.

Hope backed down the bluff. "Let's go," she said, taking Ellen's hand once more.

They drank quickly from the creek. Then they made their way along the creek bottom, stepping around some pools of water, splashing through others. Hope half expected to meet Tommy going in the same direction. Ellen began crying. Her bare feet were bleeding on the rocks. Hope herself was bleeding and sore from the reeds and their fall down the bluff. "Keep going, honey," she said.

"I don't want to."

"We have to. Now come on."

At last they reached a point opposite the ranch house. They crept out of the creek bottom and through the trees. They lay down, waiting and watching.

All looked peaceful. There were no signs of a struggle. The front door of the house was shut, despite the afternoon heat, but that could be to keep Alex from wandering off. The birds were silent, but that could be the result of Hope and Ellen's presence.

"All right," Hope said, patting her daughter's back. They left the cover of the trees and started across the open ground, toward the house.

29

Hope and Ellen moved as quickly as they could in their tired state. Their feet crunched the parched grass. The afternoon sun was hot. The house seemed very far away. The ground seemed too open.

Suddenly yells erupted behind them and to the left. The brush crashed, and Hope heard racing footsteps.

"Run, honey!" she cried, pulling Ellen along.

They sprinted for the house. Hope's arms and legs pumped furiously. The yells of the pursuing Indians acted like an invisible hand, pushing her along, giving her strength and energy she didn't know she had left.

She fixed her eyes on the closed front door of the house. Where was Rusty? Were he and Alex already dead? She prayed the door wasn't bolted. She didn't know what she'd do if it was. Ellen was sobbing for breath beside her. Something whizzed by her ear, and she realized it was an arrow.

She strained herself to the utmost, but she felt like she was moving in slow motion. The Indians' footsteps were right behind her. She heard their hoarse breathing. She could almost feel it on her neck.

Then the door swung open, and Rusty was there with a shotgun. "Get down!" he yelled, raising the gun.

Hope threw herself flat in the dirt, taking Ellen with her. Rusty fired one barrel of the shotgun over their heads. There were strangled screams and a thump as a body hit the ground. Rusty fired the gun's other barrel. The breath had been knocked from Hope and Ellen, but they scrambled to their feet as Rusty pulled his revolver and began firing it at the Indians. Hope heard another cry of pain. Then she and Ellen were past Rusty and through the door. Rusty slammed the door shut behind them and slid the wooden bolt into position. He grabbed his Sharps rifle from beside the door and began firing through the loophole. Two wounded Indians were struggling back to the trees. Others were carrying off the body of the dead brave. Rusty's first shot hit one of the carriers in the side, knocking him down. His companions ran away, while he crawled off. Rusty fired again, but he did not hit anything.

The house was shut tight inside. It was dark and hot. Little Alex came toddling in from the kitchen with his arms outstretched. He was crying, terrified by the noise of the firearms.

Hope let go of Ellen for the first time in hours. She picked up the boy and hugged him. "Oh, baby," she cooed. "Oh, it's all right now. It's all right. Mommy's here." She tickled the boy's chin reassuringly, but he kept crying.

Hope looked around. Rusty had the house ready for a siege. The fireplace was cold. The water buckets were full. The window shutters were braced tight, and ammunition was piled beside the door.

Rusty kept an eye on the trees while he reloaded the shotgun and revolver. "I seen the smoke from town and figured it was Injuns. I been waiting for something to happen here. It's been so quiet, I figured they had the place staked out. You was lucky to come out of the creek where you did."

He passed through to the house's other room, looking out the windows on that side. "Where's Tommy?"

Hope continued soothing Alex, smoothing his hair. Ellen clung to her waist. "At the fishing hole, I hope. That girl of Chance's—the one called Kansas—came to warn us about the Indians, but before we could get Tommy, the Indians came. Kansas held them off while Ellen and I got away."

Rusty gave her a look. He spoke softly, because of the children. "Kansas. Did the Indians . . . ?"

Hope nodded. She remembered the young whore's screams, and the memory made her stomach go weak. Was that to be her fate, as well?

Rusty came back to the front room, looking out each window as he did. "Smoke from town's been heavy. We won't be getting no help from there. We're on our own."

Hope put Alex down. She ladled a wooden cup of water for Ellen, then another for herself. "Ellen, you be a big girl for me and play with Alex for a while. Will you do that?"

Ellen's lower lip trembled. "Yes, Mommy."

"Tell you what. We'll make a fort." Hope put the children in a corner of the kitchen, covered by the partition wall on one side and the big cupboard on the other. She turned the kitchen table on its side and moved it in front of them, sealing them off. She handed Ellen her rag doll. "There, isn't that fun?"

Ellen nodded solemnly, clutching the doll. The girl had been through so much already. She'd thought she'd be safe when they got home, and now the danger was as great as ever.

Hope saw the frightened look on Rusty's face. She knew from Will that Rusty's family had been killed by Indians. She knew that he had frozen during an earlier attack on the ranch. She could imagine what must be going through his mind. "What happens now?" she said.

Before Rusty could answer, there was a rifle shot, and a bullet thunked into the house's adobe wall. They all ducked instinctively. Both Ellen and Alex were ready to cry. They ducked again as another shot smacked into one of the thick wooden shutters.

"Best help yourself to some artillery," Rusty told Hope.

The rifle fire was sporadic but continuous. Shots plunked into the walls and doors. In the dim light Hope lifted Will's Dragoon pistol from its wall peg. "Here," Rusty said, "take mine. It's lighter."

He handed her his Navy Colt and belt. She buckled them on. She took Will's flintlock rifle from over the fireplace, along with the powder horn and pouch of bullets. The flintlock was a museum piece now, but Will and Hope had kept it in good working order. She wished she hadn't lost the breech-loading Sharps, and she wondered if that was one of the weapons firing at them now. She and Rusty each stuck one of Rusty's old Walker Colts, the ones he had gotten from Chance, in their belts.

"I'll take the kitchen," Hope said, and she carried boxes of pistol cartridges and percussion caps into the back room.

Outside, a bugle blew, a few notes tooted off-key on an instrument that must have been captured from the army. The noise was followed by yells and the drumming of hoofbeats.

"There go the horses," Rusty said.

They looked through the loopholes to see Indians driving their horses from the corral in a great cloud of dust, waving their arms and yelling. Hope and Rusty both fired at the Indians, but the dust obscured their targets and they did not hit anything. They smelled smoke and heard the crackle of flames. The picket house and outbuildings were going up.

"Reckon we're next," Rusty said as they reloaded. He looked pale and tired. In his weakened condition, the battle had taken a lot out of him already.

Hope glanced at the children. Alex wailed with every shot. Ellen bravely tried to humor him, even though she was on the point of tears herself. "Alexander, stop that crying," she admonished, waving the doll in his face to distract him. "Stop it right now. Do you hear me?"

The dark house was like an oven. Hope was tired. Her body felt as if it had been run over by a wagon, from the fall down the bluffs. Her dress was ripped to shreds and wet with sweat and blood, and she was dirty and bleeding from head to foot. The only good part was that all the bruises hid the mark on her cheek where Chance had slapped her. She found a kerchief and tied a headband for her sweaty hair, to keep it out of her eyes.

She moved from window to window, looking out the embrasures. The embrasures were angled wide on the inside, to afford a full field of fire, while on the outside the opening was just big enough for a rifle barrel. Only a trick shot could hit a target that small at a distance, and even at point-blank range, an enemy could do no more than fire inside the house blindly. Each shutter was braced with wooden supports, and there were spare braces against the wall, in case the first ones failed to hold. With a full complement of defenders, the four windows and two doors could make the house a formidable obstacle to an attacker, but with only two people inside, the extra openings could prove a drawback.

The off-key bugle blew again.

"Here they come," Rusty said.

The Indians burst from a ravine by the creek. They came in single file, running for the house in their knee-length moccasins, carrying bows and rifles and war axes, with hide-covered shields on their arms. Their chests were painted blue and white and red, with black paint on their faces. Their long, unpleated hair bounced on their shoulders. Sunlight glinted on greasy skins. Rusty drew a bead on the lead runner and fired. The Indian threw up his arms, staggered, and dropped on his face. The others fell back. There was a ragged volley of shots from the trees. An arrow thunked into the door right next to the loophole, making Rusty jump back.

Hope watched through the back door, keeping her eyes on the trees and brush at the bottom of the hill, thinking the Indians would come from there. Nothing happened. She moved to the left side window, bumping into the stove in her haste. She peered through the loophole and saw forms slinking out of the smoke from the sheds. Hope laid the flintlock in the embrasure. She trembled with fear and excitement. This wasn't a dream, she told herself; it was really happening. The forms were very close. She aimed and fired. When the powder smoke cleared, Hope saw a brave writhing on the ground, holding his hip. She tipped the powder horn and poured powder down the rifle barrel. She rammed in a bullet, trying to hurry but not to go too fast and do a bad job. Bullets and arrows peppered the adobe house. The Indians were behind the trees near the house, sniping at the windows. In the corner, Alex was crying, while Ellen held him fearfully.

An arrow bounced off the wall near Hope's head. She whirled around. An Indian had fired his bow blindly through the loophole in the opposite window. She saw another arrow penetrate the opening. She dashed across the room, drawing Rusty's pistol from its holster. As the arrow steadied with the tightening of the bowstring, Hope wedged the pistol alongside it, cocked, and fired. Someone yelled, but whether from surprise or because he was hurt, she could not tell. Then there was the sound of retreating feet. Hope fired the pistol after the Indians, but in the smoke and confusion she could not tell whether she'd hit anything. She heard Rusty shooting from the front room.

All went quiet. Hope moved from loophole to loophole, but no Indians were to be seen. The bodies and wounded had been carried off. She saw a splotch of red blood on the ground near one window. She leaned back against the wall, catching her breath and reloading the pistol.

Smoke from the burning outbuildings filtered into the house, bringing with it the stench of charred leather from saddles and harnesses. Inside the dark building, wreaths of powder smoke further limited vision. The occupants coughed as they breathed the acrid fumes. Hope went behind the overturned table and knelt with the children. "Are you two all right?"

Alex wailed uncontrollably. Ellen blubbered, "I want it to stop, Mommy."

Hope cradled the girl's shoulders. "It will, honey. Soon."

"If Daddy was here, he'd make them go away."

"I know he would."

Hope ladled both children some of that morning's milk. She gave them some venison jerky to chew. There wouldn't be any more milk after this bucket. The cow had been killed, along with all the other domestic animals. It didn't matter, though. The people would follow the cow soon enough.

Hope sighed. Having the children here was the worst part. She wished she had left Ellen in the reeds now. How could she have been so stupid? At least the girl would have had a chance that way. She might have joined up with Tommy by this time. Tommy would have seen her through.

Outside, the bugle blew again, in that screeching, atonal blast. Shots rang out, and bullets thumped into the adobe house. Fire arrows hissed onto the roof, but the sod would not burn. One of the arrows set the west gallery roof alight, though.

Rusty beckoned to Hope. In a low voice he said, "Remember

to shoot yourself at the end, Miss Hope. Don't let yourself be took prisoner.''

Hope gulped. She nodded and went back to the window. She saw the Indians coming out of the smoke. They were advancing from all sides, while others fired from behind the cover of the trees. Hope fired the flintlock, knocking one back. Somehow her coolness at killing people no longer surprised her. She moved to the next loophole, reloading as she went. She saw dim forms pass in front of the opening, but she was too late to get off a shot. She heard Rusty's rifle firing from the other room.

Hope put down the flintlock and drew the Navy Colt. She heard moccasins on the gallery outside. She heard gutteral commands. There was a loud banging. The Indians were beating on the shutters and doors, trying to knock them in with rifle butts and pieces of wood. Hope fired point blank out a loophole, heard a scream. There was more hammering from the other side of the house. She ran there and fired. Thank God Will had built this place so strong. Both children were crying now.

She heard Rusty cursing with the frenzy of battle. He had not frozen this time. She glanced through the doorway and saw blood spreading from his shoulder. ''Are you all right?'' she cried above the shooting and hammering of wood. He waved her off, reloading his pistol.

She fired through the back door. The air was alive with savage yells. She heard the Indians digging at the adobe walls with knives and axes. She poked the pistol barrel through a loophole, trying to get an angle on the diggers. Somebody grabbed the barrel, then screamed because it was red hot. Hope fired the weapon instinctively and pulled it back inside. An arrow zipped past her.

Hope slumped against the wall, trying to reload the pistol. She could hardly see in the smoke and darkness. A stray bullet clanged off a frying pan. She fumbled with the paper cartridges. She dropped copper percussion caps. Her lungs were so filled with smoke, she thought she would suffocate. The racket both outside and in was tremendous. Part of the outside gallery was on fire. In the corner, the children were screaming, but Hope had no time for them, though she saw gouges in the table where bullets had plowed into it. She was burning with thirst, but she wasn't sure where the water bucket was anymore. Besides, there wasn't time.

There was a terrific banging from the front door. The Indians had backed a horse to the door, and the rider was making the animal kick the door in. The heavy door shook on its rawhide hinges. Rusty ran to the door's loophole, and he ducked as a pistol ball came through the other side. The Indians had been waiting for that. He poked the shotgun through the loophole and blasted both barrels into the horse's rear. The horse screamed and leaped into the air, throwing its rider, who was also hit by the shotgun pellets. Rusty ducked away from the loophole again, but not before another bullet came through, smashing his collarbone. He reeled, grimacing, and fell to the floor.

Hope rushed into the front room. Rusty looked up at her, wincing. "I'm supposed to be back here for a rest. Somebody forgot to tell them that." She knelt beside him, and he patted her hand. "It's your fight now, Miss Hope. Leave your guns here, and I'll reload them."

Hope left her pistols. She took the Colt Dragoon and the huge Walker Colt from Rusty. She ran from loophole to loophole of the house, firing out. The smoke-filled air rang with war whoops, with the crashing of wood, with gunshots and the cries of children. The Indians poked rifle and pistol barrels through the loopholes and fired into the house. Hope poked her pistol barrels back, firing in return. It was a deadly game, both sides blazing away with only a thickness of wood between them. The heavy revolvers bucked in Hope's hands. Their recoil hurt her wrists and arms. The hammers were difficult to thumb back. Her head was spinning with fatigue. The smoke burned her eyes. It choked her lungs, making her cough.

She heard new noises, noises she couldn't place. Then she looked up. The Indians were on the roof. They were digging through the sod, trying to break into the house that way. Hope ran to the front room and got the shotgun. As she did, a shaft of sunlight suddenly streamed from the ceiling into the murky blackness of the house. They had a block of sod out. Above her, she saw dim forms through the smoke and powder haze. She heard triumphant yells. She pointed the shotgun into the opening and fired one barrel, then the other. The recoil hurt her shoulder.

She heard screams and heavy thuds. Loose dirt cascaded down. There was no more digging.

"Call me if they start again," she yelled to Rusty.

"Mommy!" Ellen screamed from the other room.

Hope ran into the back. She heard wood splintering. One of the window braces had given way under the relentless hammering. The shutter swung open. An Indian climbed through the narrow opening and dropped catlike to the earthen floor, near Hope's bed. He was wearing a buffalo-horn headdress. His chest was painted clay white with the figure of an owl in red. There were diagonal black streaks on his face. He carried a war ax. All Hope could think of was the danger to her children. She rushed upon the brave, swinging the shotgun by the stock. She brought the weapon down with all her might, thwacking the Indian's head with the hot barrels, knocking him into her spinning wheel, shattering it. He tried to get up. She hit him again, and again. The headdress came off. She heard metal crunch bone. She heard the Indians outside. She saw blood splatter. She heard someone screaming and realized it was herself. The Indian half rose, putting up a feeble hand to ward off the blows, then his skull turned to jelly and he fell to the floor.

A pistol went off near Hope. It was Rusty. He had dragged himself into the passageway. Hope turned in the direction of his smoking revolver. Another Indian was slumped halfway through the open window. The air was alive with yells. Hope pushed the Indian's body back through the window. She swung the splintered shutter closed, found the extra brace in the darkness, and somehow jammed it tight against the hands pushing from the other side. There was banging on the other windows; they wouldn't last much longer. She took the reloaded pistol from Rusty and went to each loophole in turn, firing, like an automaton, trying only to postpone the inevitable.

There was a loud rumble of wheels, then a jarring crash against the back door. Hope smelled fresh smoke, heard the crackle of flames. The Indians had filled the buckboard with hay, set it alight, and rammed it against the door, trying to burn their way in.

"Rusty!" Hope cried. "Help me!"

She assisted Rusty to his feet. Bullets pinged around them. A lantern shattered. The Indians' yells rose to a fever pitch. Hope led Rusty to the door, steadying him.

She reloaded the shotgun. "Ready?" she said.

Rusty nodded woozily. With his good arm, he cocked his revolver.

Hope unbolted the door. She swung the door open, flinching against the sudden heat from the fire. She discharged both barrels of the shotgun into the smoke. Rusty emptied his pistol. Then they flung their weight against the burning buckboard's gate. Fortunately, the Indians hadn't known how to set the brake. The buckboard budged. They heaved again, Rusty almost passing out from the pain in his collarbone, and the flaming vehicle rolled away from the door. Hope pulled Rusty back inside in a hail of bullets and arrows. Hope swung the door shut and bolted it as Rusty collapsed to the floor. Hope looked through the loophole. The Indians ran up and tried to push the wagon back, but the flames were too hot for them to get close to it now. She fired her pistol into them once, twice.

From the trees, the captured bugle tooted mournfully. The Indians began leaving, carrying off their dead and wounded. Hope fired a defiant shot after them.

A sudden calm descended on the adobe house. It seemed strange not to hear the gunfire, the yells, the pounding at windows and doors. The house was boiling hot inside. The air was so thick with smoke that it was nearly impossible to see or breathe. Hope held her dress across her face to filter the acrid fumes. The shaft of light from the hole in the roof made the surrounding area seem even blacker. Looking at the block of sky, Hope saw with a shock that it was dusk. They had been at this for hours. It had seemed like minutes. Fire crackled from the buckboard outside. Dry wood cracked and popped. There was a crash as part of the gallery collapsed.

Hope bent over Rusty. "How are you?"

Rusty lay with his back to the wall, near a barrel of cornmeal. "I'll live. I think." He managed a grin. "Did I do all right this time?"

"You did fine, Rusty."

Rusty's face and clothing were black with powder smoke, and Hope realized that she must look the same way. She was more tired than she could have ever imagined. Her clothes were stiff with sweat and dirt and blood. She reloaded all the weapons, going from loophole to loophole as she did. There were no Indians in sight.

"Will they be back?" she said.

"If they know how low on bullets we are, they will be," Rusty replied. "If they don't come soon, we can expect them at dawn."

Satisfied that no attack was imminent, Hope went to the children. They were still behind the overturned table, in the space between the cupboard and wall. Alex, incredibly, had fallen asleep. All the crying must have exhausted him. Ellen huddled next to him, glassy-eyed, mumbling to her doll, reassuring it. Hope held the blond girl close.

"Is it over, Mommy?" Ellen asked in a low voice.

"I don't know," Hope said.

She brought Ellen and Rusty water, then she took some herself. It seemed she could not get enough of the tepid liquid. Hope realized how famished she was, and she cut off jerky strips for everyone, gnawing hers like an animal. In the quiet, she heard something dripping from the roof. It was blood.

Hope rose and stood over the body of the Indian she had beaten to death with the shotgun. She hesitated, not wanting to do this, then she bent and lifted the body beneath the arms. The Indian's skin was clammy, and its feel sent shivers of revulsion through her. Hope dragged the body to the back door. She opened the door and threw the body out, near the burning buckboard. She threw the buffalo-horn headdress after it. Then she ducked back inside before snipers could get a shot at her, but all was quiet.

Darkness fell. The inhabitants of the stifling adobe house waited for the Indians to attack again. Rusty dozed, exhausted and weakened by his wounds, snoring like a little boy. Hope stood guard all night, holding the children, singing to them to make them sleep. Only fear for their safety kept her awake.

Before dawn, Hope was back at the loopholes, guns ready, waiting for the final onslaught. She roused Rusty, who gamely faced the front door with a revolver. The air inside the house was stale, like the aftermath of a hundred cigars, but by now most of the smoke had drifted out through the loopholes and the opening in the roof.

Gray light streaked the eastern sky. No attack came.

The light spread across the horizon. The sun rose.

"They're gone," Rusty said at last. "Heaven help us, Miss Hope, they're gone. They had enough."

Hope sank to the earthen floor. She passed a weary hand over her eyes, and she said a prayer of thanksgiving. Then she roused herself. She got up and looked around. Inside, the house was a mess. The once-whitewashed walls were blackened and pocked with bullet holes. Plates were smashed, furniture splintered. Hope's spinning wheel was in pieces where the Indian had fallen into it. The floor was littered with cartridge boxes, arrows, used percussion caps, tin cups, glass from the broken lantern. There was a puddle of water where one of the buckets had overturned. The dripping blood from the roof had dried to a sticky brown goo. Other blood, from the dead Indian and from Rusty, was everywhere. On the fireplace mantel, between the copy of *Ivanhoe* and the arrowhead that had been pulled from Will's back years before, the wedding miniature of Hope's parents had been smashed by an arrow. She picked up the portrait and reset it, brushing away the broken glass.

She went outside. The body of the dead Indian had been dragged away during the night. Hope had never heard a thing, and she got goose bumps to think that the Indians had been so close. The burnt-out buckboard blocked the back door. The dead horse blocked the front. The gallery was half collapsed. The shutters and doors were smashed and battered. There were excavations in the adobe. The bodies of two Indians lay sprawled on the torn roof, the one place where their tribesmen had been unable to retrieve them undetected. The house itself still held, though. That was the important thing. The outbuildings were a total loss, with all their equipment. The horses were gone. The rest of the stock had been run off or killed. The smell of charred wood hung over everything. Here and there wisps of smoke still rose.

Hope went back inside. She bound Rusty's wounds, until someone could come to remove the bullets and set the broken collarbone. Mechanically, as if in routine she could find relief from the memories of yesterday, she lighted the stove. She made coffee for herself and Rusty, and she fed the children. She'd never liked coffee much, but now she longed for it. Despite the growing warmth of the day, she felt cold inside, and she poured the hot liquid into herself.

There was one more thing she had to do.

"I'm going to find Tommy," she said.

"Don't leave," Ellen pleaded. "Tommy can come home by himself."

Hope shook her head. "No, I have to go. You and Alex will be all right. Uncle Rusty is here with you. The Indians are gone. Someone will be here from Kingdom soon, to see how we are." If there's anyone left in Kingdom, she thought. Rusty looked at her, and she knew that he was thinking the same thing.

She was in a hurry. She would not rest until she held Tommy safely in her arms. She took two pistols, one in the holster that she still wore and one stuck in the belt, and she set off. She followed the creek, moving cautiously in case the Indians were still around. Her eyelids were weighted with weariness. She had to shake her head to clear her vision, and she stumbled repeatedly. Her body ached. She smelled to high heaven, and she knew she must look like an apparition. She was surprised not to meet Tommy coming down to the house. He must be playing it smart, staying put until someone came for him.

She passed the reeds where she and Ellen had hidden from the Indians. Off to the right, she saw something pale on the ground, and she jumped when she realized that it was the body of the Kansas Cow. She went on, giving the body a wide berth, not wanting to see it close up, not wanting to see what the Indians had done to it.

Her pace quickened as she neared the fishing hole. "Tommy?" she called. "Tommy, where are you?"

She moved faster. Why didn't he answer? "Tommy!"

She burst through the trees and brush to the fishing hole, and she stopped. In front of her was Tommy's fishing pole, broken. There were scattered fish bones where predators had picked his catch clean. A few feet farther on was a torn straw hat. Hope did not have to be an experienced frontiersman to read the story in the moccasin prints around the fishing hole. They told of a short chase and futile flight.

The Indians had captured Tommy.

"Oh, Tommy," Hope cried. She sank to her knees, picking up the battered straw hat. "Oh, my poor boy."

30

Chance was halfway to Fort Worth when he turned back.

He had meant to put Kingdom behind him forever. He had meant to get on with his life, as he should have done years before. He couldn't do it, though. He couldn't leave Hope. He couldn't get her out of his system. He guessed that he never would.

No woman had ever gotten to him the way Hope had, and he wasn't sure why. She was pretty, but he had known prettier. Maybe it was Tommy, he thought. That was some of it, but not all. Hope was like a splinter that had worked itself deep under his skin, and no amount of prying was ever going to dig her out.

Chance was sorry for what he'd done to her, sorrier than for anything he'd done in his life. He hadn't been able to stop himself. The years of frustration had built and built, until he had exploded. Now he'd see if he could make amends. He'd see if he could patch their old love back together.

He set his red roan Chinaco toward Kingdom. Sometimes Chance wished that Will would get killed, so that he could have Hope to himself again. Then he cursed himself. Will was the best friend he'd ever had—ever would have. He'd take Hope back any way but that one.

As Chance drew closer to Kingdom, an undefinable sense of foreboding came over him, and he urged Chinaco on faster. Then, as he topped the rise that led down to the ford of the Clear Fork, he stopped. In the valley he saw the burnt-out ruin of houses. Across the river, a large section of the stockade was blackened, and parts of it had fallen down. Little figures moved here and there, listlessly.

Chance's heart rose in his throat. He spurred Chinaco down the hill. He passed the burnt shell of Fred Thompson's house, and Tom Nye's. He clattered across the ford, which because of the drought was so shallow as to be almost nonexistent. He passed Mr. Blunden's cabin, with nothing left but the stone chimney, and Jules Villette's, with some of the terraced rows of grapevines uprooted. All around were other signs of the Indians' coming—dead animals, scattered mattress ticking, smashed furniture, spoiled food.

As he approached the fort, people came to meet him. Many of them bore wounds. A big, heavily built man was in the lead. It was Jacob Koerner, the blacksmith. "Chance!" he cried. "We're glad you are back. It was Indians, Chance, a big war party. They got Jules Villette, and Ma Richardson, and . . ."

Chance paid no attention. He rode past as if no one were there. He was afraid to ask if Hope was safe, afraid of his reaction if she wasn't. He had to see for himself, and he was determined to cover the ten miles to the Double H as quickly as possible, all the while dreading what he would find there.

As he neared the ranch, he set Chinaco to a full gallop. Then he saw the burnt outbuildings, and an inarticulate cry of pain rose from deep inside him. Hope must be dead.

He reined Chinaco to a sliding stop in front of the battle-scarred house. He threw himself from the saddle and ran for the door. To one side, he saw two fresh graves. The graves were unmarked, so they must be those of Indians. He smelled stale gunpowder and burnt wood. His heart was pounding with fear.

Then Hope was in the doorway. She looked a mess, with powder-blackened face and hair, and red-rimmed eyes. Her clothes and skin were torn and dirty and crusted with dried blood.

"Chance!" she said, and she came to him, burying her face in his chest, crying. "Oh, Chance."

He held her close, overcome with relief, stroking the back of her head, letting her soak up his strength. Only two days before she had refused to let him touch her. Now she wanted nothing more, and he did not want to let her go.

Then he had to let her go, because Ellen and Alex were running up from the creek. "Uncle Chance!" yelled Ellen.

"Chance! Chance!" Alex shouted happily.

Chance knelt, hugging both children. He looked behind them,

expecting to see someone else. Then he looked at Hope, and a worried note crept into his voice. "Where's Tommy?"

Hope stared at him. She was shaking. Tears rolled down her face.

Chance rose and grabbed her arm. "Where's Tommy?"

"The"—she sobbed—"the Indians took him."

Chance felt as if the bottom had fallen out of his stomach. His feet seemed to lose contact with the ground. His head spun.

"He was at the fishing hole," Hope went on. She spoke slowly at first, then the words came in a torrent. "They must have followed his tracks. He must not have hidden himself well enough. Or maybe he did something foolish and came out to look, and they . . ."

Chance shook her without realizing it. "How could you let him go up there by himself?"

Hope replied angrily, twisting away from him. "Me? This never would have happened if you hadn't"—she looked at the children and changed what she'd been going to say—"if you hadn't left us. Tommy would be here now, if you'd been with him. Will would never have left us defenseless that way, no matter what had happened between me and him personally."

Chance drew back, unable to meet her gaze. This was his fault, all his fault. He had thought it couldn't get any worse, but it had. It was as bad as it could possibly be. He straightened and said quietly, "How about Rusty? Is he all right?"

Hope quieted, as well. She didn't have much anger left in her right now. "He's wounded, but he'll recover. He's inside, asleep. Jake Koerner was up here to tend his wounds and see to us." Her tone grew hopeful, "Chance, they've sent Aaron Richardson to Fort Belknap for the minute men. Maybe the minute men can—"

"Hang the minute men," Chance said. His hooded eyes were filled with grim purpose. He walked back to his horse and mounted.

Hope followed him. "Where are you going?" she said.

"To get Tommy," he told her. He yanked hard on the reins and rode off.

Chance returned to Kingdom. He entered the fort and dismounted, oblivious to the people who clustered around him. He unsaddled Chinaco, rubbed him down, watered and fed him. He stripped his pack of the nonessentials he'd been carrying—clothes, whiskey, cards, portable faro layout. On this trip all he'd need would be food, ammunition, a blanket, and his buckskin jacket.

While he worked, Jake Koerner and the others told him about the raid, about how the Indians had ridden up the valley, cutting down men and women in the fields, looting the houses and stealing stock. About how they'd set the stockade on fire—they hadn't dared attack a structure that strong head on—and about how, after a desperate struggle, the flames had been brought under control. They told how the Indians had captured Jules Villette and roasted him alive in front of the stockade for the amusement of the defenders. They told how Jules had tried to sing the *"Marseillaise"* before the screams had overcome him, and how Aaron Richardson had put a bullet into him, ending his agony.

Chance wasn't interested. His energies were focused on one goal. When he had finished making up his blanket roll, he went to the stockade corral. He still had horses there, but they were stagecoach hacks, not what he wanted. George Vestry, who was absent, had the only good mounts left in Kingdom. He passed over Vestry's high-bred Morgans in favor of a snip-nosed little pinto of Spanish stock. He knew the pinto had more bottom than both of the Morgans put together. He threw a loop around the pinto's head and began leading him out.

"Hey, Evans! What the hell are you doing? Leave that horse alone."

It was Shawcross, one of Vestry's "soldiers," a big, bearded, intimidating man who hadn't forgotten how Chance had run them off the Sommerville place.

Chance ignored him. He led the horse toward the corral gate.

Shawcross laid a rough hand on Chance's shoulder. "I said, you ain't taking that—"

Chance turned and drove his fist deep into the pit of Shawcross's stomach. The air exploded out of the bearded man, and he doubled over. Chance clubbed him solidly on the jaw, and Shawcross dropped to the mud and manure of the corral. Shawcross reached for his revolver. Chance stomped a boot onto the other's hand and ground the heel down. He heard bones break. Shawcross yelled with pain. He rolled around, holding his injured hand by the wrist. "I'll get you for this, Evans. I'll get you."

Chance said nothing. He walked away with the pinto.

George Vestry's wife, Lucinda, came from her picket house. She'd seen the fight from her front door. She was not intimidated by Chance. "Mr. Evans, where are you going with our horse?"

Chance stopped. Lucinda was a well-bred woman, pretty in a cold sort of way, and he'd always thought she was too good for George. He touched his hat brim and said, "The Indians took Tommy Cooper, Miss Lucinda. I'm going after him, and I need a spare horse."

The crowd murmured. A look of pity came over Lucinda's face. "Yes, we heard about him. The poor boy. And you're going after him by yourself?"

"That's right."

"Well, of course you can have the horse, Mr. Evans, and God be with you. Is there anything else I can do?"

"I'd be obliged if you'd find me an extra grain ration for the horses, and maybe some grub for myself."

"Yes. Yes, of course. I'd be pleased to," Lucinda said. She went back into the house, beckoning one of her neighbors for assistance.

"I'll ride with you, Chance," said Jacob Koerner.

"No. You'd just hold me up."

Chance threw his saddle on the pinto. He tied Chinaco with a short lead rope. Vestry's wife brought him the rations, which he packed in fiber *morrals* and looped over his pommel. "Thanks, Miss Lucinda," he said. He mounted and rode from the fort, scarcely listening as its inhabitants wished him good luck.

He picked up the Indians' trail north of the ranch. He could have followed the tracks of the main bunch from Kingdom, but there was always the off chance that the two war parties had not been together, and off chances were something he could not afford. Sure enough, the party that hit the ranch had joined up with the main bunch on the far side of Buzzard Peak. They were headed northwest, and by their tracks there looked to be at least a hundred of them. That made it one of the largest raids into Texas in a long time.

The Indians had a day's start and were traveling fast. Chance set a hard pace, changing horses frequently. He wanted to catch them before they split up. He had not thought out what he would do then. What could he do, one against a hundred? Try to trade for Tommy, he supposed. He had no money, but the Indians might accept Chinaco, or his pistols and rifle. He could promise them more horses and cattle, too. Some of them would remember the beef contractors from the old Penateka reservation. They would know that he would deliver.

Whatever it took, he thought grimly.

He followed the Indians across the Brazos, across the Wichita, across the South Pease. They seemed to be heading for the Staked Plains—someplace on the upper Canadian, maybe. Then, just short of the North Pease, the tracks of the war party split up.

Chance cursed his luck. This time there was no marker to point the way to the Indians' destination. Once he thought he saw the prints of Tommy's moccasins, but he lost them on the trampled ground. He cut a wide circle, studying the tracks of the various groups for a long time, looking for a horse that might be ridden double. An Indian might have found Tommy's trail right away, but Chance was not that kind of tracker. At last he found what he was looking for, or thought he did, and he started after the party. There were four braves, plus a double rider and a string of stolen horses.

For a day and a half he hung onto the trail doggedly, sometimes losing it in the hot dry emptiness of the plains, sometimes losing it on the rocky ledges over which the Indians traveled, but always picking it up again.

Then, abruptly, he caught up with them.

The Indians must have decided they were safe from pursuit. They'd gone into camp in the breaks of a dry stream bed, near a waterhole. They were dancing, drinking bottles of Jules Villette's wine, singing off-key and breaking the empty bottles on the rocks. Chance watched them from the shadow of a large rock outcrop.

Tommy was not among them. The double rider had been a wounded brave, a slightly built fellow, no more than a boy.

Chance faced a dilemma. He couldn't keep following this bunch. Eventually they'd realize they were being trailed, and they'd turn on him. A hundred Indians might have admired his bravery and listened to what he had to say. Five would butcher him. There was only one thing to do.

He crept into their camp at dawn. They'd stayed up most of the night, and now they slept in a drunken stupor, snoring, with broken bottles everywhere. It was ironic, thought Chance, that Jules's beloved wine was going to help bring retribution upon his killers.

Chance killed them as they slept, cutting their throats. It was easy, and he enjoyed it. He had never enjoyed killing before. This bunch were Kiowas. He could tell by the way their hair was cut off above the shoulder on the right-hand side. One wore the feathered fur cap of the *on-de*, the elite Kiowa caste. His single braid was wrapped in otter fur, and a silver chain hung alongside his thin scalp lock. He must have been an important warrior, a chief or a chief's son. Chance had intended to capture the wounded boy and force him to tell who had taken Tommy and where they were headed; but the boy mustn't have been as drunk as the others, because as Chance approached him, he suddenly awakened, sprang up, and fired at Chance with an old Whitney revolver. Chance had no choice but to draw his own six-gun and shoot the boy dead.

After Chance had killed the Indians, he scalped them and threw the scalps away, to show his contempt. But this did not seem like enough. He was too overcome with grief and rage and frustration. So, as a further sign of contempt, he cut off their left ears, which was something the Kiowas themselves liked to do to their victims. When that still didn't satisfy him, he carved the Double H brand into each of the dead Indians' foreheads, and he lined up the bodies and left them, so that if any of their friends came upon them, they would know who did this and be afraid.

He rounded up the string of stolen horses. Most of the brands he recognized; a few he didn't. He started back for the spot where the war party had split up, determined to find another set of tracks and start over. Now he had something better than his guns to trade for the boy. But before he reached the Pease, a big storm came up. It rained for a day and a half. The same rain that saved the crops of the surviving settlers along the Clear Fork washed away the tracks of the Indian raiders. The Indians had vanished into the vastness of the plains. There was no chance of finding them now. There was no chance of finding Tommy.

Dispirited, Chance made his way back to the Double H. Hope came out to meet him. He halted Chinaco in front of her. He did not say anything. He did not have to. Tears rolled down Hope's cheeks, and Chance felt his heart wrenched even more than it already had been. Hope had been counting on him to bring Tommy back. She had believed in him. He had failed her, and he had failed his son.

He wanted to comfort her, but he could not bring himself to dismount. He felt inadequate. Without a word, he turned Chinaco away, and he returned to Kingdom. When he got there, he turned the string of horses into the corral. Then he went into his saloon, and he began to drink.

Part IV

31

1865

Hope was in the kitchen, washing the lunchtime dishes in the oaken tub. Ellen dried them with a ragged towel, while three-year-old Alex stood by, watching. Fulgencio and Rusty had gone to the stable.

It was late summer, over a year since the Indian raid. Inside, the adobe house looked much as it had before the Indians had come. Hope had painstakingly rebuilt her spinning wheel, and it stood in its old position near her bed. Hope's brown dress was patched and mended, and she had no hopes of getting a new one in the near future. Alex was bare-chested, with buckskin breeches. With his moccasins and deep tan, he looked like an Indian boy. Ellen had grown another two inches, and her once-blond hair was coming in a darker, honey color.

"Can I go now?" Alex asked impatiently. The new brood mare had just foaled, and Alex was in a hurry to go to the stable, with Fulgencio and Rusty, to see the colt. Ellen shot her mother a look, because she wanted to go, too.

"Yes," Hope said, laughing, "you can go. Ellen, finish that dish, and you go with him."

Alex started for the front door like a shot. Then Hope heard him stop. After a second he came back to the kitchen, and his small voice held a note of fear. "Mommy, there's a strange man out there. He's looking at our house."

Hope dropped what she was doing. She went to the front, drying her hands on her dress. As she reached the open doorway, she pulled the pistol from its belt on the peg.

She saw three bearded men outside, but it was the one nearest the house who drew her attention. He was tall and thin, gaunt really, and he wore a battered old hat with a bullet hole in the crown.

Hope went weak in the legs. She gripped her son's shoulder for support. In a quiet voice she said, "He's not a stranger, Alex. That's your father."

Will stood about where the gate to the picket fence would be one day. Behind him were Sam and Todd Sommerville, with the horses that the three men had borrowed in Kingdom. Off to one side, unseen from the doorway, were Fulgencio and Rusty, but the Sommervilles motioned them to stay put for a minute.

Will had heard about the Indian attack on his ranch. He'd been expecting the place to look different, and it did. Most of the outbuildings had been rebuilt, as had the gallery of the house. The adobe exterior of the house itself was pocked with bullet holes and larger excavations, where the Indians had tried to dig their way in. The shade trees had grown taller.

Will wore a blanket roll across his shoulder, as did Sam and Todd. On Will's faded brown coat were dark spots where his shoulder straps had been. He'd thrown the straps away at the surrender. At his side was a Colt's Army .44. Officers had been allowed to keep their sidearms. His trousers were a nondescript gray, all out at the knees. His high boots were unpolished, and they needed soles. Todd and Sam were dressed in similar fashion. The only article of uniform among the three was Todd's much-mended jacket of butternut gray, with its light-blue sergeant's stripes. Todd was barefoot.

When Hope appeared in the doorway, Will's breath was drawn from him. It was like finding the Grail after a long and difficult quest. Their eyes locked on one another's. Hope looked ragged and haggard, but to Will she was the most beautiful woman in the world. She put the pistol back in its holster. Somewhat self-consciously, she attempted to straighten her hair, and Will smiled at that. She smiled, too. They moved toward each other, slowly at first, almost shyly, then running the last steps and flinging their arms around each other. They hugged each other tightly, then they kissed—a long, lingering kiss that tried to wash away four years of privation and loneliness.

Finally, reluctantly, their lips parted. Will looked at her, running his fingertips through her hair and along her cheek, as if to reassure himself that she was real.

"Oh, God, it's good to have you back," she said. "I've missed you so much." She kissed him again, and she put her heart and soul into it.

Then she held him at arm's length. "You've changed, Will. You look so much older. You all do—even Todd." Her eyes narrowed, because she knew that she could never really understand what they'd been through. "How was it?"

Will shrugged. "We lost."

Sam and Todd had lined up behind Will, and Hope hugged each of them tearfully. Sam, whose face was marked with chicken pox scars, seemed touched, while Todd grinned.

Bare-chested Alex advanced on Will and tugged his pants leg. The boy had Will's fair hair and his mother's good looks. He gazed up at Will with a quizzical expression. "Are you really my daddy?"

Will knelt beside him. "Yes, I am, son. I been away at the war." Then, feeling funny because he didn't know, he asked, "What's your name?"

"Alexander," the boy said gravely.

Will nodded. He stood, smiling, and he picked the boy up. The boy was tense at first. Will tousled his hair and patted his back. The boy still resisted, suspicious of this bearded, ragged man who called himself his father. Well, that was only to be expected, Will thought.

He looked down at the willowy girl who had followed Hope from the house, and he laughed. "My God, is this Ellen? The last time I saw you, you weren't much more than a babe in your mother's arms."

He bent down, and he lifted Ellen in the crook of his other arm. He straightened, holding them both. He saw the children trade a look, then a smile, and he knew that something new and good was beginning. Ellen put her arms around his neck, tentatively at first, then holding tight.

Fulgencio and Rusty came forward now, laughing and shaking hands with the Sommerville boys, clapping Will's shoulder. Hope said, "We've been expecting you for months. Curt's been back since May. His regiment was stationed near Galveston.

Apparently they all just walked away one day and came home. We've been worried about you.''

The three ex-soldiers laughed grimly. There was not much to be happy about. Will was holding the children as if he would never let them go. He said, ''I reckon there's fellas that ain't back yet. We was camped outside Richmond for a long time, waiting for the Yanks to find ships to take us south. They finally took us to New Orleans, then Galveston. From Galveston we mostly walked back to Kingdom, or what's left of it.''

''Did any of the others come back with you?'' Hope said.

Sam shook his head. ''We're all that's left. Our regiment— Will's regiment, really, 'cause he was the commander—was down to less than a hundred men at the end.''

Will finally put the children down. He moved close to Hope and rested a hand on her shoulder. ''Chance told me about Tommy.''

Hope sighed. She nodded, eyes closed, trying not to cry. Will held her. After a minute, she stepped back. ''Come inside, and I'll tell you about it.'' She looked at her brothers. ''I've bad news for you, too, if you haven't already heard.''

32

The men sat around the table, while the two children stood shyly in a corner. Hope brought in a steaming pot of the roasted corn bran that passed for coffee. Sam and Todd looked somber. Hope had been telling them about their father's murder.

''No idea who did it, huh?'' Sam said as Hope poured the coffee.

A warm breeze wafted through the windows. The burnt aroma of the coffee partially obscured the unwashed smell of the three bearded ex-soldiers. ''No,'' Hope replied. She had not yet told them about George Vestry, about how Chance had run Vestry and his men off the Sommerville land. She didn't want trouble so soon after her brothers' return. No good would come of it. It could only end with Sam and Todd being killed, or being hanged for killing Vestry.

Will shook his head. He had taken off his hat, and it could be seen that his hair had receded at the temples. "It's a bad business, and there's going to be a lot more like it, I'm afraid." He explained to Hope, "The Yankee occupation troops are on the border and in Galveston and Houston. In the rest of Texas, it's every man for himself. There's no law, no real government. The state's in chaos. There's a lot of old scores being settled."

Hope returned to the kitchen. She brought back plates heaped with fried salt beefsteaks and cornbread. The ragged, skeletal-looking returnees tucked in eagerly. Between mouthfuls, Todd said, "We been living on handouts and what we could forage since we landed in Galveston." Then he grinned. "Come to think of it, that's what we been living on since we left here in Sixty-one."

The men kept eating, chewing loudly. There were deep lines in what Hope could see of their faces above the beards. Todd, whom she would always think of as the baby of the family, was all grown up. And Sam, who'd come out of the war a lieutenant, seemed more serious than ever.

As they ate, Will questioned Hope about the Indians' attack on the ranch. She told him how she and Ellen had been separated from Tommy, how the Kansas Cow had warned them, how they'd hidden in the reeds and made their way here. As she went on, Will looked around. It was hard to picture the desperate battle that must have taken place in this house that was now so neat and clean.

"And Chance went after them?" he said when she was done.

Hope nodded. She hadn't told the whole story about Chance's behavior, just that he'd been away from the ranch when the attack came. "He lost their trail in a heavy rain."

Will said, "If Chance couldn't bring Tommy back, nobody could." He looked grim. "Chance was drunk when we saw him in Kingdom. I think he blames himself for Tommy. Heck, it wasn't his fault."

Will had been devastated when Chance had told him about Tommy's capture by the Indians. Will wasn't a drinking man, but his first thought had been to get blind drunk, like Chance. If it hadn't been for the prospect of seeing Hope again, he probably would have. Now he rose and looked out one of the open windows, toward the northwest and the empty land called Comancheria. "We won't give up on Tommy. We'll try to get him back. Indians ransom their captives sometimes. It's just a matter of . . ."

His voice trailed off. He turned away and pretended to fiddle with the arrowhead on the mantel. He didn't want them to see him crying.

There was a strained silence in the room. The Sommervilles, Hope, Rusty, and Fulgencio all looked at one another. The children stirred uneasily.

Will composed himself. "We weren't surprised to find that the Indians attacked. We seen evidence of their deviltry as far down as Milam County, and there's more as you come up the Brazos. Blackened, deserted homes. Overgrown fields. Markers crumbling on the graves. It's a damn shame."

Hope said, "It's going to get worse still, now that the Yanks have disbanded the minute men. At least they gave us some protection."

"Maybe they'll send U.S. troops," Rusty said. "Reopen the old forts."

Sam Sommerville snorted. "That ain't what the Yanks have in mind. They want us Texas rebels to suffer some."

Will sat back down, brooding. Alex had been looking at him, as if he wanted to ask something but lacked the nerve. Now the boy pursed his lips and came close to his father's knee. In a slow, serious voice, he said, "Did you bring back a sword?"

That broke the spell. Will laughed, and he patted the boy's head. "I wasn't that kind of soldier, son. Didn't have no use for a sword in our bunch, 'cept for a couple of times at dress parades, and then I borrowed somebody else's."

Dessert was sizzling beef tallow poured into a tin plate of blackstrap molasses. The men lapped it up, running their fingers over the plate afterward and licking them clean. Todd eased himself back from the table. He patted his stomach. "Man, that was good. So what are you going to do now, Colonel?"

"I told you," Will said, "don't call me Colonel no more."

Todd grinned. "Sorry, Colonel. Old habits die hard, I reckon."

Will gave Todd a look, then lifted his brows. "The first thing I aim to do is have me a bath and get rid of this beard. Then I'm going to burn these flea-ridden clothes and put on my old buckskins, if they're still around."

"They're around," Hope said.

Will looked at her and his pulse quickened, as it had whenever he'd thought of her through these long years. He wanted her so badly that he ached, but that would have to wait until they were alone. It was still hard to believe that he was back. Home, they called it, but it did not seem like home anymore. Home was the regiment. That feeling would take a long time to go away. It would take a long time to be comfortable here again. He'd raised this house, built most of the furniture with his own hands, yet he felt like an outsider.

Todd went on, interrupting Will's thoughts. "I mean, business-wise, what are you going to do? We got nary a dollar between us."

Hope said, "There probably isn't a dollar in the whole of Kingdom—except for George Vestry, of course. He's got plenty."

"We still got cattle, ain't we?" Will said.

"*Sí,*" Fulgencio said from his chair in the corner. The pockmarked Mexican seemed ageless. Of all the people in the room, he was the only one who looked unchanged. "There are many of them. Thousands, I think. They have bred well while you were gone. They are wild as the deer and as hard to catch. But they are there."

Rusty said, "I hear there's a new hide-packing plant over to Jefferson, on the coast. They're paying four dollars a head, they say."

There were low whistles around the room.

"You was talking about taking a herd to California before the war," Todd reminded Will.

Will looked at them all. The long line of his jaw was firm set. He said, "We ain't taking the cattle to Jefferson, and we ain't taking them to California." He drew a deep breath. "We're taking them north. To Missouri."

"Missouri!" Hope exclaimed. The others looked surprised.

"I been thinking it out for some time," Will told them. "We'll sell the cattle at one of the railheads there—Sedalia is the farthest west, I believe."

"But why Missouri?" Hope said.

"Because the North has people, Hope, millions of 'em, living in big cities. They got immigrants coming from all over the world. The Yank army was full of them, and there's more to work their factories. Them people have to be fed, and we got the beef to do it."

"You'd deal with Yanks?" Rusty asked skeptically.

"They got the money," Will said.

"How are we going to get the cattle there?" Rusty said. "It must be five or six hundred miles, and we don't know the country."

"We'll find a way," Will said. "If cattle can be drove to California, they can be drove to Missouri."

Sam looked at Will shrewdly. "You'll have to raise an outfit. That costs money, too, and we got none. Half of us don't even own saddles anymore."

"I'll get us outfitted," Will promised. "I'll go to George Vestry if I have to."

That remark produced gloomy looks around the room. Hope said, "Can you be sure there'll be a market for cattle in Missouri?"

"No. It's taking a chance, but taking chances is what life's about. We ain't going to get rich sitting here staring at ourselves."

Hope felt hollow inside. Will was only just home, and already he was talking about leaving again. "When will you start?"

"In the spring. Soon as the grass is up. In the meantime, there's plenty of work to do."

While the little group discussed Will's plan, the children got bolder. Soon they were climbing on Will, tickling him, pulling his beard, laughing and giggling.

"Give your father a minute's peace," Hope told them at last.

"That's all right," Will said as he dangled a squealing Alex by the feet. "I don't mind."

At last Sam and Todd took their leave. They wanted to reach their place before dark and see Curt. Curt had married Kathy

Nye, and the widow Nye had moved up to the Sommerville place with Kathy and what remained of her family.

When the brothers were gone, a twinkle came into Fulgencio's big eyes. "Rusty, you and me, we should take the little ones for a ride. I think perhaps *Señor* Will and *Señora* Hope would like to be alone."

The children squawked in protest. Hope looked at the floor, blushing. Will could not remember seeing her blush before. Will glanced at Fulgencio and smiled thanks.

Grinning broadly, Rusty got off his chair and swatted the children with his hat. "You two beat up on your pa later. Let's make ourselves scarce."

33

1866

Just after noon, the herd was halted and allowed to graze. The steady drizzle that had fallen all day could not dampen the men's spirits. The long drive was almost over. They had considered the Indian danger over a few days ago, when they reached Baxter Springs. Now they had crossed the last big natural barrier, the Osage River. Another two, two and a half days would see them in Sedalia. Tomorrow Will was going to ride ahead to scout out potential buyers.

Todd Sommerville and Rusty rode herd on the grazing longhorns, whose hides were slick in the rain. This stretch of uncultivated bottomland was welcome. As they got into civilized territory, it was becoming hard to find good grazing, because of all the farms. The Missouri country was green and rolling, with a lot of woods. It had been Southern territory at the beginning of the war, but most of the land had been confiscated and given to Unionists, and there were still a lot of hard feelings on both sides.

Fulgencio, Sam Sommerville, and young Aaron Richardson, who was serving as horse wrangler, joined Will by the two-wheeled Mexican cart that carried their supplies and spare gear. Lije Abernethy had unhitched the double yoke of oxen from the cart. He was brewing up coffee and passing out cold biscuits. Lije didn't ordinarily make coffee for the noon halt, but today everyone was in a celebratory mood. Lije was a drifter who'd appeared in Kingdom just before the start of the drive. He was a bit dirty, and he had a habit of getting cigar ash in his stew, but he'd proved a tolerable cook—even a very good one on occasion.

Will poured a cup of the steaming coffee and sat on a fallen log. Through the rain, he watched the grazing cattle—his cattle. They had been five weeks and over five hundred miles on the trail. Just getting on the trail at all had been a miracle. The men had been hired on credit, but much had to be purchased—the camp cart, food, tools and supplies, saddles, harness, guns and ammunition. George Vestry had advanced Will the goods, but he'd driven a hard bargain. He'd asked for payment of eight hundred dollars, due on August 1, with Will's ranch the loan's guarantee. It had been the only deal Will could make; he'd been forced to take it. Now that gamble was ready to pay off. There'd been lots of times Will had thought that it wouldn't.

In the beginning, the herd had stampeded every night. Then there'd been rivers to cross, swift and deep, and treacherous with spring rains. There had been danger from Indians and outlaws. They had left Kingdom with 500 prime steers. Now there were 483. Two had been killed by lightning, five lost in stampedes, and one drowned crossing the Red. Eight had been given to bands of Indians as payment for not being attacked, though these animals had been bolters and troublemakers, whose presence in the herd had not been missed. The last casualty had been a big corkscrew-horned brindle that they'd suspected of causing the nightly stampedes. They'd shot and eaten him. After that, the stampedes had stopped.

Will sipped the coffee. He shut his eyes and let his shoulders slump. Everything smelled wet and fresh and clean. After so many weeks of constant vigilance, it was good to relax at last.

The sound of hoofbeats made him sit up. A group of riders was emerging from the woods to the right. There were twenty to twenty-five of them, armed with revolvers, Spencer carbines, and shotguns. A couple wore old Union Army jackets. A posse, maybe, chasing some of those Missouri bank robbers that Will had been hearing so much about. Their leader was an arrogantly handsome man of average height, well dressed, with catlike eyes and a flowing mustache. The men drew up near the Texans. They spread out, as if to cover the drovers in case of trouble. Several dismounted, holding their rifles.

"Now what?" Will said to his men.

He rose, still holding his coffee, and he walked toward the newcomers. "Howdy, boys. Who might you be?"

The leader smiled, showing a raft of big, white teeth. "Who are you is a better question."

"Name's Will Cooper. We're from Texas. We're taking these cattle to Sedalia, fixing to sell them there."

Still smiling, the leader shook his head. "Well, now, I'm afraid that's impossible."

Suddenly the air grew charged. "Why?" Will said.

"Ain't you heard about the quarantine? There's no Texas cattle allowed into Missouri, on account of the fever."

"What fever?"

"Texas fever. Your cows carry it, or their ticks do. It don't affect them, but it'll kill our animals up there. I'm Boyce Slidell, special agent to the governor. We're Regulators, charged with enforcing the quarantine."

"I never heard of no Texas fever," said Sam Sommerville, coming up.

Slidell flashed his teeth again. "Well, it's a fact, sorry to say."

Todd had ridden over. Now he spoke up. "Wait a minute, mister. The Colonel here's married to my sister. They got young 'uns. The Colonel's got everything he owns tied up in this herd. If we don't sell them, the Colonel will lose his ranch, his home."

"Aw," said one of the Regulators, and the others laughed.

Todd bristled, and Slidell's grin faded. "That ain't my problem, Reb. I just enforce the law."

Todd bristled more. He didn't like taking hide off a Yank.

Will knew they could never force the herd through against these odds. "All right," he said. "We'll turn them around. We'll try and sell them in Kansas."

Slidell said, "You don't seem to understand, Reb. These cows are being impounded."

"Impounded?" The truth dawned on Will and he cursed himself for having let down his guard. "You mean they're being rustled."

"I won't bandy words with Sesesh trash. Call it whatever you want, but you're leaving and those cows are staying here."

"The hell they are," Todd said, and he went for his six-gun.

"Todd!" yelled Will, but it was too late.

With a fluid motion, Slidell swerved in the saddle. His carbine cracked, and Todd was jolted backward off his horse. In the background, there was a sudden thundering of hoofs, as the cattle stampeded.

Todd lay on his back in the mud, his sightless eyes staring at the drizzly sky with a look of surprise. There was a hole in his chest.

"You son of a bitch," Will said. He threw away his cup, reached up, and dragged Slidell from his horse, slamming him to the ground. He jumped on the Regulator and began hitting him, driving his fists into that mass of white teeth, watching them disappear in a welter of blood. He hit him again and again, then there was a blinding pain, as somebody blasted the back of his head with a rifle butt.

Will moaned, rolling in the mud, holding his head. There were shooting stars in front of his eyes. He got to his elbows and knees. His head felt as if it were split open.

Slidell stood, shaking the mud from his hands and expensive clothes. He spat blood and pieces of broken teeth. Gingerly he felt the wreckage of his mouth. Another tooth wobbled loose, and he pulled that out. "You shouldn't have done that," he told Will. "You shouldn't have done that at all." He spat more blood. "Tell your men to throw away their guns."

The men were looking to Will. Even against these odds, they were willing to have a go at the Yanks. It would be suicide, though, especially as the Texans were armed with a collection of ancient pistols and rifles, most of which hadn't been cleaned since they left Kingdom.

Will rose unsteadily to his feet, shaking his head, trying to clear it. "Do as he says," he told the men.

Aaron Richardson protested, "Colonel—"

"I ain't getting nobody else killed for a bunch of cows," Will said. Then he added, "Not this time, anyway."

"Smart move, Reb," said Slidell. He sounded funny because of his puffing lips and the big gap in his teeth. "You still have to pay for striking an officer of the law, though."

"You ain't no law officer," Will said, "and you ain't no governor's agents. You're Jayhawkers—thieves and murderers. You're men who joined the irregular troops during the war because you were too yellow for a stand-up fight. That man you just killed was in every major action from Gaines' Mill to Appomattox. You ain't got half his guts."

"Don't appear like he's got any guts at all anymore," Slidell observed, and some of his men laughed. "Now, what do we do with you?"

"Hang him!" shouted one of the Regulators.

"Yeah, string 'im up!"

"String 'em all up," suggested someone else. "That way, they can't warn the next herds about us."

Slidell grinned grotesquely through his broken mouth. "That sounds like a good idea."

One of the Regulators, a big, red-bearded fellow, pointed at Aaron Richardson. "This one's just a kid, Boyce. I don't want to be part of hanging no kids. Besides, they said this big Reb's got a family. I got a family myself. I know how they'd feel if I didn't come back. You said we'd just take the cows. You didn't say nothing about no killings."

A number of the Regulators stirred uneasily, agreeing with the red-bearded man. Slidell thought it over, then he said, "All right, we won't hang them. This one's got to learn respect for his betters, though. Wait a minute, I got an idea. Hold him."

Two Regulators grabbed Will's arms.

"Come on."

They followed Slidell, boots squelching in the mud. Will's head hurt like hell. Slidell stopped. "Tie his wrists to this tree."

One of the men produced a length of rope. He tied Will's wrists tightly around the tree, cutting the circulation. The rough, wet bark of the tree trunk pressed against Will's face.

Slidell grabbed Will's shirt and undershirt, and he ripped them from his back. The torn garments hung around Will's waist. From one of the Regulator's saddles, Slidell produced a black muleskinner's whip, and he stepped into Will's vision, uncoiling it. He smiled through his bleeding mouth.

Slidell stepped away. Some of the Regulators crowded around, eager with anticipation. Others hung back, not wanting to watch.

Will heard the whip whistle as it was swung overhead. He braced himself. The whip hit his back with a loud *crack*, slicing through his bare skin like a razor. Will jumped, almost biting through his tongue. His stomach went weak and filled with bile. His legs were drained of strength. His back throbbed. He felt blood dripping from the wound.

The whip whistled again. Will tried to brace himself, but no amount of bracing could prepare him for the shock and pain as the whip cut into his back. He groaned, the breath drawn out of him. The mark of the lash was red hot. Again the whip struck. Will ground his teeth together, determined not to cry out. He fixed his eyes on the tree bark just in front of him, trying to concentrate on that one spot, trying to banish everything else from his . . .

Crack! The whip struck again. Again. Will's moans were louder. He couldn't help it. His feet did an involuntary dance with each blow, and he heard the Regulators laughing at him. Clammy sweat streamed out of his hair and down his face. His stomach was turned inside out. His legs were like rubber. The whip shredded his back, cutting through flesh and sinew, splattering blood, making his body go alternately rigid, then limp. He held out for as long as he could, then he began to scream. He was no hero like Chance. He screamed to ease the terrible pain, and the Regulators laughed louder at him, but he no longer cared. He only wanted the pain to end. He lost all track of time. Then the pain did end. There was a roaring in his ears, as if he were hearing a battle from underwater. His head spun. Then everything went black.

Will sagged against the tree. Only the rope was holding him up. His hair was dark with sweat. The flesh on his back hung in strips. Blood covered his back. It covered his torn shirt, his pants and rawhide leggings. There was blood on the tree. There was blood trodden into the mud at Will's feet.

The red-bearded Regulator, whose name was Fitzpatrick, came forward and looked at Will nervously. "Damn you, Boyce. You killed him anyway."

Slidell spat more blood through the hole in his teeth. He drew back the whip and gave Will another lash for good measure. The unconscious body twitched.

"Boyce, that's enough!" cried Fitzpatrick.

Slidell coiled the whip, using a handkerchief to wipe the blood from the leather popper. "All right," he said, "cut him down."

Fitzpatrick sliced the rope with his knife. Will toppled onto his back in the mud. The soft rain beaded his face.

Slidell looked at the rest of the trail drivers, and he laughed contemptuously. "I thought you Texas boys were tough."

The Texans looked uncowed, and for a moment Slidell thought about hanging them anyway. Fitzpatrick and his friends would raise a stink, though. It wasn't worth it. Slidell decided that he would get rid of Fitzpatrick after they sold the cattle. Fitzpatrick was big, but he didn't have the stomach for this kind of work.

"Take their horses," Slidell ordered. "Leave them one each to get home on. Take their guns, too."

"We'll be needing them guns," Sam Sommerville said. "We got to go through Indian country."

"You could also use them to come after us. Sorry, no deal."

Slidell spat blood again. His mouth was starting to hurt. It was starting to hurt bad. He wondered if he'd lose more teeth. He was afraid of what he'd see the next time he looked into a mirror. He'd always been vain of his good looks, especially his big smile. The women loved it. Now this damn Texan had made a mess of him. He wanted to put a bullet through the Texan's brain before he left. Then he thought, why bother? Why have to argue about it with weak sisters like Fitzpatrick? Like as not, the Texan would die of blood poisoning before he got home. It would be a lingering death, too, a lot more painful than a bullet in the head. That thought made Slidell feel better.

"Come on," he told his men. "Mount up. We got some cows to catch."

The Regulators rode off in the direction of the stampeded cattle. When they were gone, the Texans lifted Will and carried him back near the fire. There they heated water and cleaned him up as best they could. Fulgencio took some herbs that he kept in a pouch, and he made a paste, which he rubbed into Will's wounds. They laid Will in the two-wheeled camp cart and covered him with blankets. After that, they dug a grave by the side of the road, and they buried Todd. Then they started back to Texas.

34

At the beginning of July, Will and his men returned to Kingdom. They were tired and dispirited. It had been touch and go whether Will would live, but his grit and Fulgencio's ministrations had pulled him through. For the last hundred miles, he had been well enough to ride. Just getting out of the jolting camp cart had made him feel better.

As the men topped the rise leading to the Clear Fork ford, they stopped in surprise. The view had changed dramatically in the four months that they'd been gone. The top of Buzzard Peak had been cleared of mesquite and brush. The vegetation had been replaced by rigid lines of white tents, set in a quadrangle around a flagpole.

"Well, I'll be," said Sam Sommerville. "The army's here."

The new fort swarmed with men and animals, with soldiers and laborers erecting wooden buildings before the onset of winter. A steam sawmill buzzed. Below the hill, the town had changed, too. A community of shacks and tents had mushroomed alongside the path leading to the fort. Wagon trains churned up dust. The sudden explosion of buildings had almost surrounded the Richardsons' fields, which were across the California Road from Chance's saloon. Tinny music filtered up to the men on the rise.

The men rode down the hill and across the ford. Not far from

Jules Villette's old vineyards, which were now untended, they passed a detail of soldiers escorting an empty wood train back toward Weatherford. The soldiers were mostly fresh-faced boys from the farms and cities of the North. They wore ill-fitting cavalry jackets, and most sat their horses as if they'd never ridden before.

From his seat on the camp cart, Lije Abernethy pulled the cold cigar from his mouth and spat as the soldiers rode by. "If that's what's supposed to protect us from the Indians, God help us."

Aaron Richardson left the group to see his brothers and sisters. The rest of the men rode with the camp cart into town. The stockade was long gone, pulled down after the war. The men rode along the crowded street, not seeing a face that they knew. There were laborers and teamsters, off-duty soldiers and civilian scouts. There were the well-heeled government contractors that swarmed around any post. Many of the new buildings were tents. Half were saloons, and all were doing a roaring business, even at midday. Pianos tinkled. Knots of painted women stood outside some of the establishments, beckoning customers inside. The smells of animals and manure were strong.

"Looky," Lije marveled, "they got a ho-tel and everything here now."

A crowd of men came and went from George Vestry's store, where a sign now advertised drinks in the back. The only establishment not doing business was Chance's Kingdom. The paint was peeling from the once-elaborate signs, and the building itself had a decrepit air. The cattlemen dismounted and went inside.

The saloon reeked of dirt and decay, of damp from the leaky canvas roof. The lithograph of the Alamo was gone; only a light patch on the wall showed where it had been. The shelves were empty; the piano was warped. There was no one inside but Chance, who sat at a dust-covered table. He was drinking from a jug of homemade whiskey and idly laying out cards.

Chance rose to greet them, staggering. His face was greasy and unshaven. His black suit was wrinkled and stained, and the collar of his shirt had turned brown with filth. He smelled.

"Hey, boys. Welcome back," he said. "Drinks are on me. How'd it go?" He saw the looks on their faces and the ragged condition of their clothes, and he said, "Uh-oh. Not so good, huh?"

The cattlemen eased themselves to the waterstained bar, pouring drinks into dirty glasses. Outside could be heard the raucous noises of the town. Chance produced a dusty bottle of beer for Will. "Still got some, see? Told you I'd never let it run out, didn't I? What happened up north?"

Will sipped his beer, standing back to escape Chance's rancid breath. He told Chance about the Regulators, about Todd's murder and his own flogging. As he talked, the scars on his back began to ache. He could hear the crack of the whip again. He could feel the deep bite of the leather.

When Will was done, Chance rubbed his stubbly chin. "You want to round up some boys and go after this Slidell fellow?"

Will shook his head. "What good would it do? Them cattle are long sold by now. No sense getting more people killed, just for revenge. It sure won't help Todd none." Chance was in no shape to go after anybody, but Will did not want to hurt his feelings by saying so.

"Besides," Will went on, "I ain't licked yet. I'm going to try and get a contract selling beef to this new fort. Shouldn't be too hard. I got the biggest ranch around, and them soldiers has got to eat."

"When did the army get here, anyway?" Sam said.

"Right after you all left," Chance replied.

"Why here?"

Chance laughed. "Because Buzzard Peak's easier to defend than old Camp Cooper or Fort Belknap. The post commander's got himself convinced that there's three thousand Comanche warriors ready to swoop down on him at any moment."

The others laughed, too. Lije said, "There probably ain't three thousand Comanches in the whole world, counting women and children, with Kiowas thrown in for good measure."

"How do they get water up there?" Fulgencio said.

"They haul it up from the river," Chance said, and the others shook their heads.

A figure appeared at the saloon's batwing doors. It was George Vestry. Vestry pushed through the broken doors, then paused, getting his eyes accustomed to the dim light, wrinkling his nose at the smell. In contrast to the tattered clothing of the cattle drivers and Chance's filthy suit, Vestry looked more prosperous than ever. He now owned most of the land in and around Kingdom. He had a new house and Mexican servants, and he sent his children to expensive Louisiana boarding schools.

Vestry twirled his walking stick, and he tapped it on the packed-earth floor of the saloon. "Hello, Will. I saw that you were back. How was the trip?"

Will's men leaned against the bar. Will sipped his beer. "Could have been better."

Vestry could barely repress a smile. "I'm sorry to hear that. Does this mean you don't have my money?"

"That's what it means," Will said.

"Not even a dollar of it?"

"Not even a cent."

Vestry smoothed his thin mustache. "Is it too early to ask for that note on your ranch? Let me have it now, and I'll give you some money toward resettlement."

Before Will could reply, Chance spoke up, slurring his words. "You want that note, Vestry, you come back in August, like it says."

Vestry sneered. "I don't recall you being involved in this, Evans."

"You don't recall shooting Jack Sommerville, but that don't mean it didn't happen."

Vestry drew himself up, with a sidelong look at Sam. "Still accusing me of that, eh? Someday your loose mouth is going to get you in trouble."

"I been in trouble before," Chance said.

Sam said nothing. He had long ago concluded who had killed his father, but now that Todd was dead, revenge didn't seem so important.

"All right," Vestry told Will, "I've tried to be nice about this, but you won't have it. I can wait a bit longer. You'll never have that money by the end of the month."

Will said, "What are you going to do with my land, George? You can't sell that much of it to grangers, like you usually do. It's only good for farming along the creeks."

Vestry tapped the ferrule of his walking stick on the floor. "At first I had planned to break up the ranch for farms. Then I thought. You claim how many acres for grazing—about fifteen thousand now, right?''

''About that.''

''That's a lot of land. A kingdom by another name, if you will. An intriguing thought, no? So I decided I'd let the cattle stay. Unlike you, I can afford to wait for a good market. I'll let Mr. Blaine manage the operation, see if he has the talent for something big.''

Will and his friends looked glum.

Vestry smiled. ''I'll see you on August first, Will. Have the money, or have the deed to your property. Good day.''

He turned and walked out the door.

Will and his men left soon after. Will had to get out to Curt Sommerville's place, where Hope and the children had been staying while he was gone. Chance watched them go. He was so drunk, he could hardly stand. He had to help Will get that money. He had to help Will save his home. Chance owed it to Will. He owed it to Hope even more. It was his fault that she'd lost Tommy, and he had vowed to make it up to her as best he could. He had vowed never to let anything bad happen to Hope again.

Chance stumbled back to the table and poured another glass of whiskey. He held the glass in his trembling hand, watching the clear liquid ripple. He licked his lips with desire. Then he flung the whiskey across the room. He looked at his hands, at himself, at the saloon.

If he was going to help Will and Hope, the first thing he had to do was clean up. He didn't have the price of a wash at the new bathhouse, so he mounted Chinaco and rode upriver, where he wouldn't be observed. Chance bathed in the cold river, scrubbing himself relentlessly, dunking his head, trying to get sober. He shaved by the reflection from a pocket mirror. His hand was unsteady, and he cut himself more than once.

Chance left his shirt and suit to be cleaned by Aaron Richardson's sister, on credit. Then he started on the saloon. He sanded and polished the bar. He patched the holes in the canvas roof. He washed the glasses and tacked up the old picture of the Alamo. He repainted the signs with paint borrowed from Curt Sommerville.

The first days of sobriety were the hardest. Chance's head felt as if somebody were driving nails into it, and he threw up repeatedly as his body purged itself of liquor. He got the shakes and he ran with sweat, but he fought through it.

Will, Sam, and Fulgencio came into town to help him. Across the street, Vestry watched them working, putting in new batwing doors. Vestry jeered at Chance. "You're finished in Kingdom, Evans. You're nothing but a whiskey-soaked tinhorn. Why don't you get out now and save the town the trouble of throwing you out?" He laughed and went back into his own thriving establishment.

Chance paid Vestry no attention. He was very pale, and he'd lost weight. To Will, he said, "How's Hope taking Todd's death?"

Will looked at Sam, and he said, "Bad. Real bad. She was real fond of Todd."

Chance nodded. "Any words on that beef contract at the fort?"

Will made a sour face. "I made them an offer, but they're having some Unionist bring in cattle from Fort Worth. Reading between the lines of what the quartermaster said, I think Vestry blocked me from getting the business."

"I'm sure he did," Chance said. "That son of a bitch has been working hand in glove with the Yanks."

Sam paused in his work. "I thought he couldn't do that, being a former official of the Confederate government."

Chance snorted. "You can do anything if you got the money."

Chance's Kingdom reopened. Business was slow at first, but it gradually improved. Chance sold his homemade whiskey at ten cents a shot, to undercut Vestry and the rest of the competition. People liked the easy atmosphere of his place, and they enjoyed matching their skill at cards against the man in the black suit. Most of his customers were freighters, teamsters, and civilian contract workers from the fort. He didn't get many soldiers, and he suspected that Vestry had been able to have him declared off limits to them. Curt Sommerville helped him make the whiskey, and Sam started working in the saloon again, running the bar while Chance played poker or dealt faro bank or monte. It was hard for Chance to stay sober with the liquor flowing, but whenever he had an urge to backslide, he thought about Hope, and he found renewed determination.

The fort had given Chance's business new life, but it was going to be too late to save Will. Chance would never amass eight hundred dollars by August 1. There were only ten days to go. Eventually he might make that much on a single turn of the cards, but not yet. The high rollers were still going elsewhere. He would have to find another way to save Will and Hope.

So Chance left the saloon in Sam's hands, and the next morning, well before dawn, he put on his old ranging outfit, saddled his red roan Chinaco, and left Kingdom.

35

Chance rode southeast, toward Austin. There would be no high-stakes poker game this time. He was woefully out of practice. His fingers had not yet recovered their old dexterity. If he tried to drop a hole card or deal from the bottom, he might find himself on the receiving end of a bullet or a lynch rope. Besides, there was always uncertainty with cards, no matter how well you played. He needed something sure, and he needed it in a hurry.

In camp that evening, he sewed himself a hood from an old blanket. He cut out slits for the eyes and mouth. Then he tried it on. He guessed he would not be the first Texas Ranger to turn to stagecoach robbing.

When he reached the vicinity of Austin, he turned downcountry, along the Houston road. He found a likely spot, where the road rose through narrow, winding hills. At the crest of the hills, a coach would have to slow down. There were plenty of scrub oaks and rocks there to shield him until the last moment.

For a day Chance camped back in the hills, letting solitary travelers pass unhindered. At last a column of dust alerted him that a stagecoach was coming. He saw the coach a mile off, coming up the pass. He rode to the crest and tied Chinaco to a tree. He slipped on his hood and waited under cover. Behind him, the big July sun was setting into the evening haze, taking the edge off the heat of the day.

As the stagecoach labored to the top of the rise, Chance stepped in front of it, with cocked six-guns pointed at the driver and guard on the box.

"Stop right there," he cried, "or you're dead men!"

The driver, who could not have been more than eighteen, reined in the horses. He was not about to argue with cocked revolvers at that range. The shotgun guard, a burly fellow, bit his mustache and ran his fingers nervously over the triggers of his weapon.

"Get rid of that shotgun," Chance ordered.

The guard hesitated.

"Now!" Chance said, aiming a pistol.

The guard let out his breath, then he tossed his weapon into the brush.

"Get down from the box," Chance ordered. He walked to the coach door and spoke to the passengers inside. "Get out with your hands up, and get in a line. And don't try jumping out the other side."

The passengers obeyed. There were seven of them, five men and two women. To the driver and guard Chance said, "Ease out those six-guns and drop them."

The men did. Chance kicked the weapons away. "Anybody else carrying a pistol?"

A man at the end of the line raised his hand. He wore the flashy clothes of a gambler.

"Take it out," Chance told him. "Slow." The gambler removed the pistol from a shoulder holster and tossed it to the ground.

Chance said, "As I come to you, put your money in my hat. Everybody else, keep your hands up, if you know what's good for you."

Chance started down the line. The first passenger was a one-armed man of about twenty-five. His cheap clothes were girt with string. With his good hand, he held out some coins. There was a little bit more than seven dollars.

"You a veteran?" Chance asked.

The one-armed man nodded. "Terry's Texas Rangers," he said proudly.

"Got family in Austin?"

"Lookin' for work."

Chance pushed the money back. "Keep it."

The second man was overdressed and pompous, a carpetbagger. He held out a fat wallet, and he spoke with a New England accent. "Sir, this is an outrage, and I—"

"Shut up," Chance told him, and he dropped the wallet into his hat.

Next was a woman, looking genteel but poor. A war widow, maybe. She held out her purse, but Chance declined. "I don't rob ladies, ma'am."

Fourth in line was a Union Army major with enormous sidewhiskers, who looked nervous. He was on his way to occupation duty in Austin, probably. The sharp-faced woman beside him must be his wife. "Hurry up," Chance told him. It was hot inside the hood. Pieces of dirty wool got in his mouth, and he spit them out.

The major held out a leather purse. There wasn't much inside. Fifty dollars, maybe. Of course, soldiers were not paid much, but this major's frock coat and forage cap were made of expensive cloth. His gilt buttons shone, and the braid on his shoulder straps looked like real gold. He shifted uncomfortably from one foot to the other, while his wife looked on.

"Is this all?" Chance asked him.

"Of course it's all. I—"

"Take off your clothes."

The major looked startled. "What?"

"You heard me, get 'em off. I think you have more."

The major looked helplessly to his wife, then back to Chance. "I assure you, I—"

"Now!" Chance said.

The major unbuttoned his heavy coat. He handed it to Chance, who felt inside, looking for money sewn inside the lining.

The major said, "You see—"

"Keep going," Chance told him, dropping the coat. "Keep going till you're buck naked. Not only that, but if I don't get any money, you'll ride into Austin buck naked, too."

One of the passengers snickered.

The major sighed. His waspish wife snapped, "I told you to let me carry it. But, oh, no, you know everything."

The major sat on the stagecoach step and rolled up one trouser leg. Strapped to his calf was a bulging cloth wallet. He unbuckled it, stood, and handed it to Chance.

"The other leg, too," Chance said.

"I swear to you, I—"

Chance jammed a six-gun under the major's nose. "Do it, you son of a bitch, or I'll blow your head off. I'm tired of playing games with you."

Hastily the major sat and rolled up the other pants leg, exposing a wallet equally as big as the first. With a pained look, he gave it to Chance. Chance's heart leaped as he glanced inside. The major must have been carrying close to a thousand dollars.

"This would have eased the rigors of punishing the South, wouldn't it, Major?" Chance said. "You must have a private income."

"It's my wife's money. You see—"

"Be quiet," said the woman. "Don't tell that rebel a thing."

Chance took the heavy wallets from his hat and stuffed them into the shield front of his red shirt. "I thank you, Major. The Confederacy thanks you, as well. Consider this reparations for the way you blue-bellies have been plundering our state."

The stage driver and a couple of the passengers laughed out loud, happy to see an arrogant Yankee brought low. The major's wife glared at them.

Chance continued down the line. Next was a traveling salesman of pots and pans, who contributed slightly over a hundred dollars to the cause. The gambler was last. He gave Chance two purses, one of coins, the other of greenbacks. "Do you want my watch, as well?" he said.

"Selling watches isn't my game," Chance told him. He glanced in the wallets. Another jackpot.

There was a sudden blur of motion to Chance's left. He dropped the hat with the money and whirled. The major was pulling something from his trouser pocket. It was a small pistol. Both men fired at the same time. The major's bullet hummed past Chance's ear. Chance's bullet hit the major square in the chest, knocking him back into the stagecoach, from where he sat heavily in the dust. His wife screamed and ran to him.

"You fool," Chance shouted at the major. "You damn fool. Why did you do that?"

The major's wife cradled her husband's head, heedless of the blood that stained her dress. There was a sucking noise from the major's chest. The woman looked up at Chance. "You've killed him. Killed him, you rebel scum."

"Christ lady, I didn't want to do it. I didn't want to hurt anybody. He didn't give me a choice. He pulled a gun."

Chance half spun on his heel, sickened by what he'd done, sickened and at the same time angry at the soldier. Then he recovered his composure. "What are you looking at?" he snapped at the other passengers. "Get him in the coach, and get out of here."

"The ride will kill him," his wife protested.

"Staying here will kill him a damn sight surer. Now load up and get moving."

The guard and driver lifted the major onto the floor of the coach. They put a blanket over him, propping his head on his rolled-up frock coat, so that he would not choke on his own blood. His wife was crying uncontrollably. The other passengers were shaken as they got in. With a pistol barrel, Chance motioned the one-armed veteran to go last. He stood him off to the side, where the others couldn't see. He had retrieved the money from the ground, and now he pinched off a wad of the major's greenbacks and slipped them into the veteran's coat pocket.

"I don't want it," said the one-armed man, looking Chance in the eye. "It's blood money."

"I didn't ask you what you wanted," Chance said sharply. "Take it. Give some to that war widow when you get a chance."

The one-armed man hesitated, then climbed into the coach. The guard stayed inside with the major, while the young driver returned to the box. He whipped up the team, and the stagecoach rumbled away.

When the coach was gone, Chance removed the stifling hood. The cool evening air refreshed his sweaty face. With trembling fingers, he counted his take. Despite what he had given away, there was fourteen hundred and twenty-three dollars, plus some change. That was a fortune, and it had been incredibly easy to get. In fact, he had enjoyed it.

Except that he had killed a man.

He tried to tell himself that shooting the major had not been his fault, that he'd had no choice, but it didn't make him feel any better. He couldn't stay here and worry about it, though. There would be a posse after him as soon as the coach reached Austin. He crammed the stolen wallets into his saddlebags, and he started back for Kingdom.

He pushed Chinaco hard, doubling back, following stream-beds and rock ledges to throw off any pursuit. It was July 31 when he reached the Double H. While Fulgencio led off the weary roan, Chance presented Will a wad of greenbacks tied with a string.

"This is for you and Hope."

In front of the adobe house, Will and Hope stood stock still. They had been resigned to losing the ranch, to losing their dreams. They had been preparing to move to the country around Fort Phantom Hill, to start over. Now, literally at the last minute, they were saved. Will wiped his hands on his pants before touching the money, as if he were afraid of soiling it.

Chance beat the dust from his clothes. He ladled a long drink of water from the bucket on the gallery. His eyes searched out Hope's, but it was hard to tell what he read in them anymore. The love that had once been so obvious seemed blurred, uncertain. Certainly she would have no trouble reading the desire in his own eyes. Her dress was more patches than fabric these days, but she still glowed with that inner strength and beauty. It was all Chance could do not to take her in his arms. Lord, how he envied Will. Had it been any other man married to Hope, he would have hated him. With an unpleasant shock he realized that he might have killed him, as well.

Will turned over the thick pile of bills. "You been riding hard. Did you get this legal?"

Chance took his eyes from Hope. "No, I robbed a stage-coach," he said sarcastically. "How do you think I got it?"

"You tell me."

"I got it playing cards in Dallas, like before."

Will was skeptical. He hadn't thought Chance was up to a big game. "This is a lot of greenbacks. It's mostly Yankees that have paper money in this part of the country."

"There was a couple of Yank officers in the game. You know, rich boys with allowances." Chance laughed. "It was a combination of good luck and bad players."

"I hope that's the way it was," Will said. "I couldn't take it otherwise."

"What do you mean?"

"I got kids, Chance. What kind of example would that be for them? How could I preach honesty to them and then take stolen money?"

"How about losing your home? What kind of example is that?"

"At least we'd still be honest. They couldn't take that from us. I'd rather start over with nothing than think this was ill gotten."

Chance looked at Hope. He could tell that she agreed with Will. He thought they were both crazy. He said, "Well, set your honest mind at rest, partner, because I swear on the Bible, I didn't drop a single bad card to get this money."

Will nodded. Chance's word was good enough for him. His mood lightened. "You keep anything for yourself?"

Chance flashed his big grin, as much from relief as anything else. "Not as much as you got, but enough to restock my bar and hire some girls. I sure would like to see Vestry's face when he shows up here tomorrow."

"Ain't you staying the night?" Will said.

"If I get asked."

"You ain't got to be asked, Chance. Our home's yours. Right, Hope?"

"Of—of course," Hope said. Chance saw a funny look on her face. Maybe she was remembering how he'd tried to force himself upon her in this house. Suddenly he wondered about their son. He wondered where Tommy was and what he was doing, and there was a great pain in his heart.

It was hard for Chance that night, staying under the same roof as Hope, knowing there was only the thickness of a wall between them, longing to go to her but unable to do so. He tossed and turned and got little sleep. There were dark circles under his eyes when Vestry rode up next morning, accompanied by Amos Blaine.

"He isn't greedy or anything, is he?" Hope said. "He must have left Kingdom before first light."

Will and Hope went out onto the gallery. Politely Vestry said, "Good morning, Miss Hope. Good morning, Will." He drew up short as Chance came out, too. "Hello, Evans. I didn't expect to see you here."

"Lots of things happen in this life that we don't expect," Chance said.

Vestry turned back to Will. "I guess I don't have to tell you why I'm here."

"I guess you don't," Will said. He held out the wad of greenbacks. "Here's your money. Eight hundred dollars."

Vestry's polite look froze. He took the money.

"It's all there," Will said, "Count it."

"There's no need for that. I trust you. Do you mind telling me how you got it?"

"I reckon that's my business," Will said.

Vestry arched his dark eyebrows at Chance. "I suppose you had something to do with this."

"Maybe. Maybe not," Chance said.

Chance was disappointed. He had expected Vestry to explode with anger, but the man recovered well. He turned to Blaine. "Well, Amos, it looks like you'll have to wait to get that ranching experience." He turned back, fingering the crisp new bills. "This makes a tidy profit for me. It was an excellent investment. I'm only sorry it didn't turn out the same for you, Will."

"I'll bet," Hope said. "You won't object if we don't ask you in?"

"Not at all," Vestry said. To Will, he said, "My congratulations on saving your ranch." He touched his hat brim to Hope. "Ma'am, my congratulations. Come, Amos."

The two men turned their horses and rode off.

As they departed, Chance turned to Will. "Well, the ranch is still yours. What are you going to do now?"

Will's jaw muscles worked. He stared into the distance. "I'm going to wait till spring. Then I'm putting together another herd, twice as big this time, with twice as many men. I'm taking them north, and I'm going to sell them, and this time nothing on earth is going to stop me."

"What if Slidell and his Regulators come after you again?"

Will turned, and his look was grim. "They'll wish they hadn't."

36

True to his word, Will gathered another herd and took it north the following April.

There were twelve hundred cattle and fifty-eight horses. There were ten men, again hired on credit, with Sam Sommerville and Aaron Richardson among them. Lije Abernethy was again cook. This time the Texans were prepared for war. Besides revolvers, they carried seven-shot Spencer carbines, and Will had a new Henry repeating rifle. They weren't looking for trouble, but they weren't going to back down if trouble came.

Chance gave them the money to get outfitted, from his burgeoning saloon profits. Will did not have to get supplies and equipment from George Vestry this time. There were other stores in Kingdom now.

The day before Will went north, he rode into Kingdom to say good-bye. The town had continued to grow since last summer. Many of the tents had been replaced by buildings of wood. There were a church and a courthouse now. The people had showed their defiance of Yankee domination by naming their streets after Confederate generals—Lee, Jackson, Hood, Beauregard, Forrest. The town had long since seen its first man killed, a drunken soldier shot in a row over cards. Indeed, Kingdom was becoming noted for the frequency of gunplay on its streets and in its saloons.

Will hitched his horse and went into Chance's Kingdom. The saloon had undergone major changes, and Will sometimes wondered how much money Chance had won in that Dallas card game, anyhow. The building had been enlarged and a shingle roof added. A new walnut bar ran nearly the length of the room.

There were more gaming tables and plenty of men to run them—it was easy to hire men in Kingdom these days. The piano had been repaired, too, but most noticeable of all were the girls. Chance's welcome sign now claimed the BEST GIRLS IN TOWN. They circulated among the customers, and they plied their trade in a house behind the saloon, where the stagecoach corral used to be. The girls were certainly better looking than the Kansas Cow, but they seemed harder, more forbidding. Will knew that Chance took up with them himself, but for the life of him he didn't see how any man could find such women attractive.

Chance came up to Will. He wore his black suit, and he looked fit and confident. Will wore buckskins. He had sewn a strip of rawhide around the brim of his battered old hat, to stiffen it.

"All ready?" Chance asked.

"Ready as we'll ever be," Will said. "This is your last chance to come with us. We could use another good man."

Chance shook his head. "With business as good as it is, I can't afford to be gone that long, especially since you're taking Sam again. Besides, I told you—I hate cows."

Will grinned, and Chance said, "Hope and the kids staying with Curt?"

"Yeah. Ride out and see them once in a while, will you?"

"Sure," Chance said. "Be glad to."

"How are you making out with Vestry?"

"Same as always. He's trying to have me closed down. Says I'm running a disorderly house." Chance laughed. "Vestry's kind of a prude, you know. Having the girls right across the street from him really offends him. It's also taking business from him."

"You're taking business from everybody, it looks like," Will said, surveying the big crowd. "Any chance he'll be successful?"

"Nah. Judge Stringfellow is a Yankee—just like George claims to be these days—but he likes to come in here and visit my girls. He's already told me he'll rule there's insufficient grounds. Vestry'll have to do better than that to run me out."

Will grew serious. "You watch your back around Vestry, Chance. He don't like me, but he hates you. He'd like to see you dead, and with men like Shawcross and Lawton working for him, he's capable of doing it—especially Shawcross. I'm surprised he hasn't tried to kill you himself, after what you did to him.''

''He probably would have, but I think Vestry's held him in. Vestry doesn't want my death to look like murder. By the way, partner, don't sell yourself short. Vestry hates us both. We're the only threats to his power in this county.''

''I don't know about me so much,'' Will said, ''but that ain't the real reason he hates you. He hates you because no matter what he does or how powerful he gets, people will always like you better than they do him. And that's the most dangerous kind of hate.''

There seemed no more to say. Chance held out his hand. ''Well, good luck.''

''Thanks,'' Will said, ''I'll need it. Good luck to you, too. You may need it even more.''

The cattle started for Missouri the next morning. Will crossed the Clear Fork above Kingdom, to avoid taking the animals through town and possibly spooking them. A good portion of the town turned out to watch as, across the river, the long herd wound slowly through the red and yellow wildflowers, with the remuda and camp cart off to one side. The drovers waved their hats to the spectators. As last the drags disappeared over the hills, and only the dust of the herd could still be seen, suspended high in the bright noon sky.

37

On the last day of June, a series of violent thunderstorms rolled across the Clear Fork country. Chance wondered what it was like for cattle drovers like Will on the open prairie in this kind of weather. He could picture the stampedes, the confusion, the danger. It was not the life for him.

At last the storms ended. The night was cool after the previous sultry heat. The rain had washed away the noxious smells of the town, leaving the air sweet and refreshing. There were gurgling sounds, as water drained into the streets. In the distance, thunder still boomed dully, and lightning flickered along the horizon.

Chance put on his hat and went for a walk. He was going to see a woman. She was the wife of a freight contractor, who was out of town on a run to Fort Concho. The woman was a pleasant enough diversion, and if Chance closed his eyes, he could pretend that she was Hope.

He crossed muddy Main Street, heading for Beauregard Street and the woman's house. In the darkness, he almost bumped into George Vestry coming from the opposite direction.

Vestry's steps were unsteady. His high cheeks were flushed. His hat was off center, and several strands of greased hair hung across his forehead. He gave Chance a smug look.

Chance acknowledged him curtly. "Vestry. Don't often see you in drink."

"I don't often have this good a reason," said Vestry, beginning to smile.

"Oh? What's the reason?"

"You." Vestry's smiled broadened, and he laughed. "I'm finally getting rid of you."

The two men stopped. Other people on the street stopped, too, to watch them.

Chance was unimpressed. "Well, well, well. What kind of manly attack have you planned? Are you going to shoot me in the back, like you did that fellow in Austin? Or gun me down from ambush, like you did Jack Sommerville?"

"Even better than that," Vestry said. "I'm going to do it legally."

Vestry should have stopped there, but drink had made him overconfident. "Should I tell you? Sure, why not? What harm can it do? I've just come from the Bella Union." The Bella Union was the gathering spot for Kingdom's small band of Unionists. "I've been talking with some building contractors, up here from Houston. It seems the authorities are looking for a man who committed a murder during a stagecoach robbery near Austin last July. This was no ordinary murder. The victim was an army major. That means the federal government and the army want the killer. They want him very badly. So badly that they've offered two thousand dollars reward for information about him.''

Cold sweat prickled Chance's hair and the back of his neck. His mouth was dry. He tried to sound casual. "You telling me this for a reason?''

Vestry went on. "The murderer was wearing a hood, so the passengers didn't see his face, but they got a rough description of him. He was about, oh, your height and weight. He was wearing a red shirt and a black hat. He was also wearing a pair of Mexican *botas*, with a painted floral design.''

Chance's voice grew cold. "Say what you mean, Vestry.''

"That description fits you.''

"It fits a lot of people. A third of the men in Texas wear *botas* like that.''

Vestry shrugged. "Maybe.'' He started away, then he turned back. "Oh, I forgot. During the robbery, the major lost close to a thousand dollars in new greenbacks. Five days later, you turned up at Will Cooper's ranch with a pile of new greenbacks. Funny, isn't it?''

"I won that money playing cards,'' Chance said.

"Sure you did.'' Vestry leaned in close, so close that Chance could smell the whiskey and cigar smoke on his breath. "Oh, it was you all right, Evans. I've got you this time. I'm on my way to see Judge Stringfellow now, and give him the good news.'' He straightened. "Tell you what, Evans. I'm a generous man. I don't need to see you dead, just gone. You have a choice— clear out of town tonight, or stay and hang. Personally, I hope you're stupid enough to stay. I'd enjoy watching you swing. And the best part is, I'd get two thousand dollars for doing it.''

Vestry laughed and walked away, leaving Chance alone in the street.

Chance's chest rose and fell. His breath was heavy. His ... is opened and closed. Vestry was right. He had him.

Chance didn't want to hang, and he would not leave King-dom. He would not leave all that he had built here. He would not leave Hope. Vestry could not make him leave Hope.

Chance started after Vestry, walking rapidly in the mud. He

had no idea what he was going to do. He was acting purely from emotion. People were watching, but he didn't care.

"Vestry," he shouted. "Vestry, you son of a bitch!"

Vestry turned. He saw the uncontrollable anger on Chance's face, and a look of fear came over him as he realized the mistake he had made. He dropped his walking stick and reached under his coat for the pistol he carried there.

Chance went for his own gun. Both men fired. Something burned Chance's shoulder. Vestry staggered. Vestry raised his pistol again, but Chance fired first, and the shot jolted Vestry backward. As Vestry swayed on his feet, trying to regain his balance, Chance fired a third time. Vestry crumpled to his knees and pitched forward in the mud.

Chance stood over his fallen enemy, with his revolver smoking and thunder booming in the distance. Chance's shoulder was bleeding, but he felt no pain. People all around him were shouting. The Yankee sheriff came, taking Chance's revolver and arresting him.

Vestry lingered into the early hours of the morning before he died. Chance was held overnight, then let go. Everyone knew there had been bad blood between him and Vestry. People had seen the two men exchange words in the street, though no one had heard what was said, and there must have been two dozen witnesses who had seen Vestry draw first. Even Yankee justice had to acknowledge that Chance had acted in self-defense.

As Chance left the jail, with his shoulder newly bandaged, he was surrounded by a boisterous crowd. Most of the crowd supported Chance, but in front were Amos Blaine, Shawcross, and Neal Lawton. Shawcross stepped in front of Chance. Shawcross wore his revolver at his left hand now. He did everything with his left hand. The bones of his right one had fused from the stomping Chance had given them, and he had lost effective use of the hand. He pointed angrily. "Maybe the law's let you go, Evans, but that's not the end of it."

"All right, friend," said the sheriff, pushing Shawcross back.

Shawcross went on, waving his good hand. "Colonel Vestry ain't here to stop us now, Evans. You're a dead man."

"I said that's enough," the sheriff told him, "or I'll run you in for disturbing the peace."

Blaine and Neal Lawton dragged Shawcross away. Over his shoulder, Shawcross yelled, "Remember what I said!"

Chance went to his saloon and forted up. He knew he would have to come out and face Shawcross eventually. He'd have to face Neal Lawton, too. Lawton was Shawcross's best friend. Like Shawcross, he was big and bearded, the kind of man who went where he pleased and did what he wanted. He hated Chance, and he'd back any play that Shawcross made. Amos Blaine would no doubt join them. Vestry had made Blaine, and Blaine would want to avenge his death. Suddenly Blaine was not such an important man around Kingdom, and that would make him all the more eager for revenge.

The whole town waited for the explosion. Chance needed a plan.

Chance emerged from his sanctuary only once, taking a restless stroll during Vestry's funeral the next day, when he felt it would be safe. Either the funeral was shorter than he had expected, or he lost touch of time, because he stayed out too long, and on his way back he ran into Vestry's widow, Lucinda. Lucinda was dressed in black. She was heading for the new stage station. She was leaving Kingdom, to join her children in the east. Presumably Blaine would now look after Vestry's business interests.

Chance stopped as she approached. He remembered how good she'd once been to him, and he realized the burden that he'd inflicted on her. For all his faults, Vestry had been a good husband and father. Lucinda saw Chance, and tears flooded her eyes.

Chance didn't know what to say or do. He spread his arms helplessly. "Miss Lucinda. I'm sorry. I . . . I didn't . . ."

Lucinda just looked at him. Her well-bred good looks were pale and lined with grief. Then she lowered her eyes and swept around him.

Chance went back to his saloon. He sat by himself and brooded. He made a lot of decisions, about both the present and the future.

That night Chance went to Amos Blaine's house. He knocked on the door. Blaine answered, and when he saw who was there, he took a step back, convinced that his life was over.

Chance flashed his big grin. "Amos," he said, "how would you like to make some money?"

38

Blaine poured himself a drink. He rubbed a hand across his bald head. His house was neat for a bachelor's. On the mantel was an old tintype of his wife and son. It was one of the few items that was regularly dusted.

"How do I know this ain't a trap?" he asked after Chance had explained his idea. "How do I know you won't do for me, too?"

Chance said, "If I wanted to kill you, I'd do it right now. There's no witnesses."

Blaine downed part of the drink. Shrewdly he said, "Then how do you know I won't turn the tables and set you up, instead?"

"Greed," Chance told him. "You're smart, Amos, but not smart enough to run a big operation. You're not a leader. Left by yourself, you'll eventually run Vestry's business into the ground. Come with me and you can make big money. I have plans, and I'm going to need a right-hand man."

"I thought Sam Sommerville was your right-hand man."

"Sam won't be interested in the things I have in mind."

Blaine finished his drink. "Big money, you say?"

"You know me, Amos. I don't do things small. I have expensive tastes, and I have a lot of lost time to make up for. I'll see you get your share."

Blaine considered. The lamplight reflected off the sharp angles of his face, making a pattern of light and shadow. At last he smiled. It was a cynical smile. "All right. All right, I'll do it."

"Good," Chance said. "Now here's the way it'll be."

* * *

The next day Chance sat on a stool by the doors of his saloon. The saloon was closed and its employees had been sent home. Across Chance's knees was a sawed-off 10-gauge shotgun, loaded with Blue Whistlers. Chance watched the street. People hurried through the area between his place and Vestry's, or they avoided it altogether, afraid of trouble.

The day dragged on. About five in the afternoon, Chance spotted Shawcross and Lawton in the alley behind Vestry's store, which was also closed. They entered the bar, where Blaine had invited them to formulate plans for killing Chance.

Chance waited. At sunset Blaine appeared briefly on the street, as if getting a breath of air. He looked idly around, then he wiped his forehead with his sleeve. That was the signal that Shawcross and Lawton were drunk. Then Blaine went back into the bar.

Chance waited awhile longer, until dark. He was nervous but determined. Time and again he went over what he was going to do, mentally preparing for anything that could go wrong. At last he rose from his stool, stretched, and went out the doors, carrying the shotgun.

He crossed the street to Vestry's store. His presence attracted attention, even in the dark. People got out of his way, at the same time following him at a safe distance, to see what was going to happen.

Chance went behind Vestry's store. The single door to the bar was open. Blaine had seen to that. Chance heard the men inside, arguing. "I still don't like that idea, Roy," Lawton was saying. "Do it while he's asleep. It'll be safer. I know how to make a bomb, I seen it done in the war. We can—"

"No," Shawcross's drunken voice rumbled, "do it in the saloon. I want him awake. He crippled my hand, and I want him to see me before I kill him. I want him to know who done it. I want to see the look on his smart-ass face."

Lawton said, "I keep telling you, it's too risky. Chance is too good with a gun. I don't want to take no chances on getting killed myself. What do you think, Amos? You're bein' awful quiet."

Blaine said, "I ain't sure. There's things to be said for both ways. Here, have another drink."

Chance thumbed back the shotgun's heavy hammers. He took a deep breath. Then he went quietly in.

By the lantern light, he could see that the three men were alone, as arranged. Blaine, looking nervous, had Shawcross and Lawton at one end of the bar, with their backs turned. They were passing a bottle.

Chance strode quickly across the room, raising the shotgun to his waist. Blaine saw him and moved out of the way.

Shawcross and Lawton realized something was wrong. They turned and saw Chance coming at them. Shawcross dropped the bottle, breaking it. Chance had expected them to go for their guns, but they didn't. Neither man moved.

Chance smiled.

Chance pointed the shotgun at Shawcross and fired one barrel into his stomach. Shawcross was blown off his feet. Chance swung the weapon and fired the second barrel into Lawton. The blast slammed Lawton into the bar. Lawton hung there a moment, then he collapsed in a heap.

Both men were dead, torn apart by the close-range blasts of buckshot. Blaine stood terrified at the end of the bar. He and Chance looked at each other, and Chanced nodded. Blaine backed away and left the building. Chance removed Shawcross's and Lawton's pistols from their holsters, and he put them near their hands. Then he calmly stepped to the bar and waited for the sheriff.

This time Chance was not even arrested. He had been threatened by Shawcross and Lawton in front of half the town. Everyone had known a shootout was coming. There was some concern that Chance had provoked the fight, but since he had been outnumbered three to one by Vestry's men, he was considered within his rights to choose the time and place of battle. By the standards of the frontier, it had been a fair fight, and the verdict of self-defense was so obvious that it was useless to go through the time and expense of a trial. On Chance's suggestion, Judge Stringfellow got Chance and Blaine to meet and promise that there would be no more trouble between them, and the matter was considered at an end.

Chance went to his shack behind the saloon. He took a bottle of whiskey with him. He sat on the bed and he drank the bottle down, methodically, slug after slug. He had to have it. He had to get drunk, even though getting drunk only made him feel worse. He kept seeing the looks on Shawcross's and Lawton's faces when he had gunned them down.

Chance had been able to rationalize killing the army major and Vestry. Both men had drawn first. This time he could not pretend. This time he had crossed over the line, to murder. Not only that, but he knew that he'd do it again if he had to, and it would not bother him. He remembered how he'd once run from Nacogdoches to avoid a shootout—and been proud of himself for doing it. How could he have changed so much? What had happened to him?

He kept drinking, consumed by inner torment, until he passed out.

He was awakened by a hand shoving him roughly.

"Wake up. Chance, wake up." The voice was Will's.

Chance opened his eyes. It was bright daylight, and Will was standing over him, dressed in new clothes and hat, grinning from ear to ear. Chance's head hurt. So did his eyes. His tongue felt thick.

"We sold the cattle," Will said excitedly. "Not in Missouri, in Kansas. A new place called Abilene. We met their agents on the trail. They're begging for Texas cattle up there. We were one of the first herds in. We got twenty-three dollars a head. That's almost twenty-eight thousand dollars."

Will tossed a huge satchel of money onto Chance's chest. "Here's your share," he said, and he began laughing. "We're rich, Chance. We're rich!"

Part V

39

1874

On the first Saturday of July, as he did on the first Saturday of every month, Will Cooper took his family to town.

Will and Hope were in the front of the two-seater wagon, with the children in back—Ellen, Alex, and James, age seven. They were accompanied by Rusty Harding and a well-armed party of ranch hands, or cowboys, as they liked to be called now.

At forty-two, Will looked every inch the cattle king—gruff, stern, squinty-eyed, with a flowing mustache. He didn't like the term cattle king, but that was what people called him, and he was forced to maintain the image. He wore a dark suit and a wide-brimmed hat, and his old Henry repeater was on the box beneath his seat.

Beside him, Hope was a mature beauty of thirty-five. Beneath her fashionable hat, her reddish hair was brushed to a bright sheen, hiding the few strands of gray that had started to creep in. Her bottle-green dress was well cut but plain, and she refused to wear a bustle. She had servants now, but she could still plow a field if she had to, or chop wood, or hold off a war party.

They left the big stone house, with the locked sets of deer antlers above the doors. They drove past the corrals, past the branding chutes, out the big gate, and onto the road to town. It was the hottest, driest summer in years, and the horses raised a large cloud of dust. Occasionally they saw cattle—their cattle—grazing along the creek or resting in the shade.

In the backseat, Ellen adjusted her parasol against the sun. Ellen was fourteen, but she looked least three years older. She had budding breasts and a curved figure, and she was conscious of them. Her father was the richest man in three counties, and she was conscious of that, as well. She did not worry about her dresses growing small now. She had more dresses than she could wear, though that did not stop her from buying more. Will and Hope had indulged her every whim, perhaps as overcompensation for the loss of Tommy, perhaps because of the hardships that Ellen had endured as a child.

"I don't see why we have to take this old wagon," Ellen complained. "The new surrey's much nicer. Why did we buy it, if we're not going to use it?"

"We took it because it's faster in case we run into Indians," Will told her. Besides, he felt silly in the new surrey. It was way too fancy for his tastes.

Ellen twirled the parasol with irritation. "Oh, we won't see any Indians."

"Jeez, Sis," said her brother Alex, "don't you know we're in the middle of an Indian war? Didn't you hear about the fight at Adobe Walls?"

"That's hundreds of miles away," she said.

"The Jacksboro Road ain't," Will said, "and Indians killed a man on it two days ago. They stole some horses from Lee Dyer, and they chased one of Aaron Richardson's hands ten miles before they gave up on him. That's why we brought the extra men with us."

Hope said, "It's not just Indians, Will. Kingdom County's more lawless now than it's ever been. Robberies, horse and cattle stealing. It keeps getting worse. When is it going to stop?"

"I wish I knew," Will said.

"You had a chance to do something about it," Hope said pointedly.

"I had reasons for saying no. It ain't my kind of job. I'm a cattleman, not a lawman."

"Somebody's got to do it."

"Somebody, maybe. Not me."

They reached town. Kingdom was even more crowded than usual, with refugees from outlying ranches and farms seeking protection from the Indians, with buffalo hunters who had been chased off their ranges and were waiting for the trouble to end. Wagons were parked in every available space, loaded with furniture and valuables. Bonneted women tried to keep some sort of house, while children squalled and men played the fiddle or cards, to pass the time.

Will's wagon moved slowly along California Street, which was jammed with horses, with mule teams and ox teams, with vehicles of all size and description. People thronged the plank sidewalks—soldiers, both black and white, teamsters, buffalo hunters, cowboys, businessmen, gamblers, Tonkawa Indians, drifters, and plain riffraff. There were few women, other than whores. On one corner stood a black man playing a banjo, with his hat on a chair for money and a group of black soldiers and children in attendance.

There were six hundred permanent residents of Kingdom, though at any one time at least twice that many people were likely to be in town, due to the great number of transients. The principal streets were lined with false-fronted wooden buildings, with here and there a structure, such as the courthouse, of limestone or adobe. The town smelled of animals. It smelled of leather and sweat, of musty buffalo hides. It smelled from the distillery and the brewery. It moved to a cacophony of piano music, of yells and shouts, of neighing horses and barking dogs. By sundown there would be gunshots, as well.

Kingdom had become one of the wildest towns in the west. Brawls and shootings were frequent. There was constant tension between blacks and whites, between soldiers and townsmen, between gamblers and cowboys and buffalo hunters, all of it fueled by oceans of cheap whiskey. The law was powerless to stop the violence, though the town marshals tried their best. At one point, the desperate city council had hired a self-styled gunfighter to police the town, in much the way that Abilene had once employed the man known as Wild Bill. On his first week in office, the gunfighter had gotten drunk and shot a man in the street for refusing his order to halt. When it was learned that the victim had been deaf, the gunfighter had been dismissed from his post, and the great experiment had ended.

Will eased the wagon into a group of parked vehicles outside Sam Sommerville's store. Sam had used his share of the profits from the first cattle drive to buy George Vestry's old business. He had rebuilt the store of adobe and expanded it. He had been one of the first to enter the trade for buffalo hides, and he had a large hide yard out back. Hope took the children inside the store.

James needed new flannel shirts, and Alex wanted a mouth organ. Ellen would never buy anything from a general store, even one owned by her uncle, though she would deign to go in and order from the better catalogues.

"Meet us at three o'clock, out front of Gorman's Restaurant," Will told Rusty.

While Rusty and the hands rode off on their own business, Will crossed the busy street to Chance's Kingdom. If Will was Kingdom's most prominent citizen, Chance was its most notorious. He was famed as a gambler and a gunman. Most of the stories about him were made up, though several years ago he had killed a buffalo skinner in a dispute over cards, and before that he'd shot a wagon boss for the same reason. From time to time he disappeared up the cattle trails to the Kansas boom towns, and there were rumors of a shooting scrape in Ellsworth, but Chance never talked of it.

Chance's Kingdom had become a frontier palace. All traces of the former building were gone. Only the name was the same. The new building was three times as large, with a shingle roof. Its sign now boasted the BEST GIRLS IN TEXAS. It boasted the best whiskey and the best games, too. Trail-herding cowboys had spread its fame from the Rio Grande to the Platte. Will pushed through the gaudily painted building's batwing doors. Inside there was music, laughter, and shouting, amid a pall of tobacco smoke. On one side was the long walnut bar. Behind the bar, on the paneled wall, the picture of the Alamo had been replaced by a large mirror, with rows of bottles in front of it. There was a back room with a roulette wheel and tables for poker, faro, and other games. On this late Saturday morning, the saloon was mobbed with men of all kinds, save for the black soldiers of the Tenth Cavalry, who for the last several years had formed part of Fort Stanley's garrison. They had their own bars, their own part of town.

Will saw Chance waiting for him at the bar, with an uncorked bottle of beer. Chance's body had thickened over the years, from liquor, good food, and lack of exercise. His dark hair was liberally seeded with gray.

As Will moved through the crowd, Chance looked at his watch. He shook his head and grinned. "Eleven-thirty," he said. "Right on time, like always." He put the watch in a pocket of his silk vest, and he handed Will the beer. These visits of Will's had become a monthly ritual. They were about the only times that the two friends saw each other anymore.

Will sipped the cool beer, feeling it cut the dust in his throat. Chance motioned to the white-jacketed bartender for a whiskey.

"Want to sit down?" Chance said.

Will said, "No. Standing's fine, after riding in that wagon."

Chance pulled a fat envelope from his black coat. He gave it to Will, another act of the ritual. "Here's your half of the month's profits."

Will put the envelope in his own coat, without looking inside. He pulled out another envelope that was at least twice as thick. "And here's yours. I got thirty-five a head on that herd Aaron took to Ogallala. After the panic last year, I'm one of the few people that's got cattle to sell."

He sighed as Chance pocketed the envelope. "Alex is driving me crazy, trying to make me let him go on a drive. He has fits when I tell him he's too young. He's only twelve, and already he thinks he's my right-hand man."

Chance laughed. Will no longer went on the drives. Mostly he consigned his herds to professional trail bosses, like Aaron Richardson, or he sold them to buyers at the ranch and let them take the cattle themselves. If his own men were to conduct the drive, Rusty, who was now foreman, usually led them. Fulgencio had taken his money from the first Abilene drive and returned to Mexico, with his brother's bones, to buy a ranch there.

The two friends were approached by a bleached blonde with a fetching figure and a suggestive walk. The blonde's ruffled dress exposed her creamy white shoulders. Her hair, which was almost white, was pinned and braided in the latest style. She casually hooked her arm through Chance's. "Hi, honey," she said. "Hello, Mr. Cooper."

Will nodded. He was ill at ease around women, especially women of this kind. "Hello, Miss Julie." Julie was Chance's latest girl, the latest in a long line.

Chance smiled at Will's discomfort. He winked at the girl. "Run along, Julie. Will and I want to talk. I'll see you in a little while."

"All right," Julie said brightly. She moved off toward the

gaming tables. One benefit of being Chance's girl was that she did not have to service the customers.

"Nice girl," Chance said, watching her go.

"Mm," Will said. He saw her stop to talk with Amos Blaine. Even after all this time, it was hard for Will to get used to the idea of Blaine working for Chance. Chance said he did a good job, though. Blaine had saved enough money to buy a small ranch of his own in Hidden Valley.

Idly Will said, "Jake Koerner and some other prominent types was out to see me last week."

"What did they want?"

"To talk about all the rustling and horse stealing that's been going on. Seems there's some around here think I'm involved, on account of my ranch is hardly ever hit."

"That's crazy."

"That's what Jake says." Will looked over at Chance. "He thinks you're behind it."

Chance met Will's look. He snorted. "That's what happens when you elect a blacksmith mayor."

"He thinks you're behind the stagecoach holdups, too, and the freight robberies. He says you've got a gang and a secret hideout somewhere."

"That's the stupidest thing I ever heard," Chance said.

"That's what I told him. Him and the others want me to run for county sheriff. They say I'm the only one who can put a stop to the trouble."

"Are you going to do it?"

"No. I got enough to do with the ranch."

Was it Will's imagination, or did relief flash across Chance's face? One reason, maybe the main reason, why Will hadn't offered to run was because, deep inside, he had been afraid that being sheriff would eventually bring him into conflict with Chance.

He sipped his beer, wincing against a sudden upsurge in the noise. He could never get used to living with this racket, and he hated breathing this foul tobacco smoke. He couldn't understand why Chance liked this kind of life. "I got something else to tell you."

"Now what? Somebody think I'm behind Lincoln's assassination, too?"

"You know the army's going to campaign against the Comanches and Kiowas?"

"Know it? The soldiers don't talk about anything else. Half of 'em didn't even get drunk last payday. They were afraid they'd land in the guardhouse and get left behind."

"Well, Colonel Benedict has invited you and me to go with them as scouts, or auxiliaries, or whatever we want to call ourselves."

"Any money in it?"

"We'd be temporarily commissioned in our old military ranks, captain and colonel."

"That means you'd outrank me. You never outranked me in the field before."

"It's just a title, Chance. Don't be so touchy. It ain't like I'm going to be giving you orders or nothing, telling you when to go to bed."

Chance motioned for a new drink. He sipped it thoughtfully. "What's it been, twenty-three years, and we're still fighting Indians here? If you had told me it would be like this when we started, I'd never have believed you."

Will was bitter. "It should have ended years ago. It would have, if it wasn't for the government's Peace Policy. Our lives don't mean a thing to them do-gooders back east. All they care about is protecting 'Nature's Children.' "

"They sure aren't much of an advertisement for Nature," Chance observed dryly.

Will drank more beer. Because of the government's policy of protecting the Indians, there were hundreds more Texans who had suffered tragedies as bad or worse than Will's own. Will had never stopped trying to find Tommy. Hope had taught him how to read and write properly, in part so he could deal with Northern bankers and cattle brokers, but also so that he could write the agencies and forts to see if they had word of his son or of any captives who resembled him—although the Quaker Indian agents would not always reveal the presence of white captives, lest their charges get in trouble. So far, all of Will's efforts had proved fruitless. Tommy might as well have dropped off the face of the earth.

"The army's had it with the Peace Policy," Will said. "Colonel Benedict says they mean to finish the Indians properly this time."

"Are you going to go?" Chance said.

"I believe I will."

Chance patted his ample belly. "I haven't been in the field in years. Still, I could get up for a big killing of Indians." Chance had his own thoughts about Tommy, and they were thoughts of revenge. "All right, I'm game. When do we leave?"

"Soon as the army gets their resupply worked out. This grass-hopper plague has played hell with getting feed."

Chance grinned broadly. "This'll be like old times, won't it? You and me. You told Hope yet?"

Will nodded.

"She won't try to stop you?"

Will laughed. "Hope would probably go herself, if they'd let her."

"She'd probably do a good job, too," Chance said.

When they had finished their drinks, Chance walked outside with Will. They stood on the bustling sidewalk, with people flowing around them.

"It's really changed, hasn't it?" Chance said. "Hell, I remember this town when it was called 'Saloon.' I remember when it was so small that sometimes we used to build a fire in the street—right there—and we'd all eat supper together, roast a wild cow or buffalo. Jules Villette was there then, and Tom Nye." He shook his head. "Those days are long gone now."

Now Will was the pillar of the community. He was everybody's hero, and Chance was a gambler, a gunman. It irked Chance that nobody remembered him as a Ranger. Nobody remembered him as a hero. He wondered if that was what had driven him to his secret life of crime. Or was it jealousy, jealousy that Will, who would not have survived without him, was now worth far more, in both money and social prestige? Had his friendship for Will turned into a form of hatred? Or had he turned bad because crime was so easy and the rewards so great— or even because it was such fun?

Across the street, Chance saw Hope and the children leaving Sam's store. They waited for Will under the porch awning. The sight of Hope made Chance go tight inside, as it always did. His mouth grew dry. He lived for these moments, watching Hope from a distance when she was in town, or at some infrequent social function. It was all he had of her anymore. Hope had become like a church at which he worshipped. She had become remote, lofty, and his love for her had become ever more abstract. He never gave up hope that she would return to him, though. There was always a chance that something would happen to Will, and if it did, Chance intended to be there to pick up the pieces.

Beside Hope, Alex was playing his new mouth organ, while James climbed on a hitching post. Ellen twirled her parasol, well aware of the stares she drew from passing men. She could get her little nose up in the air, too. She was going to cause somebody a lot of trouble someday.

"Come on," Will said, rapping Chance's shoulder. "Let's cross. Say hello to Hope and the kids."

40

"I'd forgot how much fun soldiering can be," Will said.

It was a foul October evening. The rain was pouring down. It had been coming down for days. The column had gone into camp on the desolate prairie, somewhere north of the Pease. Will huddled in his yellow slicker. Rain streamed off his hat brim. "This brings back a lot of memories, and ain't none of them good."

"Just remember, it was your idea," Chance told him. Chance's head was half hidden under his drawn-up blankets. They were sitting near the small fire that served as the officers' mess, with their backs to the wind, like everyone else. A ground sheet had been spread on poles above the fire, to keep out the rain long enough to brew coffee. At that, they had been lucky to find enough burnable wood.

Will went on. "It wasn't two weeks ago this was a desert,

and we all come close to dying of thirst. Now we're drowning. What's next?''

"Snow, probably," Chance said, and the nearby officers laughed. There was nothing else to do under the circumstances.

Around them, soldiers in rubberized ponchos tended horses, huddled around small fires like their own, came and went from guard and patrol. These black soldiers were well trained and disciplined. Perhaps because blacks had few opportunities on the outside, they deserted less than whites and there were more reenlistments, which meant that the men of the Tenth Cavalry were older and more experienced than those of the average white unit. Unlike white soldiers, who wore pretty much what they pleased on campaign, the "buffalo soldiers" stuck close to the basic uniform, save for the flimsy black campaign hats, which everyone despised. Most of the men wore forage caps or wide-brimmed hats purchased with their own money in town.

The column had been in the field since early September, when five companies of cavalry and two of infantry had left Fort Stanley. Four other columns, equally strong, were converging on the Staked Plains from other posts, driving before them all the Indians who had fled the reservations and the ones who had never come in. They intended to keep the Indians on the run, giving them no peace, no time to camp or hunt. They would stay out until every hostile had been either killed or disarmed and taken to the reservations around Fort Sill.

It had been a grueling campaign. Colonel Benedict had ordered that no bugles be blown, and sabers had been left behind. The cavalry went ahead, while the infantry followed with the supply train. Every few days the two groups rendezvoused and set up a base camp, where they awaited the resupply trains from Fort Stanley. The Indians knew the soldiers were coming. From far-off buttes and mesas, their scouts saw the column's dust cloud. There had been skirmishes, with casualties on both sides. Several times the Indians had tried to run off the column's horse herd. Dispatch riders had been attacked and sometimes killed. Once the Indians had even circled behind the column and attacked the supply train. But the soldiers came doggedly on, pushing ever deeper into the trackless wastes, while their foes vanished before them, refusing to come to grips. It had been like looking for the proverbial needle in the haystack. The distances were unimaginably vast. The land seemed to have swallowed the Indians without a trace.

Will and Chance rode with Colonel Benedict and his staff. Sometimes they went out with the Indian scouts, or they went hunting for buffalo or antelope to help feed the command. They ate in the officers' mess, and in base camp they shared a Sibley tent with the other officers. In the field they slept under the stars or, as they would tonight, in the rain.

The coffee was ready. "Army coffee, gentlemen," said Harry Benedict, the one-armed colonel who commanded the Tenth Cavalry. "This will clean you out—if there's anything left inside you, that is."

Several of the officers laughed grimly. Some were breaking ancient hardtack with their revolver butts. The adjutant sat with a pencil and sodden paper, struggling over a report.

Will gratefully accepted a steaming cup of coffee from the mess attendant. "This wet weather makes my bones ache," he said. "Must be a sign I'm getting old." The weather made the scars on his back ache, too, but he never mentioned them.

Chance grumbled. "The only good thing I can say about this campaign is that I can fit in my buckskin jacket again. There's nothing like a little dysentery to get your weight down." The campaign had been hard on Chance. He had suffered everything from fever to saddle sores. The cold, damp, and frequent walking bothered his left leg, the one he'd broken years before, and he had often been left limping with pain.

The colonel, a spare, active man with a trim cavalry mustache and goatee, was sitting next to Chance. He laughed and sipped his coffee. "I must compliment you, Captain Evans. You've borne up remarkably well. I confess, I had doubts about asking you along, but you've never once complained. You've done everything that's been asked of you and more. I've known Colonel Cooper since I took over at Fort Stanley, of course. I knew his reputation as a soldier. But I knew you only by your reputation from town, a reputation that is somewhat less than flattering."

Some of the officers grunted ruefully. They had lost enough money at Chance's gaming tables. Benedict went on. "It was Colonel Cooper who persuaded me to bring you. He told me of your exploits fighting Mexicans and Indians. I had no idea you were such a hero.'' He smiled. ''I'm glad I took his advice.''

''Thanks,'' Chance said, as rainwater spilled from his hat brim into his coffee. ''Next time tell him to recommend somebody else.''

Harry Benedict was a hard-driving professional soldier. A Virginian by birth, he had stayed with the Union during the Civil War. He'd been a general then, and he'd lost his left arm at Brandy Station. After the war, the only way a crippled officer could remain in the service was by joining a black regiment. He had been determined to make the Tenth the finest regiment on the frontier. Many felt that he had succeeded.

The wind gusted, whipping rain against the men's backs. They huddled over their coffee, wrapping overcoats and blankets more tightly around them. The cold seeped up through the rubber ground sheets on which they sat. ''My son will never forgive General Sheridan for not delaying this campaign until next year,'' Benedict told the men. ''He's a senior at West Point. He wouldn't have missed this for the world.''

Chance thought that statement reflected either on the boy's youth or on his sanity. ''You come from a military family?'' he said.

Benedict laughed. ''Good Lord, no. My father was a barber in Richmond.''

''How'd you end up being a soldier?''

''It's in my blood, I guess. Something I wanted to do ever since I can remember. I studied hard in school, and my father made some helpful contacts in his work, and eventually I won an appointment to West Point.''

He spoke offhandedly, but Chance bet that feat hadn't been easy for a barber's son in prewar Virginia, where dozens of young aristocrats would have competed for those appointments.

''I love the army,'' Benedict went on somewhat wistfully. ''My only worry is that they'll make me leave. Every time there's a Benzine Board to weed out unfit officers, my status comes up because of this damned arm. I don't know what I'd do if they retired me. Hire out to some foreign army, I expect. I hear the Mexicans are always looking for officers.''

''Let's hope it doesn't come to that, sir,'' said Major Harcourt, the second-in-command.

"Indeed. More coffee, gentlemen?" Benedict smiled. "Then we can all turn in for a nice, refreshing night's sleep."

The wind gusted again. The rain fell harder.

At last the rains ended, and there was a fine spell of Indian summer weather. The column pushed past the Cap Rock, up onto the Staked Plains. Still no Indians were found, save those hovering endlessly on the column's flanks. Then Chance's prediction came true, and winter set in. There were biting northers, with temperatures plunging forty degrees in two hours. There was rain, sleet, and snow. The supplies from Fort Stanley were held up in the rear. The tents, with the little shelter they provided, could not reach the rendezvous points. Still the column marched on.

"They're out there somewhere," Benedict swore. "They have to be."

Mornings were the worst. Mornings were when you wanted to stay put and quietly slip into the warm peace of death. Every morning Will dragged his frozen body from his frozen blankets to face a frozen dawn. He had never been this cold, not even in the war. Then there had always been the promise of an eventual bivouac, of a campfire. Here the only prospect was for more cold. Will wore two undershirts, two pairs of drawers, and extra socks. He had on two flannel shirts and a buckskin shirt, a coat, a buffalo robe coat, a scarf, buffalo skins over his trousers, and thick buffalo-skin boots, like the Indians. He had stuffed the nooks and crannies of this getup with newspaper. He was so bundled up that he could hardly move, and still he was cold. Except for his leg, the cold didn't seem to bother Chance as much. He actually seemed to become stronger the longer they stayed out. He seemed to become more driven, as if he were afraid they wouldn't find any Indians.

The bad weather continued. Men and horses sickened and died. There was no grazing, and the grain was nearly exhausted. Colonel Benedict was on the point of calling off the campaign and returning to Fort Stanley when they had a stroke of luck. During a brief mild spell, one of their patrols caught a Comanchero and his wagon crossing the plain, returning to New Mexico.

The Comanchero was brought back to the column. Bruises on his face gave witness to his interrogation.

"Did he tell you where the Indian camp is?" Benedict asked the sergeant in charge of the patrol.

The husky sergeant shook his head. "He's a hard case, sir. We couldn't get him to talk."

"I'll make him talk," Chance said.

Chance pulled his sheath knife and ran his thumb along the blade. Behind his dark beard, he was grim and hollow-eyed. "A couple of you men tie him to a wagon wheel. The rest of you ride ahead. I'll be along directly."

After a while, Chance caught up to the column. The knife was in its sheath. There was no sign of the Comanchero.

"Did he talk?" Benedict said.

"He did. He said the Comanches and Kiowas have a winter camp in a canyon about two days ride south and east of here. He said they think we've gone back to the fort. He thought so, too, or he never would have tried to make New Mexico."

No one asked what had happened to the Comanchero. No one had to.

Will didn't approve of what Chance had done to the Comanchero, but he understood. Comancheros furnished the Indians with guns, ammunition, and whiskey, taking stolen money, horses, and sometimes captives in return. A captured Comanchero could expect no mercy from Texans. When Benedict sent a detail back to bury the man and get the wagon, they found that the Comanchero had been scalped.

The column turned and marched for the canyon. Soon after, a snowstorm descended on the Texas plains. There was little visibility. The column moved by compass. The wind whipped snow in the men's eyes, lashing their faces. Eyebrows and beards were coated white. The gaunt horses wanted to drift before the storm, and it was hard holding them.

The storm lasted a day before playing itself out. The wind died. During the following day there was a brief melt-off, then a hard freeze. The horses' hoofs crunched the frozen snow cutting their lower legs. Night fell, and no camp was made. The column pushed on, guided by the moon and the light of a million stars over the slivery expanse of snow.

Then Tonk scouts came in, saying that the canyon was ahead, and a big camp was in sight.

Word was whispered down the column for the troop commanders. Together with Will and Chance, the officers rode ahead for perhaps a mile, then dismounted and left their horses with some of the scouts, who were waiting there. They marched forward, mounted a low rise amid a snow-covered stand of piñon pine and scrub cedars, and they found themselves staring into an enormous canyon, shadowy and mysterious in the moonlight.

The canyon was twisting and irregular, with tree-covered rock ledges and, here and there, side canyons opening out of it. A wooded stream meandered down the middle. Strung out as far as the eye could see, on both sides of the stream, were a series of Indian villages, slumbering in the darkness. That mass of slow-moving animals must be the pony herd—yes, there was the faint tinkle of a bell mare. Somewhere a dog was barking.

Some of the officers sucked in their breaths at the sight. Benedict whispered, "Well, gentlemen, this is what we came for."

With his one hand, the colonel raised his field glasses, holding them lightly to his eyes because of the intense cold, studying the canyon. Will could feel excitement and tension rising within the little group. The only sound was the wind sighing through the pines.

Benedict lowered the glasses. "It's a big camp, Comanches and Kiowas both. Five hundred warriors, at least. I'd like to reconnoiter the ground, but there's no time. We must strike while we have the element of surprise."

He looked around the assembled officers. He tried to sound calm, but he had a hard time keeping the eagerness from his voice. "B Company are the best shots. Mr. Clark, you will take some scouts and take your men upstream. Find a way down the bluffs. Leave your horses if you have to. Form a blocking force at the far end of the village."

"Yes, sir," said B Company's commander.

"The remainder of the battalion will move to the canyon floor. Mr. Rutherford and his scouts will lead, followed by A, E, D, and I, in that order. Forward by twos on the bottom, and come onto line as soon as you clear the line of trees. A Company and the first two platoons of E will attack up the far side of the stream. D Company and the second two platoons of E will attack on the left. I Company will be in reserve."

"Damn," muttered I's commander in disappointment.

"I will ride on the far side, with E. We attack at first light. The sounding of 'Charge' will be the signal."

The men stirred excitedly. Bugle calls meant a lot to soldiers, and this would be the first bugle heard on the expedition.

"If we're discovered before then, come into action as you come onto line. Mr. Rutherford, when the action begins, you and your Tonkawas will capture the pony herd. Get them downstream where the savages cannot recover them."

"Yes, sir," said young Rutherford.

Benedict grew more intense. "There is to be no smoking, no talking in ranks. All commands are to be passed by hand signal. If there's any noise, I'll have the offender spread-eagled for a week. Is that understood?"

It was.

"Any questions?"

There were none.

Benedict pulled out his watch. He opened the case and studied the face by moonlight. "I make it three twenty-two. By sundown today the Indian wars in Texas will be over."

He snapped the watch shut and put it away. "Very well, gentlemen. Rejoin your troops. And good luck."

41

Waiting.

Horses stamped and snorted. The breath of men and animals was frosty in the cold.

The cold seeped through Will's buffalo-skin boots. It seeped through his layers of clothing. All around, the black soldiers were quietly preparing for battle, securing their equipment. Many were removing their caped greatcoats and tying them to their saddles. Though he was already shivering, Will took off his buffalo coat. He would soon be warm enough.

Like the soldiers, Will and Chance made a last check of their weapons. Besides his Henry repeater, Will had two Colt .44's, rechambered to accept the new metallic cartridges. Chance carried a pair of new Colt .45's and a new Winchester repeater. His horse was the big, black gelding that had replaced Chinaco. Chinaco had grown old, and Chance had sold him to a farmer from the new settlement of Wilcox.

Rutherford, the young lieutenant in charge of scouts, came up. He saluted Colonel Benedict, and with gestures he indicated that his men had found a way down the bluffs to the canyon floor.

Benedict nodded. He turned to Major Harcourt and gave the hand signal to move out.

The signal was passed down the column. The men started forward, leading their horses. Will felt the cold receding as battle approached. There was a growing tightness in the pit of his stomach. He'd felt it a hundred times before going into action. This time was scarier somehow. It was like the time before the battle on the Canadian, in '58. Fighting Indians was not like fighting Yankees. Maybe it was because of what Indians did to a man if they captured him. He remembered Rodolfo's body, what it had looked like.

Guided by the scouts, the battalion started down the bluffs. They had to go slowly. It was difficult negotiating the narrow switchbacks. The snow was frozen, and it turned to ice with the passage of men and shod horses over it. Every few minutes the men had to stop and chop breaks in the ice with their knives and axes, to stop it from becoming so slippery, all the while trying to be as quiet as possible. Far away, the dog was still barking.

Once at the canyon bottom, the soldiers mounted. They rode forward by company, in twos. After passing a belt of cottonwoods, they came onto line on both sides of the stream. They were about a half mile downstream from the first village.

One-armed Colonel Benedict was slightly ahead of the formation, with the bugler at his side. The colonel waved his hand, and the line advanced. In the Indian camp, more dogs were barking now, but the sleeping Indians paid no attention. They probably thought that the barking was occasioned by wolves. They never imagined that the soldiers could reach them here, in this weather.

The soldiers rode slowly forward, checking their eager horses. The sky was sullen with the promise of dawn. Ahead, dark lodges were visible against the snow and the sides of the canyon.

Benedict motioned the command to draw weapons. Each man pulled out his revolver.

The line increased speed. Their rumble grew louder in the icy snow. The camp dogs were barking furiously now. There were whinnies from the pony herd. Will thought it impossible that they had not been discovered.

There was a flash of light from the lodges, followed by the crack of a rifle shot.

Colonel Benedict turned. "Bugler, sound the 'Charge,' if you please."

The bugler snapped his instrument to his lips. He began blowing the stirring notes of the "Charge." As one, the men put spurs to their horses and bounded forward. The bugle died after the first few notes, because the instrument froze to the bugler's lips, but it was enough. The men went in yelling and cheering, fired by the sound.

Will and Chance rode side by side. For a few moments Will gave himself up to the thrill of galloping his horse through the snow. The frigid air rushed at his face. Around him, hats blew off. Ahead, there were shouts and movement. Then the cheering soldiers were in among the lodges. A form appeared before Will, and Will fired his pistol. The form dropped away with a thin scream. All around were yells and gunfire in the fading darkness. The surprised Indians were trying to fight back. Will heard the notes of an off-key bugle from ahead, as some brave tried to rally his fellows.

The soldiers swept through the first village and into the next, shooting into tipis, shooting at the running Indians. There was no way of telling sex or age in the confusion. All Indians were targets. Squaws fled with the children, while the braves attempted to cover them. A tipi was set ablaze somehow, and its flames provided hellish illumination for the battle.

The ground was more broken than it had looked from the heights, and the charge began losing some of its steam. Will saw a horse stumble and fall, landing atop its screaming rider. The cheering died, then rose again, as the men got their second wind, reloaded their weapons, and pushed on.

"Come on, men," yelled Colonel Benedict. "Come on! Keep after them!"

The dawn air was wreathed with powder smoke. There was continuous firing. The noise was tremendous. Waves of gunfire rolled off the canyon walls, magnifying the sound. All this was punctuated by the screams of the women and children, by the screams of the wounded and dying, by the cheers and curses of the soldiers.

Far ahead there were volleyed rifle shots. The fleeing Comanches and Kiowas must have reached the blocking force. More screams of terror and despair. Many of the Indians now tried escaping up the sides of the canyon. Others, cut off, sought shelter along the riverbank, standing in the icy water. Some of the soldiers had dismounted and were skirmishing with them.

The attack went deeper into the villages. How many more could there be? Will thought. A blanketed figure materialized alongside him and fired a rifle in his face. He felt the hot blast and thought that he was dead. It took a second to realize that the Indian had somehow missed. From nearby, Chance shot the figure, man or woman Will couldn't tell in the dim light and acrid murk of powder smoke.

There were more flaming tipis now. Figures ran out of the fog, Indians and soldiers. Bodies of men and horses littered the ground. Riderless cavalry mounts bounded past, maddened with fear. There was blood on the churned-up snow, turning it pink.

The dawn sky was iron gray. Flakes of snow were falling again. From ahead the Indian fire grew louder. The off-key bugle sounded again. The attack was slowing. More and more saddles were emptied. The soldiers' momentum was stalled. It was a critical moment. They musn't let the Indians get organized. The Indians had them vastly outnumbered.

"Bring up the reserve!" yelled Benedict.

I Company galloped forward. They came onto line, and Benedict rode ahead of them. He had lost his hat. His reins were wrapped around his hand.

"Now, men! Charge! Finish them!"

With renewed cheers, the men spurred forward. Will saw Benedict reel in the saddle. He saw the colonel topple from his horse, then he had to turn away, as his own horse carried him on.

The soldiers rode into the teeth of the Indian fire. The Indians wavered, then they broke and ran. The off-key bugle sounded once more, then died abruptly, as if its owner had been shot in midnote. The battle turned into a series of individual combats, as soldiers pursued their foes among the burning tipis, or down the valley toward the blocking force, or up the canyon walls.

Will saw Chance break off toward the stream, after a group of Indians who were trying to reach the shelter of the trees.

The Indians were a mixed group. Chance rode behind them on his big black horse, shooting them down in the swirling snow. A woman arched her back and twisted as she fell. An old man crumpled. A girl lay wounded, floundering like a beached fish. There was an out-of-control look on Chance's face. He was enjoying this.

Will galloped alongside his friend, trying to stop him. "Chance!" he yelled. But Chance didn't hear.

An Indian stopped to cover the retreat. It was a boy, a teen-ager. He fired his bow, too hastily for a good shot. The arrow hit Chance's horse in the chest. The big black horse reared, and Chance held on, cursing. The horse galloped ahead, maddened. It struck the boy a glancing blow, knocking him to the snow. Chance wheeled the plunging animal by main force. He fired his pistol at the downed boy, but he was out of bullets. He threw away the pistol and drew his Winchester. He tried to steady the horse.

Will looked at the boy. There was something about the boy's straight nose and mouth. Something about his rounded eyes.

Blue eyes.

Chance got control of his horse. He leveled the rifle. His finger curled on the trigger. Will rode up and pushed Chance hard just as he fired, causing the shot to miss. Chance glared at Will, wild-eyed.

"Stop!" Will yelled. "He's white!"

Chance glared at Will again, then at the boy. He almost shot the boy anyway. Then the fire in Chance's eyes banked. He felt very tired. He wiped a hand across his bearded face and he lowered the Winchester. "Christ, you're right."

Will dismounted. The snow was falling steadily. There was smoke from fires up and down the canyon. There was more shooting, scattered here, concentrated there, as the battle continued. There were shouts from soldiers rounding up prisoners. Horses ran loose. Babies wailed, women cried. The wounded groaned.

Will helped the boy to his feet. The boy looked sullen, suspicious. His eyes darted from one man to the other, like the eyes of a trapped animal. He wore only a deerskin shirt, breechclout, and leggings.

Chance dismounted beside Will. Gruffly he said, "You speak English, boy?"

The boy stared at them, uncomprehending.

"What's your name?" Chance said, repeating the question in sign language.

The boy hesitated. He looked as if he wanted to bolt and run. At last he said, "Te-han."

"Tehan," Chance said. "Means 'Texan' in their tongue. He's a captive, all right."

They looked at the dark, curly-haired boy, and suddenly both had the same improbable glimmer of thought.

Will's throat went dry. It was too much to hope for. His voice broke, "What is he—fifteen, sixteen? That's about the same age as . . . as Tommy."

There was a flicker in the boy's close-set, hooded eyes. Again he looked from one man to the other, puzzled. "Tom-mee," he said, as if he had great difficulty forming the words, as if they were forming themselves. "M . . . me."

Will didn't know what to do. He hadn't seen Tommy since the boy was two. It was Chance who recognized him. "My God," he breathed, "I think it *is* Tommy."

"You're sure?" Will demanded.

"I'm sure." There was no mistaking the boy now.

Will went weak in the knees. He said a silent prayer. "I don't believe it. After all these years, we've found him. We've found him, Chance!"

Will was crying. He wanted to embrace Tommy, but the boy's sullen attitude held him back. He was not ready to be embraced. For years Will had dreamed of this moment. He had assumed that Tommy would remember him, and that the two of them would rush into each other's arms in joyous reunion. He should have realized it would be this way. Tommy did not know Will.

He knew only a wild Indian's anger because he had been captured.

Will swallowed. "Tell him," he said excitedly. "Tell him who we are. Who I am."

But Chance had gone white. He was trembling. He was sick to his stomach as he realized what he'd almost done.

He had almost killed his own son.

42

It was night. The snow had stopped and the sky had cleared. A quartet of black soldiers sat around a fire, chanting the Comanche medicine song, beating sticks against mess tins and cups in time to the music. They had learned the song at Fort Sill, and they had adapted it to their own rhythms, their own voices. They had increased the tempo slightly, added harmonies, and turned it into something uniquely their own. The chanting made an eerie sound as it floated over the wild, snow-covered plain.

The adjutant, Captain Graham, came up to where Will and Chance were talking to Tommy. "You'd better see the colonel now, if you're going to do it," Graham said quietly.

Will and Chance nodded. They rose, motioning Tommy to follow. The boy obeyed. What else could he do? These white men would not let him stay with the prisoners of his own people. They said that the Nemenna were not his people. They said that he was white, like them, that he was the tall one's son. They had put a white soldier's overcoat on him. At first he had not believed them. His name was Te-han. His father was Tape-day-ah, who blew the white soldier's medicine horn in battle. His mother was An-ki-ma, who had been shot by the dark one. As the day wore on, however, he had become confused. Memories of another life had begun to filter through the barriers that his mind had set against them for its own protection. Yesterday he had been proud and sure of himself, soon to become a warrior. Now he was uncertain who or what he was.

Around them, as they followed the adjutant, campfires stretched through the darkness in neat rows. They were the first fires the men had been permitted in days. The frozen air still smelled of gunpowder from the slaughter of the Indians' pony herd. Over a thousand of the animals had been killed. Many of the men had wept as they shot them, but it had been necessary, perhaps the most important act of the day.

And it had been a successful day. The Indians had suffered sixty-seven dead and over a hundred prisoner, not counting the casualties their tribesmen had removed as they escaped up the sides of the canyon. The soldiers had lost eight dead and thirteen wounded, three of them seriously, including Colonel Benedict. In the battle's aftermath, the soldiers had burned the Indians' lodges and over a ton of dried buffalo meat. They had destroyed weapons, ammunition, and clothing—many of the Indians had left behind robes, blankets, even hunting shirts in their haste to flee. The surviving Comanches and Kiowas had no food or shelter and few weapons. Most of all, they were afoot. They would be forced to go to the reservations to stay alive, those who didn't die on the way.

Captain Graham was a short, peppery man with a brisk walk. The collar of his greatcoat was up, and he wore a flapped buffalo cap. He looked over his shoulder. "By the way, Captain Evans, let me congratulate you on finding your son. A great day for you, eh?"

Chance missed a step. He tried to sound casual. "He's not my son. He's Will's."

Graham stopped. It was the first time he'd seen Chance and Will since the attack started. "Really?" he said. "Major Harcourt told me one of you Rangers had recovered his son. He didn't say which one. The resemblance between you and the boy is amazing, and I just naturally assumed . . ." He shrugged helplessly and looked at Will. "I'm sorry. I guess I should be congratulating you then."

"Thanks," Will told him, flicking looks at both the boy and Chance.

Colonel Benedict lay near the doctor's fire, covered by blankets and a buffalo robe, his head propped on his saddle. He was wan, coughing. His officers were gathered around. His NCOs and many of the enlisted men were in the background, awaiting the inevitable. Some of them were crying.

"Ah, there you are," Benedict said weakly, when he saw Will and Chance.

"How are you, Colonel?" Will said, kneeling beside him.

Benedict coughed and shook his head. "I've bought it. Funny, after all the big battles I was in during the war, to get killed in a skirmish with savages."

He coughed again and rolled on his side, spitting blood and phlegm. "Take it easy, sir," said Major Harcourt, but Benedict waved him off.

"How's the boy?" Benedict asked Will.

Will hesitated. "Fine, sir."

"You're a lucky man, Will. I'm glad for you. Damn glad."

"Thank you, sir."

"I just—" He coughed. "I just want you two to know. It's been an honor serving with you."

"Thank you," Will said.

"The honor was ours," said Chance, tight-lipped.

The one-armed colonel fell back in another fit of coughing. There was a rattle in his throat now. He beckoned to Harcourt. "Don't . . . don't carry my body back, Jack. Bury me out here . . . with the men. Tell my son I . . ." He said no more. He didn't have the strength. The rattle in his throat grew louder.

The assembled soldiers, hardbitten men, hung their heads. So did Chance.

Ordinarily, Will would have hung his head, too, but not now. He was staring at Tommy. Captain Graham had been right. The boy did look like Chance. He had the same build, the same eyes, the same curly hair and sensuous mouth.

Suspicions that had been no more than nebulous wisps at the back of Will's mind all these years now coalesced and flooded over him. He remembered Hope's surprising eagerness to marry him. He remembered Tommy's premature birth. He remembered all the time that Hope and Chance had spent together while he was gone with the Rangers.

He turned away from the fire, away from the dying colonel, away from Tommy and Chance. There was a sour taste in his mouth.

This should have been one of the happiest days of his life. It had become one of the worst.

43

1876

It was well past midnight when the five young cowboys left Kelley's Saloon. Four staggered under a load of drink. The fifth had not touched a drop.

The cowboys were with a herd camped across the river, waiting to be shipped. They wore new clothes—hats, gaudy wool shirts, boots, and cheap bandannas with "Dodge City, Kansas" stitched on them. They'd paid twice the actual value for the clothes, but they'd had no choice. Their old clothes had been worn to rags on the trail, and their boot tops had been slit open when their legs had swelled from drinking too much gyp water—except for the fifth man, who wore knee-high moccasins. The men had bathed and shaved their beards. Their hair and such mustaches as they could grow had been cut. They smelled of bay rum, or they had, before they'd started dancing.

"Who's got the bottle?" asked Johnny Presnall. Johnny was twenty-one, with long arms and big teeth. A cheap cigar was clamped in a corner of his mouth.

Four-Eyes Givens, an open-faced lad of eighteen, with eyeglasses, held up the whiskey. There were giggles as everyone had another drink.

Ace Jackson was a lean, hard, straw-haired boy of twenty. He'd been up the trail more times than any of them. He drank deep and said, "Money's gone. So's the whiskey, just about. It's time to leave. You all got them trigger fingers loose?"

"You really gonna do this?" asked Four-Eyes.

"Hell, yeah," Ace said. "Don't tell me you're going to back out."

Four-Eyes adjusted his glasses, which had fallen over his nose. "I don't know . . ."

"Come on, Four-Eyes," said Johnny. "You said you was. The way we been robbed in this dump, it's the least we can do."

Four-Eyes wasn't sure. He had thought the other men were joking. "You done this before?" he asked, taking another drink.

"Sure I have," Ace told him. "I done it last year in Caldwell. Before that I done it in Wichita. Dodge City's no different from them, 'cept it smells more like buffalo." He laughed at his own joke. "Come on. You won't get in any trouble."

Four-Eyes looked unsure, then the liquor got the better of him. "All right. I'll do it if you do."

Ace turned to the man on his right. "How 'bout you, Henry?"

Henry Collinson was a twenty-year-old Englishman who had run away from home to see the American West. He was slender, with a sensitive face and a long nose. He had alert, curious eyes, even if they were dulled right now with whiskey. He weaved slightly on his feet. "The boss warned us about setting off our pistols in town."

"Bosses always say that," Ace told him. "I keep telling you, there's nothing to worry about. Hell, we'll be safe across the river before anybody even knows what's happened. Come on, Henry. You ain't a *real* cowboy till you hoo-rawed a town, you know."

Henry thought it over, scratching the back of his head. He turned to his friend. "What about you, Tom? Going to have a go at this hoo-rahing?"

The fifth man, seventeen-year-old Tommy Cooper, was the most serious of the group. He shook his head. "I don't like to waste ammunition. I'll ride with you, though."

"Good enough," said Ace.

The five cowboys started back for their horses. Tommy and Henry walked a little behind the others. They had become good friends. Tommy had come into town only because Henry was going. They made an unlikely pair, the educated young Englishman and the former Indian captive. Henry was quiet, and Tommy liked that. He didn't badger Tommy about his experiences with the Indians, as the others did. He didn't joke around and call him "Chief." The two of them pulled a lot of night herd together, and Tommy used to laugh to hear Henry trying to sing to the cattle. And laughter was rare for Tommy.

Ahead of them, Four-Eyes Givens hiccuped loudly.

"You ain't gonna puke again, are you, Four-Eyes?" Ace Jackson asked.

"If I do, it'll be on your boots," Four-Eyes said.

"That's where you done it last time."

Johnny Presnall laughed through his big teeth. "Sure took the spark out'n them dance-hall girls, didn't it?"

Four-Eyes said, "I puked even worse after you and Ace went into the back rooms with them girls."

"You just didn't have the guts to go back there with them yourself," Johnny told him.

"That's 'cause my guts come up when I seen their faces. Last time I seen beasts like that, they was rootin' for acorns out back of my daddy's farm."

The five men reached the horses. They glanced around furtively, to make sure no lawmen were looking. They opened their saddlebags, giggling and trying to look casual. They pulled out their six-shooters and buckled them on. Four-Eyes caught a finger on his buckle tang and swore, shaking his hand. Henry turned his holster upside down taking it from the saddle bag, and his pistol dropped out.

Johnny almost swallowed his cigar. "Be careful with that thing," he said as Henry picked up the pistol.

"Sh," warned Ace. "Keep it down."

The cowboys mounted their horses. They finished the bottle a last time. Four of them passed the bottle a last time. Ace finished it, and Ace tossed it in the street by the sidewalk, with a lot of other empty bottles. Johnny said, "Got them glasses on tight, Four-Eyes? I wouldn't want you to mistake me for no Man in the Moon or nothing."

Four-Eyes, who'd had all sorts of problems with the glasses on the trail, laughed. "Hell, I'm so drunk, I don't know if they're on or not."

The cowboys eased their horses into the middle of Front Street. Surrounding them in the warm night were the tinkle of pianos, the laughter of men and women, the buzz of drunken conversation. At a nod from Ace, four of them pulled their six-guns. "Remember to keep them things pointed up," Ace reminded.

"Wherever that is," said Henry.

Ace took a deep breath. "All right. Let 'er rip."

With a yell, the cowboys spurred their horses. They galloped down Front Street, along the railroad tracks. Ace fired first. The others followed his example, discharging their six-shooters into the air, laughing and shouting and hallooing. The noise of the pistols sounded loud over the rumble of the horses' hoofs. On the sidewalk, some people scrambled for cover. Others watched. Still others clapped or shouted encouragement.

They turned down Bridge Street, heading for the toll bridge over the Arkansas River and out of town. "Hurrah for Texas!" they cried, shooting wildly.

"Long live the Queen!" shouted Henry.

Tommy saw the figure first. He was running toward them, coming from the alley behind the Lady Gay. He carried a shotgun.

"Look out!" Tommy cried. "The law!"

"Shit!" yelled Ace. "Ride for it!"

The cowboys fired a last flurry of shots, then they were low on their horses' necks, heading for the bridge. As they rode past the figure, the shotgun boomed once, twice. One of the cowboys uttered a strangled cry.

"Who's hit?" yelled Johnny.

"It's Henry," Tommy cried.

The young Englishman reeled in the saddle, but by some miracle he held on, and he slumped over his horse's neck. Tommy grabbed his reins as the five men thundered over the plank bridge.

Ace looked back, shaken. The lawman could be seen in the street, calmly reloading the shotgun. "Son of a bitch," Ace said.

"He didn't have to do that," Four-Eyes said. "We wasn't hurting nobody."

Johnny fell back. "You hit bad, Henry?"

There was no answer.

The cattle camp was not far from the river. The trail crew had been asleep, save for the boss and those on night herd. Tommy's party had been the only ones in town. Now the sleepers stood, roused from their blankets by the shooting and the noise of approaching horses. Aaron Richardson, the trail boss, threw his coffee into the fire as Tommy and the others galloped up.

"What happened?" Aaron said.

"Henry's been shot," Ace said. "By the law."

"Was that you all hurrahing the town?" Aaron asked angrily.

Ace nodded, lowering his head.

They dismounted near the fire. "Help him down," Tommy said. "Easy."

Aaron and Tommy eased Henry from his horse. By the firelight, they saw that the Englishman's side was wet with blood. The sight sobered them rapidly.

"Oh, man," said Ace, sickened.

Four-Eyes said, "God damn Dodge City."

Johnny threw away his cigar.

They laid the wounded man by the fire. "I warned you about firing your six-guns in town," Aaron told them. "These Kansas marshals don't play. They just look for excuses to gun Texans. Do you know which one got him?"

"It was Boyce Slidell," said Johnny. "I seen him earlier at the Occident."

Aaron shook his head. "Slidell's the worst of the bunch, even worse than that new man, Earp. He shoots to kill. The rest of you'll be lucky if you ain't arrested come morning for disturbing the peace."

On the ground, Henry Collinson groaned. He was dying. There was nothing they could do. His side had been blown off. Bits of his ribs were showing. He lived for a few minutes more, then he breathed his last.

The men stood around the body. "He's a long way from England," Four-Eyes said. He took off his glasses, which had become misted with tears.

Suddenly Aaron turned. "Where's Tommy?"

The others looked around. Tommy was nowhere to be seen, nor was his horse.

They had not even heard him go.

44

Tommy had had one friend, and now that friend was dead. He knew what he had to do.

He rode back into town. He tied his horse at a rail on First Street. He took off his hat and left it on his saddle horn. Tommy hated the white men's big hats, just as he hated the heavy boots in which they clumped around. How could they get a feel for the ground that way?

He found Boyce Slidell in a billiard hall next to the Dodge House, playing pool and drinking beer and looking full of himself. Tommy settled outside, making himself blend into the shadows as only an Indian could. He waited.

Tommy had been sent on the cattle drive because Aaron Richardson was a friend of his father's, and his father had hoped that a few months on the trail would help straighten Tommy out. Tommy had never adjusted to being "home." He didn't like the big house. He didn't like the white men's clothes or food or customs. At school he'd been older than the other boys. They had laughed at his lack of English, at his Indian walk, at the awkward way he held books and pencils. There had been frequent fights. In town it had been the same. Tommy had been the object of stares, of whispers, of more laughter, and only his father's name and the interventions of his Uncle Chance had saved him from getting in more trouble than he did.

Tommy hadn't fit in with his family, either. They wanted him to be something that he wasn't. He knew that his father was a good man, yet somehow he felt closer to his Uncle Chance. He had vague memories of fishing with Chance, of Chance's laughter, his strength. Of his father, there were no memories at all. People said his father had been away at war, but why had he been gone so many years? If the war had lasted that long, why hadn't he taken his woman and children along?

Tommy remembered his mother. He remembered her thick hair, the soft smell of it. He remembered being held when he was sick. But for years he had thought that his mother was An-ki-ma and his father was Tape-day-ah, and now they were both dead. It was all confusing.

Most of all, he hadn't gotten along with his younger brother Alex. Alex had grown up expecting to inherit the ranch, training for the day when he would take over. He had known that he had an older brother, and that his brother might return some day, but he had never expected it to happen. Yet it had happened, and Alex had suddenly found himself pushed aside. Someone else—a stranger—was being groomed to take over. The fact that Tommy didn't want to run the ranch, that he didn't want to be there at all, hadn't mattered. The final straw had come when Tommy had been sent on the cattle drive. For years Alex had wanted to go on a drive, and now the newcomer had usurped his place there, too. There had been a fight. Alex had been game, but he'd been no match for the older and more athletic Tommy. He'd kept coming on, though, and Tommy had been forced to pound him pretty good before some of the hands had heard the noise and stopped it. Tommy didn't think the bad blood between him and Alex would ever die.

His only friend at the ranch had been Ellen. Of Ellen he had the most memories, of hours and days playing together, laughing and exploring the countryside. Ellen had grown spoiled, and she acted as if she were the queen of Texas, but the two of them shared a love of horses and a desire to be free of the constraints that society and their family put upon them.

Tommy had enjoyed the cattle drive. He had liked the open spaces, the freedom, the sense of being on his own. He had liked working with animals. Now the drive was ended and he was in a town, and he felt as if he didn't fit in again. He hated not fitting in. He wondered where in this world he did fit in.

One thing was certain. After what he intended to do tonight, he would not be able to return to his father's ranch. But, then, he had not planned to return to the ranch anyway.

He stirred. Slidell was leaving.

* * *

It had been a good evening for Boyce Slidell.

He had just won twenty-five dollars at billiards, and he had a contented buzz from the amount of beer he'd consumed. He went out behind the pool hall and relieved himself. He didn't bother with the privy. He just peed in the alley. God knows, it stank enough already.

Earlier, he'd likely started another Texan on the road to hell. He'd have to ride out to the camps tomorrow, find out who the man had been and arrest his accomplices, or—better yet—fine them on the spot and keep the money for himself.

Boyce hated Texans. To him they were all still rebels. Reconstruction hadn't been nearly hard enough on them.

Boyce had developed a reputation for being tight-lipped and stern. It hadn't always been that way. There'd been a time when he had smiled a lot. He'd had a smile that charmed the ladies right out of their shoes. Then a Texan had knocked out all of his front teeth. The wooden teeth he'd gotten to replace them were uncomfortable, and they didn't look good. Being vain, Boyce hated for anyone to see them, so he kept his mouth closed as much as possible.

He was sure he'd killed the man who'd disfigured him, though he kept seeing the man's Double H cattle brand wherever he went. People said the brand belonged to a "cattle king" named Will Cooper. Boyce didn't remember the name of the man who'd knocked out his teeth. It might have been Cooper. Maybe this "cattle king" was his brother.

Boyce would never forget the man's brand, though. Selling those Double H cattle had brought him his first big windfall. Boyce's problem was that he spent money as quickly as he acquired it. He needed constant infusions of cash to support his lifestyle. Being deputy marshal of a place like Dodge was the perfect job. He and the rest of the police force were making a small fortune, shaking down the businesses. In return, the police let the businesses charge the Texans fifty cents or even a dollar for drinks that should have been two bits. They let the citizens of Dodge cheat the Texans at cards and overprice them in the stores. They let the citizens drug and rob Texans in back rooms, and they arrested the Texans if they complained about it. The work wasn't hard. The worst that Boyce had to fear was shooting it out with some blind-drunk cowboy who'd probably never fired his gun in anger before. Usually it wasn't even that hard, like tonight.

Boyce buttoned his pants. He started back to the billiard hall. He'd play one more game, then go over to Big Lil's and pick out one of her new girls. The idea of a woman stirred him. Maybe he wouldn't even bother with . . .

He thought he heard something behind him. A movement? A footstep?

He turned to look. As he did, a hand grabbed his chin and jerked it upward. Something sliced across his throat. It was so sharp that he barely felt it. The hand pushed him away.

Boyce stood stupidly for a moment, then he realized that a warm liquid was gushing down the front of his expensive clothes. He realized that the liquid was blood, his blood, and that the thing that had slashed his throat had been a knife.

He reached futiley for the wound, trying to close it, trying to staunch the bleeding. He tried to call out, but he found himself gurgling. He was light-headed. The night sky spun above him, and then he was sitting in the wet filth of the alley. He clawed at his throat, and the blood poured over his hands, over his white shirt, over his vest and broadcloth coat. It occurred to him that he was dying. The last thing he saw was a dark-haired young man standing over him with a pleased look on his face. Almost idly, he wondered who the young man was.

Tommy wiped the blood from his knife, using the hem of Slidell's frock coat. He started to scalp the dead lawman. He grabbed Slidell's pomaded hair. Slidell's head lolled on its partially severed neck. Gripping the head with his knees, to steady it, Tommy pulled the hair back and lowered his knife for the incision.

Then Tommy stopped. What good would it do? It wouldn't stop Slidell from entering the afterlife, because there was no afterlife as the Nemenna knew it. That was what the white men told him, just as they told him he was not really one of the Nemenna. Reluctantly he let the lawman's head fall into the mud and trash of the alley.

He straightened, wiping Slidell's hair grease on his trousers. There would be a posse after him when the body was discovered, but he was confident that he could outdistance them.

Where would he go? Back to his people? No. He would not fit in with them anymore, just as he did not fit in with the whites. Besides, the Nemenna were on reservations now. Their old way of life was ended. The buffalo were gone. The land was no longer free.

He would go to Mexico, he decided. Maybe there he could start over. Maybe there he would fit in.

He walked back to his horse. He took the big hat off the saddle horn, and he tossed it away. Then he mounted and rode out of town.

45

Will and Rusty had just finished a five-day tour of the line camps. They'd done some hunting and fishing, and they'd also stopped to inspect the Wilkens Creek pasture that was being fenced with barbed wire. Will had used wire fences before, to keep out grangers, but he intended this pasture for upgrading his stock with two imported Durham bulls. The two men returned to the ranch house, dusty and tired. They found a visitor in the parlor, talking with Hope.

"Fulgencio!" Will said, opening his arms wide.

The two old friends embraced, patting each other's shoulders. Will stepped back and looked at the squat Mexican face, pock-marked, the hair still raven black. "Ten years, and you ain't changed a bit, Fulgencio. A little fatter, maybe. What is it, the air down in Mexico keeps you looking so young?"

Fulgencio grinned. "Rusty, he would say it is the grease."

Rusty laughed, and he, too, embraced his friend. Fulgencio said, "And you, *Señor* Will . . ."

"Oh, cut the *señor* nonsense. I'm just Will to you."

"You look the same also except for the . . . you know."

Will touched his thinning hair self-consciously. Rusty laughed again, and Will shot him a look.

Fulgencio wore a short jacket and pants of burnt-orange buckskin, trimmed in white leather, along with soft buckskin leggings. His big sombrero lay on a chair. He looked around the room appreciatively. There was glass in the windows, Mexican-design rugs on the cedar floors. The furniture had come from New Orleans; Sam had ordered it from his catalogues. A seven-foot-plus spread of cowhorns adorned the fireplace.

"Truly a magnificent house," Fulgencio said. "Like that of the greatest haciendas."

Will shrugged. "It's mostly Hope's doing. If it was just me, we'd probably still be living in a dugout. And you, you're looking prosperous. Business is good, no?"

"Business is good, yes. Every *gringo* from the Rio Grande to the Yellowstone wishes to be a *ranchero*. Even my scrawny Mexican cattle bring the top dollar. I have a herd of stock cattle contracted to a gentleman in Colorado, so I think, why not take them myself and visit my old friends on the way?"

"Well, we're glad you did. How 'bout a drink? Not *aguardiente*, the good stuff. Hell, I might even have one myself."

"You'll stay for a few days, won't you?" said Hope.

Fulgencio smiled. "Alas, no, *señora*. My herd is camped by the river, and as you *norteamericanos* say, 'time is money.' "

"Yeah," Rusty said. "Leave them cows around here too long, and they're apt to get rustled."

There was an awkward silence. Will could see from Fulgencio's look that he knew about the troubles they'd been having here in Benedict County—Kingdom County had been renamed for the dead colonel of the Tenth Cavalry. While Will poured the drinks, Fulgencio picked up the old arrowhead from the mantel, the one that had been pulled from Will's back years ago. "You still have this?"

"I like to remind myself of the bad old days," Will said.

Fulgencio nodded. His brother had been killed defending this ranch in those days. He could remember them all too well. "And *Señor* Chance, how is he?"

"All right, I guess. Don't see much of him these days."

"A strange man, in many ways."

They sat in leather chairs. "You ever get married?" Will said.

"*Sí*. I have a woman who is fat and gives me babies—six now—and who makes the best *tortillas* I have ever eaten. I have my ranch. It is not like this, of course, but it is enough for me. My brother's bones are nearby, and, most of all, it is in, you know, Mexico. It is home. I am content."

"We're glad for you," Hope said smiling.

"And you two. You are content, no?"

Will and Hope exchanged looks. "Yeah," Will said, but his voice lacked conviction.

There was more small talk, about families, and cattle and weather. Then Fulgencio grew serious. "I have come for more than the old times, Will. I have news of *Señor* Tomas."

Will sat straighter in the chair.

Hope's smile faded. Her face grew pale.

"Tommy?" she said.

"The *gringo* called Te-han is said to be living in the foothills of the Sierra Madre. They say he sometimes rides with a *bandito* named *El Tuerto*—'the one-eyed.' "

"How do you know this?" Will said.

Fulgencio smiled. "You are more famous than you think, Will. Even in my country they have heard of the cattle king Cooper, how he lost his son to *los Indios*, then rescued him, only to have him run away."

Will was on his feet now, pacing. "Where in the foothills?"

"They say in the uplands of the Rio Escondido. But in my country, you understand, such news is not always accurate."

Will stopped. "Fulgencio, you're a real friend, coming all the way here to tell me this."

Fulgencio shook his head. "You would do it for me. I know that."

Hope stepped forward. She laid a hand on Will's arm, but he drew back from her. "What do you mean to do, Will?"

"I'm going after him, of course."

Rusty smacked his fist into his palm. "I'll saddle up the boys. We'll get—"

"No. I'm going alone."

"Will, it's too dangerous," Hope said.

Fulgencio said, "She is right, Will. It is not like the United States. Those hills are infested with gangs of *banditos*, who think nothing of killing travelers. Wait for me to return from Colorado. My *vaqueros* and I will go with you.''

Will said, ''No, old friend. This is something I must do by myself. I don't know why. I just know that's the way it has to be.''

He glanced at Hope again. He had never resolved his suspicions about Hope and Chance. That was the worst part about it—they were only suspicions. There was no proof, and Will was not the type to confront her. Maybe Tommy's resemblance to Chance was coincidence. Maybe Tommy took after Hope's dark-haired father, Jack. Maybe he took after Will's own grandmother, for that matter. He had been through these arguments a million times. Whatever the truth was, and no matter what had happened to his relationship with Hope, his love for Tommy would never change. He had always thought of Tommy as his son, and he always would.

''When are you pulling out?'' Rusty asked.

''Tomorrow,'' Will said.

Will was up before dawn. By the light of the coal-oil lamp, he packed his saddlebags and bedroll. He jerked the strings tight on the roll and tied them. The door to his room opened. It was Hope, from her room next door. She wore a robe in the predawn chill. Her long thick hair fell about her shoulders. The lamplight caught its reddish highlights.

''You're ready?'' she said.

''Just about.''

''Be careful.''

''I will.''

''I wish you weren't going alone.''

''We been through that.''

''And what if you're successful? What if you bring him back? He's wanted for that marshal's murder.''

''Boyce Slidell? I still don't believe Tommy had anything to do with that. There's lots of people must have wanted Slidell dead. If anybody killed him, it should have been me.''

''But they found moccasin prints by the body.''

''That proves nothing, Hope. Lots of people wear moccasins. Could've been a buffalo hunter killed him. Or a drunk Indian from off the reservation.''

"Then why did Tommy run away?"

"Maybe he was going to run away anyhow. You know he was unhappy here. I'll get him the best lawyer in Texas—the best one in Kansas, too, if it comes to that."

Will picked up his bedroll and bags. He took his hat. His rifle and pistols were downstairs.

Hope stood in the doorway before him. In a low voice she said, "Will, why are you doing this to me?"

"Going after Tommy?"

"You know what I mean. You haven't touched me since you rescued Tommy. You moved into your own room right after you came back. You hardly even talk to me anymore unless you have to. Everything was so good between us, then all of a sudden it changed. What happened out there, with the army?"

Will said nothing.

"Is it something I've done? Something I've said? Why won't you tell me?"

Will almost spoke, then he stopped. "I . . . I can't, Hope. I'd like to, but I can't. It's like everything else, I guess. I got to work out the answers myself."

She put her arms around him, holding him, pressing her smooth cheek against his shoulder. He could feel her heart beating against his. But he was cold, immobile, and after a second she stepped back.

"Aren't you even going to kiss me good-bye?" she said.

He looked at that beautiful face, shadowed in the lamplight. God, how he loved her. He had loved her from the moment he'd first set eyes on her, and he knew that he would never love anyone else. But all that while, had she been in love with another man? Had she begged another man for his kisses, the way she now did for Will's?

"I'm sorry," he said. "I got to go."

He pushed past her, out the door.

She lowered her head and cried.

46

Kingdom was booming. The new Western Trail to Dodge City ran right by the town, and hardly a day passed during "the season" when there wasn't at least one herd camped across the river. Kingdom was the last town before Dodge, and the drovers came in to buy supplies and raise hell. In addition, this year there were over a thousand buffalo hunters in and around town, waiting for the annual southern migration of the herds.

Chance was in the rear of his saloon, playing poker with a skinny young cowboy. The cowboy was regarded as something of a card sharp down in Goliad County, and his fellow herders had pooled their money, over eighty dollars, for him to take on the infamous Chance Evans when they got to Kingdom.

Chance cleaned out the cowboy in two hands. The skinny young man sat looking at the table stupidly. If he'd had the time for a few more drinks, honor might have compelled him to go for his gun, to make up for being humiliated in front of his friends. As it was, he didn't know what to do.

Chance laughed and pushed the cowboy's money back across the table. "Here, son, take it. Next time, don't get in over your head. Here's an extra ten. Buy your partners there some drinks."

The skinny cowboy's friends whooped at that. The cowboy looked relieved. He took the money and moved off with his comrades. Chance looked at the well-dressed man sitting next to him, smiled and shook his head.

From the front of the saloon came a great stir. "Christ, it's a woman," said a shocked voice. Whoever she was, she must be something, because everybody was getting out of her way. Then Chance saw a tall figure, and a flash of reddish hair.

It was Hope.

Chance's heart leaped. She acted as if she owned the place,

talking to a surprised bartender who pointed to the back room, where Chance was. Rusty Harding and some cowboys were with her, a step behind and struggling to keep up.

Chance stood. Hope saw him through the crowd, and she made her way to his table.

"Hello, Hope," Chance said. "Rusty."

"Hello," Hope said.

"Hi, Chance," said Rusty.

Chance introduced his friend at the table. The man had a cadaverous look. His dark-blond hair was combed in a spit curl. His eyes were large and piercing, disturbing. "This is our new dentist," Chance said. "Dr. Holliday. Doc, this is Mrs. Hope Cooper. Her husband is Will Cooper, the rancher."

The man had risen as Hope came over. Now he inclined his head. "Mrs. Cooper. A pleasure, ma'am." He had some kind of Southern accent. Hope couldn't place it.

"Doctor," Hope said. Then she said, "Chance, I have to talk to you. In private, if you don't mind."

"Of course. Come into the office. You'll excuse us, Doc."

"Certainly," said the strange-eyed dentist. He bowed again. "Ma'am."

Chance's office was in a back room. The room was furnished in a clubby male style—dark woods and fabrics, big comfortable chairs. There were a desk, files, and other implements of business. The old picture of the Alamo, framed now, hung on one wall. Chance no longer lived at the saloon. He had a house, in the northern part of town.

Amos Blaine was seated at Chance's desk, scratching his bald head and going over some sheets of figures. He looked up in surprise as Chance and Hope came in.

Chance motioned Blaine out. "Miss Hope," Blaine said on the way. Hope did not acknowledge him.

The door closed behind Blaine. Chance turned to Hope. "Now, what is it?" They were alone. He hadn't been alone with her in years. He hadn't touched her in years. It was hard not to sweep her into his arms.

Hope looked worried. "Have you seen Fulgencio?"

"Fulgencio? Is that old horse thief in town? Why hasn't he stopped here?"

"He didn't have time, I suppose. He stayed at our house last night. He told Will that Tommy's been located. In Mexico."

She paused to let this information sink in.

Chance guessed what she was going to say next. "Will's gone after Tommy, hasn't he?"

She nodded. "He left this morning. By himself."

"And you want me to go with him?"

"Yes."

The room was quiet, save for the muffled sounds of the saloon and the street. The smell of her was strong. There was the slight rustle of her clothes as she shifted her weight. Chance wondered what she felt, being alone with him like this. He wondered if she wanted him to kiss her, the way he wanted to kiss . . .

He stepped back, to control himself.

"He needs you, Chance. I'm afraid for him."

Chance rubbed his smoothly shaven chin. He took a turn around the office, then stopped. He looked into Hope's green eyes. "I'll make you a deal. I'll go after Will if you'll promise to come away with me when this is over."

She said nothing.

"We can take Tommy with us," Chance went on. "We can start over. In New Orleans, or San Francisco, even Europe. Anywhere you want."

She looked down. Her hands were by her sides. "Chance, I can't."

"Oh, God, Hope. We been through this over and over for . . . Jesus, eighteen years now. You've done your bit for propriety's sake. It's time to do something for yourself. For us."

She looked up again. "You don't understand. I can't leave Will. I love him."

The words hit Chance like a body blow. He stared at her, jaw clenched.

"Maybe I was in love with him all along and didn't realize it. I don't know. Maybe it's something that's grown on me. But I do love him, and I would never leave him for anyone or anything."

"I once thought you felt that way about me," Chance said.

"Once I did," she said quietly. "But that was a long time ago."

"I still feel the same way about you, Hope. I think about you every day. Every night. I . . . I love you more than ever."

"You? With all your girls?"

"That's just physical. They don't mean a thing to me. You're the only good woman I ever knew, Hope. I'd have left Kingdom long ago, but I couldn't bear not being near you. I couldn't give up hoping that somehow you and me . . ."

"You've stayed here all this time because of me?" she said.

He nodded.

"Then why didn't you . . ." She remembered long ago, wanting him to propose marriage. "Oh, never mind. It doesn't matter now." She turned away.

Chance moved close to her. He hesitated. He recalled that day in the adobe house, how he'd gotten carried away. He put his hands on her shoulder, lightly, not wanting to scare her. "Come with me, Hope. I promise I'll make you happy. I know things haven't been good between you and Will."

She turned back to him, eyes questioning.

"Everybody knows it," he explained. "You can't hide that sort of thing. Come with me."

"How long would it last?" she said. "How long before you found someone younger? Another Julie, or Tara, or whoever it is you keep company with these days?"

"Hope, I swear, I—"

"No, Chance. It wouldn't work. It would never have worked. Anyway, I told you, I love Will. Love isn't something you turn on and off, at a whim. You have to work at it, through good times and bad."

He let go of her shoulders, and she moved away.

"What happened between you and him, anyway?" he asked.

"I don't know. It all started when you came back from the army expedition with Tommy. You don't think he suspects, do you? About you and me? After all these years?"

Chance wrinkled his brows. "Well, there was a sticky moment when some officer thought Tommy was my son, because he looks like me. But Will never followed up on it. He never said anything about it."

"He wouldn't," Hope said. She let out her breath. "That's it. He does suspect."

"He's been cool to me since then, but I thought it was just

because he was worried about Tommy. Has he ever asked you about it? About us?''

She shook her head.

"What if he does?"

She looked resigned. "I'll tell him the truth. I'll have to."

"It'll be the end of you two."

"I can't help that. I owe Will the truth. I owe him that much."

Chance watched her, feeling guilty because he was hoping that Will would ask, hoping he might get Hope afterward.

"And what if he asks *you*?" Hope said.

"I don't know."

"Are you afraid of the truth?"

Chance responded angrily. "Afraid of the truth? How the hell do you think I've felt the last year, watching Tommy suffer? Not being able to help him. If you knew how many times I wanted to tell that boy the truth, how many times I wanted to take him away. But I didn't. I couldn't. Because of you and Will. What it would do to you two. That was the only thing that stopped me. Not the truth."

He didn't tell her the rest. How his grief over Tommy's failure to readjust to civilized life had made him drink again. How it had made him throw himself even more into his illegal activities. As a release. As a way of hitting back at the world . . .

Hope said, "You still haven't answered my question. Will you go after Will? Will you help him?"

"Calling my bluff, huh? Well, it wasn't much of a bluff. Sure, I'll do it. You know that. I'd do anything for you."

"Don't do it for me. Do it for Will. Do it for Tommy, do it for your son."

"You didn't have to say that. You know that, too."

She hesitated. Then she kissed his cheek. "I know."

Chance swallowed. His cheek burned where she'd kissed it. His breath was coming quickly. "You'd better go now, Hope. Or I won't let you go at all."

Hoping she would stay. Praying.

She gave him a tight-lipped smile. "Good luck," she said. Then she turned and left.

Will headed south, for Mexico. He rode his favorite horse, a coyote dun with a black mane and tail named Buck, and he led a packhorse. He had crossed the Red Fork of the Colorado. Ahead of him lay Twin Mountains and the Concho. He wore an old red shirt, vest, leggings, and wide-brimmed hat. He looked like one of his hands, which was the way he liked it.

He heard hoofbeats behind him. He turned in the saddle to see another rider with a packhorse. Even at this distance, he could tell by the way the man sat his horse that it was Chance.

Will kept riding. The hoofbeats grew gradually nearer. At last Chance drew alongside him. Chance wore a white shirt, with his sleeves held up by garters. His six-guns were strapped tight, while Will's six-shooters were buckled loosely around his waist, cowboy style. They rode side by side for a minute, then Will looked over. "What are you doing here?"

"Going for a ride in the park, what do you think?"

"I think you better turn around and ride back to Kingdom. I don't want you."

"You got me, whether you want me or not."

"I'll do this myself. Tommy's my son."

"And he's my godson. If I recall correctly, that gives me some responsibilities toward him. Now, if you insist on being an asshole about this, I'll ride ahead and find him by myself. What's it going to be?"

"All right," Will said at last. "You can come. Don't say nothing to me, though."

Chance grinned. "You know me. Never speak 'less you're spoken to—that's my motto."

The two men rode on in silence.

47

"This the eleventh village we been to, or the twelfth?" Chance asked.

"I ain't been counting," Will said.

The villages tended to look alike, differing only in their setting and relative size. This one straggled alongside a clear stream in the rugged Mexican uplands, a country of agave and ocotillo, of burning days and freezing nights. It had been three weeks since they'd crossed the border at Del Rio, and they'd uncovered no trace of Te-han. No one had heard of him, or if they had, they weren't talking.

The village was a collection of *jacals*, made from poles and mud with thatched roofs, with an occasional structure of adobe. Chickens, pigs, and dogs wandered the streets. Burros twitched their tails at flies. Old *carettas* with solid wooden wheels sat here and there, as if abandoned. Half-naked children ran about or stood relieving themselves. At one corner a knot of men in serapes, smoking corn-husk *cigarittos*, watched the *gringo* riders impassively. Dark eyes stared at them from open doorways. The smell of frying cornmeal filled the air. To the rear of the village lay a cleared space, once perhaps destined as a plaza, now given over to weeds and a few goats.

Will and Chance dismounted by the adobe *cantina*. They could tell it was the *cantina* because it was the biggest building on the street. There was no sign or other means of identification. They removed their rifles and saddlebags from their saddles. They hobbled their horses, looping strings of tin cups on the hobbles. If they heard the cups jingling, they knew the horses were being stolen. They had learned that the biggest danger in Mexico was not from bandits or Indians or even disease, but from horse thieves.

They pushed aside the cowhide that covered the doorway and went in, taking two steps down. Inside, the *cantina* was dark, smelly, and surprisingly cool. Some scruffy-looking men and a woman sat in one corner. There were no other customers. Will and Chance cut the trail dust with tequila and water, served in glasses that had probably not been washed since the days of the conquistadores. All eyes in the room were on them, but they had grown used to that in the last three weeks.

Chance addressed the *cantina*'s proprietor in Spanish. "We're looking for a *gringo* who calls himself Te-han. Do you know of him?"

The proprietor, an ageless fellow in a dirty cotton shirt,

shrugged. It was the kind of shrug that indicated familiarity with the subject.

Will and Chance looked at each other.

Chance laid a silver dollar on the bar in front of the proprietor. "Do you know where we may find him?"

The proprietor shook his head. "I have heard of him. That is all?"

Chance laid another dollar on the bar. "What about the man who calls himself *El Tuerto*?"

The room grew quiet. With a sidelong movement of his eyes, the proprietor indicated the knot of men in the corner.

Will and Chance walked over. Their spurs jingled. The men watched them coming. Some were Mexicans, some were Americans. All were heavily armed. Their leader, who was American, wore a patch over his left eye. He was heavyset, almost fat. The woman sat with him. She looked neither young nor old, just tired. She wore a loose-fitting bodice and a flared skirt.

The leader's sombrero hung behind his head, revealing an unkempt mess of thinning, gray-blond hair. Around his sweaty neck was a necklace of wolf's claws. Something about the man looked familiar to Will. The man must have felt the same, because his one eye opened wide, as if he were seeing ghosts.

Will and Chance stood in front of the crude table, far enough apart to cover the bandits if trouble came. "You *El Tuerto*?" Chance asked the leader.

There was no answer. The man continued to stare.

Chance looked at him more closely. "Say, don't I know you?"

The leader reached beside him, for a crutch. He propped the crutch under his right arm, and he heaved himself upright, revealing a stiff, crippled leg. "You should know me. You gave me this leg."

"Christ," Chance said. "Now I remember. It was a long time ago. You used to be called . . ." He tried to think of the name.

"Squirrel Eye," said Will, recalling it first.

"Squirrel Eye, that's it." Chance gave a short laugh. "I never figured you to still be alive, Squirrel Eye. Never figured you to still have that leg, either."

"Young Pete saved me," Squirrel Eye said. "He saved my leg, too—not that it's much good to me anymore."

Chance looked around. "Don't see young Pete. He get married? Go straight?"

Squirrel Eye shrugged. "I got drunk one night. Shot him over a hand of cards."

Chance didn't seem surprised. "You didn't used to have that eye patch, either," he told Squirrel Eye. "That's why you look different. That game eye gave you a sleepy look before."

"The eye got infected," Squirrel Eye said. "Had to have it cauterized."

"That sounds like fun," Chance said.

"It ain't the word I'd use."

Chance and Will kept their free hands near their six-shooters. The other bandits affected boredom, but it was an act. They waited for a word, a gesture, from Squirrel Eye to move into action.

Squirrel Eye sat back down, with difficulty because of the leg. He poured himself another glass of *pulque* and grinned, revealing yellow teeth. "This is too rich. Twenty-four years since you shot me. For every day of every one of them years, I been in pain with this leg. For every one of them days, I prayed I'd run into you two again. And now you walk into my parlor. It's enough to make a man believe in God."

"Too bad young Pete isn't here to see it," Chance said.

Squirrel Eye leaned across the table, narrowing his eyes. His voice grew menacing. "We got unfinished business."

"No, we don't," Will said.

Squirrel Eye cast his good eye on Will. "You don't think I should want revenge?"

Chance grinned easily. "I think if you try to get it, I'll blow what's left of your ugly face through that adobe."

Squirrel Eye's men shifted uneasily. Hands edged toward weapons.

Will said, "We come here looking for somebody, Squirrel Eye. We heard you might be able to help us."

Squirrel Eye had been angered by Chance's remark, but his curiosity got the best of him. "Looking for somebody? Who?"

"A white boy, about eighteen. Calls himself Te-han. We heard he rides with you."

There were mutters among Squirrel Eye's men. The woman snorted derisively. Squirrel Eye said, "What's Te-han to you? You the law now?"

"I'm his father," Will said.

Squirrel Eye exchanged a look with the woman. Then he turned back to Will. "You're Will Cooper? The cattle king?"

"I own a ranch."

Squirrel Eye, or *El Tuerto*, sat back. "Well, I'm damned. I can say I been shot by somebody famous, anyway." He looked at Chance. "What about you, big mouth? What's your name?"

"Chance Evans."

There was silence in the room. Squirrel Eye's men knew that name. Then Squirrel Eye said, "Looks like you boys did all right for yourselves."

"That's more than I can say for you," Chance told him. "This place is a pig sty."

"About Te-han," Will went on, trying to head off trouble.

Squirrel Eye turned his half-empty glass on the table. "Te-han, or whatever his name is, don't ride with us no more. He didn't fit in. He couldn't take orders."

"Te-han's a loner," said one of the American bandits.

"Yeah, that's the word for Te-han," Squirrel Eye said. "A loner."

"You know where we can find him now?" Will said.

Squirrel Eye stared. "You expect me to give you the information for old times' sake?"

"I'm prepared to pay."

"Prove it."

Will reached in his vest. He dug out five gold double eagles that he had kept for this purpose. He tossed them, one by one, onto the wooden table.

Squirrel Eye reached out. Will pinned the bandit's hand with his rifle barrel. Will's right hand was on the butt of his six-gun. His thumb was on the hammer. He felt the room grow tense.

"The information first," he said.

"Sure," said Squirrel Eye, and he smiled. "Sure. Follow this stream about ten miles. Where it forks, turn northwest up the canyon. Another six miles or so, and you'll see the mountain called La Sagra. Don't worry, you'll know it when you see it. Te-han lives at the base of the mountain, with his squaw."

"Thanks," Will said. He lifted the rifle barrel from Squirrel Eye's hand. Squirrel Eye scooped up the gold coins.

Will and Chance backed out of the *cantina* slowly, ready for trouble.

"Be seeing you," Chance said.

"You never know," Squirrel Eye said, grinning. "You just might." The frowzy woman beside him laughed.

Outside, Will and Chance unhobbled their horses, glancing over their shoulders at the *cantina* doorway. "Think we'll have trouble with them?" Will asked.

"I think there's a damn good chance of it," Chance said. "We'd do well to watch our backs from here on out."

48

In the end, Tommy found them.

They had no difficulty locating La Sagra, a huge rock formation soaring above the slab-sided mountains, but they spent a good deal of time riding about it without discerning any sign of habitation.

They were beginning to think that Squirrel Eye had tricked them. They had just ridden past a ledge of overhanging rock when they heard Tommy's voice. "Hello, Father. Uncle Chance."

They turned in their saddles. Tommy was squatting on the rock ledge with a rifle across his knees. They must have ridden right by him, but they hadn't seen or heard him.

"Hello, Tommy," said Will.

"Hi, partner," Chance said. "You did a good job of sneaking up on us."

Tommy had let his hair grow long. His braids were wrapped in strips of deerskin. He wore an old deerskin shirt, a breechclout, and moccasins. His face showed no emotion. "You have come far."

"Not so far," Will said.

"How did you find me?"

"*El Tuerto* told us where to look."

Tommy looked back down the trail. "*El Tuerto* is a bad man. I am surprised that he did not rob you or try to kill you."

"He's tried that before," Chance said. "You might say that *El Tuerto*'s an old friend of ours."

"It was your Uncle Chance gave *El Tuerto* that game leg," Will explained. "A long time ago."

Tommy continued studying their back trail, as if watching for something or someone. Seemingly satisfied, he dropped from the rock ledge to the trail. Will was once again struck by the boy's resemblance to Chance—the hooded eyes, the stocky build, the compact movements.

Tommy said, "Would you like to see my l—my house?" He had started to say "lodge."

"All right," Will said.

"Come, then."

Tommy's house was located up a narrow side track, situated so that it was hidden until you were practically on top of it. It was a log cabin, snug and low to the ground, with wolf skins decorating the outside walls. On a flat piece of ground nearby was a patch of corn, almost ready for harvest. There were chickens and goats and the usual dog. Deer meat was drying on a rack in the sun.

A rather plain Mexican girl, barefoot, with a low-cut bodice, came from tending a baby goat. She stood shyly beside Tommy, in the presence of the two *gringos*. "This is Teresa," he said.

Will and Chance touched their hats. "Afternoon, Teresa," said Will.

"Ma'am," Chance said.

"This is my father and my Uncle Chance," Tommy told the girl.

The girl made an awkward attempt at a curtsey. "*Buenos dias.*"

"Teresa was a captive of the people you call Kiowas," Tommy explained, "until she escaped. Like me, she is an outcast from her society. We understand each other well."

While Tommy saw to their horses, Chance looked in the corral out back. "Those horses all have different brands," he said, returning.

Tommy showed no sign of guilt or remorse. "Taking horses is what I know. It is what the Nemenna taught me. I sell them to the local landowners. They don't ask questions." He indicated the shaded dirt in front of the house. "Sit."

Will and Chance sat. Tommy joined them, one knee raised, arm draped across it. "I have no strong drink to offer you. Teresa will bring water from the spring, if you wish."

"That'd be fine," Will said.

Teresa moved off, and Tommy said, "Is everyone well at . . . at home?"

"Yes," said Will.

"I know why you have come, of course. You want me to go back with you."

Will said, "Your mother and sister are worried sick about you. They miss you."

Tommy smiled. "And Alex? Does he miss me, too?"

"Yes, he does. He's your brother, Tom. He understands that you've had a bad time. He feels bad for resenting you. He'd like to make it up to you. It's been hard on him, too, you know."

"And the others, the ones who laughed at me, do they miss me, as well?"

"All that will get better, Tommy. It just takes time." Will leaned in closer. "Look, I know you're in trouble with the law. I'll take care of it. I know you didn't kill that marshal."

"But I did kill him," Tommy said.

Will and Chance exchanged glances. Chance wiped a hand across his jaw. Just then Teresa came back with gourds of clear spring water. She sat beside the men as they drank.

"I would kill him again," Tommy went on. "He killed my friend."

"I'll still take care of it," Will said. "I'll get you the best lawyers. I knew Boyce Slidell. He was bad. If I could have, I'd have killed him myself."

"Will I have to spend time in one of your prisons?"

"Maybe. I don't know."

"I could never do that. I would die first."

Chance spoke up. "I don't think you'll have to. I'm no lawyer, but I've had some experience in these matters, and I don't think the case will even come up for trial. You'd have to be extradited. They'd need a lot more evidence than they've got now to make a murder case, especially against the son of one of Texas's most prominent cattlemen.''

"And Teresa?" Tommy said. "Can I bring her with me?"

"Of course," Will told him. "There's no need to ask that." Will searched for something more to say, some additional argument to make Tommy come home. Finally he blurted out, "Damn it, Tommy. We want you back. *I* want you back. I've lived too long without you. I want you near me. You're my son."

Tommy pursed his lips. Teresa, who knew little English, understood the tone of the conversation, and she looked from one man to the other with a sad, sympathetic expression.

Chance watched them. If Will suspected the truth about Tommy, as Hope thought, he had said nothing about it on their ride south. But Will was the deep kind, who kept things to himself. Chance wanted to tell Tommy how much he loved him. He wished he could be like Will and say those things, instead of having to keep them secret. He wanted to say to Tommy, Come back. Come back, and we'll take them all on. You and me. We'll dare them to arrest you, to laugh at you. In a wild moment, he even thought about telling Tommy the truth and staying there with him.

But he couldn't do that. The boy's life had already been turned upside down. Another shock would overwhelm him, drive him over the edge. Anyway, what would Chance do here, hundreds of miles from anywhere? Hundreds of miles from Hope. Always it came back to Hope.

"Listen to your pa, Tommy," Chance said. "It isn't right, you being here like this. Think of all the good fishing you and me are missing. Anyway, it's dangerous here, with Apaches and bandits running loose. I don't think *El Tuerto*'s going to look favorably on anybody who leaves his gang."

Tommy looked at Will and Chance. At last he smiled wistfully. "Father, I know how you feel. I feel the same things. I do not want to hurt you, but . . . but I cannot go back."

Will said, "Look, if it's the—"

"It is not the law, my troubles with them. It is just that . . . I do not belong back there. Father, I am happy here." He looked at Teresa, who lowered her eyes. "*We* are happy. I am happy perhaps for the first time since I was a child in Texas. Those were good days, but they are like the wind that blows through the tall grass. They cannot be recaptured. I do not wish to leave this place. Perhaps one day I will come back to you, but not now.''

Will's face fell. His shoulders slumped. ''That's final?''

''Yes.''

Will and Chance stayed the night at Tommy's cabin. Tommy slept uneasily, repeatedly getting up and going outside to look around. In the morning Will and Chance saddled their horses and readied their pack animals. When all was done, they embraced Tommy and said their farewells to him and Teresa. Then they mounted their horses and rode off. They followed the track down from La Sagra. They rode down the canyon, toward the stream. They were silent for a long time.

At last Chance said, ''Maybe it's for the best, Will. What kind of life would Tommy have led back in Kingdom? How long before he got in trouble again? He's happy here. That's what really counts. His happiness.''

''I know,'' Will said. He was digging a fingernail into the leather of his saddle horn, hardly paying attention to the trail. He felt disappointed and a failure, and he wanted to be alone in his sorrow. He wondered if there was something else he could have done, something else he could have said, to change Tommy's mind.

He realized that Chance had fallen behind. He turned. Chance was halted at a band in the trail, looking back the way they had come. Will became aware of the sound of hoofbeats. He turned and started back. ''What is it?''

''A lot of horses,'' Chance said, ''coming on fast. We got trouble, partner.''

49

Will joined Chance. From maybe a mile up the twisting canyon, they heard the beat of many horses, growing louder. They could not yet see any dust.

"Think it's Squirrel Eye?" Will asked.

"That's my guess," Chance said. "Likely he intended to ambush us at Tommy's. Either he missed us there, or for some reason he changed his mind and decided to wait. I don't intend to stick around and find out." He gave Will a meaningful look.

"I know, I know," Will said. "Get rid of the packhorses."

"I lose more good pack animals riding with you," Chance complained. He swung from his horse. He got an extra box of rifle ammunition from his pack and stuffed it into his shirt. Will did the same.

"All right," said Chance, remounting. "Let's move."

They fled down the canyon. It was tricky going. The ground was rocky and boulder strewn, and they could not afford to go too fast, lest the horses be injured. Behind them, the hoofbeats grew louder still. Their pursuers had the advantage of being familiar with the terrain.

Ahead, the canyon narrowed to a pass. "They're going to catch us," Chance shouted, looking back. "If we can make the far side of that pass, maybe we can hold them off."

They made for the pass, riding as hard as they could. The hoofbeats were very close behind them now. They could see dust over the canyon walls. They lowered their heads to their horses' necks, eyes on the narrow opening of the pass. They were almost there.

A single gunshot, then a volley erupted from in front of them. Will's coyote dun Buck went down, throwing Will as he fell. Will hit the ground hard, knocking the air from his lungs, cutting himself on the rocky ground. He knew he had to get up, to get to cover, but he was disoriented. Little fountains of dirt were kicking up around him. He heard gunshots.

"Over here!" Chance yelled. He was leading his black horse into the rocks and brush at the side of the canyon.

Buck was on the ground, legs flailing, blood coming from wounds in his chest and neck. Will got up. He yanked his rifle from the pommel scabbard, grabbed his canteen from the saddle horn. He ran for the rocks, with bullets hitting all around him. A piece of stone ricocheted, slicing his cheek. He dove into the rocks by Chance's side, banging his rifle barrel sharply as he did.

"They suckered us," Chance said. He kept his head low as bullets clipped through the brush or whined off the rocks. "They drove us right into an ambush. If they'd waited about ten seconds more to open fire, we'd both be dead."

The two men were near the base of the canyon wall, fairly well protected by the screen of rocks and vegetation. From up the canyon came the sound of hoofs and the snorting of the horses, as the rest of the bandit gang came into view and dismounted. Some of the bandits took the horses, while others scrambled into the rocks on both sides of the canyon. Chance aimed his Winchester. He fired, dropping one of the bandits. A storm of bullets beat about him, and he ducked again.

He looked to see Will working at his rifle with a knife. In falling, Will had hit the Henry's soft metal loading tube, which ran beneath the barrel, on a rock, denting it.

"Damn," Will said, "it's broke. It can't be reloaded."

"That's why I brought a Winchester," Chance said. "You can't break them that way. How many shells can you fire?"

"Two, it looks like. The one in the breech and the one behind it. The spring's broke, too."

More bullets hit around them. Chance looked over the rim of rocks, marking the puffs of smoke, looking for a target. There was no sense using precious ammunition until he had something to shoot at.

"We're all right for the moment," Will said. "They'll try to get above us, though. From there they can fire right down on us, like shooting ducks in a pond."

"We can keep 'em out of there for a while, but not forever,

especially with just one rifle. Six-guns are no good for this kind of work.'' He looked at Will. ''Your six-guns *do* work, don't they?''

''They worked the last time I tried them,'' Will said.

''When was that?''

'' 'Bout a year ago.''

Chance rolled his eyes.

Just then a well-placed shot killed Chance's black horse.

''They didn't have to do that,'' Will said. Out on the canyon floor, his own horse Buck was still flailing his legs weakly, whinnying in pain as he died.

Chance was less emotional. ''It's no different than we did to the Indians. I'd do the same, if I was them.''

The firing died down. Silence descended over the canyon. Then they heard Squirrel Eye's voice, from the direction of the pass. ''Hey, boys! Didn't think I was going to let you leave without saying good-bye, did you?''

''Manners always was your fine point,'' Chance called back. He was peering through a crack in the rocks. ''If I can spot him, I'm going to drop him,'' he told Will. ''He should be standing, with that leg.''

''Maybe we can make a deal,'' Squirrel Eye yelled. ''You give me some more of them double eagles, and I'll let you go.''

''We only brought enough to buy information about the boy,'' Chance replied. ''Ain't you heard? This country's infested with bandits.''

Squirrel Eye said, ''All right. I don't mind waiting. I can take the money just as easy off your bodies.''

''See him?'' Will asked.

''No,'' Chance said. To Squirrel Eye he yelled, ''I'm telling you, you're going to be disappointed. We don't have thirty dollars between us. Why don't you all just pack up and go home while you still can?''

They heard Squirrel Eye's men laughing. ''Bold talk,'' cried the bandit leader. ''I admire a bold man. It's a pity I don't believe you. Let me know when you've had enough.''

From all around them, the firing began again. Chance wedged between the rocks, watching the puffs of smoke. He aimed and squeezed off a shot at one of them.

''Hit anything?'' Will said.

"Don't know." Just then a bullet hit the rocks no more than an inch from Chance's face. He ducked his head back under cover. "That was too close for comfort."

The bandits began making their way up the canyon walls. They were briefly exposed as they dashed among the rocks and brush and stunted trees, under covering fire. Will and Chance shot at them, winging one, dropping another. Each shot brought a retaliatory hail of bullets down on their little stronghold, forcing them to duck.

After two shots, Will's Henry stopped working. He and Chance took turns using the Winchester.

The sun rose higher in the sky, making the rocks hot to the touch, catching Will and Chance in its pitiless glare. They drank from their canteens, sweating.

"We'll have shade in the late afternoon," Will said.

Chance was watching the rocks for movement. "We won't be here in the late afternoon. We'll be dead. These bandits aren't like the Indians. They're not going to get tired and go away."

Will took another drink of water. His eyes glazed over for a moment, and he stared into the distance. "Fate's strange, ain't it? If a packhorse hadn't got noisy all them years ago, we might be in California right now, instead of getting our butts shot to pieces in some godforsaken canyon in Mexico." He sighed. "Wonder what they'll write for our epitaphs?"

"How about 'Two old men came from Texas. One was fat, and one was bald.' "

"I ain't all that bald," Will protested.

"I'm not all that fat anymore, either, but they have to write something about us." Chance fired his rifle at a moving bandit, missing but making the man drop for cover. "Damn. They're getting up there."

Squirrel Eye called to them once more. "You boys enjoying your farewell party?" The bandit chief was still somewhere at the bottom of the canyon, about level with Will and Chance. His leg and bulk would prevent him from climbing higher.

"It's not bad," Chance cried, peering out and hoping for a shot. "Be better if there were some whores."

"Changed your minds about the money?"

"We told you, there isn't any money. What the hell, you weren't going to let us go anyway."

"You may be right. At least you'd get it over with quick, though."

Chance took a drink from his canteen. The shouting made him thirsty. "Hey, Squirrel Eye! We've known you all these years. What the hell is your real name?"

There was no answer.

"Come on. What is it?"

"It's Virgil" came the bandit leader's reluctant voice. "Virgil Grimes."

"Virgil?" Chance cried. "Ha ha ha."

"Go on, shithead. Laugh. You're going to die laughing. You'll die slow, too. I'll see to that personally."

"Stop yapping and come get us, *Virgil*."

The firing redoubled. Will and Chance hugged the rocks. Chance snapped off a shot. There was no time to aim. "This is doing no good," he said.

"My turn," Will told him.

Chance passed him the rifle. Will took a breath. He raised his head above the rocks. He saw movement up the hillside. A wide sombrero. He aimed quickly and fired. He couldn't tell whether the shot hit, because bullets were pinging the rocks so close to him that he was forced to duck back.

"They shoot better than Indians, too," he said.

The bandits got even higher up the canyon wall. Bullets whined off the inside of the little stronghold now, ricocheting wildly about. The first ones plunked into the dirt at their feet.

Will tried to get off another shot but couldn't. He was driven down by the volume and accuracy of the bandits' fire. Bullets began hitting next to them. They were driven scrambling into a corner of the rocks, pressed up against them, and that last bit of safety would remain for only a few minutes more.

"That's it," Chance said. "They're just going to sit up there and pick us off now."

"No, they ain't," Will told him. He tossed the rifle back to Chance, and he drew his pistols. "If we're going to go, we'll go down fighting."

Chance grinned. "Now you're talking." He began reloading the Winchester.

Will went on. "There's two on that ledge up there, the one with the stunted cedar. We'll get them first, then we'll go for

Squirrel Eye. You never know, one of us might get lucky and get to him.'' Probably neither of them would get five feet before being riddled by bullets, but it sounded good.

Chance finished reloading. ''You know, this may sound crazy, but I think the happiest times of my life have been spent with you, like this, surrounded and waiting to be killed. Christ knows, there's been enough of them.''

Will took a last drink from his canteen. ''Chance, you amaze me. You face death without a thought. You put your life on the line for someone you don't even know. Other times you're low as a snake. How is that?''

''I don't know. I never thought about it. It's just the way I am, I guess.''

Bullets were hitting the ground inches from them. Will cocked his revolvers. ''Well, partner, this is it. See you on the far side.''

Chance grinned again. ''I don't know about that. Might be a bit hot where I'm going.''

They took deep breaths, ready to spring to their feet.

From high up the canyon side, a new rifle opened fire. They heard one of the bandits yell, ''Ow! Shit!''

''What the . . . ?'' Chance said.

More rifle shots. More yells of pain. Stones cascading, as someone fell down the hillside.

''We got help,'' Will said.

''Who?''

''Who do you think? Tommy, it has to be.''

The bandits were shouting in Spanish and English. They were confused, surprised, suddenly scared. They began firing blindly up the hillside.

''Come on!'' Will said.

Will and Chance rose and charged out. It felt funny to be on their feet again, after being cramped behind the rocks for so long. Will's legs were stiff and he couldn't get them working right for the first few strides, and then it was just like Gettysburg or Chancellorsville or a dozen other fights, and the only thing was to keep moving forward, to keep fighting as long as he could.

He made for the nearby rock ledge, zigzagging up the steep hillside. Behind the scrub cedar, he saw the two bandits. They were Mexicans. They were looking back up the canyon for their new attacker. They didn't see Will coming. He was aware of bullets hitting around him. Then he was scrambling over the ledge, firing his pistols as the bandits turned. One man spun around, throwing his rifle. The other dropped on his face. Will turned and saw Chance making for another group of bandits, firing his rifle. He saw men running away.

There were shots all over the canyon. The echoes made it hard to tell where they were coming from. Some of the bandits were fleeing. Others were firing up the canyon walls. Others were firing wildly at Will and Chance. Will had seen it happen before. A superior force, seemingly on the verge of victory, had been surprised and had fallen apart, panicking, unable to adjust. He saw a man with a Texas hat topple and roll down the hill, shot by their unknown savior.

Will scrambled over the rocks, heading back down the hillside now, looking for Squirrel Eye. Sweat poured over him. The cut in his cheek stung. A man popped up in front of him. Will shot the man, and he fell. He heard the crack of Chance's Winchester, and he saw that Chance had fallen behind, limping on his left leg.

More bandits were running. The first ones were already on their horses, galloping away down the canyon. Then Will heard Squirrel Eye's voice. "Come back here! Come back, you sons of bitches! We got 'em outnumbered. God damn you, don't leave me! Come back!"

Will dropped behind a large boulder. Just below him, Squirrel Eye was yelling at his men. Squirrel Eye was standing, propped against a slab of rock, his crutch by his side. In the confusion, he hadn't seen Will. The one-eyed bandit turned and fired up the canyon wall, cursing, determined to finish the fight himself.

Will ran at him.

Squirrel Eye turned, snarling. Will slid behind a clump of brush as the bandit fired. The bullet hummed past his head. As Squirrel Eye levered another shell into the breech of his rifle, Will came to one knee, cocking his .44. He fired, hitting Squirrel Eye in the forehead. The outlaw leader threw up his arms. He hit the slab of rock, bounced off, and fell in a lump at its base.

Will closed in. Squirrel Eye's sombrero had fallen off. His eyes were wide open but sightless. This time he was dead.

For Will, that was enough. Leaderless, the rest of the bandits were running now, and he was content to let them go. He caught his breath, reloading his pistols. He looked back up the hillside and saw Chance fire a last shot at the retreating bandits. He saw one of the bandits sway in the saddle.

Then the canyon was quiet, except for the sound of the departing horses. Will could see other horses still tied to the tree. They must belong to the dead and wounded.

Will made his way back up the hill to Chance. He felt tired and sick, the way he'd always felt after a battle. There was a sour taste in his mouth as he thought of the men he'd shot. His cheek hurt from the cut. There were bruises where he'd been thrown from his horse. The moans of wounded men sounded around him.

"Your leg all right?" he asked Chance.

Chance shrugged, reloading his rifle. "It'll do."

They waited for their rescuer to show himself. "Tommy," Will called, "come on out. It's over. Tommy, is that you?"

Nothing happened.

Will and Chance exchanged anxious glances. They started up the canyon side, searching among the rocks and trees, among the bodies of the bandits.

"Tommy, where are you?"

Will's heart was pounding. It was an effort to take each step, for growing fear of what he might find.

Finally they discovered him, sitting against a gnarled cedar. His rifle was beside him. Blood was flowing from a hole in his chest.

Will leaned against the cedar for support. "Oh, no," he said. He heard Chance cursing wearily.

Tommy must have suspected something when Will and Chance had left his cabin. He must have followed them and heard the shooting. He must have worked his way unseen into the rocks, where he could have a decisive effect on the fight. Maybe Squirrel Eye's last shot had gotten him. If Will had been a second earlier getting to the bandit chief . . .

Tommy's eyes found theirs. He smiled weakly. It was a good-natured, boyish smile, a smile that Will had not seen since before the war.

Then Tommy's head lolled on his shoulders, and he was dead.

Will's eyes filled with tears. He knelt beside the body, taking the still-warm hand, as if he could make the boy come back to life. With his other hand, he smoothed Tommy's dark hair back from his forehead.

Chance moved beside him. Something in his step made Will look up. Chance's dark eyes were blazing. His voice was filled with vehemence. "God damn you. This is your fault. If you had let me kill Squirrel Eye like I wanted to years ago, this never would have happened."

The accusation stung. Will had no reply.

"I told you that Squirrel Eye's kind had to be exterminated. But you wouldn't listen. Oh, no. Play fair, you said. Well, his kind don't play fair." Chance reached for his pistol. "I ought to . . ."

Will rose angrily, hand on his own pistol butt. "You ought to what?"

The two men faced each other, ready to draw.

"You ought to what?" Will repeated. He didn't want to share Tommy, not even in death. He knew it was wrong, and he didn't care. "What right have you got being so upset? He was my son, wasn't he?" He paused. "Wasn't he?"

Chance's chest rose and fell heavily. His lips were drawn back. He started to say something. Then he changed his mind. He took his hand from his pistol, and he turned away.

Will closed his eyes, which were still wet with tears. After a while he said, "Tommy's got to be buried. And that girl of his, Teresa, she's got to be told. There's wounded to be tended, as well. We can't just leave them here. I'd better get busy if I'm going to do it."

Chance put a hand on Will's arm. His voice was soft but firm. "We'll both do it," he said.

Part VI

50

1879

On the morning of September 11, 1879, the flag was lowered for the last time at Fort Stanley, and the garrison, which since the end of the Comanche wars had declined to one company of the Tenth Cavalry, marched out.

With bugle blowing and guidon snapping, the troops paraded down Fort Street. The men looked smart in their blue jackets and chasseur caps. Their boots, belts, and carbine slings had been heel-balled until they gleamed. They would change to fatigue dress at the first halt, but they wanted to make their last impression on Kingdom a memorable one.

The town turned out to watch them go. The firehouse band played "When Johnnie Comes Marching Home" and "The Girl I Left Behind Me." There was little cheering, for these soldiers were black, and Texans had not yet reached the point of cheering blacks. Only the town's small contingent of black whores was noticeably boisterous, and their wagons were loaded, for they would be moving, too. There would be little business for them with the soldiers gone.

Will and his family watched the troops' departure from in front of Sam Sommerville's store. Alex, now seventeen, lounged against a hitching rail with studied indifference. James, twelve, played with Sam's children, while Hope gossiped with her sister-in-law, Mary.

Will stood with Sam, in front of the three sets of double doors that formed the entrance to Sam's store. Sam had become the town's biggest merchant, and he was the largest trader in buffalo hides west of Fort Worth. He was also Kingdom's mayor, elected after Jacob Koerner's murder last year.

Sam's thumbs were hooked in his vest pockets. His short, dark beard was becoming salted with gray. The chicken pox scars were little craters on his forehead and cheeks. Sweat ran down his neck in the late summer heat. He drummed his fingertips on his spreading stomach as the troops marched by. "The end of an era," he said.

"There was times I thought I'd never live to see it," Will said. "And a couple of times I damn near didn't."

Will was still lean and erect. The long scar on his cheek, the one he'd gotten in Mexico, made him look even more grim than his reputation. He sniffed with distaste. The stink of buffalo hides was awful in this heat, though he supposed that people who lived in town, like Sam, were used to it. "You going to lose much business with the fort closed?"

"Compared to a few years ago, when there were almost four hundred men up there, yes. But let's face it, in the last year the fort hasn't meant much, business-wise. For me or the town. I'll tell you where I *have* lost business, and that's with the buffalo hunters. Last year's sales were way down, both in supplies and hides. I'm sure the herds will be back this year, though. Then, when the railroad comes through, things will really start jumping."

"You sure you'll get the railroad?"

"Positive. It's going to cost us, of course. We've made representations—that's a fancy word for bribes—to both the Texas and Pacific and the Texas Central. We're the county seat. One of them's bound to place a stop here. Then we'll be able to ship buffalo hides directly, instead of having to send them to Fort Worth. Plus, it's our intention to make Kingdom the main cattle market for all of Texas. A sort of Dodge City of our own, right here. The northern cattle trails will be plowed under soon. Those new breeds you're working with could never stand the long drives, anyway."

Will smiled. "And if the cattle trade goes bust, the railroad can always bring in grangers, right?"

Sam shrugged. "It's business, Will. Times change, and you've got to change with them. You know that if anyone does."

Will knew. The more he put up barbed wire, to keep the sodbusters and small ranchers off his land, the more he found it cut and had to put it up again. He was constantly in court, fighting to protect his range rights. He'd been forced to use the ploy of having his men file on all the local watercourses and then buying their deeds. If he didn't, some granger would file and Will's cattle would be without water, because American law did not recognize the old Spanish and Mexican custom of sharing water rights. The newcomers kept arriving, however, farmers and ranchers, and when bad weather or bad management forced them under, Will bought them out. He'd bought out so many small ranches that his foreman and roundup bosses carried books of all the brands he now controlled, just to keep track of them.

Sam went on. "The only thing that can keep the railroad from coming is this town's reputation for lawlessness and vice."

Will knew what was coming next. As if by reflex, he looked across the street to Chance's saloon. Chance was with the crowd out front, watching the soldiers, with his latest girl on his arm. He saw Will and raised his glass in salute. Will nodded to him. The two rarely saw each other anymore. They'd hardly spoken on the way back from Mexico.

Sam said, "Now, Will, I know you don't want to hear this again, but—"

"You're right, Sam, I don't."

"But we think you should run for sheriff."

"You got a sheriff."

"Ben Butler? Chance owns him. You know that."

Will said nothing.

"Will, there isn't a horse stolen or a cow rustled in this county that Chance doesn't get his cut. There's not a stage held up or a freight outfit robbed that the loot doesn't end up in Chance's strongbox."

He made sure the women weren't listening, then he added in a lower voice, "Not a person gets laid in this town, but Chance gets part of the fee. And that saloon of his is a rendezvous for every outlaw, killer, and confidence man in Texas."

"It's a big saloon," Will said. "It's a rendezvous for a lot of people, Sam. You sound just like Jake Koerner."

"And look what happened to Jake. He spoke out once too often, and Chance had Amos Blaine kill him."

"That ain't what the jury said. They weren't out thirty minutes before they came back with an acquittal."

"That's because they were threatened. Their families were threatened."

"From what I heard, it was because the state didn't make much of a case. Lack of evidence, I believe they called it."

Sam held his temper. "Will, I know Chance has done a lot for you. He's done a lot for all of us. But you're letting friendship blind you to the truth. Chance isn't the man he used to be, and he's getting worse all the time. He's got to be stopped, before he drags the whole county down with him. You're the only one who can do it, Will."

Will wasn't interested. "I wouldn't be here if it wasn't for Chance. This town wouldn't be here."

"Stop being so stubborn."

"I ain't stubborn. You show me some proof. What I want to know is, what's Chance supposed to be doing it for? He can't need the money. God knows, he's got enough coming in, between the saloon and his partnership with me."

"I don't know," Sam said. "Maybe he just does it because he likes it. Chance is funny that way."

Nearby, Hope was listening to the two men. Mary had gone into the store to roust out the children, who were running wild inside. In her heart, Hope knew that what her brother said about Chance was true. She stiffened as she realized that Chance was watching her from across the street, and she turned away from him. She still felt his gaze on her, though, and she blushed, and that made her angry. There had been a time when she had liked the way Chance looked at her, but that time was long past.

The troops were gone, turning left on California Street, toward the river crossing and their eventual destination of Fort Sill. The government supply wagons came next, then the ambulances with the officers' families. Behind them came the laundresses, then the camp followers and the assorted riffraff that always followed in the army's wake. The crowd began breaking up. Traffic flowed back into Fort Street. Across the way, Chance was gone.

"Well," said Will, "the show's over. Everybody ready to go?"

Sam laughed. In the family, Will was famous for coming to town as infrequently as possible and leaving as soon as he could.

Alex swung lazily off the hitching rail. James was still in the store, chasing the Sommerville children.

"Where's Ellen?" Sam said.

"She ain't interested in soldiers or parades," Will said. "She went riding. She goes riding most every day since she's back from that New Orleans finishing school. It's all she wants to do."

Same grinned knowingly. "Some young buck sparking her, eh?"

"Not Ellen. She don't want nothing to do with the boys around here. Don't seem to want much to do with any of us, to be honest. Just likes to be off by herself."

Hope said, "I sometimes wonder if we made a mistake sending her to that school." She kept one eye on Mary, who had at last rounded up the laughing children. "I wonder if the best education wasn't sitting up during the full moon, watching for Indians. If it wasn't plowing fields and carrying water, and learning the Bible by the light of the setting sun, like we did."

Will said, "If that's true, why did we work our fingers to the bone so our kids wouldn't have to do them things?"

Sam sensed an argument coming on. Will and Hope hadn't been getting along for some time. He said, "Oh, Ellen'll be all right. She's young. She's just feeling her oats."

"I hope you're right," Hope said.

"Of course I'm right. You stop worrying about that girl."

James came from the store. He and Alex mounted their horses. Alex rode a paint, James a dun. Alex could rope and break a horse and he knew cattle almost as well as his father. James was gawky and coltish, with a lively imagination and a liking for school.

Will handed Hope into the carriage. Sam's store was already filling with customers. "I better get inside," Sam said. "See you folks later. Will, you remember what I said."

"I'll remember," Will told him. "Don't expect nothing to come of it, though."

51

Chance eased his horse down the long slope that led to Wilkens Creek.

Ellen was waiting for him by the old abandoned ranch house. The ranch had belonged to a man named Wilkens, who'd settled there after the war and moved out soon after, because of the Indian troubles. Now all the land hereabouts was Will's. The house had fallen down; it was overgrown with weeds. Nearby, a broken-down wagon sprawled on its front axle. The long brown grass was dotted with the last of the season's sunflowers. The placid water of the creek was strikingly blue in the clear September light.

Ellen wore a green riding habit, with a tight bodice and flaring skirt. Her low-crowned hat had a veil in the back. She was tall, like her mother, and she wore her honey-colored hair in a tight bun. She had a pert nose and mouth, imperious eyes, and a confident carriage.

"Hello," she said brightly. "You're late. I thought you weren't coming."

Chance dismounted and came near her. "You didn't really think that, did you?"

She smiled. "No, I guess not. It's just that I've been waiting."

"I had to watch our soldier boys leave town. People would think it was funny if I wasn't there."

Chance staked out the horses. He and Ellen began walking slowly along the creek. Birds were chirping in the trees. Here and there insects hung in little clouds.

"It's a beautiful day, isn't it?" she said.

"It is now," Chance said, and she lowered her eyes, smiling.

Chance had been meeting Ellen like this for some time. It had started by accident. Chance had been to Hidden Valley, where he'd gone to check on a herd of stolen horses that Amos Blaine was moving into the Indian Territory. On his way back, Chance had encountered Ellen riding. They had stopped and talked. It was the first time that Chance had ever really talked to Ellen. He had realized with something of a shock that Ellen was now a grown woman, and he had been fascinated because she was so much like her mother. Ellen, for her part, had been clearly taken with Chance. She had ascertained that Chance came that way frequently, and when they met again, a few days later, it was not entirely by accident.

Since then their meetings had become regular. Chance knew that he shouldn't be doing this. He knew something was going to happen that he would regret, but he couldn't help it. He was drawn to Ellen in spite of himself. She was beautiful in her own right, but she was also so much like Hope.

Chance still loved Hope. She had become an ideal, a goal that was always just out of his reach. In a meaningless life, his love for her had given him something to believe in. It had become a Lost Cause, something to be defended at all costs, beyond all reasoning, as other men had once defended the Confederacy.

"Chance," Ellen said—she was long past calling him "Uncle"—"do you really like running that saloon?"

Chance shrugged. "It's what I do."

"Do you like Kingdom? Living here, I mean."

"I should." He laughed. "I started the place."

"No, seriously."

He shrugged again. "I've seen places I liked better."

"Why do you stay then?"

He couldn't tell her the truth. "I don't know. You don't like it here, do you?"

"I hate it, even more so since I've been away at school. I loved New Orleans, Chance. I see why you always spoke so highly of it."

"What did you like about it?"

"Oh, everything—the girls I met at school, the balls, the carriage and horseback rides, the food. The bigness of it. People there are so . . . so different. They're *civilized*. It's not like Texas, where there's nothing to do but look at cows. There's hardly any people here, and most of them can't read or write.

They bathe once a month if they're fastidious—once a year if they're more average.''

Chance grinned, and Ellen went on, laughing. "And then there's buffalo hunters that you can smell over the next hill. At least the Tonks have been moved to a reservation since I left. You don't have to watch them stumbling around drunk in the streets any more.''

They both smiled broadly. These meetings with Chance meant the world to Ellen. Chance was the only one who understood how she felt. He was the only man in town who'd taken up for Tommy, too, and that meant a lot to her. If he ran a saloon and gambling den, so what? The best gentlemen in New Orleans drank and gambled.

It was funny. Ellen knew that her mother had known both Chance and her father before she was married. Ellen suspected that the two men had been rivals for her mother's hand, and she wondered why her mother had not chosen Chance. Her father was a wonderful man. He worshipped the ground Ellen walked on. But he was dull. His talk was all of cattle and crops and weather. Chance had style and charm. He could speak of things like history and art and books. The only book Ellen's parents had in the house, besides the Bible, was *Ivanhoe*, and that had been given to them by Chance.

"Why is it you never got married?" she said. "You're the most eligible man in the county. You have been ever since I can remember. Haven't you ever found the right girl?"

Chance waited before answering. When he did, he spoke slowly. "There was a girl once. But things didn't work out."

"Who was she?"

Chance shook his head.

"Tell me," she teased. "Come on."

"I can't. It's between the lady and myself."

"Maybe you weren't ready for marriage. Maybe you hadn't really found the right girl."

"Maybe I'm not the marrying kind."

She gave him a sly look, as if she regarded that statement as a challenge. "Why don't we see you at the ranch any more?"

"I don't know. Too busy, I guess."

"We've missed you. It hasn't been much fun, with Mother and Father the way they are."

"They're still having problems?"

She nodded. "I don't know what it is. They won't talk about it."

They grew quiet. They walked side by side, very close. The sun was hot. The air was still. Ellen slipped an arm through Chance's. She began swinging their linked arms in motion to their pace. Chance's heart pounded. His stomach felt weak.

Ellen looked over. She gave Chance that tight-lipped smile that he had seen so many times from her mother. He trembled. It was like being with Hope again. It was as if time had been turned back.

"I shouldn't be here with you like this," he said. Desire surged within him. He wanted to give her a chance to get out of this. He didn't know whether he wanted her to take it or not.

"Why not?" she said.

"Ellen, I'm older than you. I'm old enough to be—"

"My father?"

"Yes."

"You're not old. You're mature. I like mature men. The boys my own age are silly. I might as well take up with Alex."

They walked more slowly. Then Chance stopped, stepping in front of Ellen as he did, letting her momentum carry her into his arms. He held her lightly. She rested her arms atop his, not looking at him, her long fingers playing with an imaginary loose thread on his shirt.

He crooked a finger and tilted her chin. Chance looked into her eyes. Green eyes.

He kissed her gently. Her lips tasted sweet and fresh.

Ellen smiled at him, then she lowered her eyes. She made no attempt to withdraw from his arms. She looked up again, and she cupped his jaw with one hand, drawing him to her and kissing him. It was a lingering kiss, a loving kiss.

"Maybe I'll be the one to tame you," she whispered.

"Maybe you will," he lied.

They kissed again, with growing passion. When Chance swept Ellen up and laid her on the ground, she realized that this was going farther than she had ever intended, and she was surprised that she didn't care. She was carried away by her own desire, by her awakening womanhood.

At one point in the lovemaking that followed, Chance mumbled, "Hope. Oh, Hope."

"What did you say?" Ellen said. She spoke as if drugged.

"Nothing," Chance rasped, and he pressed his lips on hers.

52

A week later Chance and Ellen ran away to Denver. In his infatuation with her, Chance believed it would be like running away with Hope. It would be like getting a second chance at happiness. He didn't worry about being caught. No one knew about him and Ellen. He had left town like this before, and people were used to it. People would wonder what had happened to Ellen, though. Had she been kidnapped, murdered? Chance pictured Will following her tracks, then losing them, because Chance had made sure they would be lost. He pictured Will coming to him for help, only to find that he was out of town. He pictured Will starting on another long search. Once he would have felt guilty about that, but no longer. He blamed Will for the death of his son. He felt within his rights to take Will's daughter in return.

Chance and Ellen hooked up with a freight outfit for protection, and they arrived in Denver toward the end of October. There was already snow in the surrounding high country. Denver was a real city, with sidewalks and brick buildings and street lights. Chance had picked it because it was a mining town, and they were unlikely to run into any of Will's cattlemen friends there. He figured to winter there, then move on to San Francisco in the spring.

Chance and Ellen took a room at a boardinghouse, and at first everything was fine. They got out of bed only long enough to eat. Before long, however, Chance grew restless. He began drinking and gambling, staying in the saloons till all hours, leaving Ellen by herself.

Ellen had not seen this side of Chance before. This was not what she had expected. "Chance," she said one gray afternoon, not long after he'd awakened, "we've been here two weeks now. When are we going to get married? When are we going to get a place of our own?"

Chance was shaving in the wash basin. He had a hangover, and he nicked himself, and that put him in an even worse temper. "Christ, will you stop whining about getting married? It's all you ever go on about."

Ellen held out her arms helplessly. "That's why we came here, isn't it?"

Chance finished shaving. He pressed a towel to his bleeding cheek. "No. We came here to be together. To have some good times."

"That's it?" Ellen said.

"As far as I'm concerned, it is."

Ellen was quiet for a moment. "And when the good times are over?"

"Then they're over. I'm not going to marry you, Ellen. I'm not going to marry anybody. I told you, I'm not the marrying kind."

"I thought you loved me."

"I never said that."

"You certainly implied it," she said angrily, and her voice began rising. "Do you think I gave myself to you because I was bored, because I was looking for something to do? Because I was looking for some *good times*?" Tears welled in her eyes.

Chance put down the towel. His head throbbed, and he couldn't stand clinging women. As much out of politeness as from any real feeling, he reached out to her. "Ellen, come on. Stop—"

"No!" She jerked her arm away. "Don't touch me."

Chance rolled his eyes. "I can't stand any more of this." He put on his coat and hat, and he left the room, slamming the door behind him.

Ellen went for a long walk to compose herself. When she returned to the room, she found Chance packing his traps. The smell of whiskey on his breath told how he'd occupied his time since walking out.

"What are you doing?" she said.

"Leaving."

"Leaving? For where?"

"Kingdom." There was only one place for Chance. If he couldn't be with Hope, and he knew that he never would be with her after this episode, he had to be near her. He had to be there if she needed him. Ellen was not the same as her mother. He was disgusted with himself for being crazy enough to think that she would be.

"What about us?" Ellen said.

"What about us? It's over." Chance stopped what he was doing. "Look, Ellen, I made a mistake, all right? We both did. I thought you knew what you were getting into. I thought you were grown up. But you're not. I was right the first time—I'm too old for you. All this talk about marriage is driving me crazy. You're just a kid. We don't belong together. We never did."

"Why, you . . . you . . ."

" 'Bastard' is the word you're searching for," he said.

Ellen sank into a chair. "So you're just going to leave me?"

"I'm not leaving you. I'll see you safe home. Pack your things."

"And what do I tell my parents when I get there?"

"Tell them the truth. Tell them anything you want, I don't care. Come on, I want to get out of here."

Ellen couldn't face the thought of home. She couldn't face the humiliation of confronting her parents, her brothers. The people in town, the people she disliked so much, would laugh at her. They would laugh at her the way they had laughed at Tommy, and that memory made her hate them even more. She had too much pride to go home.

"I'm staying here," she said.

Chance was surprised and, at first, a bit amused. "Staying? What will you do? Where will you live?"

"I'll find work. Women aren't slaves anymore, you know. We can hold jobs and support ourselves."

"Don't count on it." He looked closely at her. "You're not serious, are you?"

"Perfectly serious."

"Come on, Ellen. Don't be—"

"I said I'm staying, and that's final."

Chance let out his breath. It was useless to argue with her. She was stubborn, like her father. He was in a hurry, and he wanted a drink before he left town. He emptied his fat wallet onto the bed. "Here, then. This will get you . . ."

Ellen picked up the bills and coins, and she threw them in Chance's face. "This is what I think of you, and this is what I think of your money."

Chance started forward, hand raised. His face stung. Nobody did that to him. It was only with an effort that he restrained himself from hitting her. At last he calmed down. "Suit yourself," he said coldly.

He scooped up the money and put it back in his wallet. He finished packing and picked up his traps. "I guess this is goodbye," he said.

"Just get out," Ellen told him. "Get out, and leave me alone."

Chance shrugged and left.

The room was paid until the end of the week. Ellen had only a few dollars of her own. She had not brought much money, leaving that for Chance. She was not the type to contemplate misfortune, though. She had made up her mind to do something, and she was going to do it. As soon as Chance had gone, she set out looking for work.

She canvassed every employer in Denver. She visited banks, lawyers, accountants, and assayers, and she discovered that her expensive education counted for nothing. She was a woman, and no one would hire a woman. Next, she looked for work as a clerk, or behind a sales counter. The answer was the same— no women. In desperation, she tried to find employment as a seamstress or milliner, even as a cook or waitress. But those jobs were all filled, and filled by women with more experience than Ellen possessed.

The room rent ran out, and Ellen was forced to leave, carrying what possessions she could wrap in her scarf. She wandered the streets for the rest of the day, still seeking work. Her money was gone. She could not buy a meal. The day was windy and cold, and as evening came on, it began to snow. Dispirited, weary, Ellen sank down on the sidewalk, her bundle beside her.

She had no idea what she was going to do, or where she would spend the night.

"Hard times?" said a husky female voice.

Ellen looked up to see a big blond woman, wearing a sealskin coat. "Yes," she said. She wiped a cold, raw hand across her eyes, drying them.

The woman's slit eyes peered shrewdly from her porcine face. "Man trouble?"

Ellen nodded. Briefly, she told the woman her story. The snow was falling more heavily now. It had begun to coat the streets and buildings, the clothing of passersby. Shop lights gleamed faintly through the swirling flakes.

"Do you need a place to stay the night?"

"Yes. Yes, I do." Ellen rose, stiffly because of the cold.

"Come to my house. I'll put you up."

"Thank you," Ellen said.

"Don't mention it. I'm always glad to help a girl in trouble. My name is Dolly. Dolly McComas."

They began walking. Ellen's feet were wet and cold from the snow.

"You can't find work of any kind?" Dolly said.

Ellen shook her head. "Most of the people I ask just laugh at me, because I'm a woman."

Dolly nodded sympathetically. "It's a cruel world for women. Believe me, I know. Well, I can put you to work, if you like. Do you dance?"

"Yes, I love to dance."

"There you are, then. You can work for me as a dancer. I own the Palace, on Market Street."

Ellen had not grown up in a town like Kingdom for nothing. She stopped walking. "Just a dancer?"

"Just a dancer. Any other arrangements you may make are up to you. I warn you, though, some of my customers don't dance too good."

Ellen didn't see where she had a choice. At least she'd have a room for the night. If she didn't like the work, she would quit. "I'll do it," she said.

"Good," said Dolly. They started walking again. "You can rest tonight. Start tomorrow."

"I'll start tonight if it's all the same to you. The sooner I make some money, the better."

Dolly's house was a turreted brick structure on 17th Street. The door was opened by a uniformed black maid. Behind her lounged a coarse, brutal-looking man, with thinning sandy hair and jug ears, picking his nails. In the parlor could be seen girls in various stages of dishabille.

Ellen turned to Dolly. "This is a brothel, isn't it? I should have known."

Dolly brushed the snow from her sealskin coat. She took off the coat and handed it to the maid. "This is my house. This is where the girls who work for me live. Put away your things. The dinner bell will ring shortly." To the maid she said, "Show this lady to Cherry's old room. Give her Cherry's dresses. They should fit her."

"Yes'm," said the maid. To Ellen she said, "This way, miss," and she started up the stairs.

The room was small but neat, sparsely furnished. The mattress was rolled on the metal bedstead. The maid opened a lacquered armoire to show Ellen the dresses.

"What happened to Cherry?" Ellen asked.

The maid shrugged. "Too much morphine, that's what they say." Before Ellen could ask her anything else, she was gone.

Ellen put on one of the dresses. It was made of red satin, with ruffles around the bodice that left her shoulders bare. She felt silly and exposed and cheap, but she knew it was part of the business. There were red dancing slippers, too, with tarnished tin buckles. She put them on. When the dinner bell rang, she followed the sound of feet downstairs.

The dining room was crowded with girls, dressed much the same as Ellen. Dolly was not there. She must take her meals somewhere else. Most of the girls were between seventeen and twenty-two. A few looked even younger. They were plain and probably uneducated, and they had spent whatever money they had in vain attempts to make themselves attractive. The room reeked of their cheap perfume. They fell to their food with gusto, using language that would have curled a sailor's hair.

The room quieted as Ellen entered and took a chair. At the head of the table sat a wiry, dark-haired girl, better looking than the rest. She slurped stew from a spoon and regarded Ellen with bloodshot eyes. "What's your name?" she said in a whiskey-harsh voice.

"Ellen. What's yours?"

The girl ignored the question. "Where you from?"

"Kingdom, Texas."

"Texas. Shit. I got my fill of Texans in Dodge."

Ellen said nothing, looking down.

"Kingdom?" said a girl next to Ellen. "That's my favorite town. You ever work at Chance Evans's place there?"

Ellen's heart froze at the mention of the man who had gotten her into this. "I was born there. Kingdom, I mean."

"Where *have* you worked?" said the wiry girl, looking at Ellen closely.

"Oh, around."

"And you're working here now?"

"Um, yes."

"Well, let me tell you something. Don't go claim-jumping our customers. You hear?"

Ellen nodded. The bowl of stew reached her. She took some and ate greedily. She found herself watching the wiry girl at the head of the table, whom the others called Frankie. Frankie's mass of dark hair was pinned loosely, and she was hung all over with shoddy jewelry. She had a hard mouth, hard as nails. Her eyes were hard, too, large and unflinching, and there were dark circles under them. She looked as if she had seen all the hardships life had to offer; and yet, deep inside her, it seemed there was a glimmer of softness, a gentleness long suppressed or perhaps never brought out. In another life, she might have been attractive.

"What are you looking at, bitch?" Frankie suddenly demanded.

"Who, me?" said Ellen. "Nothing."

"You looking at me?"

"No. I'm just looking around, that's all."

"I don't like to be looked at—not by women."

Some of the girls laughed. Ellen turned away self-consciously. One of the girls stood and peered out the chintz curtains. "Christ, it's still snowing. Hope it don't hurt business."

"As long as Jimmie's there," said Frankie, content to leave Ellen alone for now. "Jimmie promised me a present tonight."

She wiped stew off her mouth with the back of her hand, and she stood. "Time to go. I want a drink before work."

She left the room. The other girls filed out behind her. Ellen wolfed down the rest of her stew, and she followed them.

53

The Palace was just behind Dolly's house. It was a barnlike building, whose worn floorboards were wet and smeared tonight from snowy boots. There was a bar, and tables, and a raised dias for the orchestra. From the ceiling hung a brass chandelier, and the light from its lamps reflected on the ceiling and walls. In the back of the room, a flight of stairs led to a second floor.

Dolly looked with approval at the way Ellen filled out the red dress. "The business is simple," she told Ellen. "If the men want to dance with you, they buy a ticket from Carl." She indicated the brutal-looking man Ellen had seen earlier, who sat at a box by the front door. "They give the ticket to you, and at the end of the night, you turn them in. Tickets are a dollar. Seventy-five cents goes to the house, the rest to you. You can make more money by getting the customers to buy you drinks. The girl will tell you how it works."

"I don't drink," Ellen said.

"So what? Just make them *buy* you drinks. I don't care what you do with them."

The orchestra struck up the "Thunder and Lightning" polka. The customers were from all walks of life, sporting all manner of dress. Ellen, because of her newness and good looks, was much in demand. Dancing at the Palace was a romping, stomping affair, with lots of yelling, and Ellen had to be careful of her feet. It was hot work, and hard on the legs. The few slow dances were worse. Then the men were all over her, pawing her, trying to kiss her and feel her breasts. It was all she could do to put them off without being impolite. Between dances, the men bought the girls drinks. Ellen asked for whiskey with a water chaser, and she drank only the water. Most of the girls drank what passed for champagne, guzzling glass after glass, letting it run down their chins and laughing. From time to time, Ellen saw one of the girls go up the back stairs with a customer.

Ellen was proud of herself, because the men were fighting to dance with her and buy her drinks. She was tired but exhilarated. She had done something for herself. Then she danced with a well-dressed man of about thirty, who said his name was Jimmie. Jimmie's arrogant gray eyes roamed over Ellen's body during the dance methodically, as if he were undressing her. At the dance's end, he cupped a hand and spoke in Ellen's ear. His breath was heavy with anisette. "How much to go upstairs?"

Ellen looked at him in surprise. "What?"

"Upstairs. What's it going to cost for you?"

Ellen shook her head. "I don't do that."

The gray eyes narrowed. He grabbed her arm. "Don't jerk me around. How much?"

"I said no." Ellen shook off his hand. "I wouldn't go upstairs with you if you were the last man on earth."

"Really? We'll see about that."

Jimmie walked off. Ellen saw him talking to Dolly. She was aware of looks from the other girls, especially Frankie.

Dolly beckoned Ellen over. Her fat face showed concern. "What's the matter here?" she said.

"This man won't leave me alone," Ellen told her. "He wants me to go upstairs with him."

"Then do it. He'll pay you twenty dollars. That's twice the going rate."

Ellen stepped back angrily. "You said all I had to do was dance."

Up until that moment Dolly had been friendly with Ellen. Now she dropped the act. "Go with him," she said. "Do it now."

"No! I quit."

As the music started again, Dolly clamped a hand around Ellen's arm. She dug her fingers into Ellen's bicep, until Ellen twisted with pain. Above the noise of the orchestra, Dolly said, "You can't quit."

"Why not?" Ellen said, grimacing.

"You owe me money. Five dollars for your room. A dollar for the meal you had at the house. Twenty dollars for each dress . . ."

"Take the dresses back. I don't want your trash. I've made enough to cover the room and the meal."

"You bought those dresses, and I have a signed receipt to prove it. You owe me eighty-six dollars."

Ellen struggled, eyes wide. "What are you talking about? I never signed a thing."

"That's not what the court will hear," Dolly said.

Dolly let go of Ellen's arm. Ellen's chest heaved. She felt betrayed and stupid. "You knew—you knew this would happen. You set me up. Well, you won't get away with it. I'm going to the marshal."

"Jimmie is the marshal."

Ellen's jaw fell. Dolly smiled, and she said, "If you don't go with Jimmie, he'll arrest you for nonpayment of debt. Do you know what that means?"

Ellen said nothing. She rubbed her sore arm.

"It means you'll be put in the county lockup. You'll be in an open ward, with the men, with some of the most hardened criminals in Colorado. You'll be raped in there, by whoever wants you, as often as they want you—and no one will lift a finger to help."

Ellen clenched her teeth. She was trembling. This was a nightmare. She kept thinking it would end. She kept thinking there was a way out. But there wasn't.

Dolly's smile lengthened. "When you've served your time, you'll be back on the street. You'll be a vagrant, and if Jimmie wants, he can rearrest you, and it all will start over. There's only one way to make a living around here, honey. So wise up and go with the man."

Ellen did what she had sworn never to do. She said, "Please, Dolly. My father is one of the wealthiest men in Texas. He'll pay anything you say. All you have to do is write him."

Dolly stared at her. "Honey, I've heard that line before. You're different, I'll admit, and what you say may even be true. In the meantime, Texas is a long way off, and I've got a business to run. Jimmie can give me a lot of trouble. He can close me down. He'll do it, too, if he doesn't get his way. I'm afraid you've attracted the wrong man.''

In a voice that was barely a whisper, Ellen said, ''What do I have to do?''

''Jimmie knows what to do. Room Seven's yours, in the back.'' Dolly's voice grew kindly once more. ''Go on, Ellen. It's not so bad. Get yourself a drink first, but don't take too long.'' To one of the barmen, she called, ''Harry, give her a whiskey. Put in something from my bottle.''

Ellen walked to the bar, stiff-legged. The room seemed to be whirling in the reflected light from the chandelier. The dance had stopped.

The barman poured her drink, then added a few drops from a small green bottle. ''What's that?'' Ellen said.

''Laudanum,'' the barman told her. ''Makes you feel good.''

Ellen had never tasted whiskey, much less laudanum. Frankie and the other girls were watching, though. Ellen had to show them she could drink. She tossed the drink down, as she had seen them do. It seared her throat and stomach, making her cough. The aftertaste was awful. Jimmie came up behind her.

''Better go,'' the barman told her.

Ellen led Jimmie through the crowd, toward the stairs. She began to feel relaxed, light-headed. She supposed that must be from the laudanum. The music started again, and it sounded surprisingly pretty.

They went up the stairs, to a dimly lit corridor. Ellen searched the doors for Number Seven. She heard raucous laughter and squeals from the other rooms. She found Number Seven. It was unlocked, and they went in. Jimmie followed her closely. She could feel his hot breath on her neck. She could smell the anisette. She was light on her feet. It was almost as if she were dreaming, as if there were a fuzzy, protective cloud around the edges of reality. Even sounds seemed distorted.

Inside the room, a coal-oil lamp was lit. The room was cheaply furnished, with a bed, washstand, and chair. It had a funny smell. A sweaty, sordid smell.

Ellen wasn't sure what to do next. She turned to Jimmie, who already had his coat off. She supposed she should kiss him or something, but he started tearing at her clothes, breathing hard. Her first instinct was to hit him, but she knew that this act had to be, and she let him do it. Time seemed to have no meaning, and before she knew it, they were both naked and he was pressing her to the bed, kissing her face and neck, searching her breasts and thighs with rough, insensitive hands. The smell of anisette filled her brain. She stared at the tarpaper ceiling and tried to pretend she was somewhere else.

This isn't happening. It's not happening.

It was over quickly. Mercifully. She hardly felt a thing. Afterward, Jimmie knelt astride her. The unsettling gray eyes looked down. Suddenly he slapped her face, hard. The back of his heavy ring cut her mouth. "Next time put some life into it," he said.

Ellen averted her head. She tasted blood in her mouth. She felt it running down her chin.

Jimmie got dressed. "I've a mind not to give you this," he said. He took two double eagles from his pocket and dropped them on the crumpled bed. "Next time you'll do it for free. You'll do it better, too. A damn sight better. It'll go hard on you if you don't."

He left the room. Ellen curled up on the bed, crying. She wanted to sleep. She wanted to die.

There was a loud knocking at the door. "Hurry up, Ellen," said Dolly. "It's crowded out here. I need dancers."

54

Ellen waited until nearly dawn, when the last girls had come back to Dolly's house, and all was quiet. Then she wrapped up her possessions, put on her coat, and sneaked downstairs. Her mouth was sore and puffy where Jimmie had hit her. She had no money and nowhere to go, but she didn't care. She had to get away.

She went to the front door, treading lightly. She turned the handle. The door was locked. She felt for the key on a side-board, trying not to make noise. Suddenly a powerful hand gripped her shoulder.

"Going somewhere?"

It was Carl, Dolly's bouncer. He twisted Ellen around, leering at her in the darkness.

Ellen kicked Carl's shin. He yelped and let her go. She ran, hoping to climb out a window. She knocked into a vase, and it fell with a crash. She cried out as Carl caught her. Ellen kicked and twisted in his grasp, but it was no use. She was held tightly. Carl forced a hand inside her coat and began squeezing her breast. Ellen tried to fight, and he laughed, turning her, pressing his thick lips to hers.

"What's going on?" said Dolly's voice.

Carl relaxed his grip as Dolly entered the hall, clad in a night-gown and robe, and carrying a lamp. Other girls appeared on the stairs, attracted by the commotion.

Dolly looked at Ellen's coat, at her wrapped possessions on the floor. She said, "You don't leave here till you pay what you owe me, Ellen. I don't run a slave house, but I won't let you welsh on a debt."

"You'll make paying hard, too, won't you?" Ellen said angrily. "I'll probably run up 'debts' to you faster than I can earn money. What are you going to charge me for next? Using the air in this house to breathe?"

Dolly laughed. "That's not a bad idea, is it? You're a valuable asset, Miss Ellen. Fancy girls like you don't come along often, and I don't intend to let you get away. Now, will you go back to your room, or shall I let Carl take you?"

Carl was grinning. His eyes were wide and eager. Ellen bowed her head. She knew when she was beaten. She picked up her parcel and trudged past Carl, up the stairs.

At the landing, she stopped. Frankie was there, waiting. Some of the other girls stood behind, in the shadows.

Frankie said, "You claim-jumping bitch. Jimmie's my man, and nobody takes my man."

Frankie lashed out with a fist, hitting Ellen in the nose. Ellen cried out and grabbed her face. As she did, Frankie pulled her forward and kneed her in the stomach. Ellen bent over, the wind knocked out of her. Frankie grabbed a handful of Ellen's hair, and she yanked it hard, forcing Ellen to her knees. With her free hand, Frankie pummeled Ellen's face. Ellen got her hands in front of her. She grabbed Frankie's arm and twisted Frankie's wrist, trying to break it. In pain, Frankie let go of Ellen's hair. She stepped back and booted Ellen hard in the ribs. Ellen's grip on the wrist relaxed, and Frankie pulled it free. Frankie kicked Ellen's ribs again. Ellen cried with pain. Frankie kicked her again, and again, and again. Ellen huddled against the wall, sobbing.

"Christ, Frankie, don't kill her," said someone.

Frankie stopped. She was gasping, out of breath.

Ellen gathered her strength. She lurched to her feet. Before Frankie could react, Ellen threw a shoulder into her and knocked her down the stairs. Ellen fell on the landing. Frankie bounced all the way down the stairs, hitting her head and careening off the rail, to land in a heap at the bottom. Ellen staggered down after her, while the other girls whooped to see the battle.

Frankie was dazed, but she got to her feet, just as Ellen reached the bottom of the stairs. The two girls locked arms. They rocked back and forth, kicking and pinching and scratching. Frankie tried to scoop out Ellen's eye with a thumbnail. Ellen bit a chunk out of Frankie's cheek and made her yell. Their faces and clothes were red with blood from Ellen's nose. The other girls were screaming with excitement.

Ellen hooked a leg behind Frankie's and threw her down. She fell on Frankie, hitting Frankie's face with both fists. Frankie rolled over, screaming, trying to protect herself. Ellen grabbed Frankie's hair and began banging her head on the floor. Frankie's forehead thudded against the varnished oak. "Ow!" Frankie screamed. "Ow! Ow! Stop!" There were spots of blood on the floor.

Ellen got up. She grabbed Frankie by the collar and belt. She hauled Frankie to her feet and rammed her head into the newel at the foot of the stairs. "Ow!" Frankie screamed again, and she collapsed to the floor, moaning and crying.

Ellen turned her over with a foot. Frankie's battered face and forehead were swelling. There was blood in her dark hair. Ellen said, "The next time, *bitch*, I'll kill you. So stay out of my way. Can you remember that?"

Frankie nodded, drawing up in pain.

The anger suddenly drained from Ellen. She sagged. She felt no elation of victory, only shame at what she'd done. She started to walk away, and she came face to face with Dolly.

Dolly was standing in the parlor entrance, still carrying the lamp. Carl was with her. Dolly looked at the two girls, and she stayed surprisingly calm. "If I wanted to stage cat fights, I would build a hall and charge admission," she said. "Unfortunately, my present business will not prosper if my girls beat each other to a pulp. You will both miss work tomorrow night. And it will cost each of you twenty dollars for the damages to the house."

"Shit," muttered Frankie, from the floor. Dolly turned and walked away. Carl grinned at the two girls and followed Dolly.

Ellen's voice sounded funny because of all the blood in her nose. "I can't stand that man. Why does Dolly keep him around?"

"He's her brother," Frankie said.

Later, Ellen visited Frankie's room. Ellen's left eye was swollen shut, and her cheeks were puffy and bruised. She knocked on Frankie's door, but there was no answer. She opened the door a crack. "Frankie?"

The room was a mess. Clothes and empty bottles were slung about. Frankie sat on the bed. One hand held a compress to her head; the other hand tilted a half-empty bottle of whiskey to her mouth. There was a huge, purple-black bruise on her forehead, and she was going to have a scar where Ellen had bitten her cheek.

Ellen hesitated, then she said, "Frankie, I'm sorry about Jimmie. I just wanted you to know. I didn't chase him, he came after me."

"Yeah," Frankie said dully. She took another swig from the bottle, and Ellen suddenly realized that the look on her face was not a hard look, but a look of resignation. Ellen had beaten her up, but she'd been beaten before, and she'd be beaten again. She was used to it. Ellen felt sorry for her. She resolved never to end up like that herself.

Ellen started to leave. Frankie said, "Want a drink?"

"All right," Ellen said.

Frankie handed her the bottle. Ellen took a swallow. She was getting used to the stuff. She handed the bottle back. "Thanks."

"Tell me the truth. You ain't done this kind of work before, have you?"

"No," Ellen said.

Frankie shook her head. "I knew it. That pig Dolly." She took another drink. "What do you think of the business?"

"I don't like it."

"You'll get used to it," Frankie said.

"Are you used to it?"

Frankie shrugged. "It's all I've ever done. My mom was in the game, she got me started. I worked with her for awhile. We were even in jail together once. She's dead now."

Frankie shifted the compress, wincing as she did. "This shit wasn't worth twenty dollars, you know?"

Ellen laughed, and the laughter made her bruised ribs hurt. "I know," she said.

"I got to give it to you, Texas. You did a job on me."

"You didn't do bad yourself," Ellen said.

Frankie waved a hand toward the room's single chair. "Have a seat." She passed Ellen the bottle again. "We might as well mend our wounds together."

55

Ellen never wrote her father for the money to buy off Dolly. It was too late. The damage was done. She could never face her parents again. She was determined to get away from Dolly, but she would do it on her own.

Whiskey and laudanum made Ellen's new life easier, though she worried sometimes, because it required ever larger doses of laudanum to make her feel good. Dolly had a deal with a Second Street doctor, and the girls got their laudanum and morphine cheap, with no questions asked. Ellen's nights were a whirl of dancing and sex with men she did not know. She drifted along in a dreamlike state, half in, half out of reality. She had become a whore, but she told herself there was nothing wrong with that. Her mother had known a whore once. The whore had been a good woman. She had saved Ellen's and her mother's lives.

Ellen learned the game. She learned how to keep herself and her customers clean. She learned how to moan and thrash in bed, as if in ecstasy. Most of all, she learned how to steal, for she knew that stealing was the only way out of Dolly's debt.

She particularly delighted in stealing from Jimmie. She was free to Jimmie now. She had become part of Dolly's payoff to him. Sometimes Jimmie gave Ellen jewelry and new clothes; sometimes he beat her. Sometimes he did both. She grew to loathe the smell of anisette. The only thing that stopped her from murdering him in his sleep was the thought of the penitentiary.

Ellen kept her money hidden under a floorboard. Slowly, night by night, the amount grew. She was within a few dollars of five hundred—the sum that Dolly had set for her freedom. Then, just before Christmas, she discovered that she was pregnant.

When Dolly found out, she had Frankie take Ellen to a grim-faced Swede named Mrs. Pachen, who worked out of a shack off Blake Street. Mrs. Pachen dosed Ellen with morphine and performed the operation. It was over quickly, and she sent Ellen home.

Ellen was sick and bleeding as she stumbled back to the turreted house on 17th Street. Passersby stared at her. Frankie took her arm, alarmed. "Hey, Texas, are you all right?"

"I don't know." Ellen missed a step. She felt weak, and she guessed that she would have been in considerable pain if not for the morphine. "I don't know how you're supposed to feel."

Ellen spent the rest of the day in bed. Frankie stayed with her. Terrible spasms were tearing Ellen apart inside, and she sought relief in drafts of laudanum.

That evening, Dolly visited her. "You picked a fine time

for this," Dolly said. "Get out of bed. You have to work tonight."

Ellen was pale and sweating. The bleeding had stopped, but she did not feel right. "I don't think I can work, Dolly."

"You have to. It's Christmas Eve, our biggest night of the year. We charge triple tonight, and the men will be expecting you."

"I feel bad, Dolly. Real bad."

"Nonsense, you're just tired. You can have the rest of the week off, but tonight you work."

Frankie said, "Hell, Dolly, she's sick. She needs a real doctor. That butcher Pachen—"

"She will work!" Dolly exploded, and dribbles of spit appeared on her lips. "I have promised too many people. I have promised Jimmie."

Dolly glowered at Frankie. "See that she is out there, Frankie—for both your sakes." Then she left.

Frankie helped Ellen get out of bed. "Come on, Texas. You can make it. It's just for one night. After that, plenty of rest."

Frankie fixed Ellen whiskey with a stiff jolt of laudanum. She helped Ellen get dressed. Ellen's pain receded to a numb glow. Frankie walked her to the Palace, which was decorated with Christmas wreaths and garlands and a big tree in one corner. The men were lined up in their best clothes. Ellen began dancing, gritting her teeth and trying to keep up with her wildly enthusiastic partners, knowing that later she would have sex with Jimmie and maybe get punched by him, too. It took all her strength, all her concentration, to keep going. She hardly knew where she was. The night became a blur. Gradually the blur resolved itself. It became a tall figure with a buffalo robe coat and a big Texas hat. It became her father.

Ellen came to with a start. It *was* her father. She wasn't dreaming. He was standing in front of her, grim-faced, with a Winchester rifle in his hands.

The room had grown quiet. The music and dancing had stopped. All eyes were on the tall Texan with the rifle. Ellen's head was swimming with drugs and fever. "Daddy . . . ?"

Will held out a hand. Quietly he said, "Come on, Ellen. We're leaving."

Behind Will, the bouncer Carl left his box. He strode sound-lessly across the floor, a weighted sap in his hand. Will must have had a sixth sense, because before Ellen could warn him, he pivoted and, with a sweeping backhand motion, smashed the rifle barrel into the side of Carl's head. Carl dropped to the floor as though poleaxed. Blood trickled from his nose and ear.

"Carl!" yelled Dolly. She rushed forward, bending over her unconscious brother. "What's happening here? Jimmie, arrest this man!"

Jimmie approached from the bar. He was wearing evening clothes. Ellen said, "Watch out, Daddy. He has a gun in his coat."

Jimmie stopped in front of Will, shoulders squared. Carl's fate did not interest Jimmie. Jimmie's manly pride had been wounded. His gray eyes bored into Will's, and there was a threat in his voice. "That's my girl you're talking to, old man."

"Your girl?" Will's lips curled in anger. "*Your* girl?" He jabbed the Winchester barrel into Jimmie's chest, forcing him backward. "Mister, this girl is my daughter"—another jab forced Jimmy back again—"and I'm taking her home. And if you try to stop me, you're going to find more trouble than you ever knew existed." He gave Jimmie a final shove with the rifle, knocking the marshal off his feet and onto the seat of his pants.

Jimmie went for his gun, but before he got it raised, the Winchester's barrel was in his face, with the hammer clicked back.

"Do it," Will said.

Jimmie swallowed. Slowly he set the pistol on the floor. Will picked it up and stuck it in his belt. Humiliated, Jimmie licked his lips.

Will stepped back, alert for trouble. "Let's go, Ellen."

Ellen had never seen her father like this. He did not seem dull now. "I'll get my things," she said.

"No need for that. I've got a coat and spare clothes in the buckboard. Come on."

"Wait," Ellen said. The room seemed to be reeling. She looked around for Frankie, and found her right at her elbow. "Frankie," she said. "Do you . . . why don't you come, too?"

Frankie's features softened. She seemed touched. For a moment Ellen thought she would accept. Then the hardness returned. "Hell, what good would it do? I ain't going to change." She smiled that cynical, lopsided smile of hers. "Go on, Texas. Get out of here."

Ellen left the hall. Will followed her, covering the crowd with his rifle. Outside, he helped his daughter into the buckboard. His horse was tied behind. He wrapped a heavy coat around Ellen, to keep out the December cold. Then he whipped up the team and started out of town.

56

The buckboard clattered through the darkness. The lights of the town had become a glow over the horizon.

"Do you think they'll come after us?" Ellen asked her father.

"No," Will said. He didn't think that puffed-up marshal would risk his life for a dance-hall girl, but he didn't tell Ellen that, to spare her feelings.

"How did you find me?"

"Same way a man finds anything. I kept looking. Your tracks was headed north before I lost them. I hit Wichita, Dodge, Ogallala, and a dozen other places. Nobody'd seen you, nobody'd heard of you. Anyway, it didn't make sense, you heading for them—they ain't much different than Kingdom. Then I thought about Denver. So I came here. I kept my eyes and ears open, and I heard some fellows talking about a girl called 'Texas Ellen,' at the Palace dance hall. I couldn't believe you'd be in a place like that, but I thought I should check it out, and . . . well, there you were."

Ellen shivered under the heavy coat. She wished she had some laudanum, or at least some whiskey. "How did you know I'd come with you?"

"I didn't intend to give you no choice."

Will slowed the buckboard. The horses' breaths made a frosty vapor in the dark. Will got out and put his ear to the frozen ground, but there was no sound of pursuit. There was a ranch, as waystations in that part of the country were called, not far down the road. He and Ellen would stay there the night. He peered at Ellen closely. She had looked sick in the dance hall, and she looked just as bad now. He was glad he'd brought a buckboard for her and not a horse as he'd originally planned. "Ellen, are you all right?"

There was no use lying. "No, Daddy, I'm not. I'm not well at all."

"What's wrong?"

She looked away. Tears brimmed her eyes. For the first time, she knew shame. "Well . . ." she said haltingly. "I was going to have a . . . I was going to have a baby, you see. And . . . and I . . ." She couldn't go on. She leaned into him and began crying.

Will put an arm around her. "Please, Daddy," she said. "I'm sorry."

"I know. I know." Will spoke softly, patting her back, the way he had when she was a baby. "Why did you do it, Ellen? Why did you run away?"

"Oh, God," she said, "I don't know, not anymore. At the time, I thought I was in love."

Will had known there was a man. He had found the tracks of the second horse. "Why couldn't you have told us? That's what I don't understand. Why did you have to run away?"

Ellen hesitated. "Because the man was . . . it was Chance."

Will stiffened. A disbelieving note came into his voice. "Chance? You mean your Uncle Chance? My friend Chance?"

"Yes."

She told him the story, how she and Chance had started meeting, how they'd consummated their relationship and run away. She told how Chance had left her, how she'd been taken in by Dolly, and all that had happened thereafter.

When she was finished, Will remained silent.

"Daddy, what are you going to do?" she said. "Daddy?"

"Don't you worry about that. The important thing right now is to get you away from those people."

Defensively she said, "They weren't all bad, you know." She thought of Frankie, and the others. The red dress Ellen wore, her cheap perfume and lipstick—they were all reminders of the life that she had been part of just a few hours before.

"No," Will said in a more understanding tone, "I guess they weren't."

Not long after, they reached the roadside ranch. The owner grumbled about being rousted from bed on Christmas Eve, but he saw to their animals, and his wife made Ellen a pallet by the fire, with some cold meat and drink. Ellen was soon asleep. Will stayed awake beside her until dawn, on guard.

It was late morning when Ellen awoke. She was pallid and feverish. Her dark eyeshadow had become smeared with sleep, and her thick makeup was wearing off in places, exposing bruises on the skin underneath.

"Merry Christmas," Will said.

"Merry Christmas," she replied.

"I guess it ain't much of one, is it?"

She smiled at him wanly. "It's the best one I ever had."

"Looks like they ain't after us. Want to stay here the day and rest up?"

She shook her head. "No, Daddy. I want to go home. That's all I want."

Will cleaned Ellen up, and the ranch owner's wife got her into new clothes and combed her hair in a bun, until she looked more like her old self. They had a late breakfast, but Ellen was too sick to eat much. Then Will hitched the team, and they started off.

They had not been on the road long when Ellen said, "Daddy, do you have a drink?"

"Sure. The canteen is—"

"I don't mean water. I mean . . . whiskey."

Will looked at her in surprise. "I don't carry whiskey, Ellen. You know that. I never have."

"Damn," she said, looking away. He had never heard her use such language.

Ellen was shaking, and not just from the cold. There was something she needed even more than the whiskey.

"Ellen, are you going to be all right?"

"Dad, if I tell you something, will you promise not to get mad?"

"I promise."

"I've been taking laudanum."

"Laudanum?"

"Yes, and I've got to have some now. I've got to have it real bad."

"How long have you been taking it?"

"Since I started working at Dolly's. It was the only way to get through. I would never have survived without it. But I've got to have it for the pain now. Please, Dad, at the next settlement will you buy me some? You can find it most anywhere."

"No, I won't," Will said.

"Then Christ damn you," she swore suddenly. After a second she said, "I'm sorry, I didn't mean that. Yes, I did, too. Oh, I don't know what I meant. Dad, just get me the laudanum. Please."

"No."

"Jimmie would have," she taunted.

"Jimmie, is that the fellow I knocked down? The one who called you his girl?"

"That's right."

"Well, if Jimmie wants you to have the laudanum so bad, let him bring it to you."

They drove on in silence.

57

As the day wore on, Ellen's cravings grew worse. She was shivering, and sweat rolled off her forehead at the same time. Will put her in the back of the buckboard. He covered her with his coat as well as her own. Sometimes she lay quietly. Sometimes she raved and cursed her father, demanding that he buy her laudanum, or even morphine. She threatened to leave him and go back to Denver. She threatened to sell her body for the money. He forced himself not to listen, to tell himself that it was the drug speaking, not Ellen. This behavior went on for two days, and at the end of that time, Ellen fell into a deep sleep. When she awoke, she had lost much of her craving, but she was pale and weak.

They traveled along the course of the Big Sandy Creek. There were ranches along the route, so shelter and forage for the horses were no problem, and when bad weather struck, they waited it out. They reached the Arkansas River and followed it into Dodge City. Will decided to wait there until spring. He would not risk crossing the plains with a sick girl in the dead of winter. He rented rooms at a boardinghouse run by a kindly widow, who looked after Ellen well. He took Ellen to see a doctor. The doctor was a dark-haired young man named Rossbach, and when the examination was over, he spoke to Will privately. He took off his glasses and pinched his bloodshot eyes between thumb and forefinger. It had been a long day. "Her injuries are internal," he said. "There's nothing I can do for her. She's been made a mess of."

"Will she pull through?"

The bloodshot eyes looked at Will directly. "Frankly, Mr. Cooper, I'm surprised she made it this far. It's only willpower that keeps her going."

The winter passed, and each day Ellen wasted away a bit more. Will felt helpless and frustrated, because there was nothing he could do for her. He had to watch the robust girl he'd once known grow pale and thin, in constant pain. The doctor prescribed something for the pain, but it was just laudanum, and Ellen refused to get involved with that again.

Spring came. Warm winds blew from the south. Will wanted to remain in Dodge. He didn't think Ellen was well enough to travel. But Ellen protested. "Please, Dad. I want to go home. I just want to see home again."

So Will bought a new buckboard. He made a bed for Ellen in the back, and he rigged a canvas awning to keep out the rain. They started for Texas. Ellen had grown so thin, she was hardly recognizable. Her once-rich hair was dry and brittle. Her teeth protruded from drawn-back lips. A white crust had formed around her mouth, and it pained her to drink. Will could scarcely bear to look at her. It was all he could do to keep the buckboard headed south, as mile by mile the desolate plains slipped behind them.

They crossed the Red River, then the Brazos. The weather was warm now, but Ellen stayed wrapped up, sleeping most of the time. She was feverish, and she had lost so much weight that Will could lift her as easily as he had done when she was a child.

Then one day, when the southerly breeze made the long grass wave, and the prairie was awash with bluebonnets, Will stopped the buckboard. In the back, Ellen raised her head with difficulty. "Are we home?" she whispered in a cracked voice.

Will was staring into the middle distance. There, a brindle cow stood guard over her calf, who lay in the grass at her side. Cow and calf eyed the wagon suspiciously. Will knew the cow. There was an HH brand on its flank, with two underbits out of the left ear.

"Yes," he said. "We're home."

From the back of the buckboard came a long, drawn-out sigh. Then silence.

Will hung his head. Ellen was gone.

Will wrapped Ellen's body in blankets, and he continued on. He buried Ellen on a little knoll overlooking the ranch. It was a place he used to bring her as a child, after the war, when she would ride on the front of his saddle. She would pick wildflowers there and give them to him, and he would hold her hand and point out landmarks and the dust of distant antelope, and he would tell her of all the things they would do together some day. Now there was just this one last thing to do.

Will stayed on the knoll a long time before leaving.

58

Hope was digging in her flower garden, preparing the soil for seeding when Will's buckboard came up the drive. The ranch was quiet. The corrals were nearly empty. James was at school, while Alex and most of the hands were off on spring roundup. Hope came to the buckboard, wiping her hands on her apron. Will had been gone almost seven months.

Hope looked downcast. "You didn't find her," she said.

"I found her," Will said. He was tired and travel-stained, yet steeled with implacable purpose.

"Then where . . . ?"

"I just buried her. On Lookout Hill."

"Oh, no." Hope closed her eyes and put a hand to her mouth. A less-strong woman might have collapsed, or at least have had to sit. Hope stood bolt upright, as if the very rigidity of her posture helped to ease the pain.

Will got down from the buckboard, and he put his arms around her, comforting her as the tears came. He stroked her hair, soothing her. It had been a long time since he'd held her like this, and he'd forgotten how much her feelings meant to him. He wanted to stay here with her, but he could not.

"I'll take you to the grave later," he told Hope. "There's something I got to do first."

He went back into the house. He was gone no more than a minute, then he came back. He went to the corral and saddled himself a fresh horse.

"Where are you going?" Hope said.

"To town."

He started to mount, then stopped. He wrenched the locked deer antlers from their spot above the front door. The antlers were yellow and brittle with age, but he still could not separate

321

them, try as he would. So he threw them down, and he drew his rifle from his saddle, and in a cold rage he smashed the antlers to pieces with the rifle butt. He kicked the pieces across the yard. Then he mounted and rode off.

It was late afternoon when he reached Kingdom. He hitched his horse in front of Chance's saloon, and he strode inside. Chance was not to be seen, and Will pushed his way through the unusually sparse crowd to the office.

Chance was at his desk, beneath the picture of the Alamo, going over receipts. There was a drink at his hand. He stood as Will came in. "Will, good to see you. What brings you here? It's not time for your money, but if you want it now, I can always . . ."

He stopped as he saw the look in Will's eye. At last he said, "You know."

"I know," Will said.

Will had thought about Chance every mile of the way from Denver. Jake Koerner and Sam and the others had been right. Chance had changed. Will was wrong not to have seen it, and he had paid the price. Chance had become bitter, cold, a man without life inside.

"Why'd you do it, Chance?"

Chance sat back down. He looked at his hands. "I didn't want to, believe me. But she threw herself at me, and you know how I am. I couldn't help myself. I . . ."

"You *should* have helped yourself, Chance. She was just a girl. You were the growed man. You were my friend. It was your responsibility not to let it get started. But you've never been one for responsibility, have you? You've always done as you pleased, and damn the consequences."

Chance had no defense. He looked up. "Is she home?"

"She's dead."

Chance half rose from his chair. His pale face went even paler. "Dead? How? What . . . ?"

"After you left her, she went to work in a dance hall. She got addicted to drugs. She got herself with child and tried to get rid of it. But something went wrong, and it killed her."

Chance sat back down. His voice trembled. "Will, I had no idea. I tried to get her to come back. Really, I did. I didn't want her to stay there. I never meant for any of this to . . .''

"Save it," Will told him.

Will took something from his vest pocket, and he tossed it onto Chance's desk.

It was an arrowhead.

Chance stared at the arrowhead for a long moment. It was the one he'd dug from Will's back all those years before, the one that Will kept displayed on the mantel over his fireplace.

Will said, "It's over between us, Chance. The partnership, everything. Over."

Before Chance could say anything, Will was gone.

Will left the saloon. He crossed the street to Sam Sommerville's store. The store was not crowded this afternoon. Sam was talking to a woman who wanted to return a mail-order dress. He saw Will, excused himself, and hurried forward.

"Will, you're back! Did you find Ellen?"

Sam stopped. He had never seen Will look so grim.

"I guess I'll be running for that sheriff's job, after all," Will said.

Part VII

59

The vote count began at sunset, with the arrival of the ballots from Wilcox. Within an hour, the whole town had gathered around the courthouse steps to hear the results. The crowd was not as large as it had been for previous elections. Boarded-up stores and abandoned houses gave evidence of the hard times that had befallen Kingdom.

The courthouse was hung with bunting. There were torches on the steps, and more on the gallery, where the clerks and recorder sat. This was September and just a Democratic primary election, but because no Republican had run for office in Benedict County since the end of Reconstruction, today's results were final. The county recorder was a Confederate veteran with a shattered hip, and he held his job because of that status. He rose, staggering a bit on his crutch, a victim of the long Election Day festivities, as were many in the crowd.

"Here are the official returns from today's balloting," he announced.

As was the custom, he began with the vote for city offices. Sam Sommerville's reelection as mayor had been a foregone conclusion. The only surprise was in how far the total number of ballots had fallen since the boom years. Once Kingdom could be counted on for nearly eleven hundred votes. Now there were just a few more than four hundred. Wilcox had sent at least that many ballots. After each winner was announced, the town band played "The Yellow Rose of Texas" or "The Bonnie Blue Flag," and people marched and cheered and had more drinks.

Across the street, Chance and Amos Blaine watched the procedings from the porch of the Cricket Saloon. Chance, as always, wore the finest black broadcloth. The diamond in his stickpin was real. Blaine was dressed much the same, perhaps in unconscious imitation of his boss. Both men drank whiskey from tumblers, while Blaine puffed a long cigar. A couple of Chance's men lounged nearby, their barely concealed pistols providing visible evidence of where the real power lay in Kingdom.

When the municipal results were over, the recorder announced, "For the office of county sheriff."

The crowd quieted. There was a pause while one of the clerks corrected some arithmetic. Blaine gripped the awning support with a bony hand, and he leaned forward. "Well, this is the one everybody's been waiting for."

He was right. The contest for sheriff had overshadowed the rest of the election. Chance had tried every trick he knew to throw the victory to his man Butler. He had bribed some voters; he had threatened others. At considerable expense, he had brought men into the county to swell the voter rolls. At one point, he'd even had the pompous Butler distributing food to needy families. Butler had run an aggressive, slashing campaign, attacking Will as a power-seeking cattle baron, attacking him as an enemy of the common man, debunking his war and Ranger records. Will, on the other hand, had not campaigned at all.

At the end, the county had sponsored a debate between the two men. Butler had made a long speech, citing his record, citing the number of arrests he had made, vowing to work twice as hard next term. He had promised fairness to the innocent and harshness to the guilty. He had extolled the greatness of the law, the importance of experience, his love for Texas, and anything else he could think of. He had finished to generous applause. Then Will had taken the platform. Will had cleared his throat, nervous because he was speaking before a crowd. He'd hesitated, then he'd said, "If I'm elected, I'm going to clean up this county." He'd looked at the expectant crowd, who had seemed to want more. "That's it," he'd said, and he had resumed his seat, while the crowd laughed and roared its approval. Chance couldn't help but smile as he remembered.

Now Chance saw Will's tall, lean form at the foot of the steps, with Hope and his two boys at his side, awaiting the results stoically.

The clerk handed his corrected tabulations to the recorder, who leaned on his crutch and waved the paper for silence. He took a drink from a large glass and began, "For county sheriff. Benjamin A. Butler, incumbent. Three hundred and twenty-seven votes."

"Damn," swore Blaine. Chance folded his arms philosophically. It was what he had expected.

The recorder went on, "William R. Cooper, cattleman." He paused. "Seven hundred and . . ." The rest was drowned out by a thunderous roar. People were slapping Will's back, shaking his hand. The band began playing "Dixie."

Amos Blaine pitched his cigar into the street, and he turned to Chance. The years had turned his once-angular features puffy. "I guess the game is up," he said.

"What do you mean?"

"You know. Cooper only took this job so's he could come after us. Everybody knows that. Maybe it's time to cut our losses and move on. What the hell, the buffalo hunters are gone, and they ain't coming back. Now Kingdom's losing the cattle trade to Wilcox. There's even talk of moving the county seat there. This town's drying up, Chance."

"It's just a lull," Chance told him. "The railroad's coming. They'll be announcing the stop sites any time now, and Kingdom's going to be on the list. I ought to know, I contributed my share of the bribe. Sommerville and that crowd hate me, but they come to me quick enough when they need money. Kingdom is going to be bigger than ever, Amos. And in the meantime, there's plenty of horses and cows for the taking."

Chance grinned, but Blaine looked unconvinced. "What about Cooper?"

"What about him? Will's a stickler for the law. He won't move against us without evidence, without witnesses. We've never had a witness against us yet, and I don't intend to have any now. Nothing's changed."

"But we've never faced anybody like Cooper before. You know him. He'll keep trying. He'll keep plugging away till—"

"Listen," Chance said, and his hooded eyes flashed. "I

warned Will a long time ago never to cross me. If he does, he knows the consequences.''

"You mean he'll get what Jake Koerner got?'' Blaine's eyes narrowed. "That's a tall order, Chance. He won't be easy to take out.''

"What's the matter, Amos, you scared of Will? Don't worry. If we have to take him out, I'll do it myself.'' Chance relaxed. "Now let's go back to our place. I've seen enough here.''

By the courthouse, the crowd was still celebrating. The band was attempting the "Radetzky March'' with little success. Will was still accepting congratulations from those around him. He looked over at the Cricket Saloon, and his eyes met Chance's.

Chance tipped his hat in an ironic salute. Will stared at him for a moment. Then he turned away, to shake another outthrust hand.

Beside Will stood Hope. She refused to look in Chance's direction, but he stared a long minute at her. She was trying to seem glad for Will, but her worry for him showed through. She'd be under no illusions about what this job entailed, or why her husband had sought it.

From the moment Chance had run off with Ellen, he had known that he was losing Hope forever. Whatever flickering possibility had remained that she would some day come back to him was now extinguished. Ellen's death had only made it worse. Hope would never have him now, under any conditions. And from the moment Will had put his name on the ballot, Chance had known that he would be elected sheriff. So why had Chance stayed on?

He wasn't sure, really. Part of it was because he was getting older, reluctant to start over. Part was because he was used to wealth and power, and he didn't want to give them up. Maybe he was punishing himself, too, for having failed Hope again, when he had sworn not to. Maybe he just wanted to test his namesake, chance. Maybe, having destroyed his own life, he wanted to destroy Will's and Hope's, as well.

Maybe he wanted to show the world whose town this really was.

As Chance followed Blaine back to the saloon, he smiled to

himself. Will had told no one but Hope that Chance was the
man with whom Ellen had run away. That was like Will. He
would keep this personal, between the two of them, the way it
had always been. That suited Chance fine.

60

Will was sworn in two days later. The ceremony took place
in the sheriff's office, which, along with the county jail, occupied a small building just behind the courthouse. The office had
been cozily furnished by its previous occupant, who had rarely
left it except to collect taxes and visit the saloons.

Despite the intense interest in his election, Will's swearing-
in was a low-key affair. He wanted it that way. It was attended
only by Judge Holmes, Sam Sommerville, and the two deputies
that Will had been empowered to hire. Judge Holmes was a
distinguished-looking man, whose dark hair was turning a gen-
tlemanly gray. He owed his job to Chance, and he swore in Will
and the deputies without enthusiasm. He pinned on their stars,
congratulated them and left.

Will looked at the star for a second. Then he sat on the edge
of the desk, facing the deputies. They were young men, named
Richard Alford and Burt Carmichael. One had been a law stu-
dent; the other had held various jobs around town. Will had
hired them off a list of applicants, preferring not to retain Butler's men. "Like I said when I hired you," he told them, "our
first job is breaking up the Chance Evans gang." The two deputies exchanged looks, and Will went on, "Burt. I want you to
start at the county attorney's office. Get records on all the un-
solved crimes around here for the last year—rustling, holdups,
horse theft. I want lists of the stolen property and the brands
involved, if it's stock. Get descriptions of the outlaws, too, if
any of the victims had guts enough to give them. Try and match

the descriptions to Chance's men. I want to know who pulled what jobs.''

He turned to the other deputy. "Richard, you go to Judge Holmes. He should have a drink or two in him by now, so he may be approachable. Tell him I want warrants to look at Chance's and Amos Blaine's bank records. I also want a warrant to search Chance's office, and another to search Blaine's ranch. When you're done there, help Burt.''

The two deputies hesitated. "You want us to start now?" said Alford.

"Right now," Will said.

The young men left.

When they were gone, Will seemed to relax. He got off the desk and looked around the room. On one wall was a calender with a picture of a naked girl, and he took it down. Behind him, Sam said, "You're not wasting any time, Will. I knew you wouldn't. But you're kidding yourself if you think you can get this done in a hurry. It'll take months to get those warrants from Holmes. In the meantime, he'll go to Chance with everything you're doing. To be honest, I wouldn't be surprised if one or both of those deputies were working for Chance, too.''

"I'm sure they are," Will said. "I'm counting on it, in fact.''

An uncertain look crept over Sam's bearded face. "That doesn't make sense. Chance will be a tough enough nut to crack without you keeping him informed of your every move. Besides having the judge in his pocket, he employs the best lawyers in Texas. Even if you can build a case against him, you may have it stolen from you in court.''

Will looked at the shotguns in the rack. They were dirty. "I don't intend on taking it to court," he said.

"I don't understand.''

Will turned. "I know Alford and Carmichael are working for Chance. So was everybody who applied for their jobs. All this stuff about records and warrants is a smoke screen, to keep them out of my hair and maybe throw Chance off guard. There's only one way to settle this, Sam. That's quick and neat. I said I was going to clean up this county, and I am. I ain't planning to wait no two years while this case drags through court, just to watch some judge let Chance off free at the end of it. I've satisfied myself that Chance is guilty."

"How?" Sam said, "When?"

"All the time that fellow Butler was making speeches, I was nosing around Amos Blaine's place in Hidden Valley. I saw more than I wanted to out there. That ain't a ranch Blaine has, it's more like a clearinghouse for stolen property. And the cattle wearing his own brand was all mavericked. You can tell by the slit tongues on some, and the marks where the hoofs were filed down on others, so's they wouldn't go looking for their mothers. I saw Chance out there, too—more than once. I saw him ride out with a gang of men the day them freight wagons was stolen on the Wilcox Road and that teamster killed. Another time I saw him coming in with stolen horses. Chance never could keep himself away from the action."

Will looked squarely at his brother-in-law. "You and Jake Koerner were right about Chance, Sam. And I've been the biggest kind of fool."

"So what are you going to do?"

"I'm going to take some men over to Blaine's place and close down Chance's gang."

"What do you mean, 'close down?' "

"I'm going to hang them."

Sam sucked in his breath. "That sounds like vigilante justice, Will."

"It sounds like the only kind of justice we'll get. We'll never beat Chance in court. He owns the courts. How many more people are supposed to die while we wait for help from Austin or Washington? How many more people are supposed to lose their homes because all their horses and cattle have been stole? I don't like doing this. I don't want to do it, but it's the only way. Chance and Blaine and their kind have had free run around here too long, and a lot of it's my fault. It's time to end it."

"You sure you ain't talking out of a guilty conscience?"

Will's jaw muscles worked, making the long scar on his cheek move. He thought about Ellen, and he told himself that he was not letting outrage at her fate cloud his judgment. He thought about the time that Chance had saved his ranch from Vestry, and he wondered where that money had really come from. He wondered whether all his prosperity rested on a crime. He wondered if he had cause to be so self-righteous. He wondered if he didn't bear some of Chance's guilt. Then he recovered his determination. "You know the penalty for horse theft in this state, Sam. You know the penalty for murder. What do you say we do?"

Sam took a turn around the small room. He didn't like Will's idea, but he knew that Will was right. He said, "Chance is going to know what you're up to as soon as you start raising deputies."

"I don't intend on raising no deputies. You and Aaron Richardson's the only ones I've told. I'm using mine and Aaron's boys. I can trust them, and I believe they'll follow me."

"Oh, they'll follow you, all right. They'll follow you into hell, just like we followed you in the war." Sam sighed. "Well, I was with you in the war, I reckon I should be with you now."

"I don't know, Sam. You're old for this work."

"I'm younger than you."

Will pointed to Sam's ample belly. "You're out of shape. You ain't fired a shot in anger since the surrender."

"Look, Will, I brought you into this. I bear some of the moral responsibility for what's going to happen. If me and others like me hadn't been so gutless all these years, it wouldn't have come to this. Let me share the physical danger, too."

"You might lose your job."

"I don't care. There's things more important than being mayor."

"All right," Will said. "You can come."

Sam walked to the window and looked out. It was a warm autumn morning. Little traffic moved on the small street that separated the jail building from the back of the courthouse. Sam said, "It seems funny, going after Chance. I got my start working in his saloon. He was a good friend."

"Yes," Will said, "he *was*."

Sam turned from the window. For a moment he could almost believe that they were in the army again, getting ready for a campaign. "Well, Colonel, when do we move out?"

"Next time Chance is at the ranch with his gang. I've got

Rusty watching him. Knowing Chance, we shouldn't have a long wait.''

61

It was late afternoon when the riders trooped into the woods, about two miles north of Amos Blaine's ranch in Hidden Valley. So far they had been lucky. They had been on Blaine's land for some time, and they had not been discovered.

There were twenty of them. Will and Aaron Richardson were in the lead. Aaron was thirty-one now, with a wife and family. He was out of the trail-driving business. Over the years, his ranch south of the Clear Fork had been one of the outlaws' favorite targets. These two were followed by Sam Sommerville and the rest of the men, cowboys from Will's and Aaron's ranches. Rusty Harding was up ahead, scouting.

The riders were heavily armed. They looked grim but nervous, especially the cowhands, most of whom were quite young. Both Will and Aaron had brought all their men, save for the very youngest. With the fall roundups over, the seasonal hands were gone, and the full-time men, with the feudal loyalty peculiar to cowboys, had all volunteered. Will had left Alex at home, as well, and for once Alex had been glad, when Will had told him who the posse was hunting.

The riders entered a narrow ravine. Rusty met them there with word that the way ahead was clear. Around them, the oaks and elms were at the height of their autumn color. The air was crisp, and for a moment Will might have been a boy again, in the Tennessee mountains.

"Unsaddle your horses and feed them," Will said. "We'll leave them here and go the rest of the way on foot. We'll make a cold camp near the ranch house and move in at first light."

He looked around and picked the youngest man. "Morrison, you stay with the horses."

Morrison nodded. The tender-faced cowboy was too nervous to feel resentment at being left behind.

"Will?" It was Rusty. "If you don't mind, I'd like to stay with the horses."

Rusty had just turned forty. It was hard to believe. In his mind's eye, Will still pictured Rusty as the terror-stricken orphan boy of long ago. Rusty was tall and rawboned now, and his ginger mustache held a good deal of gray. His health hadn't been good since the war, but he never complained. He had never married. Will had once hoped that he'd some day marry Ellen.

"I come as far as I care to on this," Rusty went on. He looked apologetic, as if he were letting Will down. "I know it's got to be done, but I don't want to be at the sharp end. Me and Chance has rode a lot of trails together. It was Chance first brought me out here, from old Fort Belknap. Chance has been like a brother to me. He's like family. He's like you, Will."

"I understand," Will said. If Rusty knew what Chance had done to Ellen, he would probably have gone after him by himself. "Go ahead. Stay with the horses. I wish I could."

After tending the horses, the men removed their spurs and proceeded on foot. Will knew the area well. He had chosen a boulder-strewn finger of land that jabbed into the valley not far from Blaine's house. It was the only place where they could get close to the house unobserved.

It was dusk when they reached their positions. Hidden Valley had been named by Chance many years before. Its lush grasses were dotted with copses of woodland, and pecan trees grew thick along the creek. Downstream, on the way to the Clear Fork, stood a high, rounded hill, like an entrance marker. Blaine's ranch house was on the north bank of the creek, just below a little falls. There was a large hayrick near the house, and, behind that, the corrals were filled with horses. Calves were lowing in a pen farther on. Men could be seen lounging on the house's gallery. Other men came from the corral, and snatches of greeting drifted up to the posse members on the hill. Smoke curled from the house's stone chimney.

There was a growing dampness in the air, and Will bet there

would be fog before dawn. "Make yourselves comfortable," he told the men. "No talking or unnecessary moving around."

Will set the guard, taking the last turn himself, to make sure the men were awakened on time. Many of the cowboys had blisters and sore feet. They weren't used to walking so far. They donned canvas jackets and coats against the falling temperature. They ate suppers of water and jerky, with hardtack or corn dodgers. Then they scrunched themselves into the earth as best they could, and they tried to sleep.

Will huddled against a cold bank of earth. Already he heard someone snoring. He closed his eyes, but he couldn't sleep. He kept thinking about Hope. It was strange. Now, when his mind should have been totally concentrated on tomorrow, it was wandering. It was as if, even at the end, Hope would come between him and Chance.

Ellen's death had changed things between Will and Hope once again. Will had begun to feel badly about the way he'd treated Hope these last years. He felt like a sanctimonious fool, like the crusty, unforgiving cattle king everyone imagined him to be. He had let his jealousy of Chance affect his thinking. Surely all the feelings that he and Hope had once shared had not been faked. Surely they had been good and worth preserving. Maybe he had been wrong about Hope. Maybe she had loved him all along.

She had come to him before the posse rode out that afternoon. She had looked resigned, perhaps a bit sad. "Alex told me where you're going," she'd said, and she'd given him that tight-lipped smile. "Be careful. Please."

"I will," he'd said.

She'd touched his arm. "I'll be waiting."

How much of her life had been spent waiting for him to come back from one place or another? he had wondered. And now this, the shortest but most difficult journey of all. She had looked at him then, and her green eyes had been soft and her lips slightly parted, and he'd known that she wanted him to kiss her. He had wanted to kiss her, too, but after years of abstinence, it was hard. He had become confused, and this was no time for confusion.

The moment had passed. Hope had stepped back, disappointed, eyes downcast.

"Walk me to my horse?" he'd said quietly.

She had looked surprised. "Of course."

They had walked side by side, not saying anything. Not needing to. Alex had Will's horse, a bay with a blazed forehead named Comanche, saddled and ready.

Will had swung into the saddle. He had looked down at Hope. "I'll be back," he'd said. Then he'd turned away and ridden out to join his men.

Now he stirred. He was freezing. The damp cold penetrated his clothing. It seeped into the marrow of his bones. He could not sleep, and from the coughs and sniffles and movement around him, he guessed that many of the others weren't sleeping, either. In the valley, fog was rising. The fog would shield the posse's approach tomorrow, and the absence of a breeze would keep their scent from horses and dogs, but it would also make vision difficult, increasing the possibility of confusion.

The night passed slowly. The fog thickened. It rose from the valley, cloaking the hill. At last it was Will's turn for guard. He stood. His bones were cold and stiff. He flexed himself to get the blood moving, wincing as his tight muscles stretched. He made the rounds of the small camp, until the fog took on a slightly opaque quality with the arrival of false dawn, and the birds began singing. It was time to move.

He roused the men. There were sounds of movement, low snatches of conversation, surprise from the sleepers when they saw the fog.

The men ate a hurried breakfast. They would have loved some hot coffee, but no fires were permitted. There were metallic clicks as they checked their weapons and wiped the dampness off them. Then Will beckoned them together. It was coming on dawn, though it was impossible to see much because of the fog.

"We'll go in quiet," Will said. "Sam, you and the men who've been told off surround the house. I'll go in first, Aaron second. Barney, you and Yankee Jim are next—you make sure the outlaws' weapons are secured. The rest of you come in after. Shoot any of Chance's men who move. Stafford, you got the ropes?"

The young cowboy had brought several coiled lariats in case there wasn't enough rope at the ranch to do the job. "Yeah, boss."

The men were nervous and scared. So was Will. This would be the hardest thing he'd ever done. He'd have to go straight through, without stopping. If he stopped once, he did not think he would have the nerve to start again. He could not show his feelings, though. He could not afford to appear less than strong in front of the men.

He looked around. "Everybody ready?"

The men nodded.

Will drew his sheriff's badge from his coat pocket. He pinned it on.

"Let's go," he said.

Will had taken a compass reading on the house last evening, and he was glad of it now as he led the posse down the hill. At the bottom they spread out, a line of men crossing a field in a dawn fog. How many fields had he crossed like this? How many dawns? And each time he had hoped it would be the last.

The men lost some of their nervousness now that they were actually moving. The long grass wet their boots, making their feet cold and uncomfortable. The sounds of stumbling and the resultant curses were muffled by the blanket of wetness that enveloped them. "Quiet, there," Will whispered. "Pass the word." He checked the compass and corrected their course with hand signals.

After what seemed an eternity but was probably just a few minutes, the house loomed ahead, a dimly recognized solid in the shifting sea of mist. The rush of the falls could be heard faintly. The dogs and horses were quiet. So far, so good. Will started walking faster. The rifle felt heavy and wet in his hands.

The cabin door opened.

Silently Will dropped to the wet grass. His men did the same. A figure appeared in the doorway. It was a man, lean and bald. Amos Blaine.

Blaine stepped outside, holding his head at an angle, as if he had a headache or a hangover. He relieved himself off the gallery, started to rebutton his pants, then stopped. He peered into the fog, looking right and left. Suddenly he jumped back through the doorway. There was a warning shout, and a moment later a rifle banged, and the door slammed shut.

"Come on!" cried Will. He led his men running toward the house.

A shot came from the window. Then more, red flames spurting in the mist. One of Will's men spun and fell. There was a cry as another man was hit. The fire grew heavier as more weapons opened up. Chance's men had made a quick recovery from their surprise.

"Fall back," Will ordered. "Take cover and open fire."

Will helped carry off the wounded. Rifles cracked around him as his men began shooting. They surrounded the ranch house, taking cover behind trees, or outbuildings, behind the hayrick and a boulder in the field. In the background, the outlaws' horses were neighing madly, racing around the corrals. The calves lowed, and somewhere a dog was barking.

"Aaron," Will said. "Take some men and get between the house and the corrals. Make sure they don't make a rush and get to their horses."

"Right," said Aaron, moving off.

The gunfire was heavy now. The usually sharp cracks of the rifles were muffled booms in the fog. Muzzle flashes sparkled like lethal fireflies. Will made the rounds of his command. They were just boys, and though most of them wore guns as part of their everyday attire—would not be caught without them, in fact—few had ever been in a real fight. They were jumpy.

"Who is it?" one challenged as Will materialized out of the murk.

"Will Cooper," he replied. He told this boy the same thing he told the others. "Don't waste ammunition, son. Shoot just enough to keep 'em pinned down. Aim at the rifle flashes, but don't forget to move after each shot, 'cause they'll be doing the same to you."

From the ranch house, Chance shouted, "Who the hell is there?"

The firing stopped.

Will cried, "It's me, Chance."

"Hey, Will. How are you? This sounds like an official visit."

"It is."

"What happened to the warrants?"

"There ain't going to be no warrants, Chance."

"You mean, this is it? No trial? No jury?"

"This is it. You got some boys in there ain't wanted for hanging crimes, though. If they give up, I promise to treat them fair."

"Sorry, Will. I'm not going to make it easy for you. You'll have to get us all."

Inside the smoke-filled cabin, the men looked expectantly at Chance. They were in various stages of undress, having gone right to battle from their sleep, and they were still half dazed from the method of their awakening. Some took advantage of the break in the firing to grab a drink from the water bucket. Most were hard-bitten outlaws and gunmen, with no expectation of escaping the noose. A few, however, had done nothing more than rustle a few cows, and these were more hopeful.

"Why can't we give up if we want?" asked a gangly redhead named Brinkley.

"Don't listen to Will," Chance said. "It's just a trick to make you give up without a fight. He's trying to divide us."

"What if it ain't a trick?" Brinkley persisted.

"Yeah," said a part-Mexican named Gomez. "Why should we swing for you, Chance?"

"Because our only hope is sticking together, and because I'll shoot any man that tries to yellow out."

The outlaws looked from one to the other. Then Brinkley jumped up. He threw open the front door and ran outside.

"Don't shoot!" he cried. "I give up. I give up."

Chance stepped into the open doorway with his Winchester. He leveled the rifle and fired. The bullet hit Brinkley in the back and knocked him onto his face, arms outstretched.

Chance stepped back from the door as the posse opened fire. Bullets smashed into the wood. Bullets gouged splinters from the walls and door frame. Chance kicked the door shut, and he looked at the men in the dim interior. "Anybody else want to give up?"

No one answered.

"Now load your weapons. I've been in tighter places than this. We're not done yet."

"What are we going to do?" asked Amos Blaine. The sweat was beaded on his bald head.

Chance grinned. "We're going to blast our way out."

After the fleeing outlaw was shot from inside the house, Will positioned himself with the men by the corral, anticipating a breakout. The firing had dwindled. Each side was shooting just enough to keep the other honest. Will wished they had brought more ammunition. They'd be in a hell of a fix if they ran out.

Dark figures moved through the fog toward him. "There they are!" Will yelled.

He aimed his rifle and fired. The men around him began firing, too, most of them rising to their feet in their excitement. The outlaws came with a rush, shooting as they ran. The two sides were within yards of each other. Red flashes crackled up and down the lines as the two sides blazed away. Figures crumpled. Figures spun and yelled. Stray bullets plowed into the horses behind Will. The animals screamed, running with fear and pain, trying to kick down the corral poles. There were cries of wounded men. Will looked for Chance but didn't see him in the confusion. He shot at someone just in front of him. His Winchester ran out of bullets, and he drew his pistol and began firing that. The man dropped. Bullets cracked through the air around him.

"Get back to the house!" cried Amos Blaine.

Blaine was clutching a thigh. He limped back to the house, leading a few survivors. The rest of the outlaws were down, killed or wounded. Chance must be among the casualties or back in the house already. No one had reached the horses.

There was shouting among the posse members in the fog. Sam's men on the other side of the house were still firing, nervous and uncertain about what was happening. Other men looked to the dead and wounded. Chance wasn't among them. Will smelled smoke, not only powder smoke but a dry smoke, like that from straw. He saw a red glow in the mist. The hayrick had caught fire, probably from a powder flash.

"Get everybody away from there!" Will yelled.

He ran forward, helping Aaron drag a wounded outlaw from the spreading blaze. The hay quickly became a roaring mass of flames. Sparks shot high in the air. Heat rippled outward in waves.

A sudden gust of wind blew some of the sparks onto the shingled roof of the nearby ranch house. The sparks glowed, then died, then glowed again. The roof was tinder dry, and as Will watched in fascinated horror, the glow spread, until, almost before he realized it, the whole roof was on fire.

There were shouts and curses from the house, as the outlaws vainly tried to fight the fire from inside. The fire spread to the cabin walls. Thick smoke billowed into the fog, obscuring vision even more.

"Chance, get out of there!" Will cried.

The house was ablaze now. There were more curses and screams of fear. A figure bolted from the door. He stumbled and fell in a hail of gunshots.

"Don't shoot," Will yelled. "Let them leave."

Two more figures came out, hands raised high in surrender, coughing. There was no sign of Chance or Amos Blaine. Someone was still firing defiantly from inside.

The house had become an inferno. From inside came screams. "Help me! Help me!" The voice sounded like Blaine's. He must be too badly wounded to get out. The animal terror in his voice made Will's skin crawl. "For God's sake, help me, please!" Chance must be in there, too.

Will began running toward the house. "Chance! Blaine!"

Will tried to get through the door, but the flames and heat were too intense. His clothes were singed. He was driven back in spite of himself. The air reverberated with the hideous screaming. Then there was a pistol shot from inside the house, and the screams stopped.

"Chance!" Will yelled, and tears rolled down his cheeks. He stood and watched helplessly as the house and its occupants were consumed by flames.

62

The fire had burned itself out. Only a few flames still flickered in the blackened ruin of the ranch house. The sun and breeze were combining to dissipate the fog, and the breeze mercifully carried off some of the smell of charred wood and flesh. Above Will, the sky grew bluer with each minute, and more of the valley opened to view. It was getting hot. He took off his coat.

Will's men were scattered around the ranch, their faces and clothes black from smoke. One man had taken Sam's buffalo gun, and he was shooting the wounded horses. He had to do it from outside the corral; it was too dangerous to go in. Some of the wounded animals were running in terror, while others floundered on the ground, flailing their hoofs. The unwounded animals had been maddened by the noise, and they were rearing and kicking and racing about. Another man was in the cattle pen, shooting wounded calves with a pistol.

Five outlaws lay dead outside the house. Two more were wounded so badly that they would not recover. Four would likely live, to be taken, with the two who had surrendered, to town for trial. The thought of hanging them was too much for Will now. He had seen enough violence. Of Will's men, two had been killed outright and five more were wounded, at least one fatally. Morrison, the young cowboy whom Will had originally picked to watch the horses, had his cheekbone shattered by a bullet. He lay on the ground, screaming in pain. His friends tried to ease him, but there was nothing they could do.

Will approached the smoking house. There were two bodies inside, unrecognizable globs of black and red. One of them must be Blaine and the other Chance. Will had seen burned men before, but the sight still unnerved him. He would have to get closer. He would be able to identify Chance by his pistols and by a ring he wore on his right hand.

Will was revolted, both by what had happened and by his own part in it. What an end for Chance. Will wondered if Chance had been dead when the fire started, or if he had let himself be burned alive rather than give Will the satisfaction of hanging him.

Will started into the house, kicking aside a fallen log. From the other side of the ruin, Aaron Richardson raised his voice. "Looks like one of 'em got away."

"What?" Will said.

He hurried, with Sam and most of the others, to where Aaron knelt. With a pointed stick, Aaron indicated a depression in the dirt. "See for yourself. Here's where he crawled out the window." He rose, still pointing. "Here's where he shimmied away."

Sam Sommerville was awed. "He must have crawled right past us, like an Indian. In all the smoke and confusion, no one saw him. Who do you think it was?"

"It was Chance," Will said. "No one else could have done that."

He walked over to where the lightly wounded and captured outlaws sat under guard. "Was Chance in the house when the fire started?" he said.

The outlaws were glassy-eyed and disoriented from the fight. In the confusion of battle, half of them probably didn't even know where Chance had been. "No," said one at last, "I ain't seen him since the breakout." A couple more nodded.

Will turned away. To his friends he said, "Chance staged that breakout to divert our attention while he escaped. He sacrificed those men's lives so he could get away. And here I was, feeling sorry for him."

Chance's tracks led to the creek bank, then down. There he had risen to his feet and continued upstream, past the falls.

"He's got a good start on us," Aaron said.

Will said, "He'll need a horse. Likely he'll be looking for ours."

As if in answer to this thought, a pistol shot sounded from the direction of the woods.

"He's found them," Aaron said.

There were four more shots in rapid succession.

"He's running off the rest," Will said. "Sam, you stay here with Parker, Rose, and Yankee Jim. Tend the wounded. The rest of you men, come on."

They set off for the woods. In their high-heeled boots, and with feet blistered and rubbed raw from the previous evening, running was out of the question. They reached the woods limping and sore, weary from the accumulated fatigue of the previous night and the battle.

The horses were no longer in the ravine, but Rusty Harding was. He was lying facedown among the new-fallen leaves. There was a bullet hole in his back. Will turned him over. He was dead.

"He never even had a chance," Aaron said bitterly.

Will said, "And he thought Chance was like a brother." He stood. "Get the horses."

The men got the ropes from their saddles, and they spread out. Most of the horses had not strayed far. The men began recovering them and bringing them back to the ravine, each man trading for his own when it was found.

"Can't find Comanche, boss," said one of the tired cowboys.

Aaron said, "That's probably the one Chance stole."

"He would," Will said. "All right, Aaron, I'll take yours."

Aaron gave Will the line to his chestnut gelding. It was one of Aaron's few blooded horses that hadn't been stolen by the outlaws.

Will saddled the chestnut. Around him the other men followed suit.

"No," Will told them as he climbed onto the horse. "The rest of you stay here. I'm going after Chance alone."

63

Chance's tracks led Will southeast. They crossed Double Horn Creek not far from the Sommerville place. They headed for the Clear Fork and followed that stream south.

Will reckoned himself about three hours behind Chance. He had every expectation of overtaking him before he reached the Concho. But Chance rode day and night, past old Forts Phantom Hill and Chadbourne, past the Colorado to the Concho. He stole two horses on his flight, and Will was forced to use precious time requisitioning new horses from the ranches. Still, Will reached the little village outside Fort Concho to find that Chance had passed through not two hours before. He had bought a horse and packhorse, and he had ridden west, toward the Pecos.

He wasn't headed for Mexico, then. He must know Will was after him. He must know that Will would not be stopped by the Mexican border or any other.

So where was he going? Will guessed Arizona. There was a big silver strike in Arizona. Tombstone was supposed to be a roaring town, where fortunes were made quickly and no questions asked. It was the kind of place that would attract Chance. If Chance could get to El Paso, he could hire men to take care of anyone following him.

Will rode west, following the Goodnight Trail. He hoped to have Chance by nightfall, but his horse threw a shoe and went lame. Will had to shoot him and return to Fort Concho on foot for another and a packhorse. He had lost close to a full day.

Will drove himself. From Fort Concho, it was ninety miles to the Pecos. Ninety miles without water, following a trail lined with the whitened bones of cattle and horses that had perished in that blazing desert. He reached Castle Gap half dead with thirst, then staggered the last fifteen miles to the Pecos and Horsehead Crossing.

At the Pecos, the Goodnight Trail turned north. Chance had gone west, though. Will followed him, across the river, around the southern edge of the Staked Plains. He was in a land devoid of human habitation, devoid of water and trees. It was a land of great distances and rock formations like cathedral spires. A land of cactus, Spanish dagger, and alkali dust. A land where the sun set in great storms of red and purple and gold. A land of buzzards and mirages and thirst. Always thirst. Crossing a dry salt lake, Will and his animals nearly died of thirst, and he wondered if nature might not have the last laugh on him and Chance both. Then, on the west side of the lake, when he was at the very limits of endurance, he found a spring of brackish water. Old trails told that Indians and wild animals had used this spring. A more recent trail showed that Chance had used it, too, and not long before.

Will refilled his water bag. He rested his animals and moved on. Mile by mile he gained on Chance. And with each mile he thought of Hope, as he had since he had started this pursuit. He had never wanted to get back to Hope as much as he did now. He vowed to make up to her for all the lost years. He vowed to make up for all his stupidity and lack of feeling.

Then one afternoon he found Chance's horse dead, given out from heat and lack of water. Chance was riding the packhorse now, and Will knew that he had him. That night Will made a cold camp. Fire showed a long way in this country, and he did not want to be discovered.

Late the next morning he caught sight of a distant figure on the horizon. The figure saw him and sped up. It was Chance.

Chance couldn't hope to outrun Will. He headed for a ridge-line off to the right, lathering the scrawny packhorse for all it was worth. At last the packhorse sank to its knees, put its head down, and would go no farther. Chance abandoned the animal and made for the serrated ridge on foot. Will put spurs to his horse, but Chance reached the ridge before Will could catch him. Chance clambered up the steep ridge face, and he disappeared into the boulders at the foot of a chimney-shaped rock that stood like a marker on the ridgeline.

Will reined in. It was over if he wanted it to be. He could

leave Chance here. On foot, Chance would die from thirst and hunger as surely as from a bullet or hangman's noose. Will wasn't made that way, though. It wouldn't seem right. He had started this. He had to see it to a finish.

Will studied the ridge. Great rock formations stood like proud survivors among the detritus of eroded limestone. Boulder-strewn gullies and dry washes led to the top. Here and there were patches of parched brush. Will saw no movement. Chance could be anywhere up there by now.

There was no hurry. Will cooled down his animals. He unsaddled them, watered and fed them. There was no grazing for them, so he hobbled them at the bottom of a dry wash, whose steep sides would at least provide them some shade as the afternoon wore on. He filled his canteen from his water bag, and he slung it over his shoulder. He checked his rifle and pistol and put spare ammunition in his pockets. Then he started for the ridge.

Above him, the noon sky was a brilliant blue, brushed with wisps of high cloud. He moved bent over, dodging from cover to cover, eyes alert and watching the ridgeline. It was hard going. His boots slipped in the loose shale. The canteen bumped against his side. He was sweating by the time he reached the base of the ridge. He wiped his brow with his sleeve.

Just above him, to the right of the chimney rock and below it, a great, slab-sided rock projected from the hillside. Will made for the foot of this rock. A rifle banged, and a bullet kicked up dirt at his feet. He started to run. Another bullet cracked the air near his ear as he threw himself behind the sharp angle of rock.

"Hey, Will!" It was Chance's voice. "Why are you doing this? I thought we were friends." The voice seemed to be coming from the jumbled boulders near the chimney rock. It would be hard to get him out of there.

"We are friends, Chance," Will called back. "That's why I have to do it. I feel like every wrong you've done is my fault. How many people would be alive today if I hadn't looked the other way? George Vestry . . . Jake Koerner . . . Rusty . . . Ellen? How many more, Chance? I bet even you don't know."

"I know that you wouldn't be alive, Will. Or have you forgotten that? You owe me."

"I ain't forgotten. But you cancelled that debt when you ran off with Ellen."

"How about your ranch? You wouldn't have that ranch if it wasn't for me. You wouldn't be such a big man. I made you, Will."

"I made you just as much. I let you become what you are."

From the ridgetop came a derisive laugh. "You think you could have stopped me?"

"I think I should have tried."

Will looked up the hillside, debating which way to go. If he mounted the hill on the side of the rock nearest Chance, he would be in the open most of the way. If he went up the other side, he would be out of sight, but Chance might be able to slip down the hill past him and get to the horses. He would have to do it fast.

He gathered his strength. He took a deep breath and dashed for the top of the ridge, up the right side of the huge rock. The grade was steep; the soil was loose. He was making noise, but he couldn't help it. His heart pounded heavily. He strained for breath. His thighs burned.

Then he was at the top, bent over, heaving for breath and feeling every one of his forty-eight years. Another, slighter incline to his left would put him in sight of Chance's position. He moved up, trying to be quiet. He came to the top. There was a shot, and a bullet screamed off the rock near his face. He ducked back. So much for surprise.

He dashed across a gap to a large, rounded rock on his right. There was another shot, he didn't hear the bullet. Out of sight from Chance, he squeezed himself up the crevice between the rounded rock and its neighbor. He placed his rifle atop the rounded rock and cautiously hauled himself up after it.

He lay flat, trying to ignore the burning heat of the rock. From there he had a good view along the ridgetop. He could see the desert stretching in all directions. Then he saw the white of Chance's shirt. Chance was crouched in the boulders ahead, still watching the gap where Will had come up the hill. Will thumbed back the hammer of his Winchester. He aimed and fired.

Chance jumped from his position. He ran farther back in the rocks, along the ridgeline. Will fired after him. Chips flew near

Chance's shoulder, then Chance was lost to sight again. He was somewhere to the rear of the chimney rock now.

"Damn, Will," Chance cried. "You're acting mighty ungrateful for all I've done for you."

"I told you once before, Chance. I'd rather have nothing than have what I got now and know it was come by illegal."

"Oh, come off being so high and mighty. What you're doing right now is illegal as hell. So was that little stunt you pulled at Blaine's ranch."

"I know," Will said. "And I'm resigning my office as soon as I get back to Kingdom. This is personal, Chance. I don't intend to let anybody else be hurt by you."

Will climbed down from his perch and started forward again. He moved slowly, watching each step, trying to make as little noise as possible, quartering whatever field of fire the rocks afforded him. He angled left, so he could stay between Chance and the horses below.

Slowly he came around the side of the chimney rock. He and Chance saw each other at the same time. Both fired and fell back. Chance's bullet grazed Will's hip, digging a furrow in his shell belt. Will swallowed. Another inch and his hip would have been smashed.

Will heard footsteps running away. Then, from a new position, Chance called, "Will, I don't want to do this."

"What about Rusty?" Will cried angrily. "Did you want to do it to him?"

"Christ, do you think I enjoyed killing Rusty? I didn't have a choice. At the time, I thought you were right behind me. I'd never have done it otherwise. You've got to believe that."

Will kept angling left, eyeing the rocks as he moved along the ridge line. He found a splash of blood on one of the boulders. Chance must have been hit. Will kept going. He had a momentary glimpse of Chance moving off the ridge, down the far side of the hill, circling right, as if to come up behind Will. Will moved down and over, to block him. Chance fired another shot. Will saw him but didn't fire back. It would be a waste of ammunition. There was no chance for a good shot among these boulders unless one of them caught the other unawares.

"Come on, Will. It isn't right, us fighting. Let's you and me forget all this. Let's leave Texas and everything in it. We'll go somewhere and start over. We'll go to Arizona. There's Apaches to fight there. There's silver and land for the taking. We were always happiest when it was just the two of us against the world. It can be like that again.''

"No, Chance. A man can't just take what he wants anymore. Those days have passed, and we can't bring them back.''

"All right.'' Chance's voice sounded resigned. "Have it your way.''

Will closed on Chance's last position, shading left, because he expected Chance to try and double back that way. Then he saw Chance, scurrying farther to the right—not left—and upward. Will shifted his path to intercept him, but it was like playing hide and seek. Each movement was scouted thoroughly. Each time Will stepped from behind cover, he tensed, wondering if a bullet would rip into him. He reached the point where he had expected to cut Chance off. He didn't see him. He'd had the angle on Chance; Chance couldn't have gotten past him. He listened. Nothing.

He waited. Chance did not appear. Then Will looked along the hillside, and he saw where Chance must have gone to ground. About halfway down the hill was a small cave. It was the perfect spot for a stand. Will would be able to come at Chance only from straight ahead. Chance would be inside the cave, waiting, poised for a point-blank shot when Will showed himself.

Will unscrewed his canteen top. He took a drink and found that he didn't want it. The water felt foreign in his throat. He put the canteen back.

He could still walk away from this. He could still leave Chance to his fate.

No, he couldn't.

He started down the hill, toward the cave. His boots sounded loud on the loose stone.

The angle of the hillside was steep. He steadied himself with one hand. He was beside the cave now. He listened, heard nothing. Chance would have heard him, though. Chance would know exactly where he was.

Will raised the rifle to his shoulder. His finger curled around the trigger. He was breathing heavily, in short bursts.

Now.

He stepped in front of the cave mouth, firing inside as he did, levering another round into the chamber and firing that, too.

Then he stopped.

Chance was not there.

He stepped back, breathing hard from released tension. Sweat flowed over him. He put his hand to his bearded mouth, and he looked around.

Where was Chance?

The horses.

He must have gone for the horses. He must have wanted Will to think he was going for the cave. He must have hidden in the rocks until Will passed, then slipped behind him and over the hill.

Will swore. Chance had played him for a fool, and like a fool he'd fallen for it. He began running for the top of the ridge. His tired body had trouble obeying his commands. His legs were rubbery from physical and mental exhaustion. He reached the top, breathless, and looked down. There, low and to his right, Chance was scrambling down. Chance reached the bottom and began running across the uneven ground, for the horses.

Will aimed his rifle and fired. He missed. Chance was a moving target, and Will was breathing too hard for a steady aim. Will threw himself down the face of the hill, after Chance. He was careless of his body, falling, cutting and bruising himself, twisting his ankles on the uneven rocks. Below him, Chance was running across the plain. Chance was going to get to the horses first. Chance was going to get away, and Will was going to die.

Will cursed himself. He reached looser soil and slid down, arms flailing. Ahead, Chance suddenly slowed. He was limping. His left leg had played out, the one he'd broken years before. Will still had a chance.

Will hit the bottom of the hill and began running. His rifle encumbered him, and he threw it away. He saw that Chance had thrown his rifle away, too. Will's legs were pumping. They seemed to be all over the place. His revolver thumped painfully against his hip. He slipped on loose soil, he stumbled on rocks, but he was gaining. His lungs felt as if they would explode.

Ahead, Chance had slowed badly. He approached the wash

where the horses were. Will put his last bit of effort into his
attempt to catch up.

Chance limped over the lip of the wash. Will headed for a
brush-lined gully to one side. He slid down the gully into the
wash. The bend was to his left. He ran around the bend. Chance
had cut the horses' hobbles. He was gathering the reins, getting
ready to jump on bareback. He dropped the reins, and the two
men faced each other.

Chance hesitated. Will did not.

Will drew his .45, and he thought he saw Chance grin as he
squeezed the trigger.

The bullet hit Chance in the chest. Chance yelped and staggered off balance. He pulled his own pistol, but before he could
fire, Will shot him again.

Chance dropped the pistol. His eyes met Will's. Then his legs
gave way, and he fell to the ground.

64

Will was breathing hard. His pistol was still pointed. The
blood surged wildly through his veins. He wanted to release this
built-up energy in some violent act, yet at the same time he felt
powerless to move.

Across from him, Chance lay on his back. His legs scraped
the ground weakly. An arm flapped aimlessly across his chest.
The horses had run down the wash at the sound of the gunshots.

Suddenly Will's legs trembled and went weak, as if they had
turned to jelly. He sat, heavily. His shoulders slumped. He threw
back his head and his breath turned shallow. For a moment he
did not think he would ever move again.

But he had to move. Chance was coughing, choking on the
liquid that welled from deep inside him. Will got to his hands

and knees. He stood shakily and walked over to Chance. He realized the pistol was still in his hand, and he holstered it.

Chance had been hit in the lower chest and stomach. There was an earlier wound in his left shoulder. Will sat beside him. He lifted Chance's head and rested it in his lap.

Chance coughed. A mouthful of blood dribbled over his lips and onto his whiskered chin as he smiled up at Will. "Where the hell did you learn how to shoot?"

"You taught me," Will said quietly. Then he added, "I thought you didn't believe in hesitating."

Chance laughed. "*You* taught that to *me*." He coughed again. He leaned over and spat out a glob of blood.

Chance had a stomach wound; Will couldn't give him water. He unscrewed his canteen top. He wet his bandanna and mopped Chance's grimy face and forehead. "Just hang on now. You'll be all right."

"Who are you kidding?" Chance said. "Anyway, why would I want to be all right? So you can take me back to Kingdom and hang me?"

"I . . . I ain't going to hang you, Chance. I don't think I ever could have."

Chance laughed again. "Now you tell me." Deep coughs wracked his chest with spasms of pain. Sweat covered his face. "What the hell. If you didn't hang me, somebody else would."

Chance sat up suddenly. He vomited a huge amount of bright-red blood and other material. It splashed over his shirt and trousers. Finally the liquid stopped coming. Chance lay back, pale and weak. He was fading away before Will's eyes. "You're right," he said, and his voice was almost a whisper. "I outlived my time. It was some time, though, wasn't it?"

"It was," Will said. He hesitated. "Chance, there's something I got to know. About Tommy. Was he . . . was Tommy . . . was he mine, Chance?"

"What do you mean?" Chance said. Then recognition dawned on his pallid face. "So that's what this has been about, the trouble between you and Hope all these years. Tommy."

Will pursed his lips.

More vomit drooled from Chance's mouth. He wiped it away with a dirty hand. "Of course he was yours. Whatever gave you that idea?'' Then he remembered. ''Not that army officer? You didn't pay any mind to him, did you?''

Will still looked unsure.

Chance seemed to gather all his remaining strength for one last physical effort. His jaw clenched, as with one hand he grabbed Will's arm. The fingers dug in. There was still strength in the grip. His hooded eyes were bright. ''Look, Will. I loved Hope, sure. I'll admit that now. You must have known it, anyway. But I swear on my mother's grave—I swear on our friendship—I never touched her. God knows I wanted to, but I never did. She's yours, Will. She always was and always will be.''

Will hung his head.

Chance's grip faded. His face turned chalky white. He fell back on Will's legs, breathing harshly from the fluid in his lungs. He coughed again, bringing up blood and bits of something pale. He raised a trembling hand toward Will's unshaven chin, and he flashed a ghost of his big grin. ''That beard . . . still looks like hell.''

Tears obscured Will's vision. He took Chance's hand and squeezed it. Chance squeezed back weakly.

Chance stopped coughing. He started breathing rapidly, then he let out a long sigh. His head lolled, and his hand went slack in Will's.

Will buried Chance there, on high ground, where the rains would not wash away the body. He covered the grave with heavy rocks, to keep off predators. Then he caught the horses, and he started back.

The journey seemed very long, and he remembered little of it. At last he came to the gates of the Double H Ranch. Waiting for him there was Hope. He dismounted and went to her. They looked at each other. Then they kissed, a long, lingering kiss like that of first lovers. When the kiss was done, Hope linked an arm through Will's, and they walked toward the house, together.

Epilogue

1881

The railroad did not come to Kingdom.

First, the Texas and Pacific line announced that they had decided to build their own cattle town, some twenty-five miles south of Kingdom, on Elm Creek. Next, and far worse, the Texas Central chose to make its Benedict County stop in Wilcox.

Sam Sommerville was in turns shocked, furious, and resigned over Kingdom's loss to its rival. "Their bribe must have been bigger than ours," he said at last.

Because Wilcox was awarded the railroad, the county seat moved there. Kingdom's end was now inevitable. The town had no more reason to exist. The long cattle drives were just about over, and what was left of that business had been taken by Wilcox. There was no more fort, no more buffalo hunting. Sam Sommerville was one of the first to accept reality. He packed up his store and reopened it in Wilcox. The newspaper did the same, and the rest of the town quickly followed. The saloons closed. The gamblers and their ladies headed for choicer pickings. Within a year, Kingdom was empty.

Will and Hope decided to leave Texas. Will could not bear to stay. This country held too many painful memories. He wanted to start over. Hope felt the same. She would miss her brothers, but in a way she and Will were starting their relationship over, too, and she was eager to begin.

They headed for California. Will had heard there was good cattle country south of Sacramento. "I hope you boys are up to bossing an outfit," he told his sons. "Because your mother and me intend to make time for other things. Might even be we'll do some traveling, just the two of us.''

Alex and James grinned confidently. Will looked at Hope and smiled. She smiled back, and it was as if twenty-five years had dropped away, and they were walking in the woods along Double Horn Creek.

It took Will a year to settle his affairs. He broke up the Double H ranch, giving sections of riverine land to his few longtime hands, with even more to the longest serving, Lije Abernethy, who was still his cook and who still dropped cigar ashes in the stew. The rest of the ranch he sold to a Scottish company, the Dundee Ranching Corporation. The Scots brought in an accountant to oversee the operation, and they hired Aaron Richardson, at a handsome salary, to run the ranching end of it. Others besides Aaron were staying in the vicinity—small ranchers and farmers, and men like Curt Sommerville, whose salt would always be in demand.

Will and Hope took little with them—clothes, some photographs, an old copy of *Ivanhoe*. They took Hope's spinning wheel, which still sat in the parlor, and which she still sometimes used, though no longer from necessity. It was a bright spring morning when Will turned over the house to Aaron Richardson. He sent the wagons and horses ahead with Alex and James. Then he and Hope took the buckboard, and they drove to the top of Buzzard Peak. They got out and walked among the weed-choked remains of Fort Stanley to the spot where Will and Chance had first seen the Clear Fork country, over thirty years before.

It hadn't changed much. The buffalo and antelope herds were gone, replaced by grazing cattle. Farms and ranch houses dotted the landscape, along with fences and windmills and water tanks, and there were a few roads. But the rolling hills, the woods, the streams, and the wildflowers were still there. The land would always be there.

Will and Hope climbed back in the buckboard. They drove off the hill and down Fort Street, into town. Kingdom was deserted, a ghost of itself. The buildings were boarded up or simply abandoned. They were missing roof shingles, planking, doors—anything that could be reused somewhere else. There was garbage and broken furniture in the street. As he and Hope drove along, Will seemed to hear the tinkle of pianos, the laughter of rough men and women, the clatter of poker chips.

They passed Sam Sommerville's old store. Across the street was Chance's Kingdom. The saloon's gaudy paint was faded now. The welcome sign had blown off the room, and some-one had removed the glass windows. There was nothing left inside but rats, empty bottles, and a picture of the Alamo on one wall.

Will turned the buckboard onto California Street. There was the post office, the Variety Theater, the conservatory. There was the opera house, where Ellen's dance class had given its recitals. Outside town, Will looked for the buffalo wallow where he and Chance had made their fight against the Comanches. But the wallow was long gone, farmed under, and Will could no longer remember exactly where it had been. They passed the ancient pin oak, whose spreading branches still stood their silent sentinel.

Will was quiet, lost in thought. Hope pressed a hand on his arm. Her green eyes looked deep into his. "Don't worry," she said. "Our life is going to be good. It's going to be better than it's ever been."

Will pressured her hand back. "I know," he said.

He flicked the reins and they drove on, toward California. Behind them, a gust of wind sprang up, covering their tracks with dust.

ABOUT THE AUTHOR

Robert W. Broomall has been a journalist, draftee, bartender, and civil servant. His main interests are travel and history, especially that of the Old West and Middle Ages.

In addition to his historical novel, TEXAS KINGDOMS, Broomall has written several westerns for Fawcett including DEAD MAN'S TOWN, THE BANK ROBBER, DEAD MAN'S CANYON and DEAD MAN'S CROSSING. He lives in Maryland with his wife and children.

G. CLIFTON WISLER